DEATH MARCH OF THE DANCING DOLLS

And Other Stories

Day Keene in the Detective Pulps
Volume #3

DEATH MARCH OF
THE DANCING DOLLS

AND OTHER STORIES

Day Keene in the Detective Pulps
Volume #3

Day Keene

With an Introduction by

Bill Crider

RAMBLE HOUSE

Stay As Dead As You Are, *Detective Tales*, October 1946
The Charlie McCarthy Murders, *Detective Tales*, March 1942
Doc Egg's Graveyard Reunion, *Dime Mystery*, February 1946
Death March of the Dancing Dolls, *Dime Mystery*, September 1945.
So Sorry You Die Now, *Dime Mystery*, January 1945
A Minor Matter of Murder, *Short Stories*, Dec 25, 1945
Mighty Like a Rogue, *Dime Detective*, January 1950

ISBN 13: 978-1-60543-536-7

ISBN 10: 1-60543-536-8

Series Compiled and Edited: John Pelan
Cover Art: Gavin L. O'Keefe
Preparation: Fender Tucker
Preparation: Kathy Pelan

Dancing Tuatara Press
Special Edition

TABLE OF CONTENTS

DAY KEENE IN SMALL DOSES

Introduction by Bill Crider

My introduction to Day Keene came through paperback novels. When I began to collect them seriously in the 1960s, it seemed that Keene turned up everywhere. He wasn't just prolific. He was also popular with publishers, and his books came out from nearly all of them. I have novels by Keene (originals and reprints) from an impressive list of publishers from A to Z: Ace, Avon, Berkley, Dell, Gold Medal, Graphic, Lion, McFadden, Phantom, Pyramid, Signet, Unibooks, Zenith, and maybe others I've forgotten.

When I was looking for those old paperbacks, I never thought much about Keene's background or his beginnings as a writer. For all I knew, he'd started out as a novelist, and it never even occurred to me that he might have written stories for the pulps. After all, I never saw them anywhere.

Then one day I came across an old Avon paperback by Keene. It was called *This Is Murder, Mr. Herbert*, and I bought it without even looking inside, being sure that it was yet another novel. When I got home and opened it up, I discovered that it wasn't a novel at all. Instead it was a collection of four stories from the detective pulps. Keene had been writing for years before he started doing paperback novels, and he'd specialized in the same kind of lean prose and fast-moving stories even then. I would have loved to read more of them, but at that time I was collecting paperback books, not pulp magazines, which were a little out of my price range.

Now, thanks to Ramble House, Keene's pulp stories are all being brought back into print, and people will have a chance to see not only how Keene developed as a writer but how he applied the principles of pulp storytelling in his early work.

And just what are those principles? One of the best-known is explained in the old adage that says, "Shoot the sheriff in the first paragraph." How about this one from "The Charlie McCarthy Murders":

Hart Jackson returned to Chicago to kill Flip Evans on a Friday morning. He looked like a million dollars. His eyes were clear. His face had lost its night club pallor. His clothes, while outmoded, were expensive and well cut. The first thing he did when he got off the bus was buy a twenty-cent cigar. He paid for it with his last two dimes. Then he remembered the girl and looked around—but she was gone.

It's hard to stop reading after an opening like that, all right. Here's another one, this time the first three sentences from "Death March of the Dancing Dolls":

The dead Chinese walked into Doc Egg's gold mine on the corner of 44th and Broadway at exactly fifteen minutes of midnight July the 5th. No one paid much attention to him. No one knew he was dead.

If you're like me, you're already hooked. There are some other fine opening lines lying in wait for you at the beginnings of these stories, but you can find those for yourself.

After the reader gets beyond the first paragraph, the pulp writer's job is to hold his attention. One way to do that is with memorable characters like the one mentioned above, Doc Egg, who appears in two stories in this volume. Doc is a pharmacist, and he owns his own drug store. He's short and balding, but don't let his appearance fool you. His profession was prizefighting until he won enough money to open his business, and he has a penchant for getting involved in murder.

Or how about Matt Mercer, the one-armed private-eye, married with kids, who keeps getting hit on the head and shot at? Not that getting hit on the head distinguishes him in the company of the other protagonists in these stories. It happens to all of them at one time or another.

Great beginnings and interesting characters are fine, but without a gripping plot they don't mean much. Keene could certainly plot. I'm not saying that everything that happens is plausible, but the stories will certainly keep you turning the pages, from the dying message in "Doc Egg's Graveyard Reunion" to elusive scraps of rice paper that everyone's chasing in "So Sorry You Die Now."

One thing you might not expect in Keene's stories is humor, but it's there in all of them, more in some than in others. Nowhere is it more evident than in "A Minor Matter of Murder," in which Keene has a great time with playing around with some classic noir themes. You may figure out where this one is going before it gets there, but you'll have some good laughs along the way.

But wait! There's more! Dangerous dames. Gunplay. Romance. Savage beatings. Chases. Graveyards at night. Kidnappings. Ventriloquism. These stories have it all.

Don't take my word for it, though. Read them and see. You'll be glad you did.

DEATH MARCH OF THE DANCING DOLLS

AND OTHER STORIES

Day Keene in the Detective Pulps
Volume #3

STAY AS DEAD AS YOU ARE!

CHAPTER ONE

THE GLEASONS ARE COMING . . .

THE NIGHT, FOR OCTOBER, WAS WARM. There was no wind. Even that high up in Central Bureau sweat trickled down Murphy's cheeks and glistened on his bald spot as he filled in the complaint sheet. The blonde continued to curse me—"You dirty stooge . . . You rotten leech . . . You stinking, filthy, shamus. I hope you enjoy your blood money. Why couldn't you give us a pass?"

Those weren't the words she used but that was the general idea. A matron tried to shut her up without success. Archer's wife continued to sob on my shoulder. He sat staring at the floor. I knew what he was thinking. He was wondering if it had been worth it. I doubted it greatly. Distant pastures may look greener but grass is much the same no matter where it grows.

I was still waiting for my receipt when Haig of Homicide came in and wanted to know what I had.

I said, "A defaulting cashier."

It was the same old story. Archer, with everything to live for, a nice home, a nice wife, two kids, had met the blonde in a tavern one night One thing had led to another until three days before he had walked out of his cage with a briefcase full of steel engravings, some eighteen thousand dollars worth to be exact. I had picked them up in Evanston that morning with most of the money still intact.

Haig looked at the blonde, then at Archer's wife. "The fool. The damn fool," was his comment.

I was hot. I was tired. I hadn't eaten since noon. "Aren't we all," I said sourly. "I guess the moral is 'Don't steal peanuts.' If he had defaulted with two hundred thousand, the chances are he'd have gotten away with it easily." Haig said that was debatable but admitted that two hundred thousand dollars would buy a lot of lawyers.

"Yeah. Also a lot of cops," I added.

My crack was just that, a crack. But Haig took it personally. His face coloring slightly, he told me. "I resent that, Matt. It may be you have a price. Most private agency men have. But I'll be damned if I'd sell out for *any* amount of money."

Before I could stop him, he left the office. Only the blonde picked it up. "Yair. Guys who live in glass houses," she sneered. "I see now where we made our mistake. If Bill had swiped two hundred grand he could have bought a pass for a fifty-fifty split."

I took my receipt from Murphy and followed Haig into the hall but he was gone. I had hoped to straighten things out. I was to wish I had. It just shows what words can do. That little handful in Murphy's office damn near sent me to the chair.

It was still light but night was beginning to bracket the city when I walked out onto State Street. Olson of the Morals Squad was leaning on the building. "Nice night, eh, Matt?" he asked me. "This Indian Summer is the nuts."

I said it was, got into my car and drove to the office wondering if I had a price. I doubted it. I'm no little tin God. I've looked on the wine when it was red and done my share of wolfing and singing. *But honesty is good business.*

Mable was gone but she had listed two phone numbers and a message from Sherry on my pad—

State 2131—Call Mr. Hanson of Amalgamated Under-writers no matter what time you get in. He says it is very important.

Drive 1132—A Miss Vardell phoned four times. She sounded angry or worried but refused to state her business. You can do as you like but I said that you would call her.

I dialed Jack Hanson's number as I read Sherry's message. Boiled down it said the Gleasons were coming for bridge, for God's sake to show up sober, and would I stop at a delicatessen on my way home and pick up a pound of sliced boiled ham, some Liederkranz, and a loaf of bread.

Hanson's number didn't answer. I did better with Miss Vardell. She was both angry and worried. But her name wasn't Vardell. I recognized her voice the minute that I heard it. "I thought you were in Reno." I told her.

She said, "Shut up, you fool. I'm in another jam, a bad one." She gave an address on the Drive. "Come over right away."

I said, "Just like that, eh?", and hung up. I had gotten her out of jams before. Most of them had worn trousers. And after the Archer affair, I was up to the thorax with cheaters. I wanted no part of Zola Charters. A tasty, red-haired, little dish, she was currently married to a Pittsburgh steel man whom, rumor had it, she was divorcing to marry Shad Ambler, a San Diego night club owner. Meanwhile it would seem that she was playing the field as usual.

She called back before I could get out of the office.

"Please, Matt, don't be mad at me," she begged. "This is a matter of life or death."

I said I had heard that one before.

"I mean it," she insisted. "I *am* supposed to be in Reno. Shad would kill me if he knew I was in Chicago." She began to sniffle. "And you have to get them back for me, you have to."

"I have to get what back?" I asked.

She seemed surprised. "Then you haven't talked to Jack Hanson?"

I said that I had not, that I had been out of the office all day. But that changed the color of the mare. In a lot of ways Hanson was another louse, but he threw me a lot of business. And if he was concerned in the affair, the chances were that someone had clipped Zola for her jewels. She never traveled without them and I knew that his firm insured them.

"Okay. I'll be right over," I told her.

The building was on the Drive, one of those affairs with a canopy out to the walk and a uniformed doorman to sneer at anyone who drives up in less than a Lincoln Continental. He put the burn on my six year old Ford then turned back to admire a '46 Caddy parked just beyond the canopy. I couldn't be certain but it looked like Hanson's car.

I walked over to check the license and the girl in the front seat turned her head away from me. It was Jack's car. I didn't know who she was.

"There was something you wanted?" the doorman asked.

I gave him a dirty look and walked on into the lobby. A second flunky stopped me at the elevator cage with a request for my name, who I was calling on, and if I was expected.

I said my name was Mercer, that I was calling on Miss Vardell in 7A, and that I was expected. He used the house phone to check me.

"What's the matter, you expecting a pinch?" I asked him.

He looked shocked but made no reply.

Zola answered the bell herself. She looked and smelled as pretty as usual. Tramp or not, she had what it takes, all in the proper places, and the white hostess gown she was wearing did little to conceal it.

"I've been a bad girl again, Matt," she greeted me.

I said, "So it would seem," and walked on into a sunken living room big enough to play football in. Hanson was sitting on an ottoman. Except for the fact that he was scowling at his drink, he could have passed for one of the silver-templed distinguished business men who appear in the whiskey ads. He wanted to know where the hell I'd been all day.

I told him, "Evanston. I tried to get you just before I called Zola. What gives?"

Zola began to cry. Hanson told me the story, salting it well with curses. He had reason to swear. His firm stood to lose a hundred and fifty grand. It was about what I had expected. En route from Pittsburgh to Reno to divorce her current husband in Shad Ambler's favor, she had stopped off in Chicago to kiss a boy goodbye.

She told me, between sniffles, "I just wanted to be certain that I didn't love him more than I love Shad. He's such a sweet boy, Matt."

I said to please skip the romantic details as I had a date to play bridge, also to locate some delicatessen items, including a loaf of bread. She gave me a dirty look.

Hanson continued the story. After a round of the hot spots, Zola and her boy friend, a Chicago lawyer by the name of Tennent, had returned to the apartment at four A.M. to find a masked hood waiting for them. The hood had known her jewels in detail and not content with the few she was wearing had forced her at gun point to phone the desk and ask the night manager to bring up her jewel case from the safe on the pretense she wanted to put the rings and necklace she was wearing into it.

Tennent had protested and the hood had knocked him out. When the night manager had brought the case, Zola, the gun still in her back, had taken it at the door, telling the night manager, as she had been instructed to tell him, that she might as well keep it in the suite as she intended checking out in the morning.

Hanson spread his hands in a futile gesture. "And—that's it. She called me at five this morning. I've been trying to make a contact ever since. But so far it's no dice."

Zola stopped sniffling and said coldly, "You may think you have me in a spot. I am." She pounded a little pink fist on the table. "But I want my jewels or the full amount they were insured for. And I mean to have one or the other if I have to tell Shad the whole story."

I asked Hanson if he had reported the theft.

"How could I?" he asked flatly. "She's not even supposed to be in town." He scowled at Zola over his glass. "But if I can't establish contact and make a deal with who ever pulled the job within the next twelve hours, I damn well will report it."

Zola sat down on his lap. "But you can't do that to me," she back-watered. "Shad is so jealous he's green-eyed. He'd kill me."

Hanson got up and gave her the ottoman, saying, "Fun is fun. But a hundred and fifty grand is one hundred and fifty thousand dollars. How about it, Matt? You want in on the case?"

I lit a cigarette and thought it over.

"Please, Matt," Zola begged. She stroked my coat sleeve. "Please."

I said it was my cork arm she was petting and besides she was wasting her time because if I took the case it would be for a financial and not a personal remuneration.

She took her hand away. "You're a nasty, evil minded, old man."

I admitted that could be.

Hanson made the usual offer. I had, and he knew I had, the underworld contacts that a private agency man must have to do business. How I recovered the jewels would be my own affair. But to save themselves the larger loss, if need be, Amalgamated was willing to pay one third of the appraised value of one hundred and fifty thousand dollars. It was the standard underwriter's offer. I had handled such deals for them before, but never in those brackets.

My fee would be the difference between that figure and whatever I had to pay out. It could mean quick money, and a lot of it. It could also mean a lot of grief. By becoming a party to such a deal, and bringing it to a successful conclusion, I technically laid myself wide open on three charges: receiving stolen goods, an accessory after the fact, helping to compound a felony.

A nice business this agency racket. "Okay. I'll take it," I agreed. I crossed my fingers. "But God help all three of us if anything goes sour."

It did. But that came some hours, and two dead men, later.

CHAPTER TWO

QUICK DRINK WITH A KILLER

THEY SAY EVERYTHING COMES to him who waits, including hardening of the arteries. I wouldn't know. I've always had to sweat for anything I wanted. And I was sweating now. I parked on 63rd Street, a few doors west of Maxie's and looked at my watch in the dash light.

It was two minutes of eleven. Four of the twelve hours that Hanson had agreed to wait before he yelled 'Cop' were gone. The entrance of the boys in blue would complicate any deal I might try to make. And so far I'd learned nothing. Both of my ears were sore from tapping private wires but all I had heard to date was a lot of hard luck stories. If a local lad had turned the trick, I hadn't plugged in on the right line or he wasn't boasting about it. I had sprinkled my bait behind me but the only two possible sources of information I had left were Maxie and young Tennent.

There is a combination bar and pool room in almost every town. There are a hundred in Chicago. But there is one Maxie's. Its clientele is strictly ex-State college. You can't jump an eight ball off a table without hitting an ex-con. All outsiders are discouraged.

There was the usual chatter at the bar. It froze as I walked in. I said, "Relax. This is strictly a social call."

To prove it, I bought a drink. Harry, a big, bald, ex-box man was back of the bar.

"Maxie in?" I asked him.

He mopped his bald spot with a bar towel. "So help me, Matt," he told me. "Here I am on the up and up for eight years now and I still break out in a sweat every time a cop walks in that door."

He was lying. I knew it. He knew I knew it. But it made for conversation. He peered back through the smoke at the pool tables. "Yeah. Maxie's here. He's playing snooker with Jack Stevens."

I paid for my drink and started back, stopped as I saw six loaves of bread on a shelf back of the free lunch counter.

Harry was concerned. "What's the matter? Don't the drink agree with you?"

I said the drink was fine but seeing the bread reminded me of a phone call I'd forgotten to make. I laid a dollar on the bar and asked him for a slug.

Sherry was too sweet. I could almost see the stiletto between her teeth as I explained I was sorry I had forgotten to call her but a big case had dropped in my lap and would she give my regrets to the Gleasons.

She said, "Why certainly, sweetheart. And where are you phoning from?"

I said, "Maxie's Bar," completely without thinking.

She said, "Oh, I see. You just dropped in for a loaf of bread, no doubt."

I tried to explain, but she'd hung up.

"Wife trouble?" Harry grinned.

I told him, dead pan, "No thanks. It would seem that I have some," and walked back to where Maxie was playing snooker.

A big man in his early forties, with cauliflower ears and a broken nose that he had picked up as a welterweight contender before he had discovered there was more money in being a fence, he was allergic to the law in any form.

"Yeah? And what do you want?" he growled.

I told him some conversation and walked on past the table into his private office in the rear. He followed me reluctantly and closed the door behind him. "Okay. Converse," he said sourly.

I told him not to be like that, that I hadn't come with a beef but was merely looking for some information and was willing to pay well for it.

"Information about what?" he wanted to know. "And how much is there in it for me?"

I said that would depend. There is fear among thieves, yes. But there isn't any honor. There wasn't a lad in the place that Maxie wouldn't sell, or who wouldn't sell him for that matter, if it was made worth his while. I took four fifties from my wallet and tossed them on his desk for bait.

"Who lifted the Charter's rocks, Maxie?"

He looked even more stupid than usual. "I wouldn't know," he told me. "I didn't even know they were gone. I don't read about it in the paper."

I said it wasn't in the papers as yet but that it would be in the morning. I added two more fifties. "That's yours for his name."

Maxie shook his head. "You could make it a thousand, Mercer, but I couldn't pick it up. This is the Charter bimb you mean, the red haired chickadee who used to strip at the Rialto before she married some guy from Pittsburgh?"

I said it was her jewels that had been stolen and gave him the story as Hanson had given it to me.

"And she can't describe the guy?"

"He was masked and kept his hat pulled down," I told him. "But Zola describes him as about five seven, weighing a hundred and fifty pounds, well dressed, and she thinks that he had brown eyes."

Maxie spread his hands. "Ten thousand guys you're describing. How much did he get?"

I said, "Amalgamated had them insured for one hundred and fifty thousand."

He whistled softly. "And they are willing to make a deal?"

I admitted, "If we can't recover them any other way."

He said, "Wait," and left the office.

I waited for half an hour, nursing a fifth of rye I found in his liquor cabinet and calling myself a damn fool for agreeing to take the case. *Honesty is good business,* and while what I was doing is done every day of the week I was skirting on the thin edge of bankruptcy.

Maxie came back with his shoulders sagging. "Pick up your money," he told me. "I guess that I don't earn it. I've called every lad I know who might have turned such a trick and all I get is beefs because someone beat them to what must have been an easy touch."

It was the same story that I had encountered all night. I put my money in my wallet. "But you will keep your ear to the ground?"

"I'll keep it glued," Maxie assured me.

Out in the poolroom again I considered my best next move and decided to phone Tennent before I burst in on him unannounced. Zola had promised to phone him and say that I would drop in but in her present state of mind she wasn't to be depended on.

I did her an injustice. He was up and waiting for my call. "I am expecting you," he told me. "And I think I can do you some good. I've been thinking the whole thing over ever since it happened. And I think I know—"

He hesitated.

"Yes—?"

"I would rather not discuss it over the phone," he changed his mind. "But I do want to see you. Incredible as it seems, I think I can clean up this whole affair. How soon can I expect you?"

I mentally checked his address. He lived on the near north side. "Within a half hour," I told him and hung up.

There was something about his voice I didn't like. It was too smug for one thing. On a hunch I bought another slug and called Hanson. "What can you tell me," I asked him, "about this lad Tennent who was with Zola when her gewgaws were lifted?"

"Not much," Jack admitted. "He's a young lawyer with an office in the Loop. He has a fair practice, I believe."

I asked if it was fair enough to spend the kind of folding money a lad would have to spend to squire a girl like Zola.

He said, "Frankly, I wouldn't know. Why?"

Before I could tell him a woman's voice said, drunkenly, "Wash the idea of leaving me all alone, honey, to make a phone call at this time of night?"

Jack told her to shut up.

I said I hoped his face was red. I was burned. I had reason to be. His love life was no concern of mine but the Archer affair had turned me sour on extra-marital peccadilloes. I knew that Hanson was married. I knew his wife was in Bermuda. And I didn't appreciate the fact that he was indulging his libido while I was beating my head against a wall trying to save his firm money.

"Why?" he repeated his question. "Why do you want to know Tennent's background?"

I told him because I wanted to know how much credence I could place in anything he might tell me, adding, "I'm on my way to see him now. And he just told me over the phone that, incredible as it seems, he thinks he can clean up the whole affair."

Hanson was excited. "You mean, he recognized the thief?"

I said that Tennent had intimated as much.

"Good," Hanson said. "Good. Call me as soon as you've talked to him." He paused a moment, added, "But about your fee, Matt."

I asked, "What about it?"

Hanson started to crawl. "Well, naturally, I'm anxious to save the firm as much as I can. And don't you think that the difference between what you may have to pay to recover the jewels and—"

I told him, "No," and hung up.

Tennent lived on the first floor of an old brown stone front on Rush Street that had been remodeled into swank studio apartments. There was the usual grand piano draped with a black Spanish shawl and the usual couch heaped with pillows. The ceiling was high, and beamed. There was a fireplace. That was the living room. As far as I could tell, he had the whole first floor, a hallway running back to a bedroom and a kitchen. I didn't like his looks any better than I had liked his voice which was something.

He was a boy who had never outgrown his crew hair cut. You find them in the stag line of every deb's coming-out party. Their idea of a successful business career is to marry the boss' daughter and retire.

Not that he was a fool. He wasn't. He was a cold, shrewd baby. And he was looking out for number one. I wondered how he had ever gotten himself mixed up with a blow torch like Zola Charters. His first words answered that question. He had done some minor legal work for her in connection with the last theatrical contract she had signed.

"Now get this, and get this straight. Mercer," he made his position clear. "I don't feel that I owe Zola a thing. Understand?"

I didn't, but I said I did.

He fingered the bandage on his head. "In fact the blow I received might have killed me, it did almost fracture my skull."

It still was the Indian's summer. Heat flowed in through the open windows. I was hot. I was tired. I was hungry. I had laid out eighty bucks on the case so far without finding out a thing. Hanson, with the smell of a solution in sight, had tried to weasel on his agreement. I still had my peace to make with Sherry. "Look. I'm sorry you were slugged," I told him. "But let's cut out the preamble, son, and get down to facts. You told me over the phone that incredible as it might seem, you thought you could clear up the whole affair. All right. Let's have it."

His eyes turned shrewd. "Not so fast, Mercer. I know you. I know the fees that you charge. And before I do any talking I want to know what there is in this for me."

I asked why there should be anything in it for him.

"Because I'm almost positive," he told me, "that I can hand you the case on a platter. Tell me this. Has the company agreed to pay a good sized percentage for the recovery of Zola's gems?"

I admitted they had.

"Now tell me this?" he grinned. "Did Zola describe the man to you?"

I said she had and repeated the description that she had given me.

His grin grew wider. "Nuts. He was at least six feet tall, weighed two hundred pounds, and his eyes weren't brown, they were blue. Despite the fact that his hat brim almost reached the handkerchief he was wearing over his nose as a mask, I saw his eyes distinctly as he slugged me."

I said, "So?"

He got out of his chair. "So think that over while I mix a couple of drinks. I may be wrong. But the way I see it, we have a bear by the tail."

He walked back down the hall toward the kitchen. I lighted a cigarette. He might have a bear by the tail. It turned out that he did.

I repeated his description. "Six feet, two hundred pounds, blue eyes." There was a wide divergence between his description and the one that Zola had given me, but it failed to ring any bell in my mind. Maxie had summed it up. Ten thousand lads could answer 'here' to the description, including myself, young Tennent, Maxie, and Jack Hanson.

Glasses rattled in the kitchen. I threw my cigarette in the fireplace and walked back down the hall. "Look. Nix on the guessing games. If you think you have something, spill it. If not—"

I left it there. So did young Tennent. The screen door stood open to the night, and the bear Tennent claimed to have by the tail had turned and clawed him. He wouldn't ever marry the boss' daughter. An unopened bottle of rye was slipping slowly from his fingers, he lay sprawled across the kitchen table, the wooden handle of a knife protruding from his back.

He tried to say something and couldn't. I slipped my gun from my holster, took a quick step toward the open door—then spiraled into space as a sap made contact with the base of my skull.

As my chin scraped the tile of the floor, I knew what Tennent had tried to say.

The killer was behind me. He had been waiting in one of the rooms that opened off the hall. The open screen was a booby trap.

CHAPTER THREE

JUST A LOVE NEST

CONSCIOUSNESS WAS A PLEASANT SURPRISE. I hadn't expected to come to. It didn't make sense that I had. Neither did the pool of water that I was lying in. Someone, for some reason, had poured a pan of water on my head. But whoever it was, was gone. I was alone with Tennent.

I peeled my face from the tile and looked at him. One look was enough to see he was dead. The handle of the knife had moved. It was lower in his back, just under his left shoulder blade.

I found the bathroom and washed the blood from my face. The sap had caught me on the base of my skull but the floor had gotten both eyes. They were beginning to swell and turn green across the cheek bones. It didn't improve my appearance.

There were two things I could do. I could wipe my fingerprints from anything that I might have touched or I could phone homicide. That would mean some embarrassing questions and the whole thing would come out. On the other hand I had my license to think of. Zola was nothing in my life. If her prospective husband beat the hell out of her—it might be a good idea.

Haig, I found, wasn't at Homicide, but I got him at his home. He wasn't too pleased to hear my voice. "You drunk, or what?" he wanted to know. "Calling me this hour of morning."

I said I guessed I was 'what' because I certainly wasn't drunk, but I was in a mess. Then I told him the whole story, omitting only the fact that Amalgamated, through Jack Hanson, had empowered me to pay up to fifty grand for the return of the jewels.

"And you're certain that Tennent is dead?"

I said I was positive.

"If you value your license, stay right where you are," he told me. "I'll contact the Department."

I said I would—but I didn't. Hanson lived only four or five blocks away. I wanted to talk to him to set our stories before they blew up in our faces. I didn't owe Zola a thing. But I did owe him something. And I didn't want to talk over the phone.

I parked in front of the building and went in. The lobby was sole deep in soapy water. At its far end, in front of a door that bore the legend—Janitor—the girl I had seen in Hanson's car was sniveling as a sullen-faced, older Latvian paused in his mopping from time to time to hurl a stream of invective at her.

"But I didn't. I wasn't, Pa," she protested. "Me and Mamie just went to a movie, honest. We went to the State and Lake."

He smelled her breath, said, "Bah! You bad girl. I know where you been. He married man. For shame. He don't leave you alone—I kill him."

He saw me then and shut up. Her mouth opened of its own volition, closed again as I walked on up the stairs. It was none of my affair but Hanson was playing with dynamite. I hoped he figured it was worth it.

He came to the door in a dressing gown, the silk stripe of his dress trousers gleaming dully in the half light. The eager smile faded from his face as he got a look at mine. "My God! What happened to you?"

I gave him the story, fast. A prowl car would be on its way to the dead lad's apartment by now. But being that he was home, it would take Inspector Haig fifteen or twenty minutes to get there. I wanted to be there when he did. He hadn't been kidding about my license.

"And that's the way it stacks up," I concluded. "It seems logical to assume the tech squad will find my fingerprints on that knife. No killer would pass up a chance like that. So, unless I wanted to face a murder rap, I had to spill the whole thing to Craig."

Hanson took the cigar from his mouth. "Including the fact that Amalgamated was willing to make a deal? We'll deny it."

I told him I had already figured that. I had.

He repeated thoughtfully, "Six feet, two hundred pounds, blue eyed. But why should Zola lie to us?"

I said I didn't think she had, not consciously. She had been excited. I pointed out a fact he knew as well as I did. No two witnesses ever agree on a description. But, he being a man, and a lawyer, I was inclined to believe that Tennent's had been the more accurate.

Hanson said, "Damn. If the young fool had only talked *before* he went out to the kitchen." He slipped out of his dressing gown and into a dinner jacket. "It looks like we're hooked for the whole sum now. Once this breaks in the papers whoever did the job will be afraid to try to make contact. It has passed from grand theft to murder."

I asked him if he thought he ought to call Zola.

He said, "To hell with her. If she wasn't such a little tramp we wouldn't be stuck for this loss. I hope to God Shad Ambler kills her. Of all the lousy breaks."

I said that it looked bad. It did. It was to get much worse.

At Homicide, once my eyes had been numbed by the light, it didn't bother me much. I'd been through sweat box sessions before, and this was strictly a fishing trip. Haig hadn't a thing on me. My prints *hadn't* been on the knife. The handle had been wiped clean.

"In other words," he said, "you don't know a thing about it? Your entire knowledge of the affair consists of the fact that you were engaged by this insurance firm to try and recover Miss Charter's jewels."

I said that summed it up.

Haig looked at his watch. "Jewels insured for one hundred and fifty thousand dollars." He read from the list that Hanson had given him. "An eight carat square cut diamond ring, a ninety-eight stone diamond bracelet, a pair of four carat diamond earrings, a dinner ring containing ten two carat stones." He looked up from the list. "And so on. All, with the exception of the one eight carat stone, jewels that have no outstanding characteristics and could easily be fenced."

I said I didn't get what he was driving at.

He said, "You will." Dawn was painting the windows. He slipped his watch back in his pocket. "Now tell me this. Mercer. This theft took place some twenty-six hours ago. Why wasn't it reported?"

I said I believed that Zola had explained that. But either way, it was no skin off my nose. They were her jewels.

"Were," Haig agreed. He leaned heavily on the word. "Okay. So you didn't know about it until eight o'clock last evening. You do realize that you should have reported then?"

I told him that was a moot question, that the very nature of my work was confidential and that I was more or less bound by the wishes of my client. He was building up to something. Just what I was damned if I knew.

He grew suddenly palsy walsy. "Look, Matt. I've known you for some years now. You have an excellent record both as a former sergeant of Marines and as a private agency man. You've given an arm for your country. You've helped the Department on various occasions and at the same time built up a lucrative practice for yourself. And don't think for a moment that all that won't be taken into consideration at your trial. So you were tempted. You fell. Why not come clean and get it over with, Matt?"

I said I didn't know what the hell he was talking about. I didn't.

Haig stopped being palsy walsy. His eyes turned into gimlets as he bellowed, "The hell you don't. I'm talking about your price. You went on record last evening when you brought in that lad Archer." He threw my own words at me. " 'The moral is don't steal peanuts. If he had defaulted with two hundred thousand dollars, the chances are that he would have gotten away with it.' Well, you aren't going to, Mercer. You killed young Tennent for those jewels. And you're going to the chair."

I asked if he wanted to bet. But I wasn't as confident as I sounded. My mouth was dry. Funnier things had happened. I added, "You're off on the wrong foot, Haig. I didn't kill Tennent. Remember? I'm the lad who phoned you and told you he was dead!"

Haig sneered, "Strictly as a cover. But it isn't going to work." He picked up a Department report and read off the names of most of the lads I'd talked to concerning the theft, including Maxie's. You offered them all big money. Why? I'll tell you. Because you scented a clean-up! You wanted those diamonds. And somewhere along the line, you learned it was an inside job—that Tennent, had hired a stooge to slug him and stage the robbery. So you called on Tennent, demanded a split of the loot—then stabbed him to shut his mouth."

I said, "For a handful of diamonds."

Haig thrust his face into mine. "For one hundred and fifty thousand dollars worth, all of it easily fenced."

I had taken all that I could. There was a plainclothes man on both sides of me but before they could stop me I hit Haig so hard he bounced off Sergeant Zukor. "You're a dirty, stinking, liar," I called him. "I never stole a dime in my life. And when I have any killing to do, I do it with a gun."

I tried to hit him again. I did my best. But he scrambled out of my way and Zukor and the plainclothes men beat and wrestled me back into the chair. Haig got up feeling his jaw and looking me over thoughtfully. He didn't seem sore about the blow. I reasoned later that he knew he had it coming. Like I said before, he hadn't a thing on me. It was strictly a fishing trip. Still frothing, I insisted, "All right. Let's get this over with. If one wisecrack can sour an honorable discharge and forty years of honest living, let's go over and see the D.A. Have the grand jury indict me and let's let a jury decide this."

"Cool off," Haig advised me. "It could be that we're wrong. But you did leave the apartment after I told you to stay put."

I began to see what was gnawing on him. Either he, or one of the bright boys on his squad, had reasoned that if Tennent had engineered the theft, and if I *had* killed him for the jewels, my logical move would be to stash the gems before Homicide arrived. I told the truth. "Yes. I did leave the apartment. I drove over to see Hanson and tell him what had happened."

Zukor wanted to know why.

Still sore, I needled, "Because you lads, being as dumb as you are, I thought I might need a lawyer. And it looks as if I was right."

A plainclothes man came in to the squad room and said something to Haig. He sighed and turned out the light. "Being human, we make mistakes," he admitted. "That's all for now, Mercer. But we know where to find you if we want you."

I put on my coat and walked out of the squad room. Hanson was waiting in Haig's office with one of the company's lawyers. Her face white under her make-up, Zola was sitting in a chair against the wall. There were the usual reporters beating their gums and wanting to know all about it.

One of them whooped when he saw my face. "Holy smoke! Did Haig do that to you. Mercer?"

I told the truth. "No. No one laid a hand on me." I looked at Zukor. "Except in self defense."

Hanson said he was sorry that it had taken them so long but it had been difficult to find a judge to sign the writ. The lawyer offered it to Inspector Haig.

Haig shook his head. "That won't be necessary." He drummed his fingers on the statement I had made concerning my conversation with Tennent and Hanson and asked me if I was willing to sign it.

I said I was, and did.

While I was signing it, he asked Zola if she thought it was possible that young Tennent had engineered the theft. She said that she did not, but admitted that his description of the thug might be more accurate than hers as she had been in a state of mind bordering on hysteria at the time. "I'm still hysterical," she sniveled. "I don't see why all this has to get in the papers. Can't you understand? I'm not even supposed to be in Chicago. I'm a respectable married woman on my way to Reno to be divorced."

Hanson sighed, and spread his hands. The reporters whooped. Haig blew on my signature to dry it, read from the statement, "Six feet, two hundred pounds, blue eyed. "Who knew you were calling on Tennent, Mercer?"

"No one," I told him. "That is, no one but Jack here."

"That's what I mean," Haig said quietly. He looked at Hanson. "You couldn't be mixed up in this, could you, Jack?"

"I'm involved, yes. Deeply," Hanson said. "I wrote the policy. And I'm responsible to the directors for the loss, that is, if the jewels aren't recovered."

The air in the office grew suddenly dead and still. "That," Haig said soberly, "isn't quite what I meant, Jack. Whoever lifted those jewels knew that Zola had them, knew her habits." He tapped my statement. "According to this, Tennent recognized, or thought he recognized, the man who slugged him. And the man whom he described fits your description to a T."

His lips white with anger, Hanson said, "You're mad."

Haig continued, unruffled, "More, it would seem that you, alone, knew that Mercer was calling on Tennent."

Hanson repeated, "You're mad."

"Out of your mind," Zola laughed nervously and shrilly. "I wasn't that hysterical. I've known Jack Hanson for years."

"Men," Haig continued dryly, "even high salaried men, get into jams sometimes." He looked pointedly at the company lawyer. Understand, I'm making no accusations. But I have a murder on my hands. And I'm certain that under the circumstances, Mr. Hanson won't mind telling us where he was on the night of the theft."

His face scarlet, Hanson walked the company lawyer, a lad by the name of Bedell, over to a corner of the office and talked earnestly with him for a moment. Then, his face still red, he told Haig, "I consider your veiled accusation and question as to my whereabouts most impertinent. But due to the size of the loss, and in order not to impede the investigation, on the night that Zola's jewels were stolen I was in the company of a young woman by the name of Betty Janawosky. And while the matter may prove embarrassing to her, I am certain she will so testify."

Haig persisted. "And last night, when Tennent was killed?"

Hanson took a deep breath, exhaled. "My alibi, if one is needed, is the same. I was with Betty Janawosky." He looked at me. "I believe she broke in on our conversation when you phoned me concerning Tennent Do you remember?"

I admitted hearing a girl's voice in his apartment.

Inspector Haig asked how to spell Janawosky and wrote the name on his scratch pad, "And her address?"

Hanson's voice was scarcely audible. "Her address is the same as mine. Her father is the janitor of our building."

I have no use for cheaters. But I felt sorry for Hanson. I knew how the papers would handle the story—

PROMINENT INSURANCE EXECUTIVE ADMITS
MAINTAINING LOVE NEST FOR JANITOR'S
DAUGHTER WHILE WIFE IS IN BERMUDA!

CHAPTER FOUR

A FIERY FURNACE

SCHOOL WAS OUT. That meant it was after three and I'd had six hours sleep. I lay with my eyes closed listening to the twins. They were hungry as usual and demanding that Magnolia put both peanut butter and jelly on their bread and could they have a peanut and jelly bread for Johnny,

Someone ran water in the bathroom. I tried to open my eyes, and couldn't. They felt fine but something was weighting them down. I peeled off two pieces of cotton. It was small wonder my eyes felt better. Sherry had kept cold glycerine pads on them. She was dipping fresh ones in the solution now.

I called that I was awake and she came in and sat on the edge of the bed. "Did I ever tell you I love you?" I asked her.

She wrinkled her nose at me. "Quite frequently." Her lips were cool and sweet. "Poor papa bird. Here mama thought he was on a binge and he was getting his face pushed in fighting for a worm."

She put a cigarette in my lips and lighted it. I had explained the whole thing to her before I'd gone to bed. I'd had to square myself. "Anything new?" I asked.

She wrinkled her nose. "All very disgusting. According to the noon newscast it would seem that Betty Janawosky's father attempted to kill Jack Hanson. He did black one of his eyes and Hanson had him put under a peace bond. Also your boy friend Maxie has called at least six times and wants you to call him as soon as you wake up."

I chewed over the information. The scandal would probably cost Hanson his job. He had it coming. But I was out eighty bucks on the case so far and I meant to get it back from someone. I asked if Zola's name had been mentioned in the newscast.

Sherry said it had. Her anatomy, as revealed in an old picture from her stripping days, had also been prominently revealed in all the morning papers, "She's raising hell,' " Sherry told me. "She wants either the jewels or the money."

No mention had been made of either husband, present or prospective, but young Tennent had come in for a good play. One of the papers had even advanced the theory of a possible jealousy motive for his slaying. For reasons of his own Haig had absolved me completely.

I took the phone on the night table, called the Amalgamated office, and asked for Hanson. Someone who said his name was Schaeffer answered the phone. I recognized the name. I'd seen it on checks. He was the big shot from the New York office.

He thawed when he heard my name but played it cagy when I asked if the deal was still on since I thought that I had a nibble.

"I'm afraid I don't know what you're talking about," he told me. "But the company is, of course, eager to minimize their loss and we will be glad to reimburse you for any sum you may have to pay out for 'information' that will lead to the recovery of Miss Charter's jewels."

I said to hell with that, that I wasn't laying out another dime but that if the company wanted me to I would investigate the nibble at double my standard per diem fee and phone him again when I had.

He agreed but he was still spluttering when I hung up.

The lad was waiting in Maxie's office. He said his name was Frazer and, according to Maxie, he had walked in cold, said he had read in the morning papers that I was handling the Charter case for Amalgamated and had offered Maxie half a C to arrange a meeting in his office.

He was another rah-rah boy, well dressed, six feet, blue-eyed, and would weigh in around two hundred pounds.

I thought I had it then. Haig's theory was right. Tennent had been in on the deal. It had been a fraternity affair, all for dear old Tappa Nu Keg, and the financial advantage of the two parties involved. But Tennent had gotten cold feet, tried to double cross Frazer, and had gotten a knife in the back instead.

I said casually, "I carry a gun."

Frazer smiled, white-toothed. "How original. I'm sorry that I can't say the same." He looked at Maxie. "Scram. Our agreement was that I talked to Mercer alone."

I nodded to Maxie and he left the office.

"Now," Frazer began, "don't get me wrong. I'm strictly a middle man. But you *are* interested in recovering the Charter jewels?"

I said that would depend. It did. Grand larceny was one thing. Murder was another. Still, I didn't know that he had killed Tennent and if I put the sleeve on him and it turned out that he hadn't,

I was kissing good-by to the difference between what he was willing to take and what Amalgamated would pay for the return of Zola's stones.

He read my mind. "I wouldn't. Believe me. I'm strictly a middle man."

I salved my conscience with the thought that having seen him, I could identify and pick him up if it turned out he had killed Tennent. "What's your proposition?" I asked.

"My principle," he told me, "will take fifty thousand dollars, the exchange to be made as he directs, and no questions to be asked."

I said he was out of his mind.

He read me a list of the jewels to prove he had them. "How about forty-five thousand?" he hedged.

I tried to beat him down to forty, settled for forty-five and agreed to meet him, if Amalgamated okayed the deal, at the Soldiers' and Sailors' monument in Westwood Cemetery at ten o'clock that night. Either he, or the lad behind him, if there was one, was bright. Westwood was out of the City limits, and out of Haig's jurisdiction. The monument, as I recalled it, stood alone on a rounded knoll. A stake-out would be difficult. There were a half dozen more details. I was to come alone. On reaching the monument, I was to light a match to show I had the money. The money was to be packed in a brief case, two thousand fives, two thousand tens, and seven hundred and fifty twenties. I would be permitted to check the jewels while the contact man counted the money.

I did some mental arithmetic. The whole setup was screwy as hell. Someone was doing something to someone. I didn't intend it would be me. "Okay," I agreed. "It's a deal. That is, if the Underwriters okay it. Leave Maxie a number to call. I'll let him know in half an hour."

Schaeffer, Hanson, and two directors of the firm whom I had never met before, were holding a conference in Hanson's office. He looked like a sick dog. From what I gathered they had been riding him plenty. He was out on a long, long limb and they were ready to saw it off.

I told them the deal I had made and Schaeffer hit the ceiling. He was damned if he'd do business with a thief, he'd rather pay the full loss, besides if I was as good as Hanson claimed I was, I would have beaten down the price "to say, possibly at least twenty-five thousand."

I said they could take it, or leave it.

While they tossed the money bag around, Hanson walked me out into the hall. One eye was swollen almost shut. He looked like he was about to burst into tears. "They're firing me, Matt," he told me. "Fifteen years with the firm and because I get my name in the papers, I get the boot."

I said that was too bad.

He swore. "All over a dirty little tramp like Zola. If she hadn't stopped off in Chicago to see Tennent, no one would ever have found out about Betty."

Remembering the scene I had witnessed in his lobby, I asked how her father had treated the girl.

"He threatened to kill us both," Hanson told me. "He did try to kill me. I am afraid that he may yet. Putting him under a peace bond hasn't meant a thing. He has been roaring drunk ever since the papers hit the street." He scowled at his cigar. "To keep him from harming Betty I had to ask Zola to take her in until Jana-wosky cools off."

It was his mess. I let him stew. "About the deal," I began. "Do you think—?"

"To hell with the deal," he cut me short. "I did my best. I hope the tight-fisted chiselers have to pay off the whole loss."

But they didn't feel that way about it. Schaeffer called me back into the office. It was alum in his mouth but he told me that if the deal was the best they could make, they would have to accept it. He scowled at Hanson. "I suppose the firm still has fifty thousand in its Chicago account?"

Hanson mumbled something about his getting into a scandal over a girl didn't mean he was also a thief and Schaeffer could take his job. So saying he stalked out of the office.

If it was big business, I didn't want any part of it. I felt like I hadn't bathed for a week. My five grand cut didn't seem so large. Besides, if I had figured the score correctly, the lad in back of the steal didn't mean for me to get it. I had been played for a sucker.

But two can play at that game. They say confession is good for the soul. And mine should have felt pretty good. En route from Maxie's to the office I had stopped in at H.Q. and had a heart to heart talk with Haig . . .

A cold wind had arrived with night fall. Indian Summer was over. At nine it began to rain. Black storm clouds obscured the stars. There was no moon. The only sounds were the chirp of the crickets, the hoarse booming of the frogs and the distant whistling of a freight train far down the C.M.&S.P. tracks. It was a peach of a spot and night for murder.

I sat parked half a block from the cemetery gate, waiting for ten o'clock. The forty-five thousand dollars I had agreed to exchange for Zola's jewels was in the brief case on the seat beside me.

Not that I was making five thousand on the deal. I wasn't. All I was getting was lumps. But I at least was saving my license and squaring myself with Haig.

It was Hanson, of course. It had been Hanson from the start. Haig's wild crack in his office hadn't been as funny as it sounded. I had realized that at Maxie's when Hanson's stooge, Frazer, had named fifty thousand dollars as his original asking price. No one but Hanson and Zola and myself had known the figure he had agreed to pay. A little thing, but sufficient. I mulled him over as I waited.

A high flier and a chaser, Hanson was always in need of money. He had probably been harder pushed than usual and Zola's stop-over had been a Godsend. He knew her jewels. He knew she never traveled without them. He knew his firm, having insured them for one hundred and fifty thousand dollars, would be willing to pay a third of that to save the larger fee. It had looked like a quick fifty thousand with little or no risk. Punks like Frazer come cheap. He had hired him to turn the trick, then called me in as a go-between. He knew, that with a wife and two kids to keep in nylons and jelly bread, I would jump at the chance to earn a good sized fee.

I had. Then things had begun to go wrong. As I saw it, Tennent had recognized Frazer and figured out the rest. His asking if the firm was willing to pay a good sized percentage for the recovery of the jewels was seemingly evidence of that. I, like a fool, had blabbed the potential solution to Hanson. He had sent his girl-friend downstairs, too high to know what time it was, and willing to alibi him because the little fool thought he loved her. Then he had driven to Tennent's apartment and knifed him to close his mouth. There was no need to kill me. He wanted me alive. In fact, before he left, he had thrown water on me to make certain I came to. I was another link in his alibi.

The minute hand came to attention. I got out of the car, slamming the door loudly behind me and scuffed across the gravel through the gate. Frazer had made one bad mistake in outlining the pay-off. Along with knowing the exact sum Amalgamated was willing to pay, the mistake had been what had tipped me. I was to examine the jewels while the contact man counted the money. He would have to work by either match or torch light. And figuring he counted four bills to a second, it would still take him better than a quarter of an hour. And no lad with both a grand larceny and murder charge against him was going to hang around with a detective that long—not even in a cemetery.

I expected to *see* the jewels. Then as I saw the play, whoever met me, would slug me. When I came to, Hanson would have both the money and Zola's jewels. I'd have a sour taste in my mouth and a stink on my reputation that I would never live down.

I transferred my gun from my holster to my pocket as I walked through the gate and down the road toward the monument. There was a dim light in the gate house, also a squad of Chicago cops. More were scattered around behind tombstones, squatted in the rain.

Haig had liked my story well enough to pull a lot of wires. But he had also warned me what would happen if anything went sour. I knew how he was reasoning. He figured I had a finger in the pie and was selling Hanson down the river to save my own hide.

Most of the leaves were off the trees and the bare limbs scraping together in the rising wind sounded like whimpering voices. Knowing I'll have one some day, I've never been fond of tombstones. Rain ran off the brim of my hat and down the turned up collar of my rain coat. My feet were soaked before I'd gone a block.

The monument stood on a rise. I climbed the hill and lit a match, cupping it in my hands against the rain. Then I chopped my hand back in my pocket and waited.

The once distant train whistle came nearer, shrieked for the Westwood crossing, then thundered by a block away on the south side of the cemetery. When it had passed, the croaking of the frogs seemed louder.

I put the case between my knees and lighted another match. Still nothing happened. Ten minutes passed, fifteen, then twenty.

Then a shadow wove through the tombstones, a deeper blob of black against the night, reached the foot of the hill and began to climb. I slipped the safety off my gun. But it wasn't either Hanson or Frazer. It was Haig.

Rain glistened on his cheeks His face contorted with anger, he demanded, "Just what the hell are you trying to pull, Mercer?"

I was mad as he was. "What the hell do you mean, what am I trying to pull?" Other figures began to pop up behind the tombstones. "I give you the case on a platter And now you've ruined the stake-out. With you shooting off your face so they can hear you in Evanston, how do you expect Hanson or Frazer to show?"

He said, "I don't I don't believe there is a Frazer. I believe that you invented him, just like you invented the rest of your cock and bull story about it being Hanson who killed Tennent. You just saw a good horse, and you rode it. You killed Tennent for those jewels—and you're going to the chair."

Something had gone very sour. My mouth suddenly dry, I asked him, "And just how do you figure that out?"

"It's elemental," he told me. "Old man Janawosky just proved Hanson's alibi."

"Just proved Hanson's alibi?" I was really puzzled.

"Yes," Haig said coldly. "Because of the way that Hanson had treated his daughter he just beat Hanson to death in his own apartment, then carried him downstairs and stuffed him into the furnace!"

I didn't say anything. I couldn't. I was sick. Hanson had been a heel, but it was a hell of a way to die.

CHAPTER FIVE

SOUND SHOOTING

HANSON'S LIVING ROOM looked like the Bears and the Green Bay Packers had played a night game in it. Lamps had been hurled every which way. Chairs were overturned, end tables and mirrors smashed. There were a dozen deep gouges in the plaster on the north wall. It was also well splattered with blood. The first homicide man to arrive had found the murder weapon pushed under a couch, a heavy, iron furnace shaker.

I toured the apartment with Sergeant Zukor. I had no choice. Haig had ordered me handcuffed to him. "I don't suppose," I asked him in Hanson's bedroom, "that it would do any good to tell you that I didn't kill young Tennent and know nothing about the jewels."

He shrugged. "Me, I'm just a cop. I do like I am told."

We went back to the living room. Two of the other boys brought Janawosky in from where ever they had been holding him. He was somewhat sobered now, and frightened. He admitted to anyone who would listen that he remembered fighting with Hanson and insisted the fight had taken place in his basement apartment. "But I no kill him. I too dronk. I just beat him op a bit."

Haig ignored him to talk to Assistant Coroner Vogel who had made the examination of what few charred remains they had been able to sift from the ashes.

There hadn't been much left to examine. Identification had been made by one of Hanson's dentures that had dropped through the grates into the fire pit, a large scarab ring he habitually wore, a twisted cigarette case and lighter, what was left of his watch, and by the size and shape of the remains.

Still pale and sweating, Vogel swore, "Another case like this and I resign."

It didn't bother Haig. "You were able to estimate the time of death?"

Vogel shook his head. "Hell no. This time you can me."

The district hack who had investigated the complaint said he thought it must have been shortly after ten. He thought so because the call had come into the Sheffield Station at 10:10. He had arrived at 10:29 to investigate a 'fight'. All was quiet in Hanson's apartment but the door being open he walked in, discovered its condition, and knowing of the bad blood between Hanson and Janawosky had immediately phoned Homicide.

It had been the excessive heat in the radiators that had tipped them, that and the fact they had found Janawosky lying on the floor of the laundry in a drunken stupor, his shirt and pants speckled with blood, and still clutching a coal scoop in one hand.

Haig glowered at me. "And where was I? I was out squatting in the rain waiting for a mythical contact man to arrive. You tripped yourself this time, Mercer. You put on a good act, but it failed."

I said that Frazer wasn't mythical. "You can check with Maxie on that."

He snorted, "Maxie!"

Even Vogel chuckled. Maxie's word wasn't worth a dime. And unless I could prove that Frazer did exist and had contacted me, I was out on a long long limb with twelve of my peers, a judge, and the D.A. about to saw it off. The State would contend, and successfully, that my trip out to Westwood with a brief case full of insurance money was merely an act to cover the fact that I, myself, had the jewels, having killed Tennent to get them.

There was a bustle at the door as two H.Q. men came in with Zola and Betty, and followed by Schaeffer of Amalgamated. Despite the jam I was in, I felt sorry for the Janawosky kid. She didn't look cheap now. Hanson had turned her head but she had real stuff in her. Her eyes puffed and swollen with crying, she went directly to her father, put her arms around him and kissed him.

"It's all my fault, Pa," she sobbed. "If I hadn't been such a fool, none of this would have happened."

He patted her awkwardly. "I no kill him, Betty. All I do is fight him, then got dronk on bottle of whiskey he bring down to the basement for try to make friends with me."

A time bomb started ticking in my mind. But no one else seemed to see anything strange in Janawosky's remark. Zola was to blame for that. Looking like a million dollars, and twice as hard to get, she was telling Schaeffer that while she was brokenhearted over Jack Hanson's death, he being an old and a dear friend of hers, she felt the insurance company had stalled her long enough, and she wanted either her jewels or the money.

Schaeffer looked at me, saw the cuff on my wrist and gasped. "Mercer's your boy," Haig told him. "As we see it he got Zola's diamonds. He killed young Tennent to get them."

I asked Zola if she believed that.

Her eyes were cold. "I don't know what to believe," she said, "or whom to trust." She pounded on one of the broken end tables with a greedy little pink fist. "All I know is that I want my jewels or the insurance and if I don't get it I'm going to a lawyer."

It had all been so simple all the time. It had been right in front of my nose. And I'd been too dumb to see it. But there was no use telling Haig. His mind was made up. I was guilty.

Schaeffer mopped at his cheeks with a sodden handkerchief. "You'll get your money," he assured Zola. He tapped his pocket. "I have a certified check for the loss made out and if you will accompany me back to the office to sign a release and a waiver on the jewels we'll conclude your part in this unfortunate affair."

Haig asked what he was sweating for.

"You'd sweat, too," Schaeffer said hotly, "if you had just heard the auditor's report. Hanson has been stealing us blind for years. God knows how much he's stolen. Only a thorough audit will uncover that. And if his amatory sins hadn't caught up with him so fortunately, I would be down at Headquarters this moment swearing out a grand larceny warrant."

Haig merely shrugged. "It costs dough to live like he did." He thumped the briefcase full of pay-off money and scowled at me. "How about it, wise guy? Do you still think a man can get away with it if he steals enough?"

I'd had a sufficiency of Haig. "If you were in charge of the case, he could," I needled.

His face red, he told Zukor, "Take him down to H.Q. Throw him in a cell but don't book him. He doesn't get to see a lawyer until we have a confession."

Zukor rattled the cuffs. "You heard the Inspector. Let's go."

1 was glad to. I wanted alone with Zukor—bad. There was a reason. I hadn't a thing to lose. I was sitting on a toboggan with the seat of my pants scorching. And when they had searched me out at the dead man's park, Zukor had used my own cuffs on me. He had also taken my keys. But he had overlooked the spare key in my pants watch pocket.

Zola touched my arm as we passed. "Just tell me this much, Matt. It was Bill Tennent who hired some thug to steal my jewels? Who got them?"

I said, "You were there. You should know."

She shrugged and turned away. Zukor walked me out of the room and into the elevator. Once we were in a squad car, I wouldn't have a chance. It was now or never. My left forearm and fist are cork and steel. It was like hitting him with a sledge. Zukor's eyes turned glassy, his knees sagged under his weight.

A colored girl was running the cage. I had Zukor's gun in my hand when she turned around. Her eyes mostly whites, she begged, "Don't shoot me, Mister. Please."

I told her to stop the cage. She did. Then I unlocked the cuff from my wrist, let Zukor slump to the floor and told the girl to run. me down to two. When she let me out, I told her, "Now take the cage to the roof—and keep it there."

She wasn't as frightened as I thought. The hand on the dial over the door shot up but stopped at Hanson's floor. Cursing, I raced down the fire stairs to the basement.

Two fingerprint men were still going over Janawosky's apartment. They paid no attention to me as I ran by the door. But the uniformed cop in the boiler room had plenty between his ears. He saw a citation and plain clothes the moment he spotted me.

"Hold it, Mercer!" he ordered. He slipped his gun from his holster. "Hold it or I'll shoot."

He did. But he fired his first shot over my head. And that was a bull on his part. I gave him what I'd given Zukor. He rolled with the punch and went down groggy but still conscious, feeling for his gun, and shouting, "Stop him! Haig's prisoner's got away."

I threw a slug back into the basement to discourage the fingerprint men and fought the bolt on the boiler room door. It was rusted and by the time I got it open, the cop on the floor had found his gun. He rolled over on his belly and squeezed off a burst of three.

I could have shot him. I didn't. I had nothing against the lad. He was just working for wages. He was a good cop but a lousy shot. Lead thudded into the door jamb, sending a shower of splinters into the right side of my face.

The fingerprint men refused to be discouraged. All three cops were shooting at me as I ran up the stairs to the alley. But the night being as black as it was, all three were shooting at sound.

I caromed off a garbage can and three slugs smacked into it, one of them burning my ribs. Windows were opening now. I heard a woman scream—"Here he is!"

Then a car turned into the alley, its headlights pinning me against a garage. I dived into an areaway, tripped over a child's toy wagon, got to my feet and ran on, panting.

My side hurt, but not badly. My face hurt worse. I felt like an inverted porcupine. I crossed the next street and the next, sticking to areaways and finally came out on State. A few doors from the corner of Rush, in front of an all night bar, a Yellow Cab driver was dozing at his wheel. I slipped into the cab and slammed the door. "Let's go."

He woke up with a start and slid back the glass partition. "I'm sorry, Bud," he told me. "You better flag another cab. I'm waiting for a fare."

The sirens were wailing now. Men were piling into prowl and squad cars with orders to shoot me on sight. In five minutes a snake wouldn't be able to crawl through the cordon that would be thrown around the district.

I let the driver look into the barrel of Zukor's gun. "Well, what are you complaining about?" I asked him. "Kick it over and get rolling. So you're waiting for a fare. You have one."

He got my point—and rolled.

CHAPTER SIX

WHAT'S YOUR PRICE?

THE BAR WAS SMALL, and Irish, well back of the Yards. I had changed cabs three times to get there. No one paid any attention to my face. It was that kind of a joint. There were two or three drunks who looked as bad as I did.

I bought a double rye and ten dollars worth of quarters and halves to play the phone booth in the corner. Haig had taken the five grand fee and added it to the dough in the brief case to be returned to Schaeffer but he had left me my own wallet to be checked in at the Bureau. "And I may need more," I told the barkeep. I'm calling my girl in San Diego."

He grinned, "You got it bad. Me, I never mess around with dames."

It was a typical big-shot run-a-round. Being that time of night I got Shad Ambler's Club Dreamland for four bucks but had to donate three more talking to minor punks before he came on the wire. I played my cards as I saw them. I told him who I was, that I was in a jam, and I thought he could help me.

He wanted to know why he should.

I mentioned several lads we both knew and he thawed considerably. "Go ahead. Shoot. Maybe I'll need a favor some day."

I said I had read in the papers that he was going to marry Zola Charters as soon as she divorced her current husband and wanted to know if it was the McCoy.

He swore, "Hell no. I read that story, too. But there isn't a thing to it. I don't know where my name came in. And as I get it from the grapevine, she isn't divorcing her husband. He is divorcing her and naming some Chicago man."

I had thought I was right. I was. The perfect murder had gone sour. "Thanks a million," I told Ambler.

He seemed puzzled. "That all you wanted?"

"It is enough," I told him.

I hung up, thought it over, then made another phone call, a nickel one this time.

Zola wasn't pleased to see me. She opened her mouth to scream, thought better of it, said, "Well, don't stand there in the hall like a fool. Come in. But you shouldn't have come here, Matt. Don't you know that every cop in Chicago is looking for you."

I said I did, what was more I had scars to prove it. I walked on into the living room, sat down and poured myself a drink.

She hesitated near the phone. "I really should call the police."

"Why don't you?"

"What do you want from me, money to get out of town?"

I admitted it was an idea and asked how she had made out with Amalgamated.

Her grin was gamin. "I have their check."

I added, "Also the jewels. It was a good try, Zola, but it missed. You see I've just been talking to Shad. And he not only tells me that he has no intention of marrying you but that it's your husband who's getting the divorce, naming a Chicago man."

She thought fast, admitted, "Yes. That's so. I just gave the papers Shad's name to protect Bill Tennent." She forced tears to her eyes. "But I don't understand what you mean about the jewels. A masked man put a gun—"

She stopped short as the doorbell rang.

"That should be Schaeffer," I told her. "Seeing as I was hired by Amalgamated to recover them, I phoned him before I came over and told him where they were."

She gasped, "You're mad. You're out of your mind, Matt Mercer." Her eyes grew shrewd. "And who else did you call?"

I told the truth. "No one."

Her night gown swishing about her ankles, she swept to the door and opened it. "Come in, Mr. Schaeffer." She fairly pulled him into the apartment. "I never was so glad to see anyone in my life." She locked the door behind him. "Matt Mercer is here—and he's mad."

Schaeffer looked old and grey. I offered him a drink. "Cheer up. The worst is yet to come. Wait until the dead begin to walk."

"A wise guy, eh?" a familiar voice said behind me.

I didn't bother to turn. I knew who it was.

Schaeffer's face turned three shades greyer. "Hanson!" he gasped. "But it can't be. You're dead!"

I corrected him, "No. It's Frazer his stooge who is dead. After picking a fight with Janawosky and leaving him a fifth of drugged whiskey, Jack killed Frazer in his apartment, dressed him in a suit of his clothes, put his watch and lighter and case into one of the pockets and stuffed him into the furnace along with a spare denture that he tossed directly into the ash pit to make certain the charred remains were identified as his."

Hanson, fully dressed, came into the room, a snub-nosed automatic in one hand. "I should have killed you last night at Tennent's," he admitted. "It would have saved me the job now."

"What put you wise?" he asked me.

I said it was surprising the thoughts even a dumb agency man could think when his own hide was in danger, but admitted, "You had even me fooled when the stake-out in Westwood folded due to the news of your demise. It was a crack of Janawosky's, a crack Haig somehow overlooked, that put me back on the track. You don't put a man under a peace bond then try to buy his friendship with a fifth of whiskey. And I was positive you'd pulled a fast one when Schaeffer told us your accounts were short. You've been planning this for some time. Making love to Betty was a business proposition with you. After you made your steal, you had to disappear. And what better way than to be killed by the father of a girl you'd wronged."

Schaeffer gasped, "He stole the jewels himself. He and Zola connived."

"That's right," I nodded. "Now they have both the jewels and the insurance check. They never intended to try for the fifty thousand. That was just dust in our eyes."

Zola cursed me as only a burlesque queen can curse. "We'll spend it, sucker. We'll go to South America just like we planned. And we'll have plenty for the rest of our lives."

Knowledge of sin came slowly to Schaeffer. "They're in love."

"At least what passes for love in certain circles," I said dryly. I was beginning to sweat. The affair wasn't going to suit me. There should be loud rappings on the door by now. Knowing Haig as I did, I had been positive that one of the first things he would do would be to put a police operator on the switchboard of Schaeffer's hotel in the hope I would contact him, offering to trade Zola's jewels for getaway money.

Hanson thumbed the safety on and off his gun. He seemed to be trying to make up his mind. "Believe me, Matt," he said, "I'm sorry. I didn't mean for this to happen."

I said, "Why let it?"

He shrugged. "I have no choice."

"I don't suppose that I can call Sherry?"

Zola shrilled, "And have the call traced to here? What do you think we are, fools?"

"Yes," I said quietly. "I do. Haig is right in that respect. No matter how much a man steals, it catches up with him sooner or later."

"The hell you say," Hanson sneered. "Turn up that radio, Zola. Here's the story." He outlined it quickly.

After he shot me and Schaeffer, he'd beat it down the back way and take a train directly to New Orleans, their jumping off point for S.A. He was a bright boy, make no mistake. The story she was to tell the police was a masterpiece of half truths and lies. As soon as he had gone she was to phone Inspector Haig, screaming hysterically that I had forced my way into her apartment, demanding getaway money and when she protested she had none, forced her at gun point to call Schaeffer and insist that he come over, baiting the trap with a phony story concerning new information.

When Schaeffer arrived, I demanded money of him and when he tried to call the police I turned up the radio and shot him, then, realizing it was hopeless, turned the gun on myself.

"You ought to write stories instead of thieving," I told him. "I bet you'd make more money."

Hanson ignored the crack to ask Zola if she had the story straight. She repeated it, with gestures. Coming from a pretty, crying girl, it wasn't bad.

Zola started for the radio. I stopped her. Still sitting on the ottoman, I said, "There's only one thing wrong with your story, Jack. If it's suicide, there will have to be powder burns. Also, if I have one hundred and fifty thousand worth of easily fenced diamonds, why should I come to Zola for money? Why don't I go to Maxie?"

Zola stared at me, wide-eyed. Hanson touched the jewel case in his breast pocket. "I'll leave a few small diamonds on your body. You brought them to show Zola that you had the jewels and offered to sell them all back for a third of the insurance check. More, you'd be a fool to go to Maxie. Haig probably has ten ringers in the poolroom just waiting for you to show."

"And the powder burns?"

He nodded to Zola. "Do as I told you. Turn up that radio."

She dialed in the radio full volume and a milkman's matinee blared out a blast of brass. "No," Schaeffer cried. "You wouldn't dare!"

But Hanson did—at least he tried. He took three quick steps toward me. I dived off the ottoman at his legs and the slug's whined over my head. Before he could shoot again, I pulled his legs from under him and wrestled him for the gun.

"You fool, you sap," I cursed him. "I have a gun in my pocket. I could have shot you through the cloth. But after what you tried to do to me, I want you to go to the chair."

Then heavy fists pounded on the door and Schaeffer opened it. Haig hauled me to my feet.

"You dirty, bloody, killer," he began, stopped short, his mouth gaping open as Hanson crawled to his feet and retreated across the floor. "You're dead," he managed to gasp.

Hanson scooped up the gun. "The hell you say." Mad with fear, his finger tightened on the trigger before Haig could draw his gun.

I shot him through my pocket. "The hell he doesn't. Stay as dead as you are, chump!"

Then everything became confused. I remember Zola crying, Schaeffer shaking my hand, and someone showing me the jewels they had taken from Hanson's pocket. It was hard to stay on my feet. My head and my side both hurt. I wanted to get home to Sherry.

"I was wrong, Matt. I was very wrong," Haig ate crow. "But this is going to make me look like a damn fool. And I'll appreciate it greatly if when the reporters show up you could sort of hint we were working on this together. I assure you that I'll be grateful."

"Oh, you have a price, eh?" I said. "It's pride." Then I relented. What the hell. Haig is a big shot on the Force. I have three mouths to feed. He's done me favors in the past. "You can tell the reporters anything you want to," I told him, "including that I've gone home."

Schaeffer stopped me en route to the door and pressed a check into my hand. "With my own, and with Amalgamated's, sincere gratitude."

I looked at the figure and whistled. It wasn't bad. It wasn't bad at all.

THE
CHARLIE McCARTHY
MURDERS

CHAPTER ONE

TILL DEATH DO US PART!

HART JACKSON RETURNED TO CHICAGO to kill Flip Evans on a Friday morning. He looked like a million dollars. His eyes were clear. His face had lost its night club pallor. His clothes, while outmoded, were expensive and well cut. The first thing he did when he got off the bus was buy a twenty-cent cigar. He paid for it with his last two dimes. Then he remembered the girl and looked around—but she was gone.

"Cab, sir? Carry your bags?" a redcap asked.

"No," Jackson said, and smiled thinly. "I don't believe so."

A bag in each muscular hand, he strode out of the Wabash Avenue doors of the Bus Terminal, walked north along the avenue for six blocks, then cut over the short block to South State Street and entered the first pawn shop he came to.

"I wish to pawn these bags and their contents," he told the clerk. "And I want to buy a gun. preferably a short barreled .38."

The clerk appraised the expensive cowhide bags, opened one of them and took out a ventriloquist's dummy.

He shook his head. "Can't use it."

He opened the second bag, unfolded the evening clothes and glanced respectfully at the labels. His voice, when he spoke, was regretful. "We don't sell guns, mister. And even if we did, I couldn't loan you a dime on the dinner jacket or the soup-and-fish. They cost you plenty when you bought them, but they've been out of style for seven years."

"Eight years," Jackson corrected. "But to hell with the clothes. The bags aren't out of style. I paid two hundred dollars for the pair. If I don't redeem them, you can sell them easily for fifty."

The clerk was undecided.

"Well—

The dummy on the counter sat up suddenly.

"Don't be an umpchay." The dummy winked at the clerk. "Profit is where you find it." He craned his neck around the store, then leaned back and whispered confidentially in Hart Jackson's ear, "Besides, Whitey told us that this pawn shop *did* sell guns to right guys, didn't he, Obnoxious?"

The clerk looked from the dummy to Jackson. An unlighted cigar in his mouth, Jackson's lean lips hadn't moved. Recognition lighted the cleric's sullen face.

"Oh. Yeah. Sure. I know who you are now."

He put the two bags and their contents behind the counter and jerked his head towards the rear.

The first, and one of the most important steps in Hart Jackson's plan to dispatch Flip Evans had been hurdled.

Through the ten-by-twenty-foot plate glass window in the east wall of the penthouse, Lake Michigan, forty floors below, lay as a dirty gray comforter over the unmarked graves of the men who had fought his rise to power.

"No trace of the dames?"

The speaker, a big man resplendent in white silk pajamas and a crimson Mandarin robe, turned his eyes from the window.

"No trace." Deacon Watts surveyed the other man's breakfast tray glumly. A dyspeptic little hood, he had the disposition of a viper. "They ain't no where we've looked. And the boys have combed the town."

Flip Evans piled two eggs on top of a sausage patty, loaded the whole into his mouth and rammed it home with half a slice of buttered toast.

"Have them comb it again," he ordered through the mouthful. "If that damn little tart should talk, we'll all go to the chair. Well, maybe not to the chair," he finished, modifying his statement.

The Deacon shook his head. "I ain't so sure." He picked the morning paper off the tray, turned a page, folded the paper down to tabloid size, then handed it to Evans.

"Where I got my thumb," he told him. Evans read the item:

JOLIET—Hart Jackson, formerly well-known ventriloquist and headliner of the Keith-Albee circuits, and in more recent years a night club m.c. and entertainer, was released from State Prison this morning after serving seven years of a twenty-year sentence for murder. Still maintaining his innocence of the crime, Jackson stated that while his plans for the future had been formulated, he would rather not make them public at the present time. Convicted and sentenced in 1933 for the so called 'penthouse' murder of Adoree Darling, blues singer of the swank Club Tropical, Jackson . . .

Evans laid the paper down beside his tray, his heavy blue-black jowls alive with sweat. He piled another egg on a sausage patty, then pushed his plate away. His appetite was gone.

"Now ain't that sweet? Damn the parole board to hell. I laid plenty on the line to have that lad kept there till he rotted."

Flip Evans was a former big time stagehand who had read the talkies' handwriting on the wall. If there were any of the Ten Commandments he hadn't broken, it was strictly an oversight. A good back skipper, unscrupulous, a politician, in ten years time he had coveted, perjured, blasphemed, stolen, and murdered his way to the throne once sat upon by Chicago's mightiest tough boys. The swank Club Tropical was the office from which he wove his spider webs and levied tribute.

"So what do we do about Jackson?" Watts demanded.

Flip Evans chewed at his fat lips.

"There's only one thing we can do. That guy is poison. Still—"

The phone on the breakfast table rang. Watts picked it up.

"The Deacon speaking for Flip."

His thin face brightened. "Yeah . . . yeah. Wait. . . . It's Sam," he told his chief. "He's down on Wabash Avenue and he's just seen Thelma." He listened a moment, his thin lips pursed. "I don't like it," he told Evans. "Sam says that Thelma got off the same bus Hart Jackson came up from Joliet on. He says she seems to be trailing Hart."

Evans' fat face wrinkled in earnest concentration. He asked: "The two females are together?"

"No." Watts shook his head. "Sam says he ain't seen Olga. Thelma is alone. And he wants to know should he bring her in."

"Hell, yes!" Flip Evans pounded on the table. Then, suddenly, he changed his mind. "No. Wait. We'll work it this way. Tell Sam to keep Thelma in sight and call us back in half an hour and tell us where to meet him."

"Shine, mister?" The youngster was insistent. Jackson glanced at his dusty shoes and shook his head. "No. Thanks. I don't believe so."

The youngster picked up his shine box and walked on. Jackson resumed his contemplation of the skyline. There was nothing that he could do for hours, but wait. It would be impossible for him to get into Flip's apartment. And Flip never showed at the Club until midnight.

The skyline, he decided, hadn't changed much. It was only men who changed. He thought of the change in himself and shuddered. Still a comparatively young man, his future lay behind him.

"From the top of the heap to a bench in Grant Park. Hokus pokus," he mused wryly. "And also Abracadabra."

"Oh, here you are."

The words were slightly breathless. It was the girl he had seen on the bus. She glanced nervously over her shoulder at the traffic streaming along Michigan Boulevard, then sat down on the bench beside him.

"So?" Jackson said. His fingers tightened on the gun in his pocket.

To the best of his sober recollection, he had never seen the girl before she had boarded the bus in Joliet. He had, however, known dozens of her type. She had a skin men loved to touch—and probably did. Her light gray flannel suit was form-fitting and expensive. The twin silver fox around her throat were real. In her middle twenties, her slim-flanked figure was perfection. She was vibrant, filled with life. Only her eyes were tired.

"So?" he repeated.

The girl came directly to the point. "You *are* Hart Jackson, the performer whom Flip Evans framed in the Adoree Darling killing?"

Jackson said, "Say that again."

"You are?" she persisted.

"I am."

"Then you're the man I'm looking for," she told him. "My name is Thelma Winston. I want you to marry me."

"You *what?*" Jackson asked, incredulous.

"You heard me," she said simply. She took a roll of bills from her purse and pressed them into his hand. "I'll give you five hundred dollars down. There will be more money later. Ten thousand more, in fact."

Jackson took the cigar from his pocket and wet-smoked it. A thin, reedy voice piped over the girl's left shoulder: "Well, what do you know about that, Obnoxious? We're being bribed. Ask her what's the gag?"

The girl's eyes hadn't left Jackson's lips.

"You're clever," she told him. "You're as good as ever." Her rouged lips twisted in a bitter smile. "But it isn't any gag. I'm serious."

A passing bus backfired and she winced. It was obvious that she was frightened. But some emotion greater than her fear was driving her. When she spoke again, her voice was low and throaty.

"Don't ask me how I know, but you're a right guy, Jackson. You're a man who fights for what he knows is right—a man who takes care of his own."

"Look, sis," Jackson said more gently, "what's the story?"

She shook her head.

"Not now. It's too long. I'll tell you as soon as we're married." She paused, then added: "And you'd better let me put the gun that you're carrying in my bag. Remember, you're only out on parole."

Jackson smiled. He saw the set-up now. The girl was a capable actress. She had almost fooled him for a minute.

"I'll take a chance on being picked up," he told her. "And you're serious about this marriage gag?"

"I am."

He called her bluff. "Okay, let's go."

Jackson's estimation of Flip Evans had grown considerably. It was the first time that he had ever heard of a professional night club beauty being hired to propose marriage as a lure. He had no doubt that she would lead him straight to Evans. But that was all right with him. Evans was the man that he wanted to see.

The parsonage parlor was small. A smell of frying onions filled the building. The young minister's voice droned on: ". . . authority committed unto me as a Minister of The Church, I declare that Hart Jackson and Thelma Winston are now husband and wife, according to the ordinance of God, and the law of this State: in the name of the Father and the Son, and of the Holy Spirit. *Amen.*"

His wife lifted her lips to Jackson. He saw that she was crying. He kissed her, then handed the minister a bill from the roll the girl had given him.

"So you went through with it," he told her out on the sidewalk. "Now where?"

"Wherever you want to take me," she said steadily. "I'm your wife. You still don't trust me, do you, Hart?"

"No," he admitted candidly, I don't."

She put her arms around his neck and kissed him.

He tried to hate the girl, and couldn't. Her body was soft and yielding in his arms. The tired look had left her eyes. He hadn't realized how really young and beautiful she was. He had a feeling that there was more, far more, to the affair than he could understand.

"Trust me. Believe in me, Hart," she pleaded. "I—"

Her right hand dipped into the pocket of his coat and sent his gun spinning on the sidewalk just as he heard and saw the car. Deacon Watts was leaning out the window, a sub-machine gun in his hands. Behind him sat Flip Evans.

"Why you dirty little Judas!" Jackson swore. He slapped her away from him, dove for his gun just as the car drew up beside them. The girl's suddenly outstretched foot sent him sprawling off balance to the walk. Then the machine gun began to chatter.

"No!" Flip Evans' voice boomed above the chatter of the gun. "Get out of the way, you little fool. Get—!"

A police whistle shrilled on the corner. In the distance a prowl car siren answered. The machine gun stopped chattering abruptly. The big sedan whipped in a U turn and roared off.

Jackson got cursing to his feet—then stopped. He knew suddenly why he was still alive. His wife lay on the grass between the sidewalk and the curb, the coat of her light suit stained crimson with her blood. She smiled wanly as he knelt beside her. He was to puzzle her last words for hours.

"She's your little sister now," she gasped. A spasm of pain racked her. Hart wiped away the blood-flecked froth from her lips. "Four-ten Logan Square Hotel. Please—take care . . . of Olga."

CHAPTER TWO

UNDER THE LIGHT

THE MEN LOUNGED EASILY around the room, smoking, talking. It might have been a social gathering. It wasn't. The show had been going on for hours with Hart Jackson as the main attraction. The light that shone directly in his eyes had ceased to be a light. It was a needle-pointed gimlet of pain that bored ever deeper into Jackson's brain.

"Cigarette, Hart?"

"Please."

Jackson felt the cigarette inserted between his lips, heard the scratch of a match, and inhaled deeply. But no smoke filled his lungs. Instead, an openhanded blow rocked him in his chair.

"Suppose you tell us why you killed the dame instead," Sergeant McCreary of Homicide suggested.

"But I didn't kill her," Hart protested vehemently.

"Don't give us that."

"It's the truth. Flip Evans had the Deacon chop her down. They were trying to get me."

"Why?"

"That's my affair. I'll settle that with Evans."

"You check on Evans, Jack?" McCreary called across the darkened room.

"Yeah," an unseen speaker answered. "Him and the Deacon and Sam were all in McGinty's, two bar keeps and a half a dozen customers all said so."

McCreary turned back to Jackson. "Why not tell the truth, Hart? It'll make things easier at your trial."

"I am telling the truth."

A short arm punch to his kidneys doubled him in the chair. The questioning went on.

"You'd known Thelma for how long?"

"I didn't know her. She trailed me up from Joliet."

"And asked you to marry her on a bench in Grant Park?"

"That's right."

"You think a jury will believe that story?"

"It's the truth."

Another openhanded blow straightened Jackson from his crouch.

"You lie," McCreary said without emotion. "Now, isn't it true that you've been slipping letters out of Stateville for some time, begging Thelma to marry you when you got out?"

"It is not."

"Yet she shows up on a bench in Grant Park with a marriage license in her purse less than five hours after you get out after doing seven years."

"That's the way it was."

"Why did she want to marry you?"

"She didn't say." Jackson fought the pain boring deeper into the nerves behind his eyes. "Yes, she did," he remembered. He quoted her. She said: " 'Don't ask me how I know, but you're a right guy, Jackson. You're a man who rights for what he knows is right—a man who takes care of his own.' "

A snigger rippled around the squad room.

"And that was the start of a beautiful romance," McCreary commented dryly. He tried another tack. "Just between the two of us, how much did you promise the fellows who chopped her down for you. Hart?"

"Nothing."

"You mean they did it for nothing? They were guys who's done time with you?"

Jackson tried to close his eyes against the pain. The detective who stood behind him yanked them open with a vicious tug at his hair. "Sergeant McCreary asked you a question."

"No. I mean, I didn't have her killed. I didn't even know the girl. I had no motive to have her killed."

"That's what you say."

"It's the truth."

"The hell it is." McCreary slapped his face lightly with a small oblong of folded paper. "I suppose you don't even know what this is? I suppose you don't have the least idea?"

"I do not."

"It's an insurance policy," McCreary told him. "And it's going to burn you, Hart. It's a policy for ten thousand dollars on Thelma's life—with you named as beneficiary. We found it in the poor kid's purse."

The razor-edged knife of fear began slicing at Jackson's bowels. The girl had said that there would be more money later—ten thousand dollars more. That meant that she had known or was afraid that she was going to die. He tried desperately to think, and couldn't. The light burning through his eyes had turned his brains to jelly. He gasped:

"That's new to me. I didn't know she had it."

"Be reasonable, Hart," the homicide sergeant pleaded. "We don't get any kick out of knocking you around. It's our job. Come on. Be a good fellow. Admit that *you* had her knocked off for the dough and we'll send out for some sandwiches and Java."

Jackson felt a lighted cigarette being stuck between his lips and sucked it gratefully.

"That's the fellow," McCreary complimented. "I'll send down stairs for a police stenographer now and you can dictate a confession."

Jackson shook his head.

"I can't confess. I didn't have Thelma killed."

A hard palm smacked his cheek. The cigarette went flying from his lips. The questioning went on.

"Why did you come back to Chicago?"

"To kill Flip Evans."

"You admit that of your own free will?"

"I do."

"And why do you want to kill Evans?"

Jackson's head was growing confused from pain. He told the truth.

"Because Flip murdered Adoree Darling in a drunken brawl and tried to pin it onto my kid brother, Jerry."

"On your kid brother, Jerry? I thought that you went up for twenty years on that rap."

"I did. When I saw that the frame was tight, I got Jerry out of the apartment and took the rap myself."

"Why?"

Hart Jackson had often wondered that himself. The closest to a solution that he had ever come had been the realization that Jerry was only a kid, his younger brother, and that a right guy took care of his own.

"Why?" McCreary repeated. "And why are you spilling this now when it didn't come out at your trial?"

The man under the light smiled bitterly.

"It doesn't matter now. Jerry's dead."

"Killed in a heist somewhere?" McCreary sneered.

"No," Jackson told him quietly. "He was shot down over the English Channel flying a Spitfire in the Eagle Squadron. I got the official cablegram in Statesville yesterday."

A brief, hushed silence filled the smoke choked room. Sergeant McCreary said:

"Sorry, Hart." He paused a moment, added, "Look. You've been a big shot performer. Hart. You've made more in a week than us guys make in a year. And you ain't the kind of a lug who's usually under the light in a star session. But you're in a tight spot. Your story doesn't hold water. And if you talk, well, you'll be making it easier on us all."

"But I can't talk, McCreary," Jackson protested. "On my word of honor, I didn't even know the girl. I never saw her until she got on the bus in Joliet."

"You lie," McCreary told him heavily.

Jackson closed his eyes. The detective behind him yanked them open. McCreary was holding a vague object in front of his face. It looked like a gun. It was.

"You do admit, though, that this .38 that was found not far from the body is yours?"

Jackson lied for the first time.

"I do not."

He knew now why the girl had yanked it from his pocket. She hadn't wanted him to be held by the police, perhaps sent back to prison. She had wanted him free to watch over the mysterious Olga, whoever she might be.

McCreary stifled a yawn.

"And your defense is going to be that it was Flip Evans and the Deacon who really chopped the girl?"

"It was."

"I doubt it." McCreary shook his head. "Ten, eight, even five years ago, maybe yes. But Flip's got too big for that sort of thing. And suppose you tell me this—"

"Yes?"

"Why should Flip Evans chop down his own moll?"

The light in front of Jackson blanked out briefly. He swam back through a fog of pain.

"I don't believe it. I don't believe that Thelma Winston was Flip Evans' moll!"

"Oh, but she was," McCreary told him coldly. His tone was slightly envious. "That fat gut makes them all. Everybody knows that."

The homicide sergeant snapped off the desk light and turned on the ceiling globe.

"That's all for tonight, boys." He dismissed his squad. "Hart isn't going to sing. But we've enough to ask for an indictment." He thought a moment. "The only question is, what to book him on until morning."

Hart Jackson got slowly to his feet. His lean face, bronzed by seven years of labor in a prison quarry for a crime committed by another man, was lined with pain and streaked with sweat. His eyes, blinded by his session with the light, saw only the white face of a frightened girl who had been his wife for minutes; a girl who had told him, and believed it as she said: "Don't ask me how I know, but you're a right guy. Jackson. You're a man who fights for what he knows is right—a man who takes care of his own."

His voice, a shade above a whisper, cut through the smoke-filled room like naked steel.

"Book me for murder," he told McCreary. "Book me for murder. But it won't do you any good. You can't keep me back of bars while Flip Evans is still alive." His voice slashed like a razor-edged broad sword. "Because, so help me, God—no law, no bars are strong enough to hold me!"

"The guy," a detective said, "is nuts."

"I'm not so sure," McCreary told him soberly.

One dim bulb burned in the ceiling. At the end of the short corridor, an unarmed turnkey, his chair tipped back against the wall, nodded over the midnight edition of the morning paper. Beyond him, Jackson knew, a desk screw sat doing book work. Beyond the desk screw, through still another bolted door, lay the bank of elevators that he must somehow reach. And despite his impassioned outburst, whatever he did must be clever. A forced crush-out was out of the question.

The night's business had been dull. Jackson and an old lag confidence man were the only customers in the detention cells.

"Cigarette?" Jackson asked the man in the next cell.

The man extended an arm through the bars of his cell until his groping fingers made contact with the pack.

"Keep the pack," Jackson told him. "I'm going out."

"They must be holding a convention," the old lag chuckled. "You're nuts. You're eleven floors above the street. And even if you could get out of your cell, you got the turnkey, the desk screw, and the elevator guard to dodge."

"I know it," Jackson said. He gripped the door bars of his cell and called to the dozing guard. "Hey! Turnkey. Be a pal, will you? Move me into another cell. This one is lousy with rats."

"G'wan to sleep," the turnkey yawned. "You're seeing things. There ain't no rats up here."

"No? Keep quiet and listen."

Jackson gripped his cell bars, still staring full faced at the turnkey. From the darkened corner of the cell behind him, a rat squealed viciously. It was joined by a second and a third.

"Well I'll be damned."

The turnkey waddled down the corridor and peered past Jackson into the cell.

"They must be holding a convention," Jackson told him. "Be a pal and move me."

The squealing underneath the bunk returned. The unsuspicious turnkey fumbled his key in the lock and opened the cell door.

"We used to have plenty of rats out at County," he told Jackson. "But these is the very first I've ever seen up here."

He bent down to peer under the bunk and Jackson clipped him behind the ear.

"You're clever, pal," the lag in the next cell whispered. "You ought to be on the stage."

"I was," Jackson told him.

He bound and gagged the unconscious man with strips of the blanket from his cot. Then he put on his hat and overcoat and stepped out of the cell, locking it behind him. Dangling from his right wrist was the turnkey's leather covered sap.

At the far end of the corridor, he flattened himself against the wall beside the door, and called in a credible imitation of the turnkey's voice:

"Hey, Jim! Come in here a minute, will ya? I think that guy Jackson that McCreary brought in is trying to do a Dutch!"

On the far side of the door, a chair scraped heavily on concrete. Then a steel bolt rasped on steel.

"Cut him down, you damn fool," the desk screw ordered officially. "There'll be hell to pay if—"

The sap landed with a hollow thud. Jackson caught him as he fell and eased him to the floor, his nimble fingers unpinning the shield from his chest.

"Boy," the old lag in the cell admired, "you're good."

"They can only burn you once for murder," Jackson told him.

He dropped the desk screw's gun in his pocket, pinned his shield on the inside of his overcoat lapel, then closed and bolted the big steel door.

In the outer hall, the elevator guard looked up suspiciously. Jackson paused in the doorway, his hands fishing for a cigarette as he called back over his shoulder:

"You want that Swiss on whole wheat toast or rye, Jim?"

"On rye," a voice called back from the desk at which the screw had sat. "And don't forget to stop in the D.A.'s office, and see can you get the file on that bird that McCreary just brought in."

Jackson closed the door, turned up his overcoat collar so that the silver shield was exposed, nodded pleasantly to the guard and punched the elevator button. Three minutes later he was outside on the street. His last obstacle had been hurdled. There had been no one who knew him in the foyer of the building.

The night was black and cold. But for several official cars and one lone cab parked at the curb, an occasional weary officer walking head down against the wind, and the lights in the Coffee Pot across the parking lot, lower South State Street was deserted.

Jackson paused in the doorway briefly, flipping a mental coin.

"The Logan Square Hotel and Olga," he debated, "or straight to the Club Tropical to kill Evans?"

The mysterious Olga won the toss. To the girl who had thought he was a right guy, the girl who had saved his life, he owed that much. He strode out to the curb and yanked open the cab door.

"Logan—" he began, then stopped.

The cab wasn't unoccupied. Two cigarette tips glowed in the dark. One hand reaching for his gun. Jackson started to back out.

"I wouldn't," Deacon Watts advised. "Come right on in. I've got a gun in your belly." His voice was almost cheerful. "Boy! Talk about breaks of the game. Here me and the best mouthpiece in Chicago sit freezing to death figuring how to spring you. We decide it can't be done—and you sit right down in our laps! The Club Tropical, Sam," the vicious tempered little gunman told the driver. "Flip thinks that Pretty Boy here might know where Olga is."

CHAPTER THREE

TELL HER IT'S OLGA

IT WAS THREE O'CLOCK IN THE MORNING. The cold had lessened somewhat and the frost on the kitchen window was being slowly replaced by great, flaky crystals of snow. John McCreary noticed the snow and was pleased.

"Bunny will like that," he told his wife. "She can use her new sled in the morning."

Betty McCreary cut another slice of beef from the roast that had been steaming hot at seven, and laid it on her husband's plate. Since the early days of their marriage she had accustomed her domestic schedule to her husband's hours. She slept when he slept, waited up, frankly worried, whenever he was late, to greet him with a smile.

"Better eat up and get to bed, hon." She spooned some hot lima beans on his plate. "You've had a long day."

The homicide sergeant poured himself a second cup of steaming coffee, scratched an itching stockinged foot on a leg of the kitchen table, and exhaled a thoughtful: "Yeah." He resumed the subject he had been discussing before he had noticed the snow. "You know, Betty. I mean it. That guy Jackson no more had that dame killed than I did."

"But, John. His story is fantastic."

McCreary spooned sugar in his coffee.

"That's what makes me believe it. And don't ask me how I know, but I've a feeling somehow that he's a right guy. That he—"

The sergeant stopped abruptly and tugged at the lobe of his ear.

'He what, dear?" his wife demanded.

"He told me that was why the dame said that she wanted to marry him. Maybe his story is true. Flip Evans would gun his grandmother for the silk ribbon in her prayer book."

"But then why don't you do something about him?"

McCreary grinned.

"Look, Betty. I ain't running the City. I'm just a cop. I do what I'm told to do." He paused for a sip of coffee. "Besides, Flip has his usual alibi, and there ain't no reason I know of why he should have wanted to rub out this Thelma."

"Was she pretty?"

"Well," McCreary shrugged, "you know how them dames are. It mostly comes out of jars and bottles."

"I remember Hart Jackson well," Betty McCreary mused. "He looked something like Warren Williams in the movies. I saw his act at the old Palace half a dozen times."

"He was big time," McCreary agreed. "One of the reporters told me that Flip Evans paid Jackson a thousand bucks a week when he was working at the Club Tropical. He was tops. I only wish," he went on sincerely, "there was something I could do for the guy. But he hasn't got a chance. He—"

The phone in the bedroom rang. McCreary got up from the table with a muted curse and tiptoed in to answer. The room was warm with sleep.

"That you, Daddy?" a small, sleepy voice asked from the darkness.

"Look, Bunny. You're supposed to be asleep," McCreary told his daughter. He bent and kissed her, ignoring the ringing phone. "And you'd better sleep real fast and get good and rested."

"Why?"

"Because," he confided, "it's snowing out, an' you an' me are going sled riding in the morning."

The seven year old snuggled into a sleepy ball, said "Oooo," in drowsy anticipation, and was asleep again before the sergeant had reached for the phone.

"Sergeant John McCreary of Homicide speaking," he growled into the mouthpiece.

His wife was waiting for him with worried eyes when he returned to the kitchen.

She didn't speak until he had forced his swollen feet into his shoes and buckled on the harness of his shoulder holster.

"Now what, John?"

"Jackson made good his boast that we couldn't hold him," he told her heavily. "He damn near killed a turnkey and a screw busting out of Central Bureau." He shrugged into his coat. "And that ain't all. Max Diamond has just identified him as the lad who climbed into a cab that him and Deacon Watts was sitting in. He made the cabby wheel them to the Outer Drive, and—"

"And what?"

McCreary buttoned his overcoat, tugged his hat down firmly and perfunctorily kissed his wife good bye.

"Watts is dead and Diamond is dying," he told her. "Jackson is known to be armed and the Chief is putting out a general on him. They're afraid that he'll get Flip Evans next. Orders are to bring him in dead or alive."

The kitchen door, torn from his hand by the wind, banged shut behind him. McCreary opened it again.

"Sorry," he grinned at his wife. "And tell Bunny that I'm sorry about that ride."

Crouched behind a morning paper in the front car of the two-car elevated train, Hart Jackson heard the guard call: "Damen Street. Robey Junction. Car behind for Humbolt Park."

The gesture was automatic. Except for a loudly snoring drunk who had informed the guard belligerently that he wished to go to Logan Square, Jackson was alone in the car. He stared out of the window briefly into the snow-filled night as the first car, relieved of the Humbolt Park train, got under way. Then he resumed his reading of the paper.

His escape, and the happenings on the Outer Drive, were not yet headlined. He knew that they would be in every subsequent edition. The paper had already tried and convicted him of the murder of Thelma Winston. Even a motive had been established. He had admitted he hated Flip Evans. Thelma was Evan's girl. It was assumed that he had made love to the deceased by mail. To lull any latent suspicion that the girl might have entertained, he had insisted on an immediate marriage five hours after being released from prison. As they left the church his hired gunmen, as yet unnamed, had been waiting. He had hoped to blame the murder onto jealousy by Evans. But the one mistake that trips all murderers had trapped him. In his greed, and perhaps for funds to pay the gunmen he had hired, he had insisted that the girl insure her life in his favor for ten thousand dollars. The policy had been found in her purse.

Jackson read and re-read the story. It fascinated him. He had never known that a theory so palpably absurd could read so soundly.

Annoyed, he allowed his eyes to drift to the next column. He read, absently, that:

> . . . some slight concern is beginning to be felt by intimates over the continued absence of the noted Loop Hound and elderly playboy, Fillmore Pierce. Heir to the Pierce packing house millions, the gray-haired playboy has not been seen since leaving the Club Tropical an the early hours of Friday last. Noted, however, for his eccentricities, it is believed that Pierce may have boarded a train for . . .

Jackson folded the paper and laid it on the seat beside him. He had worries enough of his own without considering the peccadilloes of elderly playboys. Then he remembered the condition of his face, unfolded the paper again and held it as a shield.

He wondered if both Diamond and Watts were dead. He knew that the driver, a young hood whom they had called Sam, had gotten away. He regretted that exceedingly. The word *"Logan"* had slipped out of Hart's mouth before he had seen the two men in the cab. Surely, Flip Evans was smart enough to supply the balance of the address. When Hart had looked in the phone book, he had found only one Logan Square Hotel.

If, Jackson mused grimly, the Deacon hadn't been so insistent on beating Olga's address out of my face with the butt of his gun, I might be dead by now and he'd still be alive.

Even now, since he had had time to think, the chronological order of the events in the cab was vague. One minute Diamond had been holding him while Watts hammered on his face, the next he had twisted the gun from the vicious little hoodlum's hand, and the cab had been filled with gunfire and the reek of cordite.

He wished he could have taken a cab to the hotel. But a cab might have proved more dangerous than the L, with every squad car in Chicago tom-catting through the night trying to run him down. Besides, they had taken his money—Thelma's money—at the Bureau. He had only the change in his pocket that they had left him for cigarettes.

"She's your little sister now."

His wife's dying words were plain above the squeal of the wheels on the wet rails. And they conjured up a picture. He saw a girl, slightly younger than his wife, dewy-eyed, innocent; perhaps a country girl on whom the jaded night club owner, tired of Thelma, as he had tired of Adoree Darling, of countless girls, had cast a speculative eye. Evans had told Thelma she was through, had sought to compromise her younger sister. . . .

Still, that didn't add up either. A man of Flip Evans power and standing seldom made a fool of himself about a girl to that extent. He didn't have to. As Sergeant McCreary had said: "That fat gut makes them all."

But then, why had Thelma wanted to marry him, Hart Jackson? Why had she insured her life for ten thousand dollars in favor of a perfect stranger? Jackson kneaded his aching temples with the fingers of one hand. It all came back to the mysterious Olga. Since Flip was so determined to find her, she was the girl who held the key.

The el car jerked to a sudden halt. The drunk sat up and looked around him blearily.

"Logan Square. All off," he announced.

His hat brim tugged low over his battered face, Jackson walked to the end of the car.

"Er—is there a hotel right around the Square here somewhere?" he demanded of the guard.

"Sure." The guard ceased unhooking the chains to point across the vast expanse of snow that was Logan Boulevard. "Right over there where you see that neon light, bud. That's the Logan Square Hotel."

It had been two nights now, Olga Winston reflected soberly, since Thelma had been gone. And she was lonely, she was frightened, she was hungry. She was so hungry that she couldn't sleep.

She stared at her reflection in the dressing table mirror. She saw a plump, white body clad only in sheer silk hose, a pair of filmy step-ins, and a wisp of a brassiere. She thought she looked a trifle pale and added more dry rouge.

It added considerably to her color, but did nothing for the rumbling in her stomach. Her rouged lips thrust outwards in a pout. Thelma had promised to come back by the next morning. And still she had not come.

Olga tugged her stockings tighter. It would soon be dawn. Thelma's diamond wrist watch said twenty minutes after seven. No. The other hand was the long hand. That made it twenty-five minutes of four. It was early morning again and she hadn't eaten for hours.

Still seated at the dressing table, she raised the blind cautiously and peered out. Underneath the L Terminal the red neon sign still blinked provokingly:

TERMINAL RESTAURANT
Steaks and Chops

She considered the matter carefully, then pouted:

"I could eat and come right back to the room, and Thelma wouldn't even know that I'd been gone."

Out on the vast expanse of white, a man struggled across the parkway, his body bent against the wind. As she watched, he paused beneath a street lamp and looked directly at her window. She dropped the blind and picked up her purse. It wasn't fair for Thelma to stay away so long. Nor was it fair for Thelma to leave her so much money, then make her promise not to spend it.

Determined, the girl stood up. As she did, the brassiere slipped down around her tummy. She hitched it up and the filmy step-ins dropped from her unformed hips. She trailed it across the floor dressed only in a pair of stockings that fitted her like boots. Thelma's clothes simply would not fit her.

Her own warm underthings, soft woolen dress, and ski pants were piled carefully on a chair. She struggled into a suit of long woolen underwear.

"I'm hungry, and I'm going to eat," she told the mirror.

Then she remembered her promise.

"Promise now, sweetheart," Thelma had insisted, holding her close to her. "Cross your heart and hope to die?"

"Cross my heart and hope to die," she had promised. "I won't leave the room 'till you get back."

Tears coursed between the freckles that the rouge would not quite hide. She didn't want to disobey Thelma. She didn't want to die. But she was *so* hungry—so awfully hungry.

It was then that she had the idea. She didn't know why she hadn't thought of it before. The phone number was easy to find—it was printed on a patented noise-maker from the Club Tropical, where Thelma worked.

"Shore six-one-o-o," she told the desk clerk over the phone, then added a tardy, "Please."

"Club Tropical," a man's voice said as the connection was completed.

"If you please," she said distinctly into the mouthpiece, as Aunt Naomi had taught her, "I would like to speak to Thelma."

There was a brief pause at the other end, then the man's voice said:

"Why—sure. Just a moment, please. I'll call her to the phone."

But it wasn't Thelma's voice that answered. It was the voice of the big fat man who had made the gray-haired man's face all bloody.

"Say, Thelma's busy right now," he apologized pleasantly. "But she asked me to take the message. Who is this calling? And what is it you want me to tell her?"

"This is Olga calling," Olga told him. "And tell Thelma to please come home. Tell her that I'm hungry and very lonesome."

"I'll see that she comes home right away," the man assured her. "But—er— where are you calling from?"

"Why, from the Logan Square Hotel," Olga. told him primly. "Thelma knows where I am. She—"

The little girl stopped speaking suddenly and hung up the receiver. She did not know exactly why, but she knew that Thelma would not be pleased. Tears flooded her blue eyes. She threw herself on the bed and cried. She was lonely. She was hungry. She was frightened. Even playing grown-up-lady in her sister's clothes had lost all of its charm. She was, after all, only seven. And until Aunt Naomi had died, and the neighbors had sent her to Thelma, she had never been in a city before.

CHAPTER FOUR

COME AND GET IT!

THROUGH THE PLATE GLASS of the inner door of the foyer, Jackson could see a gangling, youthful clerk reading a detective magazine back of the hotel desk. His hat tugged well down over his face, he strode into the lobby.

"A room for the night," he told the clerk, "preferably one on the fourth floor."

"Yes, sir." The youth creased the page in his magazine, laid a registration card down on the desk, and extended a pen. He saw that Jackson had no luggage. "And that will be two dollars in advance, please."

Jackson swore softly. He had forgotten that he had no money but the silver in his pocket.

"Look," he began. "I—"

The buzz of a police call coming on the air cut him short. A small, desk radio began to squawk:

"Calling all cars . . . calling all cars. This is a repetition. Be on the alert for Jackson . . . he may be in any section of the city. Pay attention . . . he is thirty-eight years old, five-feet-eleven inches tall, weighs about one eighty. He is light complexioned, brown hair, smooth shaven. It is believed his face may be badly marked from the struggle in the cab. When last seen he was wearing a smartly tailored but outmoded black Chesterfield overcoat with velvet tabs, and a fawn colored beaver hat. . . . This man is armed. . . . This man is armed. Be careful. Shoot first and question later. Shoot first and question later. This is an order. P.D.C."

Jackson felt the clerk's eyes upon his face.

"Think you'd know me if you saw me again, son?" he smiled.

"Sure. I'm the guy they're looking for." He rested the barrel of his gun on the desk. "But you just do as I say and you won't be hurt."

The clerk gasped: "Yes, sir."

"And don't try to be a hero," Jackson warned him. "I'm on the kill tonight."

The clerk believed him. Jackson locked him in a linen closet on the second floor after binding and gagging him loosely. The hotel was small and if the terrified clerk hadn't lied, he was the only night employee. Two floors above, a light shown through the transom of 410.

Jackson knocked softly on the door, called: "Olga?"

The door opened almost immediately. He was prepared for almost anything but what he saw. Her taffy-colored hair stood out in twin braids from her head; her plump little body was sheathed in a woolen union suit, and her freckled cheeks were stained with tear-smeared rouge. In her childish voice she said: "Ess?"

"Why," Jackson smiled. "I—"

The baby's face lighted hopefully.

"I know who you are," she told him. "You're the big brother that Thelma went to find."

Jackson entered the room and closed the door behind him.

"That's right," he told her soberly. "That's just who I am." His sharp eyes swept the room. "You're all alone?"

The child brushed off a tear that was balanced on her nose, then nodded at a big stuffed rabbit that sat upright in a chair. She looked very frightened and tiny.

"Except for Peter Rabbit."

"Hello, Peter," Jackson said.

"Hello, Hart," the stuffed rabbit answered him. "Just imagine meeting you here."

The child stood staring, first at Hart, then at the rabbit.

"Aw. You did that." A smile brightened the tear-stained little face. "I know you did, a-cause stuffed rabbits, even Peter Rabbits, can't talk."

"Is that so?" the rabbit scoffed.

The little girl squealed delightedly.

"Make him talk again," she pleaded.

"Later, perhaps," Jackson smiled. He sat down and swung the child up on his lap. "Look, honey," he told her. "Thelma *did* send me to you, and I want you to trust me."

"But where's Thelma?" she demanded.

"Why—why, she couldn't come to you right now," Jackson evaded with an averted face. "She—you've been alone in this hotel . . . how long?"

"Two night-times and two days," she told him earnestly. "An' I'm hungry." She began to cry. "It isn't fair for Thelma to stay away so long."

"Here, here," the stuffed Peter Rabbit chided from his chair. "Big girls your age don't cry."

The child forgot her tears and laughed.

"How do you do that?" she demanded, looking first at Hart, then at the rabbit.

"If you're a good girl, I'll show you," Jackson promised. He tightened his arm protectively around her. "Look, Olga. How long have you been in Chicago?"

"About a week. Ever since Aunt Naomi died and the neighbors sent me to Thelma." She seemed to notice his bruised and battered face for the first time. Her tiny finger-tips explored the bruises. "Somebody hurt you."

"Yes," Jackson admitted, "they did." A vague picture was growing in his mind. It was for this baby's sake that Thelma had wanted to marry him. It was for this baby's sake and the desire to protect her against something, possibly the death that she herself feared, that Thelma Winston, Flip Evans' moll, had insured her life for ten thousand dollars in his favor. "Suppose, honey," he cuddled the little girl in his arms, "you tell me just what happened from the time you got into Chicago." He added as a clincher, "Thelma said you should."

Olga thought a moment, then began:

"Well, first I lost the address that Mrs. Bladen—she's the minister's wife—pinned on my coat. So, instead of going right to where Thelma lived, like I was s'posed to, I went to the place where she had written Aunt Naomi she was working. Then . . ."

The child's voice rambled on. The story was incredibly simple. Jackson mused grimly, as she told it, that he might have known what it would be.

"And 'en," the child concluded, "when the big fat man who had made the gray-haired man's face all bloody saw me hiding back of the clothes basket where I was waiting for Thelma, he was going to do something bad to me, too. But Thelma picked me up an' runned away."

"She was okay." Jackson said, paying tribute quietly to the slain girl's memory. "She was people."

The little girl began to cry again.

"But now I'm hungry. An' why *doesn't* Thelma come back? The bad fat man where she works said he would tell her to."

Jackson sat up sharply.

"You called the club?"

The big blue eyes were worried behind their film of tears.

"Ess. I got so hungry."

Jackson stood the child on the floor.

"Get your clothes on, sis," he ordered. "We've got to leave here—fast."

He knew Evans wouldn't waste any time. He couldn't afford to allow the child to live, especially now that he had gunned her sister.

"But, mister—" Olga protested. "I promised Thelma—"

"Hush," the stuffed rabbit chided. "Hurry."

Her puzzled eyes on the stuffed rabbit, the little girl fumbled into her dress and shoes, then pulled on her ski pants. Jackson sat thumbing through the phone book. When he found the name he sought, he wrote it and the address on a hotel envelope, added a hasty scrawl, signed it, sealed the envelope and tucked it securely Into the little girl's overcoat pocket.

"Have you any money, sis?" he asked her.

"Ess," she boasted. "Thelma left me lots of money." She opened the miniature purse on the dresser, "I got five dimes, an' a nickel, an'—"

Jackson added the silver from his pocket.

"That ought to be plenty, honey," he told her as he buttoned her overcoat. "You know what a taxi-cab is?"

"Uh-huh."

"Well, there's a lot of them across the street in front of the elevated train." He showed her the envelope in her pocket. "And if by any chance some bad men should try to stop us, I want you to run as fast as you can, get into a taxi-cab and tell the driver to take you to the address on this paper. You understand?"

She nodded brightly.

"Uh-huh. An' will my sister Thelma be there?"

"No," he told her soberly. "She won't. But there will be a nice lady there who—"

He stopped short as a car roared up before the building and stopped. Jackson raised the blind a trifle. Four men got out of the car, leaving a fifth at the wheel. He strode to the side window, unlocked it, and looked out. Three feet away, a shadowy fire escape led down to the snow-banked ground. Jackson turned and knelt beside the little girl.

"Look, sweetheart. Now I don't want you to be frightened, but some bad men are coming in. So listen to me carefully. Here's what I want you to do."

With his hand in his side coat pocket, Sam Harvey peered around the hotel lobby. He was still wearing a crimson welt from the barrel of Jackson's gun, earned when he had escaped from the death car in the Outer Drive.

"Funny there's no clerk," he grunted.

"To hell with the clerk." The hood behind him shook his head. "I don't like this baby killing stuff, but come on. The room number is four-ten. Flip called back after the kid hung up."

They punched the button in the elevator and rode in silence to the fourth floor.

"That's the room." Sam Harvey slipped his gun from his pocket and pointed at the light shining over a transom. "If you guys are squeamish, let me handle this. If that brat should squawk, we'd all be out of jobs—and worse."

He rapped sharply on the door of room 410.

"Ess?" a childish voice demanded.

"This is a friend of yours, Olga," the hoodlum whispered. "When Thelma heard that you were hungry she sent me over with some sandwiches and milk."

"Ess?" the voice repeated.

Harvey cautiously tried the door. It was locked.

"Well, open the door," he demanded.

There followed a moment of silence.

Then a little girl's voice said primly: "No. You go away. Thelma said I shouldn't open up the door until she came."

The four hoods looked at each other.

"Look, kid." Harvey changed his tactics. "We ain't got no time to waste. Come on, now. Open the door."

"No," the little voice said firmly. "You are a bad mans. Go away."

One of the hoodlums snorted. Harvey said: "To hell with this."

He backed across the hall, bunched his shoulder muscles and lunged against the door. The wood splintered from the lock and he lurched into the room followed by the others.

"Welcome," Hart Jackson told them from the bed. His gun barrel rested lightly on one knee. "Come and get it."

The four hoodlums froze. Sam Harvey gasped "Hey—what is this?" His eyes darted around the room. Except for the man on the bed, it was empty. "Where the hell is the little girl?"

"Girl?" Jackson repeated, puzzled. "What little girl? You fellows must be drunk."

"They're baby killers, Hart," the stuffed Peter Rabbit added from the chair across the room. "Go on. Give yourself a treat and mow 'em down."

CHAPTER FIVE

ROUNDER'S LULLABY

THERE WAS ALMOST NO OTHER TRAFFIC on the street. The big squad car roared down the slippery car tracks through the pelting snow screaming like some predatory beast. McCreary, sitting with the driver, kept the siren wailing. Behind him, the three other members of his squad sat leaning on their rifles.

"Cut north on Humboldt Boulevard," McCreary told the driver, "west on Palmer, then north again on Kedzie. We'll make better time that way."

The driver merely nodded, his eyes glued to the narrow lane of light the fog lamps carved out of the snow.

"Think Jackson meant the Logan Square Hotel?" Nelson asked from the rear seat.

"He could of," McCreary grunted. "At least it sounds as if he was headed out this way."

Ed Woods, the squad's sharpshooter was indignant. "Hell. If that guy Diamond was going to die anyway, why didn't the doc hype him so he could have told us what he knew?"

"Okay, okay, Herman," McCreary soothed him. "So what did he know? Just one word—Logan. For all we know, Jackson could have been headed for—"

The sergeant stopped short as the radio crackled, then went on to tell them what they already knew.

"Calling all cars . . . calling all cars. Max Diamond just died. This makes the third murder for which Jackson is wanted. He must be found. This is an order. P.D.C."

Harry Bennet sighed. "Sure. He must be found. And that announcer sits on his fat kanetta while we're out finding him. I should have ought to joined the navy."

"You should kick," McCreary told him. "I was going to take my kid sled riding in Lincoln Park this morning." He turned half around in the seat. "Say, did I tell you guys what Bunny said at breakfast yesterday morning?"

His squad groaned in unison: "Yeah."

Nelson chuckled.

"Hell. You even told it to Jackson when we were booking him down at the Bureau. What's the matter, John? That guy got the eye on you?"

"Well—" McCreary maintained his now almost untenable position that Hart Jackson had deserved a better break than he had gotten—"I still don't think the guy's all bad."

"Of course not," Bennet assured him. "The guy's practically a sissy pants. He gets out of stir this morning after serving seven years for one murder rap, and by," Bennet looked at the luminous dial of his watch, "four seventeen a.m., all he's done is have one dame bumped off for her insurance, slap over a turnkey and a screw, and bump off one hoodlum and one mouthpiece."

McCreary said nothing more for blocks. Then he admitted curtly: "Okay. So maybe I was wrong. But if he'd only knock off Flip Evans before we catch up with him, the whole damn city would be better off."

"A lot of Pollys would sleep better nights," Ed Woods agreed. "If Flip Evans ever coughed, they'd have to build another wing on Stateville."

The car radio came on again: "Calling H.Q. Homicide . . . calling H.Q. Homicide . . . Sergeant McCreary call your bureau . . . Sergeant McCreary call your bureau. P.D.C." The squad car skidded to a stop before an all night restaurant.

"Now what?" McCreary grunted as he eased himself out of the car. He saw the coveted lieutenancy for which he and Betty had hoped for years washed down the drain of a trial board. "If some precinct station hack from Shakespeare or West North Avenue has corned Jackson while we were waiting at the hospital for Diamond to talk, there's going to be hell to pay."

He came back through the ankle deep snow on the run.

"The Logan Square Hotel—and fast," he ordered. He added, as the great black car screamed down the street: "Jackson was there in room four-ten not fifteen minutes ago."

"Yeah?" Bennet scoffed. "And how does H.Q. know?"

The big sergeant's eyes were worried. "Because Thelma's baby sister told my wife."

"Thelma's baby sister *what?*"

"Told my wife. At least that's what the Chief said."

"But look," Ed Woods demanded. "Who knew that Thelma had a baby sister? And who sent her to your wife?"

McCreary clung to the side of the rearing car as it skidded off of North Avenue onto Humboldt Boulevard with only two wheels biting at the pavement. As the car straightened out, he gasped: "Jackson knew it. The Chief said that the baby, a little girl about seven, told my wife that Jackson sent her."

"Well I'll be damned." It was an admitted under-statement. "But where did the kid come from? And why did Jackson send her to *your* wife? How do you puzzle that out?"

Sergeant McCreary leaned on the siren. "I don't," he told Woods crisply. "If I was that smart, I wouldn't be risking my life in this jalopy. I'd be sitting in a nice steam-heated office smoking a fat cigar as the Commissioner of Police."

The exterior of the club remained unchanged. A great white barn of a building, it squatted, two stories high, among its towering neighbors of the Gold Coast. It had been, originally, a riding academy and a livery stable. In some ways, it hadn't changed.

A uniformed doorman, well bundled against the cold, stood under the bright red canopy. The parking lot across the street was filled with cars. A hot conga seeped through the heavily curtained windows. If one listened closely one could hear the faint click of a spinning ivory ball on the second floor. The Club Tropical seldom reached full swing until three a.m. From four-thirty until five every morning the band was on the air with The Rounder's Lullaby. The club's policy was simple. It catered to the wealthy venal. It sold anything—for a price.

A block from the club, Sam Plarvey slowed the car, asked, not very hopefully: "You want I should drive to the service entry?"

The cold barrel of Jackson's revolver nuzzled the hoodlum's ear. "I said the main door, Sam. Undoubtedly your boy friends have broken out of that bathroom by now. And if they have, Flip should be expecting us."

The gunman braked sullenly to a stop in front of the crimson canopy. The doorman opened the door, saw who was in the car, and backed rapidly through the drifting snow to a phone on the wall.

"I wouldn't," Jackson warned him. "I've enough odds against me now."

A spurt of flame leaped from the car and a little geyser of snow kicked up at the doorman's feet. The sound of the shot was swallowed by the wind.

"Into the club ahead of me, both of you," Jackson ordered. "And don't try to make a break. Flip is the lad that I'm after—but they can only burn me once for murder."

The two men shuffled through the door. His gun in the pocket of his coat, Jackson followed closely behind them. He had no illusions. He knew that the odds were one hundred to one against him. He felt somehow vaguely regretful. This morning it hadn't mattered. Now death didn't seem so sweet. Flip Evans' fat, leering face kept becoming confused with a pair of blue, baby eyes.

"Do it again," she had told him.

"I intend to," Jackson thought wryly. "Only this time I'm not going to throw my voice. I'm going to throw lead."

He had been right. The hoodlums he had locked in the bathroom had escaped. He was expected. Pierre, the headwaiter, immaculate in white tie and tails, stopped them at the velvet chain that kept out the immonied hoi polloi.

"Right this way, if you please, Mr. Jackson." He smiled thinly. "Mr. Evans is waiting in his office."

Jackson hesitated briefly. Exclusive of the gambling rooms, there were, perhaps, sixty or seventy couples in the place. And Evans wouldn't want the show-down in the open. It would be bad for business. Nor would Evans dodge a show-down. *He had to face the music. He had to know what had become of Olga.*

"Follow Pierre," Jackson told Sam and the doorman.

Pierre leading, the four men strode down the narrow, dimly lighted lane that separated the booths against the wall from the bank of tables that lined the small dance floor. No one paid them the least attention. At four o'clock in the morning, the habitués of the Club Tropical were concerned with more personal matters.

Fat old brokers mauled young, hard-eyed, blondes—and called it dancing. Cheaters kissed in darkened corners. Over all, the drums pulsed throbbingly. It was savage, raw, and brutal. Jackson wondered how he had ever stood the fetid air.

Opposite the last booth but one, and directly across from the raised dais of the band, Pierre paused to speak to a couple at a table. The men behind him stopped perforce.

"Darling!"

The voice was feminine and shrill. The girl rose from the shadows of the darkened booth and flung herself at Jackson.

"Darling," she repeated, kissing him full on the lips and winding both of her arms around his neck. "I thought you were never coming."

Jackson knew it for what it was the moment that she spoke. He tried to break her strangle hold with one hand while his other drew his gun. Then someone struck him from behind. He fought a wave of sudden vertigo and staggered towards the booth.

"No. Keep him out of the booth," he heard Pierre whisper tersely.

But the headwaiter spoke too late. Jackson was already in the booth, his gun torn from his hand, savage fists punching brutally at his face.

"No!" he heard the headwaiter speak again. "Don't shoot him. Flip's got to know what he done with the brat."

Jackson felt eager hands try to tear him from the comparative safety of the booth. He clung to a table leg. "As a gunman," was his last conscious thought, "I'm a damn good ventriloquist."

Then everything faded out.

Flip Evans' face was a fat and evil full moon in the half light. He sat across the table in the booth flanked by a gunman on each side. Jackson found he was next to the wall with Sam Harvey at his right side. His aching hands released the table leg and he sat up.

"Well. Little Sir Galahad's come to life again," Flip Evans jeered.

The pummeled man stifled a groan and tried to focus his eyes on Evans.

"And you thought," Evans continued, "that you were going to walk right in and shoot down Flip Evans, eh? Just like that."

"Just like that," Jackson mumbled.

"Give him a drink to clear his throat," Evans ordered.

Jackson gulped the double Scotch and felt much better.

"Okay. Now talk," Evans told him. "What did you do with Olga?"

"Olga?" Jackson asked.

"He's going to be tough," Sam Harvey warned.

Evans nodded placidly. "I expected him to be. But it he won't talk here, we'll take him up to the penthouse and he'll sing like a little bird before we're through."

"Why not your office, Flip?" one of the gunmen suggested.

"No." Evans shook his head. "Not after what happened here last week. This guy is as hot as a strip-peeler with the itch, and some nosey down-town squad might come busting in." He leaned across the table and slapped Jackson's puffed and swollen face. "What did you do with the kid?"

Jackson said, "I'd like a cigarette."

Harvey looked at Evans. He nodded and the hoodlum stuck a lighted cigarette in Jackson's lips.

"Better make it easy on yourself and talk, big boy," he warned him. "You haven't got a chance."

Jackson sucked at the cigarette until its tip was a glowing flame, then exhaled slowly. "No. Perhaps not," he admitted. "But you don't dare to kill me until you learn what's happened to the little girl."

"Don't bank on that," Evans warned him. "It—well, it doesn't really matter now. With Thelma out of the way, it's my word against the kid's."

But he wasn't as confident as he sounded. Jackson could tell that by the slight hesitation in his choice for words. He looked over at the dais upon which he had stood so many times. The band had stopped playing abruptly. A slim-faced lad in evening clothes was standing at a mike looking at his wrist watch. His words, when he spoke, came faintly:

"Heigh ho and a merry-oh, all ye stayer-uppers," he said, going on the air. "This is Lex Haven, ye old sinful maestro from the Club Tropical, calling all sinners to our morning session of the Rounder's Lullaby. Fill up your glasses, kiss the girl in your arms—and bring her to see us sometime."

The band swung into the number.

"You ought to get a new M.C. or have a P.A. system hooked up with that mike," Jackson told Evans critically. "Hell, unless they're sitting right on top of him, your customers in the club can't even hear what that lad is saying."

"Never mind what I ought to do," Evans growled. "You aren't fooling anyone. Stop stalling for time. Are you going to tell us where Olga is, or ain't you?"

Jackson, cigarette smoke wreathing his face, spoke without moving his lips. "I *ain't*. So take me up to your penthouse and try to beat it from me."

"Okay," Flip Evans agreed. "We'll do that little thing." He growled at the gunman beside him. "You and Joe go up to the front of the place and start a phoney fight. While the customers are watching you, we'll waltz Hart out the back way of the club and up to my apartment."

"But what if he yells copper?"

"He ain't yelling copper." Evans grinned. "The coppers want to burn him."

CHAPTER SIX

"DIE, DAMN YOU, DIE!"

"ON YOUR FEET," EVANS ORDERED. Jackson slid out of the booth. The lights on the band stand had been dimmed. Lex Haven was crooning into the microphone in the glow of an amber spot. But none of the customers were watching him, or listening. Their interest had been diverted by the noisy fight at the front end of the club.

"Come on. Get going. Out through the kitchen door." Sam Harvey prodded Jackson with the gun barrel.

Jackson turned obediently—then made his break. He was half way across the dais to the musician's door before Harvey had caught up with him again. The gunman rammed his gun viciously into his ribs.

"Out the way you were told, lug," he whispered hoarsely.

Jackson, breathing hard, his thin lips compressed in disappointment, ignored him to stare over Lex Haven's shoulder at the mike, then out past it at the scores of merry makers who were unaware that murder was being hatched before their eyes.

"And don't try to yip," Harvey warned him hoarsely, "or I'll burn you down right where you stand. Get going!"

Reluctantly, Jackson yielded to the pressure of the gun and walked back the way that he had come. Evans sighed, in relief: "That's better. I was afraid for a minute that you might try to yip into that mike. Now out the kitchen door and no more breaks. You're just making it tough on yourself."

In the kitchen, Jackson stalled again.

"Look. Let me slap him down, Boss," Harvey pleaded. "We can get a couple of the boys to carry him."

"Okay," Evans agreed. "I'll count three. One—"

Jackson said, "Don't bother." He moved reluctantly out the back door of the Club Tropical into the blinding swirl of wind-blown snow.

He hadn't far to walk. The boiler room door of the towering apartment building that Evans owned was only a half block down the alley.

There was no one in the alley or the boiler room. No one saw them enter. Evans unlocked an inside door that opened into a private elevator shaft that led up to his penthouse.

"You've ridden this old gray mule before," he kidded Jackson.

"That's right," Jackson admitted glumly. "On the night that you murdered Adoree Darling and tried to pin it on my kid brother."

Harvey slapped him.

The cage shot upwards swiftly. Few people even knew of its existence. Unless he was pressed for time, or wanted secrecy, Evans seldom used it. Ordinarily he used the regular tower elevator.

The penthouse was comfortably warm. Evans took off his coat and called: "Togo."

There was no answer and he called again. Sam Harvey went in search of the valet.

"Togo ain't here. Chief," he reported. Then he added with a grin, "You must have come home too early."

Evans scowled and tossed his coat upon a couch. "Okay. So he's fired. But let's get to work on Jackson. We've got to find that brat before she talks."

"I thought you weren't worried," Jackson scoffed. His moment of weakness was gone. He'd die if he had to die, but he meant to take Evans with him. He had returned to Chicago to kill him—all hell couldn't stand in his way. "I thought it was your word against a baby girl's. And you always pay off. She doesn't."

"Watch him, Flip," Harvey warned. "That guy is bad. He means to go out trying."

"That's right. I'm going out trying," Jackson said. "I've killed two men tonight, and there's one to go. I told the Law that they couldn't hold me until I'd killed you. And they couldn't."

Evans laughed.

"I'm not the Law. And I'm not a punk like Diamond, or the Deacon. The name is Evans." He nodded to the sullen gunman who had accompanied them. "All right. Go to work."

The hoodlum strode across the room and swung a right at Jackson. It went wide by inches as the big man sidestepped, then pivoted on his toes and hooked a short, hard left, toughened by seven years of chipping stone, into the hoodlum's stomach. It sent him crashing backwards through a set of ornate French Windows opening out onto the terrace. Joe lay in the snow with only his feet inside the room.

Evans looked at Harvey.

"Not me," the gunman shook his head. He balanced his gun in his hand. "Not unless it's okay to shoot him."

Flip Evans considered the matter.

"Flip is afraid to let you shoot me, Harvey," Jackson scoffed. "Because if he can't get his hands on Thelma's baby sister, he's afraid that when she tells her story, some smart homicide dick like McCreary will put two and two together and add up to Fillmore Pierce."

"So what?" Evans growled. "How did I know that the brat was hiding behind a hamper? I didn't even know that Thelma had a sister."

"But she did," Jackson told him quietly. "And if Thelma hadn't grabbed up the kid and run, well, they both would probably have left the Club Tropical in the laundry truck with Pierce. That was why Thelma looked me up. She knew that I hated you. She knew I was a right guy. She was afraid to go to the cops because she knew your pull, knew how witnesses against you have a habit of disappearing. And she knew that sooner or later, you'd get her. That was why she was willing to give herself to me and insure her life in my favor for ten thousand dollars beside. She died before she could tell me. But she knew I'd take care of the kid."

"Okay, Sam," Evans said heavily. "Shoot him. But shoot him in the legs. We've *got* to make him talk. We've got to get our hands on that brat."

Harvey raised his gun.

"Drop it!" a crisp voice behind him ordered. "Drop it! This is the Law!"

The gunman whirled towards the voice and fired—at nothing. There was no one there. He turned back screaming: "Damn you, Jackson! You—"

The heavy chair hurled by Jackson smashed full into his face and his gun skittered across the carpet as he fell. Evans and Hart dived for it at the same time. First one man almost had it, then the other—then it skidded out of reach onto the terrace.

Evans, briefly on top, smashed his great fists into Jackson's swollen face.

"To hell with a gun. Talk, damn you, talk! Where's Olga?"

Jackson arched his back and heaved. The fat man hurtled over his head to land on his feet with a cat-like agility.

Both men had forgotten the gun. Jackson had stored his hate for seven years. For the first time in his life Flip Evans was afraid—afraid of the electric chair. They circled each other warily, a berserk bull elephant brought to bay by a lean tiger.

"Sure I killed Adoree Darling," Evans boasted. "And I killed Fillmore Pierce last week when the old playboy caught me cheating. And the Deacon gunned out Thelma when we were making a try for you. And I'll kill the brat as soon as I can find her."

Jackson's fists smashed full into his face.

The fat man tried to close. Jackson stepped back quickly. He knew the power in those arms. Once they had closed around him, he was through. He stepped in and out again, both fists smashing home.

Evans grunted in pain but kept on coming. Each breath was a tortured sob torn from his laboring lungs. Then he took a hard right to the jaw and a left to the heart as he moved toward the desk. There was a gun in the drawer. A moment more and the desk was between them and the gun was in his hand.

"All right. Die, damn you, die!" he bellowed. "To hell with the brat. Let her talk. I'll fight the rap in court if I have to. What's more, I'll beat it, too!" His fat finger tightened on the trigger.

"That's enough! Drop that gun," a crisp voice behind him ordered.

Evans' lips curled in a contemptuous grin. "I'm not Sam Harvey, you cheap trickster," he bellowed at Jackson. "Don't try those gags on me."

His knuckle whitened on the trigger. Then the gun went flying from his hand to thud against the wall. The fat man turned slowly, unbelievingly.

Sergeant McCreary stood in the terrace door blowing the spent gasses from his gun. Behind him stood his squad.

Evans looked at his gun."

"I wouldn't try to pick it up, Flip," the homicide sergeant warned him. He nodded pleasantly at Jackson. "Hi there, fellow."

Evans, his knees refusing to hold him, sat down on the edge of his desk, sucking at his wounded hand. "How long have you fellows been out there on that terrace?"

"Long enough," McCreary assured him. "Ever since your Jap let us in. And even if you retract your confession to the killing of

Adoree Darling, Pierce, and Thelma Winston, we've enough to work on, so it won't make much difference."

Evans' fat face purpled with rage. "So it was the brat who tipped you to come here."

"No," McCreary told him truthfully. "It was Jackson."

"Jackson?"

"Sure." Harry Bennet grinned. "And were a lot of milkmen and barflies surprised when, right along with Lex Haven's Rounder's Lullaby, they hear a man whispering in the mike, 'This is Hart Jackson, wanted for murder, speaking. Call the nearest policeman. Hurry. I am on the band stand of the Club Tropical. But I won't be here long. Tell the police to go to Flip Evans' penthouse!' "

"You mean," Evans bellowed, "that when Hart made that break down at the club—why, damn you! I was watching you! You didn't even move your lips! You—" He broke off, incoherent.

"So with what Olga tells the wife," McCreary went on, "we put two and two together, come up here and beat you to the draw."

Nelson stepped in through the French windows pushing Togo the Jap before him.

"This should teach you a lesson, Flip. If you ever wiggle out of this rap, which I doubt, don't let a smart ventriloquist like Jackson get so close to a sensitive mike."

"Why, damn you!"

Insane with rage, Evans hurled himself at Jackson before McCreary could stop him. Jackson pivoted as the fat man reached him and swung a hard right to his jaw in self defense.

Unable to stop, Evans smashed into the huge plate-glass window. There was a crash of splintering glass. Then man and window disappeared into the night.

Ed Woods finally broke the ensuing silence. "That saves us a lot of time sitting around Court."

Jackson turned away, sickened.

"Okay," he told McCreary quietly. "It was what I came back to town to do. I said I'd kill him and I did. You'd better take me down and book me for murder. I'm really guilty this time."

McCreary studied the fine points.

"N-no. I wouldn't say that," he decided. "Sure. We'll have to take you down. But the way that matters stack up now, you shouldn't have much trouble. Hell. We had you locked up on a bum rap when you crushed out. And, being kidnapped by the Deacon and Diamond, you had to kill them in self defense."

Jackson said, "And that filthy rat Evans—"

"I'm not decided," McCreary told him frankly. "But," he paused, "If it wasn't suicide, I never saw more justifiable homicide." The rest of the squad nodded.

Jackson closed his eyes briefly and saw the smiling blue eyes of a little girl. Hell, he wasn't through. Now that he had something to live for . . .

"Hokus pokus, and also Abracadabra," a bust of Shakespeare said soberly from the bookcase. "Look. If it isn't against regulations to stop on the way to the Bureau, and if one of you guys would loan Jackson a couple of bucks, I think that he might buy a drink."

Four pairs of hands reached for their wallets.

"You know"—McCreary winked at Jackson—"I think that antique Charlie McCarthy has made a sale!"

DOC EGG'S GRAVEYARD REUNION

CHAPTER ONE

"I'LL KILL YOU YET!"

THE FACT THAT THE EGG was hardboiled had nothing to do with the case. Neither did the battered watch nor the carpenter's square for that matter. But if Detective Al Penny hadn't been shrewd enough to total them correctly, the chances are a hundred to one that Glenda Hall would have burned as scheduled and the death of the naked man who staggered into the Manhattan Bar would have stayed in the unsolved file until green grass grew on the grave of the youngest patrolman on the Force.

The heavy grey fog rolled in through the Narrows at nine o'clock that morning. By ten it had crept as far north as 42nd Street. It covered all lower Manhattan but it was thickest on the Hudson River. Here, ferry bells jingled sharply. Look-outs cursed. Fog horns moaned continuously. The fog had settled on the river like a shroud.

Deep in the hold of the rusty freighter riding out the fog at anchor off Bedloe Island, Bart Irish lifted his head off the moldy blanket that had been his only bed for months and listened carefully. There was no one in the hold but himself. There was no sound but the sloshing of bilge water, the squeal of a rat, and an occasional creak and scrape as one of the heavy crates shifted to the right.

When the mate had brought him his meager meal the night before, he had boasted that they would be back in New York by morning. Irish looked at the luminous dials of his watch, the only object of any value they had left him. It was a few minutes after ten. The ship was in the river and anchored. He could tell by the way it rode. This was the last chance he would have. It was now—or never.

If he could reach shore and someone who would recognize him, he could beat them. If he could live to say three words. If even his body would wash ashore—

His once handsome face a criss-cross of unhealed wounds, his features battered beyond recognition, he fumbled in the blanket for the key he had made from a spoon, and worked open the door in the bulkhead cautiously.

Above him stretched a long spidery series of ladders. He gritted his teeth against the pain and began to climb. The ladders seemed endless. A sudden fear assailed him. There was no daylight overhead. What if the hatch was still battened down?

Then the fog rolled down to meet him, and he knew that the hatch was open. He climbed on doggedly. His dying didn't matter. He was already dead. It was the living who counted.

Somehow he had to reach shore!

Now he was on deck. He peered around him cautiously. A fog-shrouded figure was peering anxiously over the aft rail. He thought he could see the captain on the bridge. None of the crew was in sight.

Weaving slightly with the roll of the ship he crossed the deck to the lee rail and stood a moment staring at the wraith-like spires of Manhattan while he summoned strength for the plunge into the black icy waters below.

His moment of hesitation was fatal. His small pig eyes red with anger, the mate loomed largely out of the fog and spinning him around crashed a heavy fist into his jaw.

"Try to pull a fast one, would you?" he panted. "My God you're going to make me kill you yet." He kicked the prostrate man heavily, then grabbing him by the shirt tried to pull him to his feet only to have the rotted fabric tear, leaving Irish stripped to the waist. The sight of the white, emaciated, flesh gave him an idea. He stripped the limp figure of its trousers and its shoes and threw them over-side. "Now try to take a powder." He kicked him again. "Get up!"

Numb with pain, Irish got to his feet and stood, unsteadily, clinging to the rail. "Now get back below," the mate ordered.

Instead, summoning the last of his strength, Irish vaulted the rail, fell seemingly endlessly through fleecy fog, until the cold, black waters of the bay closed over his head.

When he broke water again, angry lead wasps were stinging the water around him. His arms felt too heavy to lift but he forced himself to swim. Then one of the lead wasps found him and drove him under water. When he came to the surface again, from somewhere high up the sheer side of the freighter a voice was saying hoarsely:

"I think I got him that time. But lower a boat. Let's make sure."

It would be so easy to die, Irish thought. All he had to do was cease struggling and allow the swift current of the icy water to sweep him out to sea. If the tide had been coming in he might have chanced it. But it wasn't. The tide was going out. And somehow he had to reach shore. If he didn't live to talk, at least his body must be found.

Across Water Street, jutting out into the river, the huge pier shed stood half completed. The fog had halted all construction for the day and Mickey's Manhattan Bar was crowded. Steel men, masons, and carpenters, vied with each other for places at the polished wood.

Off duty, Detective Al Penny was discussing the potentialities of atomic power with Mickey when the fat bar owner's eyes bugged suddenly from his head.

"Now I've seen it all," he admitted.

A boisterous laugh ran the length of the bar.

Penny turned his head and his grey eyes slitted as they swept the apparition in the doorway. His hair matted with oil and slime, a nude, emaciated figure stood in the doorway, gesticulating feebly.

The bar owner shook his head. "What some guys will drink!"

"He's not drunk. He's hurt," Penny told him. "That's not mud, that's blood on his shoulder." As he spoke he strode forward and wrapped a supporting arm around the weaving man's torso. "Easy makes it, sport. What's happened?"

Irish tried to speak and couldn't. Blood oozed from his lips instead. He raised one hand to his jaw as if it hurt, then the last of his strength expended, his knees gave away and he crumpled in Penny's arms.

The young detective lowered him gently to the floor, issuing crisp, curt orders. "Get me a blanket to wrap him in. And a double slug of whiskey. He's cold as ice, like he just came out of the water."

The barman got a blanket from the night watchman's cot. Mickey knelt beside him with a bottle, yelling to the barman to call an ambulance.

One of the barflies peered over his shoulder. "Boy, what a brawl he's been in. His face looks like raw hamburger."

Penny forced a drink between the unconscious man's blue lips. "Any of you guys know him?"

A steel man shook his head. "Geez no. His mother wouldn't know him with his face in that condition."

A brawny carpenter edged forward. "He looks like he might be a sailor. Maybe he fell off some ship and got caught in the propeller."

"I doubt that," Penny said. "He'd be in even worse condition. Besides that doesn't explain the bullet hole in his shoulder."

The carpenter lost interest. "Oh, well. Them merchant seamen is always fighting. Usually over some dame. It looks to me like maybe someone came home unexpected."

There was a ripple of nervous laughter and Irish opened his eyes.

"That's a sport," Penny encouraged him. "Hang on, chum. There's an ambulance on its way."

Three words—that was all he had to say. Irish opened his lips and tried. Again only a bloody froth came forth.

"He's trying to tell us something," Mickey said.

Penny unclipped his pencil, wrapped the dying man's fingers around it and placed his note pad under the pencil. It was futile. The man was too far gone to write. With a tremendous effort of will he raised his hand to his jaw instead and tried to focus his eyes on Penny's.

"Somebody hit you?" the detective asked. "Is that what you're trying to tell me?"

Irish made a faint negative gesture. A new and sudden fear took hold of him. These men didn't recognize him. He was beaten up too badly. He had been away too long. His fingerprints were not on record. After a casual autopsy, he would be buried in a Potter's field grave and no one would ever know his story.

As if reading his mind, Penny asked, "Can you tell me your name, bud?"

Bart Irish. It was an easy name to say. He had said it ten-thousand times. His lips formed the letter but no sound came.

"Bill?" Penny asked.

Again Irish made a negative gesture.

"How about who shot you, chum?" Mickey asked. "Can you tell us that?"

A mason said, "The poor devil can't talk for the blood in his throat."

In dying desperation, he focused his eyes on the watch on his wrist and made a weak gesture of his arm.

"He wants you to take it off," Mickey said. "Maybe his name is engraved on the back."

Penny unstrapped the battered watch and scrutinized it closely. It was an inexpensive waterproof watch badly battered from long wear. There was no name on the back or inside the cover. "Watch?" Penny said, uncertainly. The dying man shook his head and the young detective added shrewdly, "Time. Is that what you want me to know?"

Too weak to nod, Irish blinked his eyes, then looked hard at the piece of steel hanging on the carpenter's leg, suspended by a loop in his overalls.

Penny, following his eyes, slipped the steel from the loop and said, "Ruler?"

"That's a square," the carpenter told him scornfully.

"Square," Penny corrected.

The dying man blinked again and turning his head with a tremendous effort looked at the bar now deserted by everyone but the barmen on the far side.

"Touch things on the bar," Penny ordered the nearest barman. "Glass? Bottle? Salt? Stein? Beer? Hard-boiled egg?"

"That's it," Mickey cried. "He blinked."

Penny held up a hand, and the barman tossed him an egg. The detective regarded it thoughtfully then laid it on the floor with the watch and the square where the dying man's hand could touch it.

"Square time egg. What the hell," a burly newcomer in a sailor's pea jacket said. "That doesn't make sense. The guy is out of his mind. He oughta be locked up in a looney ward."

"Shut up!" Penny said curtly. The eyes of the man on the floor were glazing fast. Only his will was keeping him alive. Penny put his lips to his ear and asked, "Anything else now, bud? I don't get it so far."

Irish didn't hear him. His sense of hearing had failed. His sight was going fast. But he still had one thing to do. With the last tattered fragment of his strength, he picked up the hard-boiled egg, moved it to the four and one-half inch mark on the square—and died.

Disgusted, Mickey got to his feet dusting at the knees of his trousers. "Now I *have* seen it all. To hell with State Control Board. Belly up to the bar, boys. This one is on the house."

Only Penny remained where he was. The dead man had tried to tell him something. He had died thinking he had succeeded. His moving of the egg to an exact spot on the square had been a gesture of triumph. It had meant something to him.

The young detective mumbled, "Time—square—egg—four and one half." He ran the first two words together. "Times Square," then looked sharply at the marking where the dead man had placed the egg. The half inch mark was also four-eighths, or four inches four—44.

Penny got to his feet. "What the hell! I should have gotten it right off the bat. It's plain enough. He was trying to tell me to pick up Doc Egg! You know, the little bald guy who owns the big drug store on the corner of 44th Street on Times Square."

The fat owner of the Manhattan grew excited. "You mean that Doc Egg killed him? Is that what he was trying to tell us?"

Penny pulled the blanket up over the dead man's face. "Well, it's a cinch that *he* isn't Doc Egg," he said dryly.

CHAPTER TWO

LEAD—COMING UP

A BRIGHT-EYED, BALD LITTLE MAN in his late thirties with the suspicion of a paunch, Doc Egg was reputedly worth a million dollars.

To out-of-towners and the uninitiated, his glittering emporium on 44th Street was merely another drug store, surprisingly well-stocked. To those in the know, it was a gold mine, but few begrudged him his good fortune.

Born into an impoverished family on New York's lower east side, he had wanted a pharmaceutical education badly enough to fight for one. And he had fought! In his day, as a leading featherweight contender, he had fought such men as Tony Canzoneri, Benny Bass, Kid Kaplan, and Johnny Dundee. And every dime that his bruised and battered flesh had earned had gone into his dream.

Broadway both liked and respected him. His drug store was a mecca for the sporting and theatrical crowd, and for the underworld as well. He never forgot a favor or forgave a slight. If he couldn't whip a bully with his fists, he used whatever was handy. He and Lieutenant Dan Carter of the Times Square Homicide Detail had been friends since they had been boys.

Carter's summation of his friend was terse. "You treat Doc right and he'll go to hell for you. You cross him and it's you who takes the journey."

If Egg had one weakness, it was pretty women. "They cost a man plenty," he'd explain with a twinkle in his eyes, "but it's damn pleasant spending."

The long lunch counter had been filled since shortly after eleven. So had the prescription department. His deft fingers compounding a complicated prescription, Egg told Ray Harley, his head pharmacist, "It never fails, eh, Ray? All the good things of life come at once. It's either feast or famine."

The other man chuckled. "The better to enjoy them both." He quoted, " 'Feast and your halls are crowded; fast, and the world goes by.' "

"Ella Wheeler Wilcox," the little druggist named the source. It was a game of never-failing amusement to them both. He typed the doctor's instructions on a label and pasted it on the bottle. "Thought you had me, didn't you?" He spun the bottle through the slot to a waiting clerk and picked the next prescription off the spike. "Not me. Me and Gene Tunney. Books were our ruination. Who knows? I might have been champ, if I hadn't learned to read."

Harley said, "Tunney *was* champion."

His deft fingers flying, Egg pointed out. "Yeah. But Tunney had a bicycle."

Sho-Sho, the colored porter, put his head through the swinging doors and announced, "They's a bum out heah, Doc, who wants to see you. He say he used to know you."

"He probably did," the little man admitted.

Harley added, "And you'll fall for his sob story, as usual."

Egg held up a finger dramatically. " 'He jests at scars, that never felt a wound.' "

"Romeo and Juliet, Scene 2, Line 1," Harley told him.

"I'm a son-of-a-gun," the little druggist admitted. "You watch. I'll get you yet."

He strode out through the swinging doors and shook hands cordially with the ragged man who had asked to see him, a former fighter who had befriended him in his own lean days. Egg stopped the other man's hard-luck story before it was well started. "When you were in the money, Charlie, who used to stake me? Here." He slipped a thick sheaf of bills from his wallet and pressed them into the other man's hand without even bothering to count them. "And when that runs out, you let me know. If you don't, I'll look you up and take you on for a round or two." Feinting with his left, he tapped the other man's chin lightly with his right. "And don't think I couldn't do it."

As he watched Charlie toddle out on his heels, an amused voice behind Egg observed dryly, "Just a little brother to all the bums on Broadway. When are they going to canonize you, Egg?"

The little druggist spun on his heel to face the good-looking, well-dressed, young lawyer who was sitting at the end of the counter struggling manfully to down a bromo-seltzer. "Oh, it's you. Still drinking your breakfasts, eh, Wayne? When are you going to cut it out and grow up?"

A brilliant, if dissipated, young criminal lawyer, Wayne Chandler ran lean white fingers nervously through his hair. "I'm being a damn fool and I know it, Doc. But they're going to burn that girl. And she believed in me. She trusted me." A shudder shook his body. "Every time I sober up I see Glenda's face."

Egg was sincerely sympathetic. "Tough. I can imagine how you feel, kid. No chance of a commutation?"

"None," Chandler told him. "I just got back from Albany. Glenda goes to the chair as scheduled, tomorrow night." He spread his hands in a futile gesture. "They didn't try that girl for murder, Doc. They tried her reputation."

Egg drew himself a cup of coffee and joined Chandler at the counter. "Tough," he repeated.

It had been, from many angles. The case of the State of N.Y. vs. Glenda Hall had been one of the most hotly-discussed that the Street had ever known. As her trial lawyer, Chandler had made an emotionally brilliant, if unsuccessful defense. Picturing her as a misunderstood, poor little orphaned rich girl with none of the normal natural family contacts, starved for love, he had run the emotional scale in vain. A jury of twelve of her peers had found the petite playgirl of the international set, and heir to the fabulous Hall fortune, guilty of murder in the first degree. Since the jury failed to recommend mercy, a death sentence was mandatory.

With everything to live for, she had to die. Married a half-dozen times since she was seventeen, at twenty-five the beautiful madcap's life was over. Her taste in husbands had been broad. The first had been a count. The second an aviator. The third and fourth businessmen. The fifth had been Bart Irish, the West Coast gambler and racketeer. Her sixth husband, and the man whom she had been convicted of killing had been Doug Rapp, a too-handsome New York actor, whom she had married a few months after being officially notified by the State Department that Irish had been executed by a South American firing squad during an unofficial gun-running junket of his own.

The State had charged and had proven that she and Rapp had quarreled constantly since their marriage, that his sole interest in her had been her money and that he had continued to meet other women. It had produced reputable witnesses to testify that she had told them the marriage had been a mistake, and that as soon as it was possible she meant to rid herself of Rapp.

And this, the State contended and proved, had happened on the night of August 12, 1945. Her gun had been found beside his body in her palatial Sutton Place apartment. The servants testified that the Rapps had quarreled bitterly earlier in the evening and that she had made several threats to shoot him if he didn't stop humiliating her.

It had been a difficult case to defend. The girl's only defense had been intoxication and the contention that some time during the night of the murder, the shadowy figure of Bart Irish had sat down on the side of her bed and had assured her that everything was going to be all right.

Chandler made wet circles with his glass "I was a fool to bring in that ghost angle," he admitted. "But she insisted on it."

Egg nodded. "If Bart had been alive, he would have killed that rat all right. But he could hardly come back from the dead to do it." He slipped from the stool to refill his own cup. "How about you, Wayne? Think you could stand a cup of Java?"

The young lawyer smiled wryly. "It couldn't make me feel any worse."

"Cheer up," Egg told him. "We all have to go some time." He quoted, " 'The glories of our blood and state are shadows, not substantial things; There is no armour against fate; Death lays his icy hand on kings.' " He reached for a cup and saucer. "Coming up, one cup of coffee." He glanced over his shoulder as he drew it. "You want it black, or—"

The bald little druggist stopped abruptly, staring at the burly, evil-faced seaman who had suddenly materialized behind the lawyer. Chandler turned to see what he was staring at and the lawyer's eyes went round and wide.

"No," he pleaded. "Don't."

The cup of steaming coffee in his hand, Egg looked from the seaman's small, blood-shot eyes to the heavy-calibered automatic that he was holding, partially concealed by the short skirt of his pea jacket. "What's the idea, chum?" he asked quietly. "If this is a stick-up, you've come to the wrong counter. I don't keep any money back of the soda fountain, as you can see."

"You are Doc Egg?" the seaman demanded.

Egg poised on the ball of his toes. The other man meant to shoot him. He had read too many telegrapher punches not to know. "Yes. I'm Doc Egg," he admitted. "But—"

The cup of boiling coffee in his hand left the saucer, as he flipped it straight as a shot into the other man's face. Screaming with pain, the seaman triggered wildly. Lead smacked into metal. A heavy impact spun Egg around, hot liquid streaming down his side.

"He's got me!" Egg thought, then realized it was coffee and vaulted the work table and counter in pursuit of the now-fleeing seaman who was battering his way through a cluster of screaming women shoppers who had just come in the door.

As he passed the cashier, she held out the gun that was kept below the cash register but Egg had no chance to use it. Crossing Broadway against the heavy stream of fog-blinded, slow-moving traffic, the seaman was lost in the heavy grey mist.

To make certain, Egg crossed the square. But the man was gone. Returning, spitting pungent curses, he started to slide the gun across the cash desk, only to have Lieutenant Dwyer, who was temporarily replacing Lieutenant Dan Carter as head of the Times Square Homicide Detail, reach out his hand and pick up the gun.

"Just a minute, Doc. Let me see that."

Egg eyed him hotly. "And what's eating you? If you were on the job instead of hanging around those bookie joints that don't exist, things like this wouldn't happen."

Standing just back of Dwyer, Al Penny asked, "Did you kill him, Thistlewaite?"

His temper still at the boiling point, the little druggist swore, "No, but I damn well will if I ever get my hands on him. No lad can come into my store and—" He stopped short, staring at Penny, as he realized what the other man had said. "What the hell are you talking about?"

Lieutenant Dwyer dropped the druggist's gun into his pocket. "It would seem that you tripped up, Doc. That lad you shot and dumped into the river wasn't dead. He lived just long enough to put the finger on you."

Egg shook his head. "Now wait, just a minute. One of us is crazy. What lad did I shoot where and into what river did I dump him?"

"We don't know where you shot him or why," Penny admitted. "But you beat him up plenty first. And like the lieutenant just said, he fingered you before he died."

The druggist started a hot retort and thought better of it. He had never liked Dwyer. Dwyer had never liked him. An ambitious man, the detective was known on the Street as an honest John, but a lad who would arrest his own mother if he thought it might earn him a citation. Instead of replying hotly, he asked quietly, "This is a pinch, Dwyer?"

The detective hesitated. The little druggist's arm was long and reached into high places. "Let's put it this way," he compromised. "We'd like to have you come down to the morgue with us and identify a stiff."

"Fine," Egg said curtly. He motioned to Chandler who was still sitting on his stool as if too stunned or terrified to move. "You'd better come along with me, Wayne. It looks like I might need a lawyer."

The young lawyer, moving like a sleep walker, elbowed his way through the crowd of curious that had formed around the cash desk.

"Snap out of it," Egg ordered. He regarded a wet trouser leg ruefully. "All he hit was the coffee urn. And it was the top toppling off that smacked me."

"It was a tall slim boy," Chandler told Dwyer. "For no reason at all he walked up to the counter behind me and shot at Egg four times."

The druggist started to correct the description and let it go. He could correct it later. Few men, under strain, could make an accurate identification. He could. If he had been an artist, he could have drawn the seaman.

He had been a tall burly man weighing perhaps two hundred and fifty pounds. His hair had been black and close cropped. His ears were small and set close to his head. There was a white scar over his nose and his eyes were small and blood-shot from excessive addiction to whiskey.

"I'll leave a man here to investigate the shooting," Dwyer promised the lawyer.

"Sure," Egg scoffed. "Who knows? Maybe the sailor will come back and leave his address."

He insisted on being allowed to change his coffee-stained suit to one of the several outfits that he kept in the prescription room. "Pinched again," he told Harley in parting. The pharmacist grinned. " 'I know not whether laws be right or whether laws be wrong. All that we know who lie in gaol is that the wall is strong.' "

Egg snorted, indignantly, "In Oscar Fingal O'Flahertie Wills Wilde's hat!"

In the squad car, en route to the morgue, he demanded more details.

"You know as much as we do, maybe more," Lieutenant Dwyer said dryly. "It's just lucky that Lieutenant Penny, here, was in the Manhattan Bar when the lad walked in." Penny described how he had gotten his name.

"That was clever," the little druggist admitted. "But before you get your hopes too high, I don't believe I've killed anyone lately." He pressed his forefinger to his temple in mock thought. "At least, not that I remember."

The morgue attendant, forewarned, had the body on a slab and waiting. Chandler started in with the two detectives and Egg, stopped at the door, his face pale and dotted with tiny beads of perspiration. "I don't think I can take it," he admitted.

Egg pulled the sheet from the corpse's face and studied the battered flesh intently.

"You know who he is. You killed him," Dwyer accused.

Egg ran a pink plump palm over his shining bald spot. "No. I didn't kill him," he said quietly. "But I do know who he is."

"Who?" Penny demanded.

"He's a ghost," Egg told him, thoughtfully. "He's a man who is supposed to have died, eight or nine months ago. In other words, he's Bart Irish, the dead husband whom Glenda Hall claimed she saw on the night that Rapp was killed."

"You're crazy!" Dwyer scoffed. "And even if he is Bart Irish, why should he point a finger at you, if you didn't kill him?"

"There you have me," Egg admitted. He studied the dead man's face trying to read some message in the sightless eyes. "It could be there was something that Bart wanted me to know."

Al Penny pulled the old saw, "Dead men tell no tales."

"Sometimes they do," Egg corrected.

CHAPTER THREE

DEATH-HOUSE DOLL

HERE THERE WAS NO FOG. During the morning it had rained heavily. That afternoon a cold wind sweeping down from the north had driven all outdoor workers inside and transformed the prison yard into a sheet of ice that stretched from one wall to the other.

Glenda Hall turned from the small barred window in her death-house cell, harsh sobs racking her slim body. It wasn't fair. They couldn't kill her. She hadn't harmed anyone. All she had done was live her life as she had wanted to live it. Doug had been a rotter but she hadn't killed him. There had been no reason for her to kill him. There were other ways to get rid of a husband. That was what divorce courts were for.

She wondered why Chandler hadn't brought out that fact at her trial. Or had he? Everything had been so confused.

The ample figure of the matron filled the door of her cell. "Company, Glenda."

The condemned girl wiped her eyes and covered the tear stains with powder. It never hurt a girl to look her best. Even tomorrow night when she—

Tears welled through the powder and trickled down her cheeks. "I don't want to die," she sobbed. "Don't let me die."

Egg had seen the girl's picture a hundred times but this was the first time he had met her. Guilty or not, he thought, it was sacrilege for the State to destroy such loveliness. "This is Doc Egg, Glenda," Chandler introduced him. "And while we don't want to raise your hopes too high, something happened this morning that makes us hopeful that we may get you at least a stay of execution.

The heiress shook hands soberly with the bald little druggist. "You're a detective, Mr. Egg? You found out who killed Doug?"

"No," Egg admitted. "I'm just a John Q. Taxpayer, Glenda. But I was a friend of Bart's. And it would seem Bart wasn't executed, as believed. Where he has been in the interim, we do not know.

But he was shot to death this morning on or near the New York waterfront.

She clasped and unclasped her hands. "Then I *did* see Bart that night."

"The hell of it is we have no way of proving it," Chandler said glumly. "If the lad in the morgue is Bart, he died without saying a word. What's more, we have only Doc's identification. Irish was shrewd enough never to leave his fingerprints around so we can't prove his identity by either the local or the F.B.I. files."

"That lad in the morgue is Bart," Egg said flatly. "And there must be a hundred people on the West Coast whom we could get to identify him."

"By tomorrow night?" Chandler commented contemptuously.

Egg winced. "No. Not by tomorrow night."

Glenda asked, "You think it was Bart who killed Doug?"

"We don't know," Egg admitted. "But we do know that Bart Irish was alive after he was reported executed. He *could* have been in the apartment that night. He *could* have killed Rapp. And when we leave here, Wayne is going on up to Albany and ask the governor for a stay on the grounds of new evidence having been uncovered."

The announcement failed to lift the girl's spirits. "A stay won't mean a thing. If Bart had killed Doug he wouldn't have run away and let me take the blame. Bart wasn't that kind of a man."

"See? What did I tell you?" the lawyer demanded of Egg. "All we're doing is torturing her."

Egg ignored him. "That's one of the things I wanted to hear you say," he told the girl. "Knowing Bart fairly well, that's about how I had it figured. But you *did* see him that night, Glenda?"

"I think I did," she said simply. "I'm positive I did. Doug and I had quarreled. He'd struck me. I was so furious with myself for having married such a beast that I drank until I didn't know what I was doing." She added, "But that was in my own room with the door locked."

"Then how did Bart get in to sit on your bed?" Chandler asked.

She shook her black curls. "I don't know. But I woke up and saw him sitting there. He said, 'It's been pretty rugged, hasn't it, baby? Well, don't you worry anymore. You close your pretty eyes and go back to sleep. Daddy is home again. And he's going to take care of everything."

Chandler said, "You can see what that did to a jury. It practically convulsed them."

Egg shut him up with a look. "Think hard, Glenda. What else did Bart say?"

"Nothing," she said. "That was all." She added, "Except that he had a phone call to make—he didn't say to whom."

"And then—?"

She said, "Bart kissed me and walked through the wall. And the next thing I knew it was morning and a detective was shaking me and asking me why I'd killed Doug."

Chandler protested, "If this might lead somewhere I wouldn't mind. But we're just torturing her, Egg."

The little druggist persisted. "Two more questions. Who has reason to hate you, Glenda?"

Her eyes grew round. "No one that I know of."

Egg asked his second question. "And how much would you estimate your personal fortune to be, Glenda?"

She said frankly, "I wouldn't know exactly. It's in a trust. And there are thirty or forty million dollars, or some such sum as that. Why?"

Egg said gently, "Because if your story *is* true, and I believe it is, someone doesn't like you, Glenda. Who gets the money if you die?"

She said promptly, "My cousin, Vera Hall. You see, I can't give or will away the principal. That's in the trust. The money has to go to someone in the blood-line. And Vera and I are the only ones of the Hall family left. Why? What difference does my money make?"

"For one thing, it convicted you," Egg said dryly. "The chances are if you had been a chorus girl or some small-town married tramp you not only would have been acquitted, you'd have been swamped with theatrical contracts!"

An hour later at the Ossining station he told Chandler, "Well, you go on up to Albany and see what you can do about a stay."

"And you?"

"I'll head back to town." Egg admitted, "I don't know just what my next move will be. But that girl no more killed Rapp than I did."

Chandler made a wry face. "If only you could prove that."

"Hell. Part of it is elemental," Egg told him. "There were maybe fifty men in the Manhattan Bar who heard Al Penny puzzle out the fact that Bart had been trying to name me—among them, according to Al, a couple of seamen."

"I still don't see it," Chandler said.

"Then you ought to buy glasses," Egg told him. "I had never seen the lad before. He had never seen me. He had to ask me if I was Doc Egg. And there was only one reason in the world for that pig-eyed sailor to try to blow me apart with his .45."

"He knew the cops were on their way, and he was afraid you'd identify Bart?"

"Now you're cooking with atoms," Egg told him.

The address that Glenda Hall had given him proved to be a college girl's club in the East Sixties. After speaking to Miss Vera Hall over the house phone, Egg was asked to wait in the parlor for her.

It was difficult to believe that they were cousins. There was a slight family resemblance, but where Glenda was small and well-formed, her cousin was tall and angular. Her lips were thin. Her expression was prim. She wore thick-lensed, horn-rimmed glasses and her hair was braided tightly and wrapped around her head.

"If you are a reporter," she opened the conversation, "I do not wish to speak to you. While I feel just too terrible about Glenda, I do not feel that I am in a position to give any interviews to the papers."

"You mean, as the future heir to the Hall fortune?" the little druggist asked meekly.

She said, "Don't be insulting."

"I didn't mean to be," he protested. "I'm not a reporter. And I'm not a detective." He repeated what he had told Glenda. "I'm just a John Q. Taxpayer who is interested in seeing that your cousin gets a square deal."

The angular girl said, primly, "She was tried by a jury of her peers." She sat twisting at one of her ringers.

There was something about the girl that bothered Egg, but he couldn't place it. He hadn't liked her on sight. He liked her less the more he talked to her. She wore no makeup and her face had a greasy sheen.

"You mean by a jury of men and women with very human failings and the usual poor man's prejudice against anyone with forty million dollars," he corrected. "I don't think she killed Doug Rapp."

Vera Hall pursed her lips. "A jury decided she did. Glenda has always been a willfully wicked girl." She smiled, superiorly smug. "And though I doubt if a man of your type has ever heard the quotation, it states very plainly on the Bible that 'Whatsoever a man soweth, that shall he reap'."

"Yeah," Egg said dryly. "Galatians. Chapter VI or VII, I believe." He knew now what bothered him about the girl. She was playing a part. He got to his feet, lighted a cigarette and walked to the parlor door. "Look. If I may make a suggestion in parting—before you start throwing Biblical quotations around, you should be a little more careful of your personal looks, Miss Hall."

"And just what do you mean?" she demanded.

"Your toss-a-quarter-in-the-drum get-up," he said dryly. "When I phoned upstairs, you were in such a hurry to wipe off your make-up that you missed some. There is still quite a smear of lipstick on your lower lip."

Out on the street, he turned and looked back at the parlor window of the club. The girl's face, pressed to the glass, was a mask of hate.

"I've got something," Egg decided. "But I'll be damned if I know what I've got!"

On a hunch he stopped in at the first cigar store that he came to, called Ben Morris on the City Desk of the *News-Telegram* and asked if as a personal favor he would have some one check the paper's morgue for any information they might have on Miss Vera Hall.

"Hell. I can give you that right now, Doc," Morris told him. "Along with Glenda's obit, we're running a Cinderella story on Vera. She's the daughter of Glenda's father's youngest brother. And while Glenda has always been very generous as far as money is concerned, the kid has been supporting herself as a librarian in a little up-state town."

"How about the boy friend angle?"

"There isn't any, as far as we know."

"And you're sure she's the right Vera?"

"Positive. Her fingerprints have been on file with The Federal National Bank, trustees of the Hall estate, ever since she has been a baby. Why? What's eating on you, Doc?"

"Nothing," Egg lied. "I just wondered. But look, Ben. About that Bart Irish angle. I—"

"Nix, Doc," the city editor stopped him. "You better go back and take another look."

"That lad is Bart Irish," Egg swore.

"You prove that," Morris chuckled, "and I'll not only smear it all over the front page, I'll buy you the best drink in town. It might have worked. But we got a tip that it was just one of those things that smart lawyers like Chandler figure out to get their clients a stay."

Egg demanded, "You got a tip? From whom?"

"A little bird," Morris chuckled, and hung up.

Egg replaced his own receiver and stared thoughtfully at the phone. Someone wanted Glenda Hall to die damn badly.

Night had become complete while he had been inside the store. He started on back to his own store, remembered that Dwyer had impounded his gun to check a test shot against a possible slug in the dead man, and turned east toward his own apartment to pick up another gun.

There was no mail in his box. He rode up in the automatic elevator, wishing he had told Chandler to call him at the drug store as soon as he had contacted the governor. During the few minutes he had talked to Glenda, the girl had gotten into his blood. It was small wonder that Bart Irish had been crazy about her.

His face darkened as he thought of the big soldier of fortune. Irish had been murdered. He had been shot in the back. He had been cruelly beaten, and from the looks of his emaciated body had been held prisoner on a semi-starvation diet for months.

"I'll get the sons, Bart," Egg promised.

He unlocked his door, walked in, reached for the light switch and froze, as a sixth sense warned him that he was not alone.

"Don't be bashful, Egg," a harsh voice chuckled. "Come in. Although I can't say that you're among friends."

An unseen hand closed the door behind him. A second hand flipped the light switch, and Egg found himself staring into the muzzle of a gun held in the ham-like hand of the pig-eyed seaman who had tried to kill him.

There were two other men in the room, also seamen, from their manner of dress. Both were armed. Egg calculated his chances. He had none. It was three armed big men against one aging featherweight.

"So, what's the big idea?" he asked.

One of the seamen slapped his thigh in moronic mirth. "He wants to know what's the idea?"

"Search him," the biggest of the trio ordered.

Rough hands patted Egg's pockets, armpits, and thighs. "He's clean," the seaman reported.

"Then get on with it," the big man ordered. The man to whom he spoke took a long oval packet of greasy paper from a small black case and clipped a length of slow-burning fuse to the substance it contained. "And as you and I will probably see a lot of each other for the next few days, you can call me Horse," the big man told Egg.

"You're a jackass if you think you can get away with this," Egg said sharply.

The seaman made a swipe with his gun that caught Egg on the side of the cheek and knocked him off his feet. He scrambled back, only to be knocked down again. He knew now how Irish had gotten those bruises. Whoever Horse was, he was the man who had held Irish prisoner, who undoubtedly had shot him in the back.

The man who had been working on the fuse observed, "He's a game little bugger. I seen him fight Benny Bass."

"That's past history," Horse told him. "If you're finished there, touch it off and let's go," he said. As he spoke, he struck Egg again and the little man went down for the count.

When he came to he was sitting in a car perked a half a block from the building. Horse saw that he was conscious, and forced him to turn his head so he was looking out of the rear windows of the car. "Watch sharp. It's going to happen any minute now."

As Egg watched, the front wall of his apartment building seemed to bulge in a gigantic bay, then erupted in a cloud of yellow, oily smoke in an explosion that shook the car and shattered every window in the whole block.

"Just good old fashioned T.N.T.," Horse told him. He chuckled as the car began to roll, "The cops will be looking for pieces of you all over town." He smashed the little man brutally in the face. "But I doubt if they'll find any."

CHAPTER FOUR

AN EGG AND A RAT

EXCEPT FOR THE SQUEALING OF THE RATS the silence was the silence of the tomb. It was to be his tomb. Huddled against the steel plates of the hold, the moldy blanket wrapped around his shoulders in a vain attempt, to keep out the cold, Doc Egg cursed bitterly, if futilely.

A few of the pieces were still missing but he saw, or thought he saw, most of the picture now—too late. This was the prison in which Bart Irish had been held. It was to be his prison until the freighter moved out to sea. Then a blow on the head would suffice for him, and his body tossed overside would be but another speck in the flotsam and the jetsam floating on the broad swells of the grey Atlantic.

In an attempt to fight the cold, he got to his feet and paced the ten short feet one way and ten feet back that the length of stout rope around his waist permitted. His feet were free but his hands were tied. The Horse was taking no chances.

"Bart getting away damn near cost me a fortune," he had cursed. "But you ain't getting away, little man, not until I get my share. You're almost as good a club as he was."

Egg considered the situation. Even if he was free, he still couldn't prove a thing. It would be his word against the man who wanted Glenda to die. And that would be soon, he thought glumly.

It had been night when they had brought him to the ship. The last time the door to the hold had been opened, he had seen a faint patch of daylight over head. Some hours had passed since then. It was early afternoon of the day on which Glenda was to be executed.

A newspaper rustled underfoot and he kicked at it savagely. The Horse had gotten a big kick out of showing him his own obituary. The headline of the story read:

PROMINENT BUSINESSMAN DIES IN
MYSTERIOUS APARTMENT EXPLOSION

The accepted theory had been that he had been experimenting in the small laboratory he maintained in his apartment and had made a fatal mistake. There had been pieces of a body found. The Horse and the man behind him had seen to that. Some drunken bum lured to the apartment had died before he even knew what struck him.

Egg considered his obit. On the whole it had been complimentary, but it had devoted far more space to his gambling and to his affairs of the heart than it had to his business success or to his dozen and one private charities.

The little man quoted bitterly, " 'The evil that men do lives after them; the good—' "

He stopped short, struck by a sudden thought. Bart had left him a message. What's more, he knew where it was. He closed his eyes and recalled Detective Al Penny's description of Bart's death—

". . . He tried to speak and couldn't. Blood oozed from his lips instead. Then he raised one hand to his jaw, as if it hurt, and crumpled in my arms."

Desperate, Egg walked to the ring bolt in the wall, then raced into the darkness in an attempt to snap the rope. The jerk pulled him up short and slapped him into the deck plates like a lassoed steer instead. Bruised and bleeding, he tried it again. Both the ring bolt and the rope held. His hands tied in back of him, he couldn't reach the bolt or work on the knots.

He was lying panting on the floor when the moronic seaman brought him his noon meal. It consisted of a watery bean soup, a huge piece of fat pork, and a few slices of stale bread.

Egg remained silent. The man kicked him in the ribs and departed, locking the hold door carefully behind him. As soon as he was gone there was a concerted rush of rats for the food that he had placed on the deck plates. Egg kicked them away savagely, not because he wanted the food but because he hated rats of all kinds.

"Me and Poe's guy in 'The Pit and The Pendulum,' " he thought glumly. He started up in sudden hope, sank back. The lad in the Pit had tried smearing the rope that bound him with grease in an effort to get the rats to gnaw him free but the attempt had been unsuccessful. It had been the razor sharp pendulum itself that had freed him.

Still, it was worth a try. Anything was better than just sitting down meekly waiting for the Horse to collect his share of the booty, steam out to sea, and kill him.

He felt for the fat pork with his fingers and allowing as much slack as he could, rubbed the fatty meat on the rope where it rose to the ring bolt in the plates. For a long minute nothing happened, then he heard the patter of feet and felt the weight of a dozen bodies on the rope. When they had gnawed off that portion that interested them, only a few strands of the hemp had parted. He rubbed it with the meat again, more thoroughly this time. Again and again, he repeated it patiently, until the meat was gone. Quite a few of the strands were parted but the rope still held.

He limped up to the side of the ship grimly, then raced into the blackness for one final try. With a sharp snapping of its fibers the weakened rope parted, and instead of jerking him to a halt, allowed him to catapult across the hold and smash heavily into an emptied packing case.

He lay stunned, but free. The next thing to do was find some sharp surface with which to cut the rope around his wrists. He found it in a buckled deck plate and sitting with his back to it sawed his wrists across the steel heedless of the damage that it was doing to his flesh,

His hands free, he tried to untie the rope from around his waist but his fingers were too slippery with blood. The rope would have to wait for a knife. Feeling around him in the dark until he found a short length of two by four that would serve as a club, he took his place beside the door in the hold to wait. If the moronic seaman ran true to schedule, he would return in fifteen minutes for the plate and spoon. The Horse was taking no chances, he had informed the little druggist. Bart Irish had formed a key of a spoon, and he meant to see that Egg didn't.

The waiting in the dark seemed endless. With a sick sinking of his heart, Egg realized that if the Horse should return with the seaman, he couldn't fight them both. But he could try.

After what seemed like hours, he heard heavy feet descending the steel ladder. How many feet he could not tell. He took a fresh grip on his club and raised it. If there were two of them they might take him, but they would know that they had been through a battle royal.

A key grated in the lock and the moronic seaman came in, flashing his light before him. He was alone. Egg brought down his club and the man fell without a sound. Before he was settled on the plates, Egg was astride him, feeling for the knife he should be wearing in a sheath at his side. The little man grinned as his fingers felt it. His luck had turned. It was there.

Armed with the knife, he climbed the steel ladders cautiously. Long before he reached the top he could see by the position of the sun that it was much later than he had thought. It was closer to three o'clock than noon.

The ship lay aside a loading shed. There was no one on the bridge. A seaman, the collar of his pea jacket turned up against the biting cold that was sweeping down the Hudson, was standing on the gang-way watching something in the loading shed beyond. Egg considered rushing him, then reconsidering, went over the side and hand over hand down a taut hawser to the loading pier. A stevedore saw him but made no comment. Stowaways were common.

In the pier shed, out of the biting cold, the little druggist paused briefly in the washroom to wash as much of the blood from his hands and his face as he could, then walking boldly past the gate guard, who was talking to a girl, he whistled down a cab and gave the address of his store.

There were no lights in the window. The big front doors were locked and in the middle of the glass was a neatly-printed, black-bordered card stating formally, for all to read—

> Closed In Respect To the Memory of
> Egbert Thistlewaite, familiarly known
> to all Broadway as Doc Egg

Cursing softly, Egg unlocked the door and walked in. Deep in the shadows of the store, Sho-Sho started up from the box on which he was sitting, saw who it was and his eyes rolled wildly:

"No?" he cried. "You go back where you came from. You cain't come in heah no more, Doc. You are daid."

The little druggist punched him lightly. "Don't you believe it, Sho-Sho. Don't you ever believe it until you see me stretched out in my coffin. And don't you believe it then until the coffin is six feet underground!"

Still grey with fear, still refusing to believe that he was real, the boy stuttered, "Yyy-yes, sir. Jjjj-jus' as you say, Doc."

Hearing voices, Harley opened the swinging doors leading into the prescription room. Wearing a business coat instead of his usual white jacket, he looked old and worried. But the hand that rung Egg's hand was strong. " 'Peace, peace!' " he said with deep emotion. " 'He is not dead, he doth not sleep!' "

"They damn near had me," Egg admitted. "And *you* have. Father Divine?"

"No. Shelley," Harley told him. "But in the name of all that's holy, what happened, Doc? How in the world did you get out of that apartment after it exploded?"

"I wasn't in it when it exploded," Egg said dryly.

He stripped off his bloodstained clothes and told Harley what had happened, as the other pharmacist cleaned and bandaged his cuts and painted his contusions.

Slipping into a clean shirt and a freshly pressed suit, he said crisply, "Now I'm on my way to the morgue. Glenda burns at midnight and I haven't much time to work. But once I get the Medical Examiner to perform a second autopsy, I can not only positively identify the corpse as Bart's, I can blow the whole thing sky high."

Harley was worried. "I'm afraid that if saving Miss Hall depends on the body you are out of luck, Doc. I read in the noon *News-Telegram* that an uptown undertaker had claimed the body as soon as the police released it. The way the story read, he had received an anonymous letter containing funeral expenses from some woman who said she had read of the affair in last night's paper and wanted to save the body from burial in Potter's Field as a gesture to her own missing son."

"And the police released it?"

"I believe they did."

Egg swore, "Then they are damn fools or some money changed hands. If you remember that undertaker's name, get him on the phone and ask him if he's buried the body."

He finished dressing and dropped an old gun into his pocket that he had thrown into one of the drawers, meaning to have a faulty firing pin repaired.

Harley returned and reported, "His assistant says that he is at the cemetery now and that undoubtedly the interment has taken place."

Egg considered his bloody overcoat and slipped into a light-weight camels-hair topcoat instead. "Then I'm on my way to the D.A. to get an exhumation order. They know that I'm out of that hold by now, and they're gambling for too high stakes to cut and run. If Glenda burns before I can expose them, they win. The law won't dare admit that it burned an innocent girl. So it's a rat race for Bart's body now—with no holds barred!"

He strode through the swinging doors, came back. "And for Pete's sake, Ray. Turn on the lights. Call up the gang. Get them back on the job. And take that damn card off the door." The little druggist repressed a shudder. "So help me, it gives me the heebie-jeebies!"

An opinionated, white haired man in his middle fifties, Marston, the District Attorney, was sorry but he was forced he said, to refuse Doc Egg's request for an emergency exhumation order.

He polished well-manicured nails upon his palm "Really, I am sorry to refuse you, Thistlewaite, but I'm tired of having you Broadway characters try to run my office."

Egg pounded lightly on his desk. "In other words rather than admit that it some money was passed to release that body so soon, you'll let an innocent girl go to the chair."

Marston smiled smugly. "You're being fantastic." His smile faded. "Also insulting. I prosecuted Glenda Hall myself. Her guilt as found by the jury, was an open and shut affair. And your contention that she is innocent is a reflection on my integrity."

Egg ran a hand over his bald spot keeping his temper with an effort. "And the bombing of my apartment, kidnapping me and holding me in the hold of a ship—"

"Has nothing whatsoever to do with the Hall case," Marston broke in coldly. "I promise you a thorough investigation of both charges, but you must realize that a man in your position on Broadway, a confidant of the sporting and the underworld alike, naturally makes enemies, and—"

"Hold it right there," Egg stopped him. "I didn't come here for a lecture. I came for an exhumation older and a stay of execution. Do I get them or not?"

The District Attorney stood up behind his desk. "I said that I promised you a thorough investigation of your charges."

The little druggist's temper slipped its leash. "A hell of a lot of good an investigation will do a dead girl! And to hell with you, too. If I can't save her inside the law, I'll find some other way."

Purple with anger, the D.A. pointed to the door. "Get out or I'll throw you out!"

Egg shaped his hat to his head. "If I had the time to spare," he told him, "I'd take you up on that." He walked out of the office, slamming the door so hard that the pebbled glass in it shattered. The best he could say about Marston was that the man was personally honest but a fool.

In the foyer of the building, he stopped beside a phone booth and consulted his note book. He had to have some quasi-legal assistance in what he intended to do. But Dan Carter was out of town.

His searching finger stopped beside the name of Al Penny. The home address and phone number he had given was a nearby Times Square Hotel. A moment later he had him on the phone.

"That's right. I'm not dead after all," he assured the young detective. "But look, Al, I need some help. What's more I have to work fast. And I'll be perfectly candid about it. If I can swing this, and you help me, I'll guarantee you a lieutenant's shield. If we fail it will mean that you'll probably be kicked off the Force."

Penny asked, without hesitation, "What do you want me to do?"

"Help me dig up the corpse identified as Bart Irish," Egg said crisply, "and get it up to Sing Sing before they burn Glenda Hall at midnight"

The young detective said firmly, "Then I'm with you all the way. There's something phoney as hell about that whole deal and I'll be damned glad to help you prove it."

When they had completed their arrangements to meet, Doc Egg consulted his note book again, hesitated briefly, then made a second phone call.

CHAPTER FIVE

A GRAVE MATTER

AT THE FOOT OF THE TOMBSTONE-DOTTED HILL, the Hudson coiled north like a huge grey-scaled snake in the pale light of the early morning moon. There was no sound but the whimper of the wind through the pines and the far-off howling of a dog.

Crouched back of a huge stone cross, Al Penny turned the short collar of his coat up around his neck against the wind and peered anxiously into the dark. "Maybe we'd better not wait," he whispered hoarsely. Maybe they're not here."

"They're here," Egg told him tersely. "And they're waiting in back of one of those stones for me to show up and start digging." He looked at his watch. It was a few minutes after eight. "It's a matter of who breaks first. If they think that I've lost my nerve, *they'll* start digging. And when they have Bart's corpse this time, they'll get rid of it for good."

They waited in tense silence, Egg staring at the luminous dial of his watch. The minute hand swung to fifteen, down to twenty-five, hesitated on thirty. The little druggist leaned forward to tap Penny's shoulder and tell him that they had cut it as fine as they dared when a spade clanked musically against a pick in a small clump of pine not far distant.

His voice was clear on the frosted air as the Horse announced, "Okay, you guys. Let's get going. The little guy lost his guts. He didn't dare show up." His voice was heavy with scorn. "He didn't know we'd be here, and I guess he was afraid of breaking the law." There was a moronic chuckle in the dark.

"It seems I didn't kill the moron," Egg whispered.

Penny slipped his gun from his holster. "Wait," Egg cautioned him. There was a muted sound of digging now with an occasional and metallic clang as his pick struck a stone.

"It shouldn't take long," Penny whispered. "All they have to do is remove the clods."

Egg nodded, straining his eyes into the moonlight. There were three men digging but the man he had hoped would show up had failed to come.

The third man asked, "Why do you suppose the little guy didn't go to the law after he got out of the hold?"

"What could he prove?" the Horse scoffed. "The big shot took care to see that we all had alibis when we picked him up at his apartment. And the whole crew will swear that he never was near the ship. That's the beauty of the whole thing, see? Any story he tells is fantastic. And if he does go to the law with it, the chances are that he'll wind up in a booby hatch."

The moron wanted to know how about the shooting in Egg's store.

"That was a mistake," the Horse admitted. "Either I shouldn't have been so open, or I shouldn't have missed the guy. But if I'm pinched for it, so what? The gun I used is on the bottom of the river and there aren't two guys who saw it who could identify me."

"Stop talking so much and dig," the third man said. "I don't see why they didn't cremate the guy."

The Horse explained, "The big shot was afraid that someone might be suspicious if the body was to be destroyed. But they figured that this way, if anything went wrong, they could always dig it up again." There was a thud of metal and wood. "I'm down to it," the moron said. "Clean out those clods at the other end there and hand me that pry bar."

"After we take him out we fill in the grave again?" the third man asked.

"That's the idea," the Horse said. "That way no one is the wiser that he's gone."

Egg waited for the sound of protesting nails as the lid of the plain pine box in which Bart Irish had been buried was lifted. Then he slipped his gun from his pocket and tapped Penny on the shoulder. "Okay. This is it, Al. Let's go. But let's get as close as we can before we call them."

A giant and a feather-weight shadow, they slipped from cover of tombstone to tombstone until they reached the small clump of pine behind which the three men were working.

As Egg looked out from his cover, the Horse was just lifting Irish from the box. Egg waited until the big seaman had laid his burden on the ground and picked up his shovel again. Then he stepped out from behind the pine and ordered, "This is it, Horse. Go ahead. Reach for your gun. I'd love to see you try it."

Al Penny appeared on the far side of the grave. "That goes double. Which one of you ghouls wants it first?"

Frozen statues in the moonlight, the Horse was the first to move. "Well, it seems that I had you wrong, little man," he told Egg. "Your intestines were all right after all."

The third man whimpered, "I told you I saw him fight Benny Bass. Now see what you've went and done. We aren't going to be rich after all. They'll burn us, that's what they'll do."

The Horse was no coward. "Shut up!" he ordered. Without moving his body, he turned his head to Egg. "How's about making a deal, Egg? How's about cutting you and your friend in. There's plenty in this for us all."

"Bart was my friend," Egg told him. "Pick him up now, Horse, and carry him to my car. We still have a long drive ahead and we haven't any time to waste."

The big seaman laid down his shovel, stooped as if to pick up the dead man, then grasping his shovel by the handle rushed at the little druggist swinging the deadly steel over his head. "To hell with that. If this ever breaks, we burn!"

Egg squeezed the trigger of his gun and the faulty pin missed fire. Hearing the click, Al Penny triggered a shot at the big seaman's back. He hit him but failed to stop him. In an attempt to avoid the flailing shovel Egg had stepped in under it and he and the Horse went to the frozen ground together in a tangle of flying fists and threshing legs.

Emboldened, the moron hurled his pry bar at Penny and the detective shot him through the shoulder just as the third man, desperate with fear, caught at his arm and pushed him back over a tombstone.

"Kill 'em!" the Horse shouted.

He tried to pin Egg to the earth so he could pound his face to a pulp, but it was like trying to pin a weasel. His bald head gleaming in the moonlight, the little druggist twisted and turned and wriggled out from under, using his fist, his knees, his feet, and the barrel of the gun in his hand with deadly effect. But it was an- unequal struggle. The other man outweighed him by a hundred and twenty-five pounds.

The gun knocked from his hand by his fall, Penny was desperately trying to recover it while his frightened opponent battered at his face and body with the strength and fear of desperation.

Sobbing with fear and pain, the half-witted seaman alternated between the two struggling groups, striking blindly, with the pinch bar that he had recovered, at any head that showed.

His hand still inches from his gun, Penny felt the man on top of him collapse as his head was split open by the bar.

"Kill 'em! Kill the sons!" the half-witted seaman babbled. "I just killed one good, Horse!"

He lifted the pry bar over Egg's head as it showed briefly, and Penny without stopping to rise snatched up his gun again and shot him through the heart. The heavy bar clattered to the frozen earth and he followed it silently.

The Horse turned his head briefly at the shot and Egg seized the diversion to wriggle out from under him and scramble to his feet.

"Keep away from him, Doc," Penny ordered. "Leave me a clear shot."

The big seaman spat. "And to hell with you, too, Mister!"

Bent almost double to present a smaller target, he leaped the open grave and raced for the shelter of the trees with Penny's bullets spitting harmlessly through his coat tail and his sleeves.

Damning his own poor shooting, the detective fumbled in his pocket for a fresh clip of shells and the Horse turned back abruptly, a gun in his hand now. He leveled it on Penny, backed a step to steady his aim, tripped over Bart Irish's corpse and sprawled backwards just as Egg's faulty gun struck fire and the heavy .44 slug caught the big seaman above the belt buckle. He went down screaming in pain.

"That was close, too close," Egg panted. He nodded at the third seaman. "Is that lad going to live?"

"I doubt it," Penny made a snap judgment.

"Then we've got to keep the Horse alive until he talks," Egg said. "We'll take him with us in the car." He started to leap the grave, stopped. "But let's get this straight right now." He pointed to Bart Irish. "Have I been within ten feet of him?"

Penny shook his head. "You have not."

"I couldn't have touched him or planted anything on him."

Penny raised his right hand. "I'll swear that on the Bible."

Egg nodded grimly. "Remember that. Now carry him to the car. Put him in the back seat. Then come back for the Horse. You'll have to ride with them. I'll drive."

As the younger man left with his burden, Egg looked at his watch.

He fought a wave of weariness. He couldn't let down—not yet. An innocent girl's life was at stake. The icy roads would make for bad driving. But everything would depend on their reaching the prison in time. They *had* to be there by midnight. Even two minutes delay would be fatal.

CHAPTER SIX

WITH THEIR BONES

THE WARDEN'S OFFICE WAS THICK with smoke and fragrant with whiskey breaths. Reporters sent to cover the execution talked in terse, nervous whispers. His white hair gleaming under the bright overhead lamp, District Attorney Marston attempted to console Chandler.

A nervous wreck, the young lawyer had reached the point where whiskey had ceased to bite. There was nothing he could do twit sweat out the last few minutes.

"Come on. Don't take it so hard, Wayne," Marston urged him. "You can't win every case. And the girl is guilty as hell. If I didn't know that, I wouldn't have asked for the death penalty. It's not as if you'd failed an innocent client."

Chandler looked at his watch. It was five minutes of twelve. He looked up to see Jensen, the warden's secretary, standing in the now open doorway.

"If you gentlemen will follow me, please," Jensen said. "It is time that we take our places in the execution chamber."

There was an unwilling shuffle of feet out the door and down the short corridor to the death chamber.

Ben Morris summed up the general opinion. "Damn it. Even if she killed ten guys, they hadn't ought to burn her. They could have given her life."

Kirk Tone of the Record said, "I was tipped that there was some lug on the jury who swore he'd hold out for a year if they didn't vote to burn her."

The D.A. heard him and cleared his throat nervously. "Nonsense. The law is very clear in case of premeditated murder. An intelligent jury merely did its duty as laid down by the statutes."

All talking ceased as they entered the chamber. The electrician was standing by his switches talking calmly to Warden Gault, whose usually bronzed face was a pale lemon color.

Then the door to the death house opened and a priest walked

into the chamber followed by two matrons with the petite black-haired girl between them. She was frightened, but she refused their offer of aid, and walked steadily if slowly. She had kept her promise to herself to look her best on the last night of her life and a collective gasp rose from the watching men as she came in.

Few had ever seen anything more beautiful. Even in the simple prison house dress that she wore, she was the last of the Halls.

She saw the chair, stopped, forced herself on and stopped again as angry voices rose in the corridor just outside the chamber door.

"I tell you you *can't* see the warden," Jensen protested. He lowered his voice to a hoarse stage whisper. "Please, man. Stop making a scene. They're just about to electrocute her."

Egg's voice said clearly, "They are *not* going to electrocute her!"

His face grimy with mud and clotted blood, and lined with strain, the little druggist shook off the warden's secretary long enough to yank open the door of the death chamber.

"You, Ben, Tone, Court, Murphy. *They're burning an innocent girl and I can prove it. Do I get a chance to talk or not?*"

Jensen attempted to pull him out of the doorway and Egg struck at him savagely.

In the clamor of voices that rose, Egg's clear tone cut them cleanly. "How about it, Warden Gault? If you put that girl in that chair and pull that switch after having been warned, you're not the man I think you are."

District Attorney Marston cried, "The man is crazy. Call the guards and have him thrown out."

Gault strode from the switch to the door. "No. Wait." He held up his hand for silence and the death chamber grew still again. "You're sober and in your sane mind, Thistlewaite, and you have proof that Miss Hall is innocent of the crime for which she is about to be executed?"

"I am. And I have," Egg told him.

Some of the color returned to Gault's face. "Then of course we'll listen to you. Just what is this proof?"

Egg pointed down the corridor to where Al Penny, accompanied by two guards and a prison doctor, was pushing a stretcher toward the chamber. "The body of Bart Irish is exhibit A. Al Penny and I just killed two men to get it and when I saw him last, a third man who is known by the nickname of Horse was talking his head off to the prison doctor in an attempt to trade the truth for an emergency operation."

The prison doctor nodded curtly, "That is so, Warden Gault. He claims that Glenda Hall is innocent of the murder for which she was convicted."

"Go on," Gault told Egg.

The little man looked at Al Penny. "Okay. Say your piece, Al."

Penny showed the Warden his shield, said, "I've been with Doc Egg all evening. I was with him when we recovered the body. And I can swear that at no time has he touched it."

"What are you talking about, man?" Marston demanded sharply.

"We'll come to that," Egg told him. He change his mind. "No. We might as well start with it." He turned to the prison doctor. "Would you mind feeling inside the dead man's mouth, Doctor, and removing the gold cap that you should find just back of his right eye tooth."

The doctor did as he was requested. The cap came off easily. He looked at it, looked at Egg. "Why, there seems to be something in it."

"I thought that there would be," Egg said. "I've known for years that Bart had that cap. He used to joke about it as his secret compartment. And just before he died he kept calling attention to his jaw hoping that someone would understand."

"What's in it?" Gault demanded.

Egg said, "I imagine it is a confession of murder. I wish I could pin Rapp's death on someone else but I am afraid that Bart killed him when he returned to find him not only married to but abusing Glenda, after a false report of his own death."

Warden Gault took the gold cap from the doctor, extracted the small piece of paper it contained and after unfolding it read aloud, "I, Bart Irish, killed Doug Rapp."

The little druggist broke the silence. "There would have been more to the message if there had been more room. But I think I know what happened."

Breathing heavily, the D.A. said, "Go on."

"As I said, Bart returned," Egg began. "He found Rapp married to Glenda and abusing her. So, he killed him. Then, just as Glenda testified at her trial, he unlocked the door of her room, went in and sat down on her bed for a moment and assured her that everything would be all right."

"But, man," the D.A. protested. "Rapp was killed nine months ago."

"That's right," Egg agreed. "And I know where Bart spent those months. He spent them as a prisoner in the stinking hold of a freighter. Yesterday morning, he managed to escape but in doing so he was shot and killed before he could tell anyone his story." The little druggist looked at Marston, demanded, "If a smart man killed another man and had a fair chance of pleasing the unwritten law successfully, where do you think he would go immediately after the killing."

"To see his lawyer," the D.A. said promptly.

"That's right," Egg agreed. "And that's where Bart Irish went." He looked at Chandler. The lawyer was sitting on one of the benches, his face buried in his hands. "How about standing up and facing it, Wayne?" Egg asked him. "You might as well. You've come to the end of a long and crooked trail. And I'll be damned if you didn't have me fooled. I thought you were on the level."

Chandler lifted his face from his hands. "You can't prove a thing."

"No?" Egg asked. "I can prove it was you who had Bart's body released so you could get it planted and forgotten. I can prove that you were the only man other than Al Penny who knew I was going to dig it up tonight. I can prove that when you left me at the Ossining Station you didn't go to Albany and attempt to get a stay on the basis of the new evidence we had uncovered. You came back to town on the same train I was on instead, warned your girl friend that I would probably look her up, and also gave Horse and his cutthroats orders to kill me. Unfortunately, for you, they double-crossed you by taking me back to the ship, just as they'd done with Bart."

"As they had done with Bart?" Gault asked.

Egg looked at the big man on the stretcher.

"That's right. When Bart left Glenda he went to Wayne's apartment, told him what he'd done and asked him to defend him. Whether Wayne had already made plans to loot the Hall estate or whether that shrewd mind of his conceived the whole thing that moment is something he'll have to tell us. Anyway it was a natural. Bart had been reported dead. No one had seen him at the apartment. All that Wayne had to do was get him out of the way, reset the scene a little and Glenda was perfectly framed."

The girl spoke for the first time. "I didn't do it. I didn't."

Egg forced a smile for her. It wasn't difficult. "No. That's right. All you did was sleep."

"But this er—Horse?" Warden Gault asked.

"He was the mate of a deep water freighter," Egg said. "Chandler had probably done business with him before. And as I see it he undoubtedly agreed to give Horse so much for dropping Bart into the middle of the Atlantic. But learning who Bart was and what Chandler intended to do, Horse kept him alive instead and used him as a club over Wayne."

"I get it." Gault nodded. "As long as Bart Irish was alive and in his hands, this seaman, Horse, could demand any share of the Hall fortune that he wanted and Chandler wasn't in a position to refuse."

The young criminal lawyer got to his feet. "Idiotic nonsense, all of it." He laughed. "You've explained everything, Doc, but just how I intended to get my hands on the money."

"That's the simplest part of it all," the little druggist told him. "You made love and married Vera Hall before the news got out that she was next in line for the forty million dollars. She practically told me that this afternoon when she sat twisting a nonexistent wedding ring that she had just taken off along with her make-up because you had phoned her to do so, wanting me to think her a religious bachelor girl with no interest whatsoever in men."

Chandler made his futile gesture with his hands. "Okay. I think I made a good try. But it would seem you have me."

Al Penny forestalled the D.A. "Never mind, Mr. Marston. I'm making the pinch."

"On what charges?"

"Murder, accessory to murder, kidnapping, and body-snatching, among other things," Penny grinned. "Doc Egg said this would get me a lieutenant's shield. And I'll be damned if I don't think it will."

There was a rush of reporters for phones. Ben Morris stopped beside Egg. "How did you ever think of that cap on Bart's tooth?" he demanded.

Egg grinned, "Bill Shakespeare told me."

The editor eyed him dubiously, "What are you giving me, Doc?"

Egg quoted, " 'The evil that men do lives after them, The good is oft interred with their bones.' And so it was with Bart Irish. He died in an attempt to clear Glenda, and they buried him with his confession still in his head!"

DEATH MARCH OF THE DANCING DOLLS

CHAPTER ONE

KILL ME—OR ELSE

THE DEAD CHINESE walked into Doc Egg's gold mine on the corner of 44th and Broadway at exactly fifteen minutes of midnight July the 5th. No one paid much attention to him. No one knew he was dead. Wu Sin did not know it for that matter. But he *was* dead. He had been dead for twenty minutes and, as with Humpty Dumpty and the King's men, not all the great surgeons and physicians in New York could have given him life again. The 4th had been a long, hot day. Night had done little to lessen the heat. Wu Sin's entrance found Doc Egg, with his shirt sleeves rolled over his forearms and his bald spot glistening with perspiration, back of the store's long fountain giving the sandwich man a breathing spell.

As Wu Sin plumped his ample posterior down in a stool in front of the sandwich section, the bald headed little druggist, who had wanted a druggist's education badly enough to fight for it with his fists, was deftly spreading chicken salad onto a piece of toast. He added lettuce and mayonnaise, cut it into quarters, knifed it onto a plate, garnished it with potato chips, two olives, and a slice of pickle and slid it down the work bench.

"Toasted chicken salad. Pick up."

Gandy, of the middle section, slid it onto the counter.

From the far end of the fountain, Kearney called, "A ham on white, One Swiss, rye. A club."

His hands never still, Egg repeated, "A ham on white. One Swiss, rye. A club." He picked up a soiled sandwich plate and coffee cup from the counter in front of Wu Sin, wiped the tile with a damp rag, and replaced the dishes with a glass of iced water. "And what will yours be, Sin?"

Big for a Chinese, six feet and proportioned accordingly, Wu Sin eyed the druggist with ill-concealed contempt. "In my country," he informed Egg, drunkenly, "the owner of such an establishment as this would rather die than to so lose face as to do the work of a Number One boy."

Egg glanced at the other man sharply. Even across the counter the whiskey fumes were strong. A fairly recent arrival on the Broadway scene, a plunger and a gambler with seemingly unlimited resources from which to draw, the big Chinese had made few friends among men who accepted him at face value. He was arrogant and overbearing. No one knew his background. There was one man, and only one man, in America whom he had admired—Wu Sin.

"So what the hell?" Egg thought. "The man is drunk." He said, aloud, "You don't say, Sin?" As he spoke he slipped three slices of bread into the toaster and fanned white and rye bread on the work board. "A good thing you aren't home then. If you were, you'd damn well go hungry."

The hour was late. The majority of customers at the counter were midnight regulars, gamblers, actors, chorus girls, reporters. A wave of laughter rippled along the stools.

Wu Sin's black eyes narrowed. "I do not care to be laughed at," he told the druggist.

Egg nodded, matter of fact. "Most of us don't," he admitted. "Pick up a ham, a Swiss. And you said that you wanted what, Sin?"

"I didn't say," the Chinese answered coldly. "When I decide I will tell you."

A warning bell rang in Egg's mind. Wu Sin didn't want to eat. He wanted trouble. Egg searched his mind for some slight he might have offered the man. He could find none. He seldom gambled for high stakes, he had never gambled with Wu Sin. The few times he had met him had been at various night clubs and bars. Once the Chinese had been with Morry Glade, the returned Flying Tiger, now running for District Attorney. Another time he had been with Cal Ambler, a war correspondent who had covered the Chinese front.

He began working on the club sandwich. "Okay. You do that," he said.

Wu Sin sat toying with his water glass. "This glass," he complained, "is dirty."

Egg picked it up and glanced at it. It was clean, fresh from the sterilizer. He was hot, tired. His natural inclination was to tell Wu Sin to take his business elsewhere. For the sake of peace, he shrugged instead. "That could be," he admitted. He replaced it with a fresh glass and resumed working on the sandwich.

Disappointed, the Chinese searched through the menu and ordered the most complicated three-decker sandwich he could find. Egg made it deftly, glancing at the clock. He had a date with Yvonne at one. The little French star of the Chez Paree had phoned shortly after eleven, and had told him excitedly that it was imperative she see him.

Egg sliced chicken for the sandwich he was making for Wu Sin, amused, thinking, "She's probably seen a mink coat she wants. She would, on the 4th of July."

He had long since given up trying to figure out the idiosyncrasies of pretty women. They had cost him a lot of money. But it had been pleasant spending. The sandwich finished, he slid it across the counter, drew a cup of coffee to go with it, and told the sandwich man who had returned from a much-needed cigarette: "Okay, Charlie. You can take over. I want to check the registers." He walked out from behind the counter and behind the long row of stools toward the front of the store.

As he passed Wu Sin, the Chinese spun around on his stool and grabbed the little druggist by the shirt front. "This sandwich stinks," he said. "And, for that matter, so do you."

The buzz of conversation at the fountain ceased abruptly.

"Look," Egg told the big man quietly. "You've had a few too many, Sin. You've been trying, God knows why, to pick a fight ever since you came in. Now either eat your sandwich and scram, or else."

"Or else what?" the Chinese sneered. He deliberately rubbed his knuckles across Egg's bald scalp.

It was a mistake on his part. The good-natured little druggist had no cheeks left to turn. Instead he brought up a right from the floor and knocked the big man off the stool into a display of cheap canvas over-night bags.

Bill Cleary, Egg's store manager hurried up. Egg nodded at the fallen man. "Drag him out and put him in a cab, Bill. I think he lives at the Winterset Arms over on West 34th Street"

"Right." Cleary knelt beside the man on the floor. "Come on, you." His truculence changed to worry as the big man refused to stir. He felt his wrist, then pressed his finger tips to the big man's throat. There was no pulse. Cleary looked up white-faced. "Hey. Doc," he stammered. "This—this guy is dead!"

Egg said, incredulous, "Dead?"

"Yeah, dead. Stiff as a board," Cleary told him.

Her face lined with strain, her black eyes wide with fear, Yvonne DuPree (born Jennie Shillinger in Flatbush) nervously paced the spacious living room of her swank Button Place apartment, her high heeled mules making small dancing sounds on the parquet flooring.

Why didn't Doc Egg come? Damn him for a fool. She had told him that it was important, and what had he told her?

"As soon as I close the store. I'll be right over, baby."

One o'clock might be too late. Five minutes from now might be too late. She studied her face in the mirror, trying to assure herself that the little man could protect her. He was important. He knew important people. He and Lieutenant Bill Cassidy of Homicide were pals.

Twin tears of self pity rolled down her carefully madeup cheeks. Why should this happen to her? She had come a long way from Flatbush. Now, suddenly, the bonds and stocks and jewels that she had in her safety vault, the furs that hung in her closets, the knowledge that she had done well, no longer gave her comfort. The dead couldn't spend money, they couldn't wear furs; they had no need of expensive apartments.

She crossed the room, her silk-sheathed legs flashing out from her negligee, and slumped on the sill of a tall casement window. Doc could protect her. He had to. Once she was in his arms she would tell him everything, including her own crude attempt at blackmail. That had been her big mistake, calling attention to herself. She should have let well enough alone.

The oppressive July heat was a moist blanket that made it difficult for her to breathe. Somewhere, out on the river in the night, a tug boat tooted mournfully. One jeweled hand sought her throat. A snatch of doggerel that they had sung as kids in Flatbush came back to haunt her—

Oh when you see the hearse go by,
You know that somebody's going to die.
The worms crawl north, the worms crawl south,
The worms crawl into the dead man's . . ."

The little black-haired dancer began to pace the floor again, wondering morbidly what death was like, wondering how it would fed never to dance again, never to be loved, to lie cold and still, alone, on tufted satin.

She screamed aloud. "No! Doc won't let him kill me! I won't let him kill me!"

She wouldn't wait for Doc. She'd contact the District Attorney. She'd smear the whole thing all over the front pages. She looked up the number in the phone book, poured herself a drink, then picked up the phone. There was no reassuring tone signal. There was no buzz, no sound at all, nothing but an ominous dull silence. Opalescent drops of perspiration standing out against her rouge, she clicked the phone cradle frantically. The dull, deadly, silence continued. The switchboard did act answer. Her phone wire had been cut.

Frantic, she raced to her bedroom and snatched a small pearl-handled automatic from a drawer of her dressing table. Death was near her. She could feel his cold fingers on her limber spine, the lobes of her ears.

"Go away," she screamed. "Go away."

In a frenzy of fear she emptied the clip in the automatic at nothing. The small calibered gun made dull popping sounds unheard outside the apartment. Still clutching the empty gun, she made a round of the apartment. Both doors were locked and bolted. She closed and locked the window that she had opened.

Some of her terror left her. She had fooled him. Death could not get in. She looked at the watch on her wrist. It was twelve forty-five. Doc was always prompt. He had said he would arrive a few minutes after one. He would keep his word. So her phone wire had been cut. So what? She was ten floors above the street. Her doors were locked and bolted. She was safe until Doc came.

She poured herself another stiff drink of whiskey and her terror turned to anger. Who the hell did the big stiff think he was? Frighten her, would he? She'd show him. She'd nail him in the chair, that's what she'd do. She sat down at her desk in the living room, took a piece of paper from a drawer and made a list of things she meant to tell Doc.

Her body was beautiful; her handwriting and spelling were not. They were still seventh-grade Flatbush. In a crabbed, school girl, hand she wrote:

China
When I was with the Dancing Dolls
What I seen in Chunking

In Calcutta
In Rangoon
The Flying Tiger who gave Nellie a Bracelet
Black market.
What Nellie told me.
Who killed Federal Agent Crimp.
About what I wrote him.

The last notation made her think of the note she had received. She took it from the neck of her negligee. It read simply—

So you think you know something about me that's worth a lot of money, eh? Well, maybe you do, baby. But your terms are a little high. What do you say I drop by and talk it over with you tonight?

The note was typed. There was no signature. There was nothing in it about murder. But the moment it had come she had phoned Doc. *She knew.* Nellie had known. Nellie had known more than she did, and Nellie was dead. They had found her on Riverside Drive with her neck snapped like a match stick. Yvonne began to cry. Why hadn't she let well enough alone?

She poured another drink. It was five minutes of one. In five minutes she would be safe. Doc would take her to the D.A. and she would tell him the whole story.

She poured a fourth drink, giggling at her reflection in the mirror. Tears had streaked her mascara and her rouge. She repaired them, drunkenly. She wanted to look her best for Doc. He was a nice little guy. But all men were fools.

The knock on the door, a double break that was as habitual with Doc Egg as the red carnation in his button hole, came at exactly four minutes after one. Relief surged through the weeping girl. "You're late. You're four minutes late," she called as she crossed to open the door.

The man outside the door chuckled. "Don't tell me you were counting the minutes, gorgeous?"

The bolt already shot, the key turned in the door, the knob half-turned, Yvonne paused, fearful, an icy hand squeezing her heart. The voice sounded like Doc's voice. Still—

"How do I know you're Doc?" she panted.

The tall man outside the door, turned the knob the rest of the way, pushed the door open and walked in. "You don't," he told the girl, quietly. "As it happens, I'm not. But I believe I was expected."

Yvonne backed from him, too terrified to scream. Then she remembered the gun and clicked it, futilely, at his chest

Unsmiling, he slapped it from her hand, then lifted one of his own hands to her throat. "Goodbye, baby," he told her. "Thanks for dropping me a line. If I hadn't gotten your note, I'd never have known you knew."

Her eyes bulged from her head; her tongue filled her mouth, corking off all sound; her backbone arched in pain, as she kicked feebly at his shins. Then her body, sagged limply. The killer allowed her to sink to the floor, his fingers tightening on her throat until the thing he had come to do was finished.

Satisfied that she was dead, he crossed to the desk and picked up the sheet of paper on which she had written her notes and stuffed it into his side coat pocket. There was still the note that he had written her. He searched the desk, her bedroom, the floor and her person, before he found it.

He stuffed it into his pocket with the notes that she had written. There was nothing to tie him to the murder. The past was as dead as the pathetic little heap of flesh and silk staring with bulging, sightless eyes at the high-beamed ceiling of the living room she would never see again.

On sudden impulse, he folded her hands over her chest. "I'm sorry, kid."

Then he turned out all the lights, closed the door quietly behind him, walked down the hallway unseen and descended the service stairs.

CHAPTER TWO

GRAVE STUFF

THE NIGHT CONTINUED HOT. Those New Yorkers not so fortunate as to live in petit-house apartments, slept with all of their windows open, on fire escapes, or in the parka.

A tall, thin man with a boyish smile, Cal Ambler was waiting on the steps between the green lights of Centre Street when Egg and Cassidy reached it.

"What's the big idea," he demanded, "of breaking into my unrest? Who's dead?"

"Wu Sin," Lieutenant Cassidy told him.

Ambler fell into step beside the pair. "No! Who killed the lug?"

The little druggist glanced at his watch. It was one thirty-five. "They say I did," he told Ambler. "Look, Bill. How's about calling Yvonne again?"

"There's a phone in the Commissioner's office," Cassidy pointed out. "But you've called her fifteen times, and all you got was a busy signal."

"That's what worries me," Egg admitted.

It was cooler inside the building. Ambler asked, "You kidding about Wu Sin?"

"No," Cassidy said. "I'm not. He barges into Doc's place shortly before midnight, acts nasty all over the place and when Doc lays one on his chin, the big guy lays down on the floor and dies."

"G'wan," Ambler scoffed.

Egg said nothing at all. He was hot. He was tired. He was sick of the whole affair. He was also technically under arrest. By the time the affair was cleared up it would be three o'clock in the morning and Yvonne would be sore as hell. She was probably sore now. She had probably lifted her receiver off the hook. That's why they kept getting a busy signal.

In front of the Commissioner's office, Ambler protested, "But why drag me down this time of night?"

"You knew him in China, didn't you?"

"Slightly," the correspondent admitted.

"That's why you're here. The only two guys Doc could remember who were friendly with Wu Sin were you and ex-Flying Tiger Morry Glade."

"Nix on that friend stuff," Ambler protested. "Morry can speak for himself. But as for me, let it ride that I *knew* the guy."

Most of the reporters and pic men who had been at the store had beaten Cassidy and Egg to the Commissioner's office. Egg was greeted with good-natured banter by the newsmen. He had staked most of them at one time or another.

The Commissioner shook hands gravely. "Sorry to see you in a mess like this, Doc. But we'll clean it up as fast as we can. You do admit you hit him?"

The little druggist ran a palm over his bald spot. "With everything I had."

Cassidy hastened to add, "But it was strictly in self defense."

The Commissioner was as hot and tired and irritated as the others. "All right, Lieutenant," he said rather sharply. "Never mind the Damon and Pythias angle. No one is going to railroad Doctor Thistlewaite."

Egg looked slightly surprised. He always did when some one called him by his name. He heard it so seldom. His first name was Egbert but during his days in the prize-ring the fans had cut it to Egg, and Doc Egg it had remained.

Morry Glade had been sitting on the sill of an open window. He walked over and shook hands. "Good for you, Doc. Remind me to buy you a drink. You know how I like and respect the Chinese. But I've wanted to slug Wu Sin for two years."

As tall a man as Ambler, handsome, virile, the former Flying Tiger and local attorney was resuming his interrupted legal career in a hotly-contested fight with the incumbent District Attorney. In his middle thirties, a former playboy, Glade was known as a bad man to cross.

Doc Egg shook hands, grinning. "Stop electioneering, Morry."

"I mean it," Glade said sincerely. "Wu Sin was a rat."

Ambler nodded glumly. "I say 'Amen' to that."

The Commissioner resumed his seat, looking first at Ambler, then at Glade. "That's why we requested you two men to come down here." He swept the room with his eyes. "This, perhaps, is extra-legal. But most of us know Doc Egg. He's a respectable businessman who, on innumerable occasions, has been of great service to the police."

Ambler grinned, "Hear, hear!"

The Commissioner continued, "In the present instance, as I see it, the dead man was an alien. That's why I asked that Doc be held in technical arrest." He looked at Ambler and Glade again. "That's why I asked you here. His Embassy will probably raise hell in the morning on general principles and I'd like to know more of his background." He pointed a finger at Glade. "You say this Wu Sin was a rat?"

The former Flying Tiger nodded. "He was. I don't know how he got into the country in the first place. When I left Chunking, they were talking of putting a price on his head. He was the local version of an Al Capone in the Black Market."

Ambler nodded. "That's straight from the feed-box, Commissioner. Morry knows, and so do I. I damn near fell over when I saw him in New York. I did play him up a bit and feed him a few drinks, but I was after a story. You see, the real hot shot of the Chinese black market was reputed to be . . ." he hesitated, looking at Glade.

"Go ahead and say it," Glade said. "The real hot shot was reputed to be a former Flying Tiger." He added. "I never did believe the yarn, and I was hoping to disprove it."

Egg said, quietly, "So that's where he got the dough he was spending. I should have hit him harder."

The Commissioner said, "It would seem that you hit him hard enough. You can prove it was self defense, Doc?"

The little druggist shrugged. "He hit me first. And I've a store full of witnesses to prove it."

The Commissioner tapped his desk with his pencil. "You'd object to spending a night in jail, Doc?"

"Strenuously," Egg admitted. "But make up your mind. Book me so I can get a lawyer busy on a writ, or turn me loose." He looked at his watch. "I didn't ask the guy to come into my drug store. I tried to avoid trouble. And what happens? I have to clip him anyway." He mopped at his pink bald spot, looking like a chubby little cupid. "And now I'm an hour late for a date. What kind of justice is this?"

The office rocked with laughter. Even the Commissioner smiled. "Well, far be it from me to block the course of true love. Now I know that this Wu Sin had an unsavory record, I doubt the

Chinese Embassy will raise much fuss about it. So I'll see what we can do."

He left the office to consult with the D.A. on a more private wire. Egg used his phone to call Yvonne again. This time the operator told him: "I am sorry, sir. That line is out of order. We have asked the building superintendent at that address to request the subscriber to place her receiver on the hook."

Egg hung up, grudgingly. "I tell you she's sick or something," he complained to Cassidy.

"Okay, okay," the homicide lieutenant soothed him. "As soon as we get through here I'll run you out there in a squad car."

The Commissioner returned with the medical examiner walking at his heels. He was no longer smiling. "What kind of poppycock are you trying to feed me, Doc?" he demanded.

"You're over my head," Egg admitted.

"You hit him and he died?"

"That's right."

"You didn't poison him first?"

Egg chuckled. "No, I didn't think of that."

"Then suppose, Doc," Pete Meridith, the medical examiner, asked quietly, "you tell us *how the cyanide got in his stomach?*"

The little druggist gasped, "Cyanide?"

Meridith nodded. "Enough to kill ten men."

The office grew suddenly still. Egg, embarrassed, colored slightly. "You're crazy, Pete." He repeated the story that he had told fifteen times before. "Wu Sin walked into my store. He spent maybe five minutes trying to pick a fight. He took maybe two bites of a sandwich. Then he got really tough and I had to clip him." He snapped his fingers. "And cyanide kills like that."

The Commissioner said, pointedly, "That's what Meridith's pointing out. No one but you served the dead man. Why not give us the *true* story, Thistlewaite?"

Glade said, quickly, "You don't have to talk, Doc."

The little druggist shook his head. "Nix. What goes here? Who's trying to hang what on me? I clipped him, yes. But I didn't poison the guy. I had no reason to."

Ambler stepped in in his defense. "What if he did? Wu Sin was a rat. He deserved to die. He——"

"Shut up, you fool," Glade stopped him. "You want a lawyer, Doc?"

Egg rubbed at his bald spot. "It looks like I'm going to need one. But, believe me, this is over my head."

A few of the reporters scurried for phones. Most of them stayed. An awkward silence followed. The Commissioner seemed relieved when his phone rang. He picked it up, said, "Yes?" and handed it to Lieutenant Cassidy. "Your office calling."

Cassidy cupped the receiver to his ear, said, poker-faced, "I see. He did, eh? Okay. You go ahead. We'll be right out." He hung up.

"More murder," Cassidy said quietly.

He looked at Egg. "You were right. Someone's got to Yvonne. The building superintendent just found her on the floor of her apartment—dead."

Ambler uncoiled his long form from the chair in which he sprawled. "Yvonne?"

Glade lighted a cigarette with fingers that shook slightly. "Not that pretty little black-haired girl who came to China with that U.S.O. troupe, The Dancing Dolls?"

Egg closed his eyes briefly. He made no claim to clairvoyance, but Yvonne had been excited when she had phoned him. She had wanted him to come right over. She had beets in China. A few minutes later Wu Sin had walked in and tried to pick a fight Now Yvonne was dead. So was Wu Sin. Only a fool could fail to recognize that the two deaths were connected. Yvonne had wanted to tell him something, something so important that someone had killed her to seal her lips.

He opened his eyes and walked to the door of the office. "I wouldn't try to hold me if I were you," he told Commissioner Blake. "It would seem that I didn't kill Wu Sin after all. I believe it can be proven. I hope to prove it before this thing is over. Right now I've another little matter to attend to."

"I'll help you," Ambler said quietly.

"Ditto here," Glade said. "We all thought a lot of Yvonne."

Blake cleared his throat angrily. "Now, see here. You especially, Thistlewaite. Just what do you intend to do?"

"Get the guy who killed her," the little druggist told him simply. Blake started to protest, thought better of it. The bald headed little ex-fighter swung a lot of political weight

"And when you find him," Meridith sneered, "you'll mix him a cyanide cocktail?"

"I'd know how," Doc Egg admitted.

CHAPTER THREE

KILLER IN THE DARK

OUTSIDE THE WINDOWS OF YVONNE'S APARTMENT, a gray sluggish snake, the East River, rippled through the heavy slumber of the last hours before dawn.

The apartment blazed with light, throbbed with conversation. Pic men snapped latent fingerprints. Tech men dug slugs from the walls and powdered each planed surface. Reporters asked questions that no one present could answer. At a nod from Lieutenant Cassidy, two wagon men lifted the dead girl onto a stretcher. Her arms were still folded on her breast. Death had wiped the terror from her face. She looked like a tired, sleeping angel.

Egg covered her with a sheet, his plump face working. "Goodnight, my sweet," he said simply.

He turned abruptly, walked to the window and stood staring at the river. When he turned again she was gone. There was only a grotesque outline chalked on the rug to show where she had lain. Cal Ambler squeezed his arm. "Take it easy, Doc," he said gently to the little man.

"I'm all right," the little druggist told him. He walked over to the dead girl's desk, sat down in her chair and toyed with a sheet of stationary lying on her blotter. "We all get it sooner or later." He wrote her epitaph. "She had her faults, but she got a bang out of life."

Morry Glade lighted a cigarette. "She was a good kid. The fellows overseas worshipped every inch of the ground that pretty little kid danced on."

"Strangulation, of course," Meridith reported to Cassidy. "And I'd say, judging from the fact that he only used one hand, that you're looking for a powerful man."

Meridith shook his head helplessly, mopped the sweat band of his straw sailor. "Damn it. Walking dead men with cyanide in their stomachs, Chinese black markets, Flying Tigers, strangled butterflies. It doesn't make sense."

Egg folded the sheet of paper, absently, into a child's toy plane. "No one saw him, of course."

"Do they ever?" Cassidy asked. "But with death established as occurring a few minutes either side of one o'clock, she must have let him in thinking he was you."

Ambler suggested, "Maybe we're going at this wrong, tying in her death with that of Wu Sin's."

Egg got to his feet, folding the plane into a wad and stuffing it into his pocket. He looked at Cassidy. "You're going to try to back trail Wu Sin, that is shortly before he showed up at the store?"

Cassidy nodded. "I am. I'm also going to check on Wu Sin with Washington." He swung to Morry Glade. "This mysterious head of the Chinese black market was a former Flying Tiger?"

"Allegedly," Glade admitted. He puffed hard at his cigarette. "Personally, I never thought so. But whoever he was, using Wu Sin as a front, he coined more money than they mint."

Egg hesitated, asked, "And there are how many former Flying Tigers in New York?"

Glade thought a moment, told him, "Four, not counting myself." He named them on his fingers, "Hanson, Beyers, Smith, and Carson."

Cassidy asked for their addresses and wrote them down. "And while all this was going on, G-2 did what about it?"

"They sent over a federal agent named Crimp," Cal Ambler told him.

"And what happened to him?"

"He caught lead fever," Glade said dryly. He hesitated, added, "But look. I'm inclined to agree with Ambler. Maybe we're going at this wrong. I fail to see how Yvonne's death ties in with that of Wu Sin."

Egg explained, "Yvonne wanted to tell me something. Someone didn't want her to. So they sent Wu Sin to start a brawl with me to keep me occupied until she could be taken care of. And to make sure that he didn't talk they fed him a pony of cyanide before he started out."

Cal Ambler scoffed, "That won't wash, Doc." He snapped his fingers. "You said yourself that cyanide kills like that."

"It does," Egg agreed. "But it could have been put in a capsule that didn't dissolve until it had been in his stomach for fifteen or twenty minutes." Ambler admitted that could be so.

The little druggist put on his hat and walked slowly to the door. "And you're going where?" Cassidy demanded.

"To wake up Sol Levy," Egg told him.

"Sol Levy?" Morry Glade puzzled.

Egg nodded. "Yeah. When you caught their act in Rangoon, there were how many Dancing Dolls?"

"Six," I believe Glade said.

"You wouldn't remember their names?"

The lawyer shook his head. "That I would not, that is, their last names."

"Sol should know them," Egg said. "I believe that I remember hearing Yvonne say he booked the act." The little druggist pointed out, "All of the girls were in China and India. Yvonne was no smarter than the others. And if she found out something she shouldn't have known, maybe one of the others did too."

"I see what you mean," Ambler said. "And it's well worth looking into." His mouth grew wry. "It's surprising what some men will tell a pretty girl, especially if they're drunk."

Egg agreed to meet Cassidy for breakfast in two hours and left the apartment Ambler and Glade left with him. On the darkened street in front of the building, Ambler shook hands and said, in parting: "I'm sorry as hell, Doc. I know what she meant to you. And if there is anything, *anything,* I can do, you let me know."

Egg said he would.

"That goes double," Morry Glade said.

They left him standing in front of the building, one walking north, the other south. Egg realized with a start, almost of amusement, that both men were slightly worried for fear they might, despite their proffers of help, become involved in the affair. Both of them had spent years in India and China. Both had known Yvonne.

He stared after them thoughtfully, his amusement fading. Both were big powerful men. Either man could have choked Yvonne with one hand. Murder had no friends. He doubted anything would come of it, but he made a mental note to check into their respective whereabouts the hour Yvonne had died.

He walked slowly toward a two block distant subway kiosk. He had no illusions as to his own position. Because of his political weight, because he liked him, and because as yet there was no known motive for him to have killed Wu Sin, the Commissioner had allowed him to remain at liberty. But unless the case was cracked, his free time would be short. The press and the public would demand that he be held while the investigation continued.

Wu Sin had died in his store, of cyanide poisoning and he was, after all, a druggist.

He thought of Yvonne as he had seen her last with her hands folded on her bosom. She had not folded them herself. It was an unusual gesture for a killer. He wondered if perhaps he was wrong and Ambler was right, that the two deaths were not connected. Maybe a woman had killed her.

He doubted it greatly but he searched his mind for any quarrel of which Yvonne might have told him. He could remember none. She had few girl friends. The only ones of whom she had ever spoken had been a Marguerite and a Nellie. Both had been Dancing Dolls. He tried to remember their last names. It didn't matter. Sol would know.

He paused in front of an all night restaurant across the street from the subway kiosk. There were several cabs parked at the curb, their drivers parked inside on stools eating their last meal of the night.

A cab would be faster than the subway at this hour. He walked in and ordered coffee, asked, "Who wants a Times Square haul?"

A fat hacker at the far end of the counter told him through a mouthful of french fries, "I'll take you, Doc. Soon as I finish supper."

"Swell," Egg told him.

As he spooned the sugar in his coffee he heard another driver ask the fat man, "Who's the bald headed dressed up little guy?"

"Egg, Doc Egg," the fat hacker told him scornfully. "Don't you know nuttin'? He used to be bantamweight champ. Now he owns the big drugstore down on forty-fort."

"Oh," the other driver said in awe. "He's the guy who killed the Chink, huh, with one swat of his fist."

"Yair. That's the one."

Both men kept their eyes on their plates. Neither men bothered Egg with questions. That's what I like about New York, he thought, almost everyone minds his own business. It would be different, though, once the papers carrying Yvonne's death were on the stands.

Sipping his coffee, he searched his pockets for a paper on which to write the questions he intended to ask Sol and came across the sheet of stationery that he had folded into a model plane. He unfolded it and flattened it on the counter, studying the engraved heading—

Yvonne Du Pree
10 North Button Place

She had been so proud of the address. "Just like the Premier of England," she had told him. "Only his is 10 Downing Street."

Smiling wryly, the little druggist printed—

China Dancing Dolls
Names Addresses

He weighted it with his pencil and sat waiting for the fat hacker to finish his meal. One of the girls who had danced with Yvonne might possibly know something. They had been a welcome novelty to the women-starved men in the East. And, as Ambler had pointed out, it was surprising what some men would tell a pretty girl, especially when they'd been drinking.

A blast of the big electric fan at one end of the lunchroom swept the counter and skittered the paper to the floor. Egg picked it up, weighted it with the pencil again, then rubbed his eyes. His penciled notations had faded, leaving merely the indentions in the paper. I'm losing my mind, he thought.

He retraced the word China, stopped and turned the paper over. The notes that he had made were on the other side. *This was something that Yvonne had written!*

His hand shaking with excitement, he traced the indentations, read—

China
When I was with the Dancing Dolls
What I seen in Chunking
In Calcutta
In Rangoon
The Flying Tiger who gave Nellie a bracelet
Black Market
What Nellie told me
Who killed Federal Agent Crimp
About what I wrote him

These were notes that Yvonne had made, things that she had meant to tell him. The last, "About what I wrote him" had a strangely ominous ring. The little fool had attempted to blackmail someone, and that someone had strangled her.

He searched the paper feverishly for further indentations, possibly a name. There was none.

The fat hacker waddled up to the cashier, picking at his teeth. "Whenever you're ready."

Egg folded the paper carefully and put it in his wallet. He wanted to talk to Cassidy, show him the notes. But he could do that after he had talked to Levy. He knew he was on the right trail now. "Let's roll," he told the hacker. "You know where Sol Levy, the theatrical agent, lives?"

"Yair," the hacker told him. "In a kind of a studio-like, back of his office on 45th."

There was a beauty shop downstairs. The upstairs office windows of the two story building were dark, too. Egg paid off the driver of the cab and walked into the un-lighted foyer. By lighting a match he saw that there were four names in the hall. One was a racing service, one a modiste, one a sign concern, the fourth Sol Levy. He found the bell and pushed it hard. He could hear it ringing faintly. He rang it again, a third time.

"Yeah?" a sleep-fogged voice asked seemingly out of nowhere.

Egg put his lips to the speaking tube. "This is Doc Egg, Sol. I hate like hell to bother you this time of morning, but I have to see you. It's important"

There was a pause at the other end. Then the speaking tube said, metallically, "My God. Between business being lousy and taxes and drunks waking you up all hours of the night, it's getting so a guy can't get no sleep at all. Come back in the morning, Doc —around noon."

"I *have* to see you," Egg insisted. "Look. I'll make it worth your while."

"Okay," the voice gave in wearily. "Come on up."

There was a clicking sound as the inner door was unlocked. Egg caught the door just in time, pushed it open and walked up the dark, smelly stairs, striking matches from time to time.

As he reached the second floor a light shone faintly through the glass door of the rear office, as if reflecting from the living quarters behind it.

The legend on the glass read: "Sol Levy, Entrepreneur".

"Whatever that is," Egg thought. He rapped briskly on the glass.

A distant voice called, "You started this. Come in. And lock the door behind you."

Egg tried the door. It was unlocked. There was an old fashioned key in the key hole. He locked the door as he had been instructed and crossed the vacant office toward the cracked door through which the faint light was showing.

"Again, I'm sorry, Sol," he began, stopped as he reached the middle of the office, the short hairs on the back of his neck raising. The light in the other room had winked out. A door squeaked on unoiled hinges. A floor board creaked as if some heavy weight had just been placed upon it. A darker blob of black was moving slowly toward him through the dark.

The little druggist needed no diagram. He'd walked into a trap, like any dumb sucker might. The voice he had heard had not been Sol's. It had been a clever impersonation.

"Stand where you are or I'll shoot!" Egg bluffed.

The black form continued to come closer. He knew, and Egg knew that he knew, that he seldom carried a gun.

He backed a step and huge fists reached out of the dark and battered at his face. Egg covered as best he could, sank a right, then a left, into the other man's middle. The man grunted but did not give ground. It was a pee-wee fighting a giant.

Egg ducked and wove in vain. Hard fists found his face, his body, knocked him to the floor and down again as quickly as he got up. It was like fighting in a nightmare, shadow-boxing with a shadow that landed sledgehammer blows. There was no sound but the splat of their fists and their heavy breathing.

"I can't take this long," Egg thought. He spat out a mouthful of blood, asked, hoarsely, "Who are you, killer?"

There was a taunting laugh in the darkness. That was all. Then a huge arm swung like a scythe. Egg felt the quick nausea in his stomach that always preceded a blackout. His legs rubber, he sank to his knees, his battered head a throbbing boil. Then the heavy fist landed again—and nothing mattered . . .

The little druggist lay face down on the blood-slippery floor, his battered features cradled in one elbow. Certain that his victim was out, the killer knelt beside him, searching his pockets until he found what he was seeking.

Then he said, "I'm sorry, Doc," and drove his fist into the face of the unconscious man.

CHAPTER FOUR

FROM MORGUE TO MORGUE

THE SWEET, CLOYING, STENCH OF BLOOD was thick. The heat grew greater momentarily. Doc Egg tried to move, and couldn't. His whole body felt paralyzed. He opened his eyes with an effort The room was brightly lighted now. The blood he had smelled was his own. There was a pool of it under his cheek.

He had been out for at least two hours. It had been dark when he had come in, it was daylight now. The new day's heat was pouring through the window that he couldn't see. He inched his cheek onto the back of one hand and called, "Sol!"

There was no answer. He had not expected one. He knew what had happened to Sol. Sol lay dead in the room beyond. The miracle was that he himself was still alive. It was through no virtue of his own. Someone knew that he had been headed for Sol's place.

He decided to rest another five minutes, then try to move again. If his back wasn't broken he should be able to. The killer had missed this time. He hadn't been thorough enough. He had failed to allow for the amazing vitality that had enabled Doc Egg to dig a gold mine out of the prize-ring with a pair of pillows.

It was then that he heard the crackle of flame, smelled smoke. Two hours hadn't passed. It wasn't daylight. The killer had been thorough enough. The building was on fire. He had been left to roast alive.

Sweat standing out on his forehead, in bloody bubbles, he forced his will to move his legs. His back wasn't broken. That was all he wanted to know. He forced himself to his feet and stood, swaying, in the center of the office.

Sirens were wailing in the street now. The flames were between him and the stairs. He studied the locked office door. He could break the glass and yell for help. But no one on the street below would hear him and the increased draft would only fan the flames that were licking at the flooring and the rotten woodwork of the walls.

He weaved back into the living quarters of the place instead. Sol Levy was through booking talent. Wearing a blood-stained, old-fashioned nightshirt, the agent lay on his back on a rumpled studio cot. His eyes were closed. He might have been asleep. He wasn't.

The bloody brass candle stick with which he had been killed lay on the floor beside him. The little druggist staggered by him toward the rear window that he hoped opened on a fire escape, stopped at the glint of gold in the dead man's fingers. Painfully, he opened them and retrieved a bit of chain at the end of which dangled a Phi Beta Kappa key.

His already slitted eyes narrowed. He dropped the chain and key into his pocket, thought of his wallet, and while the flames licked along the floor toward him like greedy snakes made certain that the paper with Yvonne's notes on it was gone. It was.

His battered lips twisted into a grotesque semblance of a wry smile. The Broadway Confucius had summed it up when he had said: *"A man fool you once, shame on him. A man fool you twice shame on you."*

He was disappointed in the window. It opened on a four walled court instead of a fire escape. The office and the far half of the studio were a mass of flames by now. The heat had grown intolerable. He broke the window and the flames surged closer. There was a one-story shed roof to his right. He climbed through the window, hung by the sill with his fingers and dropped. The jar set his head to throbbing but the air was cool.

Flames were leaping from the window through which he had escaped. As he lay, panting, they licked up to attack the roof. It was only a matter of minutes before the whole thing would cave in. He crawled across the shed, lowered himself into a narrow areaway and limped out to the street.

There was the usual clamor and organized confusion of a big city fire. Captains were issuing curt orders. Firemen were coupling, lugging hoses, erecting ladders to the adjoining roofs. Three streams of water were already playing on the building. A crowd had materialized out of the gray of dawn. The fat hacker was shouting to a gray-haired battalion chief. Doc Egg caught the words:

"He's in there, I tell you. The little guy. Doc Egg what owns the drug store over on forty-fort."

The battalion chief eyed the flaming hell in indecision. Even as he watched, the stairs fell and the front wall bulged out. He shook his head and turned away to give an order to two waiting chemical men. Their heavy boots clomping on the walk, their rubber coats rustling, they brushed by the little druggist and clomped down the areaway from which he had just emerged. They returned a moment later to report that the rear roof had caved in.

Egg started forward to make known the fact he was alive, and changed his mind. By staying dead, temporarily, he was harming no one.

It still was dark but there was a growing grayness in the east. He couldn't stay where he was. His store was only a block away.

The next person he met might recognize him. He limped wearily down 46th to Sixth Avenue. There was a Yellow Cab on the corner. He didn't recognize the driver.

"Take me down to the Bowery," he told him.

The hacker looked at his battered face and blooded clothes suspiciously. "You got any money, pal?"

Egg took a bill from his wallet and handed it through the glass partition.

"Been pitchin' one, eh?" the driver grinned.

"Yeah," Egg said, soberly. "I guess I have."

He got out at Chatham Square. The Bowery awakened early. He bought a suit of clothes, a shirt, a tie, and a change of linen. Then he asked the way to the nearest Turkish Bath.

The bearded store keeper told him, dry washing his thin hands, added, "Class I can always tell. You been pitching one, no, Mister?"

The little druggist walked out without answer. He thought, too late, "I should have told him. 'No. I've been catching one'." He could still feel the impact of the other man's big fists.

After a steam bath, a plunge, and a massage, he felt almost normal again. His face was still puffed. His eyes were swollen to slits. But no irreparable damage had been done.

He collected his watch and money from the cashier, sent back a tip to the rubber. It was full daylight now. The streets were crowded with early morning workers. He glanced at his watch. It was seven-thirty. Bill Cleary would be opening the store. He smiled wryly. Unless they kept it closed in his honor.

He hailed a passing cab. The hacker pulled his flag. "Yeah. Where to, chum?"

Egg spoke the thought in his mind. "The morgue." He amended his destination. "That is, I mean, the *Morning Eagle.*"

The driver clashed his gears. "Make up your mind, chum."

Old man Leary at the *Eagle* morgue knew Doc Egg well. He looked up, frightened, as the little man walked into his dusty cubicle.

"It's me, Dad. And I'm not dead," Egg said. "As with Mark Twain, the report of my demise was much exaggerated."

The old man lay down his sheers with trembling fingers, cackled, "You can't burn a man who's born to be hanged." He added, seriously, "I'm glad. I—well—"

"Forget it," Egg said gruffly. He produced a pint of whiskey he had bought and slipped it across the counter. "That's to make up for what you'll miss at my wake. Now tell me all you know about a dame named Nellie."

Dad Leary, known as the morgue keeper with the encyclopedia for a mind, ran his nicotine-stained fingers through his tousled hair. "Well, there was Nell Gwynne who was the mistress of . . ."

"This one's more modern," Egg broke in. "She was a member of the Dancing Dolls, a U.S.O. show that toured India and China. Somewhere over there, China most likely, a Flying Tiger gave her a diamond bracelet. I want to know who he was and why he gave it to her."

Leary grinned, "Well, I think I could answer your last question, Doc, but," he palmed his chin. "Let's see—Nellie. The name *is* familiar." He snapped his fingers. "I've got it." He pulled a volume from the wall and thumbed through it. "Bellevue picked up a dame identified as Nell Hawley on Riverside Drive five days ago. That's her picture there. They found her at the foot of an embankment with a broken neck."

The little druggist studied the picture. The dead girl had been a sultry blonde with a too big mouth and too bold eyes. The story gave a hotel address, the Exchequer on Central Park South. Leary chuckled, "They call it that because it takes a fortune to stop there."

Doc Egg asked, "Who claimed the body, Dad? Do you know?"

"That's the funny part of it," the old man said, "no one. The last I heard she was still over at the morgue."

"I see," Egg said, then asked off-hand, "You wouldn't know where Morry Glade lives, would you, Dad?"

"The Exchequer," Leary said promptly. "He—" the old man stopped abruptly. "Hey, what gives, Doc?"

"I'm beginning to wonder," the little druggist evaded the question. In quick succession he asked for information on the four former Flying Tigers the young attorney had named last night.

Leary had to look up only one. Hanson was working as a test-pilot for a Long Island plane manufacturer. Beyers, of the wealthy Scarsdale Beyers, was resting on his laurels. Smith was taking a drink cure. Carson, the flyer he had had to look up, had advertised two days before for a financial partner in a machine shop he had opened.

And that, thought Egg, pretty well lets them out.

"How about Wu Sin?" he asked.

Leary cackled, "You should know. It says in this morning's paper that you killed him." He added, seriously, "We haven't a thing on him, Doc. But there was an F.B.I. man in the other day asking if we had."

Egg thanked him for his information and pledged him to silence. "I want to stay dead for a few hours longer," he confided.

Out on the street again he bought a morning paper and read his own obituary.

Former Bantam Weight Champion and Broadway Character Passes

The expression had always irked him. "I hope," he scowled, "that I threw a natural."

The obituary was more than complimentary, and had probably gathered dust in the files for months. It told how, a poor East Side boy without friends or influence, he had fought his way to a championship and an education. The only thing new that had been added was the statement that the fire in which he had died was of mysterious origin.

All that was on page eight. The front page was in direct contrast, screaming:

Druggist Slays Chinese With Cyanide

The story was as inane. Having no other motive the rewrite man had ascribed the motive to a quarrel over Yvonne, whose death was headlined in its own right: DANCER MYSTERIOUSLY MURDERED!

Doc Egg read on, enthralled. According to the *Eagle's* re-write man Wu Sin was a Chinese Mandarin who had fallen madly bat hopelessly in love with the little dancer during her far Eastern tour and had followed her to the United States where he had found that she was going out with a former prizefighter turned druggist. Then the rewrite man had waxed lyrical: . . . *outraged by this sacrilege to his little broken blossom* . . .

Egg crumpled the paper into a ball, stuffed it into a Sanitary District trash can and whistled down a passing cab. Once the full story broke, a lot of faces would be red.

He wanted to see the girl in the morgue—a girl to whom a Flying Tiger had given a diamond bracelet—a girl who had lived at a swank hotel where the rates began at ten dollars a day, and whose body still lay unclaimed in the city morgue.

Then he wanted to contact Cassidy. It wasn't fair to Bill to stay dead. True, he had no proof. But he knew who the killer was. Hs knew who had killed Wu Sin. He knew who had killed Yvonne. He knew who had killed Sol Levy and left him to die in flames. Between Bill and himself and the federal men they could work out proof some way.

In front of the morgue he told the driver, "Wait," and hurried in. Jim Maxell, the cold-room attendant, stood up, pop-eyed. "You're dead!"

"Don't bet on it," the little druggist told him. He took a ten dollar bill from his wallet and passed it to Maxell. "I want to see that blonde, Jim. The one that they picked up on Riverside."

Still trembling, the attendant led the way into the vault and pulled out the drawer in which the dead girl lay. "This time, all right," he complained. "But don't never do that to me again, Doc. How the hell did you get out of that fire?"

"That," Egg said, unsmiling, "is a long, hot story."

He stood studying the dead girl's face and body. She had been beautiful in life; she was beautiful in death. The man who had killed her had had to fear her greatly to snuff out such a life. Doc doubted *he* could have done it. Long limbed, slim waisted, smiling even in death, she was the kind of a girl to whom men would have told things, drunk or sober. "Nice, eh?" Maxell admired. "We don't get her kind every day."

Egg stooped and examined her wrists. Her arms were tanned but there was a white circle around her left wrist. "What about the diamond bracelet she was wearing?" he asked Maxell.

The attendant rubbed his nose. "G'wan. Maybe she had one, maybe not. But by the time that they get to me, they're lucky they still got the gold in their teeth."

The little druggist shrugged, thanked him, and left the morgue. After the chill damp of the place, the sun felt warm and clean. He lit a cigarette, savoring its flavor. It was good to be alive. To hell with the stink it stirred up. To hell with handling it himself. He'd contact Bill Cassidy at once and blow the case wide open. He walked to the waiting cab at the curb, reached for the door handle and froze.

The driver was not the same one he had left. A broken-nosed hood, known around town by the name of Reynolds, was regarding him coldly over the barrel of a blue-steel automatic.

"You were right the first time," he said curtly. "Open the door. Get in."

Egg hesitated and a second hood in the back seat of the cab leveled a sawed-off shotgun at his head. "You hoid what he said."

"Nix," Egg protested. "You can't get away with this. You'll burn."

Reynolds grinned, disclosing snags of yellow teeth. "Not for killing you," he jeered. "You're dead. Says so in the papers."

CHAPTER FIVE

CORPUS DELICTI

ONCE EGG WAS INSIDE THE CAB the second hood, Mopey, discarded the sawed-off shotgun for an automatic. He sat at the far end of the seat holding it leveled on Egg's middle.

"G'wan. Give me trouble," he snarled, "And see what happens."

Egg looked from him out the window. After weaving uptown through traffic, they were crossing the Washington Bridge. He recalled grimly that Morry Glade had a cabin in the hills somewhere up back of Bear Mountain.

"I won't give any trouble," he said quietly. "But you're running a hell of a risk rolling this heap over to Jersey. You better watch out or the O.P.A. will get you."

Reynolds laughed so hard that he almost rammed into the rear of another car. "We better watch out," he repeated, "or the O.P.A. will get us."

"You watch your driving," Mopey warned him.

On the New Jersey end of the bridge, Reynolds drove for another half mile then turned up a lonely side lane and parked back of a battered blue sedan. "Change here for all points north," he told Egg.

Mopey prodded the druggist out of the cab into the other car. "And don't try nothing," he warned.

He'd changed to the shotgun again. Egg regarded it thoughtfully. Resistance would mean suicide. Both of these men were killers. They were acting under instructions; they were being well-paid to dispose of his body. But under their snarls and their banter, they were nervous. An attempted break on his part would only mean they would drop him where he stood. It was summer. The sun and the day were warm. Life was sweet. He climbed meekly into the rear seat of the other car.

Reynolds drove carefully, avoiding any overt act which might attract the attention of a state patrolman. A few miles past Haverstraw, Egg made his first bid for freedom.

"How much you boys getting for this?" he asked.

"Plenty," Reynolds told him.

"I'll double it if you let me go," Egg offered.

Reynolds considered the offer.

"Don't listen to him," Mopey snarled. "We was told he'd pull that gag. It's the future we got to think of."

The little druggist shrugged and settled back in his seat. Reason was futile as resistance. Both men were morons. God only knew what cock-and-bull promises had been made to them. It was as hopeless to talk sense to them as it was to a pair of monkeys in the zoo.

He sat watching the passing country side. The fields, the hills, the woods, were green and lush. Life, even the tough parts, had been sweet. He had enjoyed every minute of it. He thought of the women he had known, his mind lingering on Yvonne. If there was any life after death perhaps he would see her again. He jerked himself up with a mental start. "Cut it out, Egg," he warned. "You're getting morbid."

"You say something?" Mopey asked.

Doc Egg shook his head. "Nothing you'd understand."

He sat forward on his seat, whipping his senses alert. No fight was ever over until the last bell rang. He'd been on the canvas before and gotten up at the count of nine.

Mopey sensed the change and warned him, "Don't you go getting no ideas." Egg didn't bother to answer. Sometime before the end he would have one chance, he hoped. If it came, he meant to take it.

Just north of Bear Mountain, Reynolds stopped the car to study a signpost, then turned off on a secondary road leading up into the hills toward Lake Popolo. Egg knew this section well. He'd had a summer cottage on the lake until the government had taken it over as reserve reservoir for West Point. Glade's cabin, as he recalled it, was on the crest of a hill overlooking Cat Hollow.

There were few farms or houses on the road. Reynolds turned, again, on to a dirt road and the wilderness closed in. There were no farms or houses now. The trees reached out to whip at the car with their branches as it scurried past them like a frightened rabbit.

It seemed incredible that such a wilderness could exist within so short a distance of the metropolis of the world.

Reynolds spoke his mind. "These kind of places give me the creeps. Who'd want to live out here."

"I would," Egg said quietly.

Reynolds roared his laughter. "He would. He'd like to live out here. Catch on, Mopey?"

"Mind your driving," Mopey said.

The lane leading up to the cabin was rutted and overgrown with weeds. There were no other tire-marks on the clay. In front of the cabin, a two-room affair with a big open porch, the name Morry Glade was neatly lettered on a huge flat stone. There was no other car in the clearing. The place had a deserted look. There was no sign of life but a robin chirping on a ridge pole.

"Out," Mopey ordered Egg, "This is as far as we go."

He prodded the little man around the cabin. Egg tensed his muscles for one last desperate try, relaxed as he saw the piles of sand and gravel and cement sacks standing beside a half-finished cistern. The killer was taking no chances. He was tying up every end.

Reynolds took off his coat, cursing the heat that beat down on the clearing like a blowtorch. "This I don't see the sense of," he complained. "We coulda dropped him in the river just as well."

"Stop griping," Mopey ordered. "We'll do like we were told. You start mixing the stuff."

Grumbling, Reynolds connected a hose to an outside water tap while Mopey prodded Doc into the shade of the building and sat down on a stump where he could watch him. "One move and you get it," he warned.

Egg sat with his back to the building, watching the sweating hoodlum mix the concrete that was to cover him. From time to time he glanced at Mopey, hoping the heat would make him drowsy. Seemingly unaffected, the hoodlum sat alert, the shotgun across his knees. A maggot of a forlorn hope began to gnaw at Doc Egg's mind. "Hot work, eh, Reynolds?" he called.

The hoodlum cursed him, threw down his shovel, and drank from the running hose. The hose lay in the sun. The water was hot. He spat it out in disgust. "If I only had some beer," he complained.

The little druggist forced himself to chuckle. "A hell of a lot of good that would do you." He inclined his head toward Mopey. "Your pal here would probably drink it. He seems to be the boss."

Stooping for the shovel, Reynolds rose empty-handed and glared at Mopey. "Yeah. Hey, look. Why should I do all the work? You mix some of this here cement stuff, Mopey."

Mopey cursed Egg but got to his feet, handed the shotgun to Reynolds, and took off his coat. "Okay, okay. Keep your shirt on. We're getting enough for this job to throw in a little muscle."

While Reynolds sat down on the stump he mixed sand, gravel, cement, and water vigorously. He was using too much water and the sloppy mixture persisted in running off the platform.

Egg watched him for perhaps five minutes. The hoodlum's face was red with his exertions. His shirt was black with sweat. Egg pointed out, "You're using too much water. That stuff won't harden for a month. Also, you're using too much gravel. A 2-2-2 mix is plenty for a job like this."

Mopey threw down his shovel in a rage. "All right, damn it to hell, wise guy. Seeing that you know so much about it, you can mix your own grave."

Egg shook his head. "Hell with that."

Reynolds clicked back the hammers on the shot gun. "Do like Mopey tells you. Get out there and grab that shovel or else."

Seemingly unwillingly, Egg got to his feet, folded his coat neatly on the bank, walked out and picked up the shovel. The weight felt good in his hands. It wasn't much of a weapon against an automatic and a shotgun—but it was better than his hands alone.

"Now let me get this straight," he asked as he mixed sand, cement, and gravel deftly. "After this is mixed, then what?"

"Then you go into the cistern," Reynolds jeered, "and we shovel it in on top. Catch on? You being already dead in that fire on 45th, the guy what's paying us to do this don't want no *corpus delicti* bobbing up."

The heat grew more intense. The pile of materials was dwindling. A drowsy hush had filled the clearing. He glanced at the two hoods from time to time. Reynolds was openly sleepy but Mopey was alert. There was little hope he would drowse.

"You're getting how much for this job?" he asked.

"Five grand," Mopey told him.

The little druggist thought of the 4th of July's receipts in the fat wallet in his coat. In a hurry to go to Yvonne, instead of making a trip to the night bank, he had merely picked out the large bills, stuffed them into his wallet, sacked the rest and put it in the store safe. And the day's business had been good.

He straightened with a shovel full of wet cement "That's chicken feed. I'll give you six grand and a half right now to let me go."

Reynolds came awake at that "Yair?" he jeered. "And where you going to get it?"

Egg nodded at the bank. "I've got it right in my coat."

Both hoods got to their feet.

"I'll have a look see," Reynolds said.

"We'll have a look-see," Mopey corrected.

Egg stood gripping the shovel until his hands ached. This was it. He wouldn't have another chance. Reynolds tucked the shotgun under his arm to leave both hands free to examine the wallet.

"He's got it!" he crowed. "His wallet is stuffed with C notes!"

"Halvers," Mopey demanded. He clutched at the bills with one hand, the hand holding the automatic dropping to his side.

"Reynolds," Egg called softly. His mind still on the money, the hood turned. Egg had moved five feet closer and the shovel full of wet cement smacked the hoodlum in the face with an impact that knocked him from his feet, one barrel of the shotgun discharging as it struck the ground.

Cursing, Mopey whipped up his gun and fired. Taken by surprise, his slug went wide of its mark. The long-handled heavy shovel in Doc Egg's hands did not. Before Mopey could shoot again the shovel had completed its downward swing with all of Egg's strength behind it. The steel made contact with flesh and Mopey's head cracked like a rotten melon.

Whimpering with fear, clawing the wet cement from his eyes, Reynolds snatched up the shotgun and fired blindly. The shots pattered against the leaves of a near by oak tree, rousing an outraged gray squirrel to noisy chatter.

Unable to raise the shovel again in time, Egg jabbed at Reynolds' face with the handle end. It was a mistake. Reynolds went to the ground, blinded, but his groping hand landed on the automatic that had dropped from Mopey's lifeless fingers. He emptied the clip at Egg. Two of the slugs went wild. The third tore off the lobe of the little man's ear. The fourth and fifth hit the shovel, knocking it from his hands.

Egg kicked at the hood now on his knees. "Make me mix my own grave, would you? Why you nit-witted moron—when I get through with you . . ." Egg stooped to pick up the shovel.

Screaming with terror, still half-blind, Reynolds got to his feet and ran. He didn't run far. The shin-high wall of the cistern that was to have been the other man's grave tripped him. His body hurtled forward. The back of his neck hit the opposite wall. There was a sharp crack, a thud—then silence.

Still breathing heavily. Egg felt his ear, decided it wasn't serious and picked up the bloodstained bills that were fluttering on the ground. It had been close. It never would be closer.

A drowsy silence had descended on the clearing again. The squirrel had ceased to chatter. The robin had flown away.

Egg replaced the wallet in his coat, folded the coat over his arm, and walked back to the parked car humming softly to himself. The dead men couldn't hear him. The squirrel in the oak tree didn't know it. But the tune that he was humming was

'There'll be a hot time in the old town tonight.'

CHAPTER SIX

I'M SO SORRY YOU DIED

THE WEATHER REFUSED TO BREAK. Afternoon merged into night, still hot and sticky. The lights of greater New York blinked on. Whole families migrated hopefully to the parks.

From 44th Street to Columbus Circle, hard faced gamblers, actors, reporters, those in the know, stood in front of the Astor Bar, the Brass Rail, Lindy's, Reubens, and a dozen similar hang-outs discussing the events of today and the night before. Doc Egg's name was on almost every tongue, woven through a conversational tapestry of the dead Chinese and the dead dancer who had been found with her hands folded on her breast, as if in prayer. The affair by now had become so garbled that no two conversational or news stories matched.

. . . The little druggist had died in the fire that had taken Sol Levy's life. . . He had not died in the fire. . . . Dad Leary and Jim Maxell swore that they had seen him at a later hour . . . Dad Leary was a drunkard . . . Jim Maxell was a publicity-seeking liar.

However, as Morry Glade, immaculate in summer formal dress, pointed out to a group of City Hall men in front of the Brass Rail, "Even if they don't find his body, that won't prove that he wasn't in the building. The hacker swears that he saw him go in. No one saw him come out And the battalion chief just told me that what with all of the oils and paints and chemicals that sign concern had illegally stored in the basement, he doubts they'll find a sign of either man. That is, unless they sift the ashes."

One of the pay-rollers asked, "You think he slipped the poison to the Chink on account of the dame like it said in this morning's *Eagle?*"

Glade shrugged his well-tailored shoulders. "I wouldn't know. It doesn't sound like Doc. But I wouldn't know."

Weaving slightly, his coat draped over his arm, Cal Ambler joined the group. "Hi, Phi. You old Beta Kappa," he greeted Glade drunkenly. "Come on. I'll buy you a drink in memory of Doc."

Glade's fingers fumbled at his vest where his chain and key usually hung. "No thanks, Cal. And no offence meant, but I'd say you'd had enough."

"Great little guy, Doc." Ambler shook his head sadly. "Killed, thash what he was. Murdered, I bet you."

The attorney lighted a cigarette. "That could be," he admitted. "We know that somebody killed Yvonne. We know that Wu Sin was poisoned. And if the case doesn't break by then, if and when I win the election, as District Attorney, I'm going to rip this whole thing wide open."

Ambler patted his shoulder, "Atta boy. Vote for Morry Glade." He added, not so drunkenly, "And you're goin' send him to the chair, the dirty killer? Even if he is a former Flying Tiger?"

"You're drunk, Cal. Go home," Glade said.

"I've been drinking," Ambler admitted.

Hat Carson the bandleader of the sweet band at the Old Fashioned joined the group. "What have you guys been up to?" he asked.

"What do you mean, what have we been up to?" Glade demanded.

Carson wiped the sweat band of his panama. "Well, don't bite my head off. I thought it was a gag. But Bill Cassidy just phoned my hotel room and wanted to know which one of you guys cried in your beer when we give with the sentimental stuff."

The group laughed. Glade said coldly, "The heat's affected his mind."

Ambler struggled into his coat. "Speaking of beer, that reminds me . . ." He staggered on down the street.

"A nice guy," Morry Glade knifed him. "But he can't hold his liquor. Being a big-time correspondent has gone to his head as well as his purse. The next thing we know he'll write a book on Pink Elephants and Flying Tigers that I knew in China."

The group on the sidewalk howled.

"I just thought I'd tell you," Carson said.

Two blocks up the street and three beers later, Ambler, yawning widely, turned East and into the lobby of his second-class hotel, "Poor Doc Egg," he told the clerk. "He's dead. And nobody would lishen to me. But I bet I know who killed him. Heesh a prominent man in thish town."

"Sure. Sure, of course, Mr. Ambler," the desk clerk humored him.

Ambler shrugged his shoulders hopelessly and staggered into the elevator. "I know who killed Doc Egg," he confided to the operator.

"Ain't you the clever one, Mister Ambler?" the colored girl smiled brightly.

The big man made a wry face, fumbled his key in the lock of his door and walked in. The room light was on. Sitting in an easy chair in his shirt sleeves, Doc Egg told him: "Don't be frightened, Cal. I'm not a ghost. I'm not dead. But right now, as I see it, you're the only man in New York who can help me."

Ambler passed a hand before his eyes, then walked into the bathroom. There was a sound of running water. Four or five minutes later he emerged toweling his face and hair—and sober. "Don't do such things to me, Doc!" he protested. "How did you get here? Where have you been?"

"I walked up the service stairs and used a skeleton key," Egg told him. "Where I've been is a long story. You sober, Cal?"

The big man sat on the bed facing the little druggist "I could even use a drink," he admitted. "I don't know when anything has hit me harder. Give."

Egg told him the story of his movements from the time he had shaken hands with him in front of Yvonne's apartment up to and including the bloody fight at Morry Glade's cabin in the hills.

With a reporter's keen mind, Ambler evaluated the story. "Mopey and Reynolds could have been hired by anyone. But this man you fought with at Sol Levy's. You recognized him as Morry?"

"No," Egg admitted, "I did not," He held out the piece of broken chain and the Phi Beta Kappa key. "But I did find this in Sol's hand."

Ambler weighed it in his palm. "Glade is Phi Bete. And I noticed tonight that he wasn't wearing his key. But why come to me, Doc? Why not go directly to Bill Cassidy?"

"Bill is an officer of the law," Egg pointed out. "His hands are tied. And what can I prove? Morry knew I was going to Sol's. Someone attacked me in the dark and set fire to the building. I found a key that may or may not be his. Two hoods who never once mentioned his name took me to a cabin in the hills that 'happened' to be his. He could claim I was framing him."

"He could that," Ambler admitted. "But he was a former Flying Tiger. He did meet Yvonne and undoubtedly this Nellie, of whom you speak, in China. He does live at the Hotel Exchequer. And someone is putting up a lot of dough for his campaign." He eyed the little man shrewdly. "Just what did you have in mind, Doc?"

Egg rubbed his bald spot. "I'm dead. That is, I'm supposed to be. Why couldn't we kidnap Morry, take him back out to his cabin and beat a confession out of him."

Ambler lighted a cigarette. "Yeah. I see what you mean. Bill Cassidy wouldn't be much help in an affair like that. It would probably mean his tin. Remember you're crossing a State line."

The little druggist shrugged. "I'm dead."

"But I'm not," Ambler pointed. "Supposing something went wrong."

Egg assured him. "Nothing will go wrong. For Yvonne's sake, Cal," he pleaded.

The big man got off the bed. "By God. The dirty filthy rat. Burning's too good for him. Okay. I'll give it a whirl. But tell me this. How are we going to get ahold of Morry?"

"That," Egg told him, "is simple. Listen . . ."

At fifteen minutes after two, Egg said, tersely, "Here he comes. Walking. I knew he would."

Ambler nodded grimly from the front seat of the car. "When I call him over, clip him. Clip him hard." A moment later he leaned out of the window, called. "Hi, Phi. What you doing up this time of night?"

Glade chuckled. "Well, I'll be damned." He walked over to the car. "What are you doing, haunting me tonight—"

The name Cal remained unspoken as the bald headed little druggist clipped him deftly with the dead Mopey's automatic. Glade sagged to his knees. Egg tugged him into the car beside him, slammed the door, said crisply. "Let her roll, Cal."

At Washington Bridge, Cal asked, "The big heel come to yet?"

"I've gagged him," Egg reported.

"Good," Ambler said.

At the crossroads where Reynolds had paused to study the signboard. Ambler turned up into the hills without pausing, and a short while later up the lane leading to the cabin. His hands were shaking as he braked the car and got out. "I almost wish I hadn't let you talk me into this," he admitted. He reached into the rear of the car and dragged Glade to his feet. The attorney's eyes were furious above the gag. "Walk, you heel," Ambler ordered.

He pushed him ahead of him on up the path. Doc Egg followed, dry twigs snapping under his heels.

Breathing hard, the little man said, "There's probably not another soul within ten miles of here, I'll get a confession all right."

Ambler shrugged, braced Glade against the cabin wall and fumbled his keys from his pocket. One of them fit the door. The interior, one large living room, had stored the heat of the day. "Open some windows," Ambler ordered, "while I light a light."

Egg opened four of the windows, one on each side of the cabin, turned from the last one to find Morry Glade pushed down on a couch and Cal Ambler, in the feeble glow of an oil lamp, staring at him coolly over the long blue-steel barrel of a shiny Colt revolver.

"What's the idea? Egg asked.

"You'll find out in a moment," Ambler said dryly. "Drop the gun and drop it damn fast, Doc."

Egg dropped his gun, puzzled. "But, Cal—"

"Don't Cal me," the other man said. "I'm leaving here. You're not. I'm going to put the slugs through your head that that dumb pair of hoods I hired should have put through it when they first picked you up outside the morgue this morning."

The little druggist ran a palm nervously over his bald spot, his green eyes wide. "You—you don't mean it, Cal, that—"

"That's just what I mean," Ambler said. "You suspected the wrong lad, Doc. *I'm* the lad Yvonne tried to blackmail."

"And you killed her!"

Ambler waved the little man back with his gun, chuckling, "Yes, I killed her—almost the same way I killed Nellie."

"But I don't understand," Egg protested.

"It's very simple," Ambler explained. "You see I'm the lad who gave Nellie a diamond bracelet in Rangoon during a moment of drunken generosity, incidentally telling her I was a former Flying Tiger who was heading the Chinese black market. But it seems that she wasn't as dumb as that federal agent Crimp they sent over—the one I was forced to dispose of . Nellie put two and two together and tried to bleed me. She also blabbed to Yvonne." He shrugged. "It was a rather nasty chore. But there was only the one thing I could do."

Glade broke the light rope around his wrists and tore the gag from his mouth. "You filthy scum. Not content with killing both girls, you tried to pin it on me."

"That's right," Ambler agreed. "And I think I'll still succeed." He motioned with his gun barrel. "This is your cabin, is it not?

And will Bill Cassidy's face be red when they find your bodies here along with Mopey and Reynolds. You're a hell of a prospective D.A., say I."

Still wide-eyed, Doc Egg asked, "And it was you who killed Wu Sin to keep me occupied until you could shut Yvonne's mouth?"

Ambler nodded. "Rather cleverly, I thought. You see, Sin had been my agent in China. He, too, was bleeding me. So I slipped him a cyanide capsule telling him it was vitamin B and sent him to brawl with you and incidentally to die in your store."

"And I came to *you* tonight for help," Doc Egg said quietly.

"Also a confession," Ambler chuckled. "Well you've got one. The Levy affair, you see now, was a mistake. But after committing two murders another one didn't matter. He *did* know the other girl's name. Nellie *might* have talked to one of them. And it seemed such a beautiful chance to shift the whole thing on Morry."

"Too bad for your sake it flopped, Cal," Glade told him coldly.

"Oh but it didn't," Ambler grinned.

"Oh but it did," Doc Egg corrected, no longer wide-eyed. He lifted his voice slightly. "Okay, Bill. If you have his confession recorded, that's all we need."

Cassidy's face appeared at one of the windows. "Check."

Slit-eyed with anger, Ambler lifted his gun, opened his fingers and let it fall as a voice in the window behind him ordered, "Drop it, sucker. You don't know me. But my name is Vic Inglis. I work for the old man with whiskers. And Joe Crimp was a pal of mine."

Ambler pointed his accusing finger at Glade. "That snatch that Doc talked me into was a phoney. You knew. You knew all the time!"

Morry Glade shook his head. "No, only since a few minutes after Doc had Bill Cassidy call Hal Carson and asked which of us cried in his beer when he gave us with the sentimental stuff."

"You see," Egg said quietly. "I thought it was you, Cal, ever since I found Morry's Phi Beta Kappa key in Sol's hand. It had too perfect a plan. And thinking back I could see how every move that you made was phoney as hell, all pointing suspicion at Morry. The cleverest thing you did was to lay low with the money you made in your rotten racket. But you made one *bad* mistake."

It was difficult for Ambler to speak. "And that was—?"

"Folding Yvonne's hands on her breast," Doc Egg said quietly. "Only a fool or a sentimentalist would have taken time to do it. Neither you nor Morry are fools. But you are sentimental. Hat confirmed that. You're one of those guys who weep over songs about dear old ma and you probably haven't even written home in fifteen years. Your kind usually cries the hardest. A real man doesn't have to."

Cassidy reappeared in the doorway. "I guess we're ready to go, Doc."

The bald headed little druggist shook his head. "No, not quite." He slipped out of his coat and folded it neatly on a chair. "I have one last little thing that I want to do for Yvonne." He crossed the room to Ambler. If she knew it, she was pleased. He did what he could do thoroughly.

SO SORRY YOU DIE NOW!

CHAPTER I

DANGER, DEAD MAN!

DAWN BROKE HOT AND DRY. The wind was still from the west.
Night had failed to dispel the heat. North Clark Street awakened
sluggishly. Here and there a bum crawled from a dingy doorway to
panhandle the early work-bound crowd for the price of breakfast
and a shot of rot-gut. Merchants appeared and began to take down
their shutters. Porters opened the doors of the tawdry saloons and
night clubs.

Still heavy-eyed with sleep, Irv unlocked the door of his pawnshop. He was glad that Jessie and the children were out of the heat.
He was looking forward to Saturday night when he could join
them in Benton Harbor.

"Morning, Irv." The passing mailman handed him a sheaf of
letters. He hesitated, added, "I see you got a letter from Steve Pulos. I thought Steve was dead."

The pawnbroker sorted his mail. "He is. Matt Mercer got the
official notification over two weeks ago." He found the letter. The
censor's stamp had almost obliterated the post date, but he could
decipher the word May. The letter had been delayed three months
in transit.

The postman sighed, "Like hearing from the dead, eh, Irv?"

"Yeah," Irv agreed.

He turned back into his pawnshop. It still seemed impossible
that big, good looking, hard-living, hard-drinking, skirt-chasing,
Steve Pulos was gone. His kind didn't die. They lost an eye, or a
leg, or an arm like Matt Mercer, but they came back to haunt their
favorite bars and grow into local legends.

He slit the envelope. It contained a torn strip of rice paper covered with Japanese characters or symbols, and a brief note in
Steve's own hand. Irv put on his glasses and read the note. It was
like Steve. It was brief and to the point. It read:

Dear Irv:

We're starting another big push soon and I have a hunch I can't shake that I may cop mine this time. If so, and Matt should receive official notification, please show him the enclosed scrap of Japanese poetry. It means a lot to me. I took it off a Jap Intelligence Colonel at Tarawa, and from the way he objected to having a bayonet stuck into his guts, it must have meant a lot to him, too. If Matt doesn't hear, save it for me until I get back and we'll have a laugh and a drink together.

Your pal,
Steve.

The pawnbroker studied the characters. He wondered what they said. They must be pretty good to mean a lot to Steve. The big Marine hadn't cared much for poetry. No-limit poker games, quart-sized jugs, and pint-sized blondes, brunettes, and red-heads had been more to his liking.

He looked at his watch. It was only a little after eight. He could still catch Matt at home. The phone was in the cage at the rear of the shop. Here the air was heavy with the smell of moth balls and musty leather.

Irv laid the two bits of paper on his ledger and dialed Mercer's number. The heat settled solidly around him. He mopped at his forehead with one hand, then reached up and jerked the hanging cord of the ceiling fan. The sudden gust of air swept the scrap of rice paper from the counter just as Magnolia, the Mercer's colored maid, answered.

Irv told her that he wished to speak with Mr. Mercer, and stooped to retrieve the scrap of paper that had fluttered in between two unredeemed suit cases. The paper evaded his fumbling fingers. He swore, then straightened suddenly as two men entered the front of the shop.

Both were black haired, well-dressed orientals. They claimed to be Filipinos. Seemingly well supplied with money; they had haunted the cheap bar next to the pawnshop for the last two months.

"You open for business?" one of them asked.

He unstrapped his wrist watch as he spoke and the pawnbroker smiled inwardly. No matter who they were, if they hung out in bars, sooner or later they wound up at Uncle Irv's. That was how he had met Matt, and Steve, and Harry.

He cupped one hand over the mouthpiece of the phone and nodded. "Yeah. I'll be with you in a minute, just as soon as I finish this phone call."

The larger of the two men slipped a gun from a shoulder holster. "Let's make it right now," he said crisply. "Hang up that receiver!"

The pawnbroker did as he was ordered just as Mercer's voice boomed, "Hello!"

"So. It's a stick-up," Irv said wryly. He raised his palms shoulder high. He had been stuck-up before. He was insured. His life was worth more than his money. "Okay. Go ahead. Take what you want. My wallet is in my left hip pocket."

The smaller of the pair walked back to the front of the store, locked the front door and pulled the shade. The man with the gun told Irv, "To hell with your wallet. Where's that letter you just got from Steve Pulos?"

The pawnbroker's eyes narrowed slightly but he made no reply.

The hood who had locked the door retained and walked into the cage beside him. "Here it is," he told his partner. "Pulos told him to get in touch with Mercer. That must have been Mercer he was calling." He searched the desk, demanded, "Where's the poetry?"

About to nod at the scrap of paper wedged in between the cases, Irv suddenly changed his mind. His money was one thing. Steve's confidence was another. Friendship couldn't be insured. And Steve had wanted Matt to see that scrap of paper.

"I don't know," he lied. "I was just wondering that. I guess Steve must have forgot to put it in."

The little hood drew a gun and slapped him with the flat of the barrel. *"Where is that scrap of paper?"*

He shook his head stubbornly and the hoodlum struck him again. The pawn-broken crumpled to his knees, blood streaming from a broken nose. "I don't know," he insisted. "Why? What the hell is this all about?"

The second hood came into the cage and kicked him in the groin. "That's just a sample," he told him, "of what you're going to get unless you talk."

Writhing in pain on the floor, the pawnbroker still insisted, "I don't know what you're talking about."

Both men rained blows on his head. He attempted to cover his head with his arms. The smaller of the pair kicked him in the stomach. "Talk. And talk fast," he snarled.

Through a fog of pain, Irv heard, or thought that he heard, someone hammering on his front door. He opened his mouth to call, "Help!" and the flat side of an automatic blotted out all consciousness.

The young carrier was new to the job. His parcel post delivered, at least in the Hooper Block, he breathed a deep sigh of relief. As he crossed the walk to his truck parked at the curb, a black-haired, hard-faced, little man stopped him.

"Pardon me, carrier," he smiled, "but my name is Mercer. I have an office on the tenth floor of the Hooper Block. Do you by any chance recall if I got a parcel this morning?"

Eager to please, the carrier opened his metal-backed book. "If it was registered or insured, I'll have a record, Mr. Mercer. Otherwise—" He ran his finger down the list of names, "Yes, you had a package, Mr. Mercer. Your girl signed for it."

The man thanked him and the carrier walked on to his truck. The man walked to a parked sedan and reported, "It came this morning. It's up there."

The cold-eyed Eurasian in the back seat warned him, "Don't take any chances with Mercer. He's tough. Kill him if you have to. But get that package, understand?"

The hood said that he did. A second hood climbed from the car and inclined his head toward the lobby of the building. "There's Mercer now."

The little hood lighted a cigarette and studied Mercer through the match-flare. The former first sergeant in the Marines was a big man, six-feet-two, in his middle forties. His hair was grizzled. His face had been tanned to the color and consistency of leather by years of tropical outpost duty. His left arm was cork and steel. He had lost the arm that it replaced in a so-called "incident" on the Yangtze five years before Pearl Harbor.

"He looks tough," the little hood admitted.

"He *is* tough," the Eurasian told him.

Mercer bought a handful of cigars at the counter, lighted one, and stepped into an elevator. He felt like hell. He had been drinking too much, for one thing. He and Sherry had quarreled about it that morning. He made a mental note to phone and apologize. She was right as usual. He couldn't do Steve any good by staying drunk. Besides, as Sherry said, he was no longer a hell-raising first sergeant in the Marines. He was a married family man and it was up to him to set an example for his twins.

A plain, blunt man who believed in calling a spade a damned dirty shovel if need be, he disliked riddles. His phone call of that morning still annoyed him. He could think of no reason why anyone should call him to the phone, then fail to answer when he spoke.

Even the legend on his door, "Matt Mercer—Private Investigations," failed to lighten his mood. The whole thing had gone sour. While untrained punks were dying, he was sitting on his prat.

He unlocked his door and went in. His girl did not arrive until ten. He didn't care if she ever came. He scooped a handful of mail from the floor and strode on into his private office.

Steve's death had hit him hard. They had enlisted together as punks. They had gone through boot training together. Side by side, for twenty years, they had fought and drank their way through a half hundred jungles and a hundred water fronts. Now Steve was dead. The big, good-looking skirt-chaser was a mass of putrid flesh in a shallow grave scooped on the beach of one of the Gilbert islands.

He took a bottle of rye from his desk and half filled a water glass. Maybe now that Steve was dead, the Corps would take him back. Good first sergeants were hard to come by. He recapped the bottle with his artificial hand. The Corps doctors were fools. He could do anything with his artificial hand and arm except feel. And he didn't want to "feel" Japs, he wanted to kill them.

Not very hopefully, he dialed the local Marine Corps office. They might have received an answer to his latest appeal to Washington. They had. The Marine lieutenant in charge informed him regretfully that one-armed men could not be inducted for combat service. However, in view of his past experience and the fact that he both spoke and read Japanese, if Mercer would care to consider a commission and a desk job—

Mercer told him where he could put his desk job. As an afterthought, he told him to put the desk there, too. He banged the receiver back into its cradle and looked up to see a black-haired, unsmiling, little man standing in his doorway.

"So who are you? And what the hell do you want?" Mercer asked him.

"I am Mr. Sarangani," the little hood introduced himself. "And this is Mr. Meangis," he introduced his partner.

Mercer scowled. The men looked like Filipinos. But the names they had given were the names of islands southeast of Mindanao. "So—?" Mercer demanded.

Sarangani continued, unsmiling, "So we know that you have it. You will please to give it to us and there will be no unpleasantness.

"Unpleasantness?" Mercer asked hopefully.

He started to open the top drawer o£ his desk and Meangis stopped him by flipping his gun from his holster. "You will keep your hands on your desk, Mercer. We know all about how tough you are. But a .45 is even tougher."

Sarangani closed the door. "Where is it?" he demanded.

Mercer exploded, "Where is what? What the hell are you talking about?"

Meangis smiled thinly. "I think you know. We want the parcel from Kansas City that the postman delivered this morning."

"One of us is crazy," Mercer said. Meangis bent as if to strike him with the gun and Mercer added, thinly, "I don't think I would if I were you."

The man's beady black eyes glittered. "I am going to count to three," he said, "then—"

Mercer stood up behind his desk. "Then what?"

Sarangani said quickly. "Let us be sensible, gentlemen. We know you have it," he told Mercer. "You are the only man whom Sergeant Steve Pulos would trust. Pulos took the map from Colonel Osaki by force. In doing so he violated every tenet of international law. But, if you will please to return it to us, we will forget the matter."

Mercer's big shoulders squared. "Ringtails, eh?" he said, smiling. "I thought that they had you boys all rounded up and tucked away in concentration camps. Hell. No wonder the Corps doesn't want me back. I'm getting old. I can't smell Jap like I used to."

Sarangani's black eyes grew opaque. "You just signed your death warrant, Mercer." He flipped a quick shot as he spoke, then screamed.

A gun had appeared in Mercer's hand from nowhere. Sarangani's slug had clipped Mercer's ear lobe. But Mercer hadn't missed. Sarangani stood a moment, gaping incredulously at the gun, then took two quick steps forward clawing at the hole where his right eye had been.

Meangis ran screaming from the office, Mercer's gun yammering at his heels. There was no one in the hallway. The hood ran for the stairhead. Mercer started to follow, ran into the curious office girl who stepped out of Doctor Metzger's office, and went sprawling to the floor.

He picked himself up, cursing, and pounded on down the stairs. The sound of running feet had died away. Nine floors below a door opened into an alley that led to Dearborn Street. Mercer ran down the alley to the street. The hood was not in sight.

A woman shopper saw the gun and screamed. Mercer slipped it back into its holster, walked the few feet to the lobby of the building, and dialed Inspector Haig of Homicide.

"This is Matt Mercer, Haig," he told him. "I want to report a homicide. I just killed a Jap in my office."

"You what!" the Inspector demanded. He added, not unkindly, "Look, Matt. Why don't you sober up? I know how you feel about Steve, but—"

"I mean it," Mercer said coldly.

"No kidding?"

"No kidding," Mercer said grimly. "There were two, but one got away. I'll wait for you here in the lobby."

CHAPTER TWO

THE DISAPPEARING CORPSE

INSPECTOR HAIG HAD BEEN A DETECTIVE for thirty years. He had been on Homicide for twenty. If man was made in God's image and likeness, most of those whom he met in the course of a day were counterfeit. He liked Matt Mercer as well as his slightly envenomed nature would permit him to like anyone. Followed by his squad, he stepped into an elevator, eyeing Mercer's torn earlobe.

"And you had never seen either man before?"

"Not that I know of," Mercer told him.

"Then what did they want of you?" he demanded.

"It," Mercer told him. He realized the statement sounded silly and added quickly, "They said that they wanted a package that had been sent me from Kansas City. They said that Steve had taken it from a Colonel Osaki by force, but that if I would return it, they would forget all about the matter."

Haig looked at him sharply but said nothing.

Mercer had expected to find a morbidly curious crowd at his door. There was none. His office door stood ajar. He strode through it on into the inner office and stopped.

He had shot Sarangani through the eye. The bullet had entered the man's brain. But there was no corpse on the floor.

Lieutenant Carlson looked at Haig. Haig looked at the whiskey bottle on the desk, then told Carlson quietly, "Check with his neighbors, Jim."

Mercer flushed. "To hell with that. I'm not crazy. And I'm not drunk. Two Japs bust in and tried to put the heat on me. I shot one and chased the other down the stairs."

Haig asked him to describe them.

Mercer said, "They looked like Filipinos. They were short, black-haired, and wiry. But both of them were Japs." He described both men and the scene in detail.

Haig listened quietly. By the time that Mercer had finished, Carlson had returned. He shook his head at Haig's unspoken question.

"No one else saw them," he said. "I asked the elevator boys and the starter and the neighbors on both sides of the halls. The only one who even heard any shooting was the office girl next door. She said that Mercer bust out of his office wild-eyed, waving a gun around his head; and cursing. She tried to get out of his way and couldn't. She says that he knocked her down and the smell of whiskey was so strong that you could cut it with a knife."

"So—?" Haig asked Mercer.

The big former Marine's face had turned a dull brick red. "There were two Japs," he insisted. "I shot one, and one got away. I chased him down the stairs, then called you from the lobby."

"So, where's the body?" Haig demanded.

Mercer admitted, "I don't know. I—"

Haig interrupted, "Look, Matt. This isn't official. I should run you in, but I won't. Instead, I'm going to take your guns and give you a piece of advice. Cut it out, boy. Sure. Steve was your pal. But grief and rye don't mix. It's got you seeing things." He slipped Mercer's gun from its holster and located a spare in a desk drawer. "When you sober up, drop around and I'll give these back again."

He strode out, followed by his squad. Mercer stood in the center of his office staring at the floor where the corpse should have been. There was something strange about it. Then he realized that the throw rug in front of his desk was gone. Whoever had removed the corpse had simply rolled it in the rug.

He turned to call after Haig, then changed his mind. To hell with homicide. He could handle this himself. He strode down the long hallway to the freight elevator and pushed the button savagely.

When the colored boy stopped the platform at the floor, Mercer took two half dollars from his pocket and handed them to him. "What," he asked, "did the man look like that took out a rug to be cleaned about fifteen minutes ago?"

The boy scratched his poll and considered. "He ain' very big, Mister. He kinda little, an' black haired, an' squint eyed."

"That's all that I wanted to know," Mercer told him.

He walked back to his office swearing softly. That much of the puzzle was solved. The smaller of the two Japanese had not fled out the alley at all. He had merely turned off several floors below, doubled back when Mercer had passed. rolled his partner in the rug and carried him down on the freight elevator.

"Drunk, am I? Crazy, am I?" Mercer snorted.

His girl had arrived when he returned and was sitting at her desk studying the inscription on a neatly tied paper carton. "Doctor Metzger's girl just brought this in," she told him. "She said that there's a new carrier on, and she signed for it without even looking at the name."

Mercer took the package from her. The return address was— Army Effects Bureau, Quartermaster's Corp., Kansas City, Mo. It was the package the hoods had been after. He had an idea what it contained.

The girl continued, smiling, "She also said that you were roaring drunk and had been shooting up the building."

Mercer told her, "According to Haig, I'm also crazy. Get my house on the wire will you?"

He set the box on his desk and closed the inner office door. When his phone rang, he told his wife, "Look, hon. You're right, and I'm sorry as hell. Staying potzed won't help Steve. Now, let me talk to Magnolia, will you?"

He asked the maid if she had tried to recall the voice. She told him that the more she thought about it, the more she thought that it might have been Mr. Irving calling.

He thanked her, hung up, and told his office girl to get him Irv's pawnshop on North Dearborn. Clancey of the East Chicago Avenue Station answered.

"No, you can't talk to Irv," he told Mercer. "A couple of hoods beat him up this morning. He's in the hospital now and I'm here checking with his clerk to find out what was stolen."

Mercer asked to speak to the clerk. He told him that the contents of Irv's wallet and the safe seemed to be intact. There seemed to be no reason for the beating. Mercer could call the hospital if he cared to but the ambulance surgeon had said that it would be twenty-four hours at least before the pawnbroker could talk. Besides multiple contusions, his jawbone had been broken.

He cut the strings on the box and unwrapped it. It contained Steve's dress uniform, his watch, a much thumbed diary, a beautifully hilted sword, and a Japanese officer's automatic, patterned after a German Luger.

Mercer examined the clip. It was filled. He dropped it into his side coat pocket. Haig had taken his guns. Now Steve had sent him one from the grave. The big Marine was getting a bang, if the dead could know such things.

He forgot his promise to Sherry, poured himself a drink and thumbed through the diary. It had been started just before Guadalcanal.

He looked up, annoyed, as his door opened. Mary, his office girl's eyes, were round as saucers. She told him, "A Mr. Morgan and a Miss Fariday want to see you." She added, "You know, the picture star."

Mercer knew Morgan, well. He was a high pressure publicity man. He didn't care to meet Miss Fariday. "Tell them I'm not taking cases," he growled.

Morgan pushed by the girl. His face was lined with strain. "I think you'll see us," he said.

The picture star followed him into the office. A pint-sized blonde with big blue eyes, the girl looked like she had been crying.

Mercer waved them to chairs. "Okay, Let's have it. Who's stolen the family jewels now and what do you want me to do about it?"

The actress didn't seem to hear him. Her blue eyes filled with tears. She was staring at the uniform in the box. "That—that is Steve's uniform?" she asked.

Mercer nodded curtly. "So what?"

Morgan lighted a cigarette with fingers that shook slightly. "So meet Mrs. Pulos," he told Mercer.

Mercer made a noise with his mouth and tongue. "Of all the jackals," he told Morgan, "you press agent lads are the worst. You'd sell your mothers down the river for a column of black type."

The actress stroked the uniform.

"It's the McCoy," Morgan told Mercer. "You know that U.S.O. tour that Miss Fariday went on about eight months ago?"

Suspicious, Mercer asked, "So what?"

"So—that's when I met Steve." The actress began to sob softly. "It was in Brisbane, last January. Steve had a fourteen day leave." Tears rolled down her cheeks. "But—but we'd only been married for forty-eight hours when he had to return to duty."

Mercer said, "Baloney!"

The girl continued, "I asked him to keep it a secret. I—I wish now that I hadn't. I—I loved him so. And he's dead."

Mercer looked over her head at the door. "Where are the photographers?" he asked Morgan. "Boy. I can read the headlines now—STARLET SECRETLY MARRIED TO DEAD HERO!"

Morgan got up heavily. "Okay, wise guy. We'll prove it!"

The actress fumbled in her handbag.

"You see, I had a letter from Steve this morning. It—it was three months old." She fought her sobs. "He—he asked me to give you this."

She laid a torn fragment of rice paper on his desk. He picked it up and studied the brush Strokes. They read:

"By the great Walled City is a tree that sheds plum blossom petals like drifting purple snow down to the ancient bosom of the Pasig.

Mercer considered. The Pasig was a river that flowed from Laguna Bay to Manila Bay. The old Walled City was on its south bank across from the commercial and the warehouse district of Manila.

"So what's this supposed to mean to me?" he asked the girl.

"I don't know," she admitted. "I don't read Chinese or Japanese, or whatever it's written in."

"And the letter from Steve—?"

She dried her eyes. "That's personal. Steve asked me to bring the enclosure to you. You have it." She walked to the door, calling over her shoulder in parting, "I don't give a damn what you or anyone thinks. But I was married to Steve."

Morgan followed her to the door.

"It was a good try and a good act," Mercer told him. "It could have meant headlines for your client."

Morgan didn't bother to answer.

Mercer chuckled as he slammed the door. Morgan seldom missed a trick. He knew that Steve had been partial to pint-sized blondes. He knew that—Struck by a sudden thought, Mercer thumbed back through the diary to the month of January. On the 15th, Steve had written:

Proposed to Jennifer Fariday this morning, and believe it or not, she accepted me. The Chaplain has agreed to marry us this afternoon. Oh, Boy! I can see Matt's eyes popping out now. Imagine a lug like me married to a picture star. But this is for keeps. So help me.

Moving lightly for so big a man, Mercer crossed to his office door and yanked it open. "Miss Fariday and Morgan?" he demanded.

His office girl said, puzzled, "They went right on through." Mary added, "She was crying."

Mercer hurried out into the hall and up to the elevator bank. An elevator was just discharging a passenger. "Down!" be ordered the operator.

The boy protested, "But Mr. Mercer. This car is going up!"

Mercer rammed the gun in his pocket into the operator's back. "Down! And no stops!" he ordered.

Frightened, the boy obeyed.

Mercer reached the lobby in time to see the girl's blonde head bobbing through the doorway. By the time he had reached the doorway she and Morgan had reached the curb. A black sedan drew up beside them and the thug who had fled from his office stepped out and ordered them into the car at the point of a vicious looking gun.

Morgan began a protest and a lounger loafing at the curb fanned him with a sap. The men worked deftly, swiftly, loading the limp body into the car.

Mercer ran toward the car shouting "Stop!"

He caught a fleeting glimpse of Miss Fariday's face and that of a cold-eyed Eurasian. Then the car roared into motion. The sap swung a second time. It caught Mercer flush on the temple and stretched his full length in the gutter.

When he came to a patrolman was shaking him. The big man got slowly to his feet and brushed the dust from his clothes. "What," he asked tentatively, "would you say, if I told you that I wasn't drunk, that I was trying to save Jennifer Fariday the actress from being kidnapped by a slant eyed Jap?"

"I wouldn't say a thing," the patrolman said frankly. "But I would call the wagon and have you taken to the psychopathic ward."

Mercer smiled without mirth. "Yeah. That's what I was afraid of."

CHAPTER THREE

MR. SATAN

THE PATROLMAN DISPERSED THE CROWD. Mercer thought of the box and diary lying unguarded on his desk and returned to his office glumly. The whole affair failed to make sense. All that he really knew was that he was one hell of a detective. Whatever it was, this thing was big. He should have realized that when Sarangani and Meangis had first entered his office.

It hurt even to think of Steve. Steve had been married to the actress. The girl had leveled with him, and he had let her down. In the elevator, he considered calling Haig, and decided that it would do no good. The Inspector would never believe him. Haig thought he was on a binge. He would haul him down to the psych ward and make him play with blocks. Whatever was done for the girl and Morgan, he would have to do himself.

The box, the diary, and the scrap of rice paper were still lying on his desk. He put the paper into his wallet, poured himself a drink, and thumbed through the diary again. There was nothing in it to give him the slightest clue as to why Steve had sent him the paper.

He called the local office of G-2, identified himself and asked Colonel Myers if he knew of a Japanese Colonel of Intelligence by the name of Osaki.

Meyers told him the name was common, but that he believed that a Colonel Osaki had been mentioned in dispatches as one of the principal looters of private business firms after the fall of Manila. He promised to check on the man and phone Mercer in a few hours. "Something in our line, Matt?" he asked in parting.

Mercer told him he wasn't certain and hung up thoughtfully. Manila had been a wealthy town. The Japanese puppet government had taken over the banks but there had been a lot of private money. He took the rice paper from his pocket and re-read the Japanese characters.

"By the great Walled City is a tree that sheds plum blossom petals like drifting purple snow down to the ancient bosom of the Pasig."

"The hell you say," he grunted.

The words did not make sense. In the first place, plum blossoms were white, not purple. Still, Sarangani had mentioned a map. He had said that Steve had taken the map from Colonel Osaki by force. The scrap of rice paper was torn unevenly. It could be that joined with each other, the two pieces would have some meaning. It would have been like Steve to have torn the thing in half, each piece to be delivered to him separately.

He locked the box and the diary in his safe, told his office girl to take the rest of the day off, and took a cab to Irv's pawnshop.

Irv's clerk was gone, but Clancey was still on duty. "The captain thought it best," he told Mercer, "to keep the place locked until Irv is conscious at least. You know," he confided, "now-a-days, you don't know who to trust."

Mercer agreed with him and asked him his theory concerning the beating.

Flattered, the patrolman led the way to the rear of the shop.

"Now mind you," he admitted, "I don't know why they beat up Irv the way they did, but 'tis just as plain as the nose on my face that it was an attempted stick-up."

Mercer doubted that very much. Irv had been stuck up before. He was insured. It was something more than a stick-up.

Clancey took a position in the cage. "Here is the way I think it happened. Irv was standing here going through his morning mail when the two hoods come in. One of them threw a gun on him through the grill. The other one stepped back here and sapped him. Then both of them beat him up."

Mercer asked, "How do you know there were two of them?"

Clancey confided, "The porter next door saw them. You see, he banged on Irv's door to borrow his window squeegee and the two of them took out the back." The patrolman dropped his voice even lower. "He said it was two Filipinos who've been hanging out in Burke's bar for a couple of months. Probably planning the job. And then his banging scared them off."

Mercer said, "Yeah." He knew at least a part of what he had wanted to know. The hoods had been Sarangani and Meangis. "You searched the place?" he asked Clancey.

"Every inch of it," Clancey boasted.

Mercer tried to reconstruct the scene in his mind. The morning mail had just arrived. There had been something in it to make Irv want to phone him. A vein in his temple began to throb. That something could have been a delayed letter from Steve containing the other half of the torn rice paper. He took the scrap of paper from his wallet and laid it on the ledger convenient to the phone. Irv had dialed his number. It had been hot. Mercer looked up at the fan and demanded, "The ceiling fan was on or off when you got here?"

Clancey thought a moment. "It was on."

Mercer reached up and pulled the cord. The circular sweep of the air picked the rice paper from the ledger and fluttered it a few feet to a pile of unredeemed suitcases. Sweating with excitement, Mercer retrieved it and began to move the cases, over Clancey's protests. There was nothing between or behind them. If the other piece of rice paper had been wafted there by the fan, Sarangani or Meangis had found it. They weren't the type to run from porters. They had what they had come for when they left.

Clancey scowling after him, Mercer turned in to the bar next door. Burke reached for a bottle of rye.

"No," Mercer shook his head. "Make mine a short beer instead."

Burke drew the beer and continued discussing the affair next door with a white haired customer. "Two months they hung out in here," he told the man. "They seem like nice lads. They square all their tabs. They act like gentlemen. But then, right after the mailman comes this morning, they clip next door and try to stick up Irv. They'd been planning it for two months, see? And they'd have done it, too, if the porter hadn't wanted to borrow Irv's squeegee."

Mercer sipped his beer. "The mailman say anything?" he asked.

Burke stared at him, hard. "By God. I just thought of that. He did. He told me that Irv had got a letter from a dead guy, your old partner, Steve Pulos. You think it could have any connection?"

"Yeah," Mercer admitted. "I think that was what they were after. Now tell me this. During the two months that they hung out in here, did they mention where they were living?"

The saloon man thought a moment, shook his head. "If they did, I didn't hear 'em."

Mercer paid for his beer. On the sidewalk, he stopped to light a cigar and found that the white haired customer had followed him out of the bar. "These two lads that Burke was speaking of," he said. "Did they look like Filipinos?" He described them.

"Those are the lads," Mercer said.

The other man said thoughtfully, "Well, of course I don't know for certain, but I saw the little guy come out of the Mavis several times, and it could be that they lived there."

Mercer thanked him and stared down the street at the Mavis Hotel sign. It was two blocks away, a short stone's throw from the river. A former theatrical hotel, it asked its guests few questions. It was patronized chiefly by the riff-raff of the street and down-at-the-heel minor hoods and drifters.

He walked toward the hotel, debating. Every minute that he stalled increased Miss Fariday and Morgan's danger. Once whoever was behind all this learned that the actress had turned over the torn scrap of rice paper to him, the logical thing for the unknown master-mind to do would be to slit Miss Fariday's and Morgan's throats.

A clever detective, like the ones that he read about in fiction, would stroll into his favorite bar, sit down and deduce a solution over a half dozen drinks of rye. But Mercer had never pretended to be clever. He solved his cases the hard way.

There was no one in the lobby of the Mavis. "You have a Mr. Sarangani and a Mr. Meangis living here?" he asked the clerk.

Thin-lipped, jaundiced-eyed, the desk clerk on duty looked up briefly, then back at his racing form. "Never heard of them. Bud. You must have the wrong hotel."

Mercer turned to go, turned back and described both men in detail. "They look like Filipinos, but they're Japs."

The clerk didn't even bother to look up. "So what does that make me?"

Mercer caught him by the coat front with his artificial hand, dragged him half across the counter, and slapped the sneer from his lips. "Is that enough, or do you want more?" he asked.

The clerk whimpered, "Okay. I'll talk. How was I to know you was a cop? Sure. Those guys used to live here. They lived here for three months. But they scrammed out early this morning. An' a couple of hours later I hear that they are the two guys who beat up Irv."

Mercer insisted, "Their baggage is still in their room?"

The clerk nodded.

"And I'm the first lad to run them down?"

Half strangled the clerk nodded again. Mercer released him and demanded the key to their room. For once he had gotten a break. No two men could live in a room for three months and not leave some clue as to their true identity and connections behind them. All that he needed was enough to convince Haig that he wasn't crazy.

The ancient cage creaked to a stop on the fifth floor and the colored elevator boy pointed down the dingy hallway. "Room 510 is right down that way, Mister. It's jist around the bend, there. The last room in the hall."

The paint and paper was scaling from the walls and ceiling. The carpeting was torn. The hallway smelled of many things. As a precautionary measure, Mercer rapped on the door of 510.

As he waited, a door across the hallway opened and a stringy-haired blonde smiled at him falsely. "Looking for someone, handsome?"

"I'm sorry, sweetheart," Mercer told her, "but I'm two weeks behind on my homework."

She snorted, "Wise guy, eh?" and slammed the door.

Chuckling, he let himself into room 510. The shade of the single window was drawn. Clothes were tossed carelessly on chairs. The bed had not been made. The room had a shut-up, musty smell. He stepped inside, and closed and locked the door behind him.

He knew that he had made a mistake as soon as he had locked the door. *There was someone in the room with him, A trap had been cleverly baited and he had walked into it like a fool. The white haired customers in Burke's had been a stooge. The desk clerk had been acting. Even the blonde across the hall had served to throw him off his guard.*

His hand streaked for his side coat pocket, froze as a suave voice suggested quietly, "I wouldn't if I were you, Sergeant Mercer. You are covered from all sides."

The door to the bathroom opened. Meangis filled it, a sawed-off double-barreled shotgun in his hands. Another man appeared in the doorway that connected 510 with the adjoining room. Over his shoulder, Mercer could see Miss Fariday and Morgan. The actress and her agent were gagged and tied to chairs.

"It looks like I bobbled," Mercer admitted.

"So it looks," the suave voice agreed.

Mercer turned to face the man. He was the black-haired, thin-faced Eurasian whom he had seen in the sedan. "And who the hell are you?" he asked.

The Eurasian smiled without mirth. "I could be Doctor Fu Manchu, but I'm not. You can call me Mr. Satan."

He cracked an order in Japanese. Meangis handed him the sawed-off shotgun, emptied Mercer's pockets and piled his findings on the bed. A second Japanese sorted through them carefully.

Mercer thought, *"Haig is right. I'm crazy. The hard stuff has finally rotted my brain. This isn't happening. It can't be. I'm in Chicago, not Tokyo or Kobe. Clark Street is five floors below me. The Loop is just across the river. We were at war with Japan. And there aren't any Japs in Chicago. They're all in concentration camps."*

The Japanese who was searching Mercer's belongings took the scrap of rice paper from Mercer's wallet and handed it to the man who called himself Mr. Satan. Meangis resumed custody of the shotgun.

"Go ahead. Make a break," he taunted Mercer. "I would love to shoot your head right off your shoulders."

"I don't doubt that," Mercer admitted. "Where is Sarangani? In the river?"

Meangis asked Mr. Satan, "That is it?"

"I can't tell," the Eurasian said. He took the torn scrap of rice paper, for which Sarangani and Meangis had slugged Irv, from his own wallet and laid it beside the other. In the dim light of the room, Mercer could barely decipher the brush strokes. They read:

> *One comes at noon to the true sport where Legaspi breathed his last and all is mother of pearl and golden silence.*

To the best of Mercer's recollection, Legaspi had been the Spaniard who had conquered the Philippines and founded Manila in 1571. The affair made less sense than ever.

Satan tried to fit the pieces of paper together. Their torn edges did not match. He swore quietly for a moment, then told Meangis, "No. We merely have two thirds of the map now. The middle half is still missing." He stared, cold-eyed, at Mercer. "Start talking, Sergeant. Where is it?"

Mercer told the truth. "I haven't the least idea. I don't even know what you're talking about. This is all a lot of Japanese to me."

Satan swung back to Meangis. "It was in that bundle from the personal effects bureau. And *if* it hadn't been for that stupid carrier, and *if* you and Sarangani hadn't blundered—"

Mercer interrupted to ask if he had heard the *if* about the dog and Satan struck him across the bridge of his nose with a blackjack.

"Always the superior while man," the Eurasian jeered. "Always quipping, even in the face of death." He added crisply in Japanese, "Drag him into the other room."

His mind fogged with pain, half blind with blood, Mercer allowed himself to be walked into the room where he had seen Miss Fariday and Morgan. He doubted that he would leave it alive. If the white-haired customer in Burke's had been a stooge, no one knew that he had come to the Mavis. The gang could cut his throat, drop him into the river, and no one would be the wiser.

CHAPTER FOUR

ONE EYE, ONE EAR—

STRIPPED TO THE WAIST, his legs tied to the rungs of the chair that he straddled, Mercer felt sweat streaming down his broad chest in blood-stained rivulets. It beaded on the mat of hair and glistened on the heavy straps that held his artificial arm in place. The questioning, it seemed, had been going on for hours.

"Ready to talk?" Mr. Satan demanded.

Mercer looked from him to where Meangis stood with the muzzle of the shot gun pressed close to Steve's wife's temple. He had been warned that the Japanese would shoot at his first outcry.

"No," he shook his head. "I guess I'll just sit tight."

Satan threw the hose on the floor in disgust. "What do you hope to gain by stalling? Just tell us the combination of your safe where Sergeant Pulos' personal effects are stored—"

"And you'll cut my throat," Mercer finished the sentence for him.

Satan lighted a cigarette and studied the actress thoughtfully. "We have been going about this in the wrong manner," he decided. "The Americans make fools of themselves where women are concerned. Tear the dress from that girl's back. We will beat *her* instead."

The actress strained at her bonds, her eyes grown wide with fear. Morgan gargled a protest against the knotted towels that gagged him. Mercer's face grew black with anger. He attempted to stand up, chair and all, and Satan struck him with his fist.

"Yes," the Eurasian smiled. "I believe that this will work."

Mercer sawed at the rope on his wrists with the steel fingers of his artificial hand. It was now or never. Steve's uniform and diary were in his safe. But he doubted that either one contained the missing portion of the map for which the Eurasian was searching. The uniform would have been steam cleaned and de-loused. The diary would have been inspected by a censor. To give Satan the combination of the safe would merely prolong the agony. When they failed to find the missing portion of the map, they would resume their questioning. He knew no more than they did.

He studied his chances for survival. Satan was superintending the rebinding of the girl. He caught his yellow fingers in the neck of her dress. There was a sharp, ripping, sound, and the bare back of the girl lay exposed.

Meangis, who had laid his shotgun on the bed to help the Eurasian handle the girl, made a foul remark. The third Japanese, who had stooped to retie her ankles to the chair rungs, laughed toothily.

This was Steve's wife. Mercer gripped the back of his chair, raised it as high as he could from the floor by rising on the balls of his feet, then sat down hard, the full weight of his two hundred pounds acting as a pile driver. The seat and back broke into pieces. The chair-legs spread and snapped. His wrists were free. His ankles were still tied to the chair legs, but the rungs were not connected.

Meangis leaped for the shotgun. Raising the shattered chair-back, Mercer brained him with the heavy wood, tore the shotgun from his hands, and rolled just as the third Japanese, screaming with fear and anger, emptied an automatic at the spot where he had been. The slugs thudded soddenly into the already dead Meangis.

Still on his back, with no time to bring the butt of the shotgun to his shoulder, Mercer emptied one barrel of the gun into the screaming man's face and blew off half his head. The butt of the unsupported gun kicked back against Mercer's right cheek and almost smashed his check bone.

Ignoring the pain, he got to his knees and searched for Satan. The Eurasian was standing in the doorway that connected the two rooms. Indecision clouded his face. Mercer knew what he was thinking. Dead men couldn't talk. The Eurasian wanted him alive. As Mercer brought the shotgun to his shoulder, Satan stepped through the door and slammed it shut.

Cursing, hampered by the chair rungs still dangling from his ankles, Mercer heaved himself to his feet and followed, only to fall sprawling as Morgan, striving to get free, fell chair and all in his path.

As Mercer fell, the shotgun discharged. By the time he fought open the door, the Eurasian was gone. The Japanese automatic that had belonged to Steve still lay on the bed where Meangis had put it. Mercer snatched it up and raced on out into the hall.

The blonde stood in her doorway, screaming shrilly. Satan was twenty feet down the hall. Mercer flipped a quick shot at him and missed as the blonde caught at his arm.

He tore loose and rounded the bend in the hallway in time to see the Eurasian outlined against the stairhead. He triggered a second time and the firing pin clicked dully. He stuffed the gun in his belt and ran on. By the time he had reached the stairs, Satan had disappeared into the gloomy well. It was useless to pursue the man, hobbled as he was. More, the Mavis was a rabbit warren of stairs and passageways where a man could hide out indefinitely. He would have to call in Haig. Haig would believe him now.

He returned to room 510 and through it to the other room. Morgan still lay struggling on the floor, his face purple with his efforts to free himself. Miss Fariday had fainted.

Mercer tore the gag from her mouth, untied her, then carried her to the bed.

When Mercer had removed the gag from Morgan's mouth, Morgan's first words were, "Now maybe you'll believe us."

Mercer nodded grimly. "Yeah. I believe you," he told him. "Me and Inspector Haig." He searched Meangis' pockets for shotgun shells, thumbed two into the barrels of the shotgun and emptied the gun out of the window of 510.

Haig studied the dead men with interest. They were undeniably Japanese. "So I was wrong," he admitted to Mercer. "I'm sorry I took your guns."

"You damn near killed me," Mercer scowled.

Haig demanded, "But what is it all about?"

"A plum tree with purple blossoms," Mercer told him sourly. "You've sent for Colonel Meyers?"

"I have," Haig nodded.

Mercer sat down on a window sill and scowled at the working tech squad through a blue cloud of cigar smoke. He had killed three men. His life had been attempted twice. He had been beaten for two hours—and he still didn't know the score.

Lieutenant Carlson came in and reported, "I sent Jones and Murphy to the hospital with Miss Fariday. The Doc couldn't find anything wrong, but she was hysterical."

"She had a right to be," Mercer said. "If you guys had listened to me—"

"Okay. So I pulled a boner," Haig admitted. "The boys can print it in headlines if they want to." He swung around to Morgan. "You don't know any more than you've told me?"

The agent said that he did not. "All that I know," he repeated, "is that when we left Mercer's office, I was slugged. I came to tied to a chair and gagged. When they found that we didn't have what they wanted, they started baiting a trap for Mercer."

Haig asked Carlson, "The boys haven't picked up that white-haired guy, the desk clerk, or the blonde?"

"Not yet," Carlson reported. "They all seem to have scrammed when Satan did."

Haig snorted, "Satan!"

Morgan crossed the room to Mercer, rubbing his still numb wrists. "Look. My only interest in this affair is Miss Fariday. And Steve Pulos had no right to endanger her life the way he did. Neither have you, for that matter. Why don't you give them whatever they want. I won't feel safe concerning Miss Fariday until they do."

Mercer exploded "I haven't got what they want. And if I did have, I wouldn't give it to a bunch of slimy Japs."

Colonel Meyers of G-2 strode briskly into the room, nodding to Haig and Mercer. "So it was in our line after all, Matt." He studied the dead Japanese with interest. "Start at the beginning, Matt. Who are these lads, and why?"

"It began," Mercer said, "with the slugging of Irv." He detailed what had happened as he knew it.

Meyers asked Morgan, "This letter your client, Miss Fariday, or I should say, Mrs. Pulos, received. There was nothing in it that alluded to her portion of the map?"

Morgan answered, "Nothing, outside of asking her to deliver it to Matt Mercer." He thought a moment, added, "No. I'm wrong, As I recall he said that he had taken the enclosure from a Colonel Osaki, and that it had meant a lot to the Colonel."

Meyers smiled wryly. "I don't doubt that at all." He turned to Mercer. "I was right about Colonel Osaki. He had a private looting party through Manila. We thought at the time that the money and jewels had gone into the Japanese exchequer. But this throws a new light on the matter."

Haig whistled. "You mean he kept the loot for himself."

"It appears that way," Meyers said "He obviously buried at least a good share of it for his own personal use when things had quieted down." He asked Mercer to repeat the two portions of the map as he remembered them.

Mercer wrote them out word for word. "I'm no mental giant," he said when he had finished, "but here's the way this thing looks to me. This freak plum tree on the bank of the Pasig is the starting point. The true spot where Legaspi breathed his last, and all is mother-of-pearl and silence, is the hiding place of the loot. The missing portion of the map tells how far it is, and in what direction from the plum tree."

"That sounds right to me," the G-2 Colonel admitted. "And that's just about the way a clever Jap would record a hiding place—a word map that wouldn't mean a damn thing to anyone but himself."

Haig demanded, "Then how did Sergeant Steve Pulos get on to it."

Mercer shook his head. "God knows. But the big Greek was smart enough to nail a horse shoe on a house fly. Maybe he squeezed it out of a prisoner who had been on the looting detail. He went into action shortly thereafter. He knew the information was too valuable to keep on his own person until he could contact G-2. That's why he sent one scrap of paper to Irv and one scrap to his wife."

"But the third half," Morgan protested. "What did he do with that?"

"I wish I knew," Mercer said simply.

"Concerning this Eurasian," Meyers said. "Describe him?"

"He's about five feet ten and a half. Thin to the point of emaciation. Fair skinned, black haired. Black, piercing, eyes and well-modeled black eyebrows that slant upward toward his temples." Mercer thought a moment, added. "He's a Jap. But he looks more like a high caste Hindu."

"That sounds like Nagasaki," Meyers said. "And if it is, this thing is big. He was in charge of all of the Nips' South American espionage. The last that we heard of him, however, Chile had interned him."

"You can check on that?"

"As soon as I get back to the office." Colonel Meyers hesitated, added, "But now, can you tell me this, Mercer? Steve Pulos got the map from Colonel Osaki. It is obvious that Osaki is dead. Even if he was alive, he wouldn't dare admit that he had crossed up his own government. *Then how did Japanese Intelligence get in on this? How did they learn that Steve Pulos had the map? How did they learn that he had sent it back to the Slates in three pieces?"*

Mercer's head had begun to ache. He had been a long time without a drink. "I don't know," he admitted. "I'm not that kind of a detective."

The phone in 510 rang. Lieutenant Carlson answered it. "It's some dame who wants to talk to Mercer," he told Haig. "I put Kelly on the switchboard and he says she sounds like she's crying."

"Take it, Matt," Haig said.

"Yeah? Matt Mercer speaking," Mercer growled into the phone. "Oh. It's you, Sherry." His back stiffened suddenly. "What!"

In the sudden silence of the room, Sherry's sobbing voice was clearly audible through the two rooms. "Two men in a car," she sobbed. "Magnolia had the boys out in the park. They knocked her down and took the twins." She fought hard to control her sobs and failed. "Then—they told her to tell me to call you at the Mavis." Her last words were a sobbed prayer. "Oh, Matt. Do something, please. They took my babies."

Mercer said, "Don't, Sherry. Hang on to yourself. I'll be right home."

He hung up and turned to face Haig. "They've got my boys."

Haig knew what the four-year-old youngsters meant to Mercer. "Nagasaki?" he demanded.

"Yeah." Mercer fumbled his hat from a table and turned blindly toward the door. Before he reached it, the phone rang a second time. "Yes. This is Mercer speaking," he admitted in answer to the query.

The Eurasian's voice was cold. "Your wife has phoned you?" Mercer told him that she had. The other man continued. "So sorry. It is extremely distasteful to me to have to go to such lengths. But you must understand by now that this is a matter of great importance. It is now almost two o'clock. I will give you eight hours in which to consider the matter. Be in your office at midnight. I will contact you again. At that time you will either turn over to me the missing portion of the map or I will return your sons to you, one ear, one eye, one nose at a time."

Mercer protested, "But—"

"If the police should attempt to interfere before that time, I need not tell you what will happen."

"But—!" Mercer was talking to an empty line. The Eurasian had hung up.

Haig said, grimly, "We'll turn out the whole Force. I'll have every prowl and squad car in the City—"

"You'll do nothing," Mercer cut him short. "They'll kill my boys if you do. To hell with the Force. You wouldn't believe me before. Now I'll handle this my way."

Colonel Meyers asked, softly, "But what are you going to do?"

"I don't know," Mercer admitted.

CHAPTER FIVE

I'LL CALL YOU AT MIDNIGHT

IN MERCER'S OFFICE THE ONLY SOUND was the big man's heavy breathing and Sherry's muted sobs as her frantic fingers cut the dead Marine's dress uniform to pieces.

"It *has* to be in one of the seams," she sobbed. "It's the only place we haven't looked."

Mercer put down the diary and rubbed his swollen eyes. "Yeah," he agreed, not very hopefully.

Ben Morgan looked at his watch, said grimly, "We've only another half hour before the call comes in."

"It has to be in one of the seams. It *has* to," Sherry sobbed.

Mercer looked at his wife. He wished he could comfort her. But at a time like this, words meant nothing. He picked up the sword, twisted and pulled at the hilt. It contained no secret hiding place.

He thought, *"Advising other people not to deal with kidnappers is one thing. When it happens to you, it's different. To hell with anyone else. I'd give all of Manila to get my boys back safe."*

Her eyes swimming with tears, Sherry asked. "They won't mistreat them, will they Matt?"

"Of course not," he assured her. His throat felt dry and constricted.

"And we *will* get them back?"

Mercer came to a decision. "We'll get them back," he promised. "You'll have your boys in your arms by twelve-thirty."

Morgan said sharply. "You say that as though you believe it."

"I do," Mercer said. He rested his head in his hands for a moment. "Do me a favor, will you? Step down to the drug store on the corner and get me some five grain quinine capsules."

"I'll be glad to," the agent said. "I'll do anything I can to help. That's why I'm sticking around." He turned in the doorway, puzzled. "Did you say quinine capsules?"

"Five grain," Mercer nodded. He explained, "I'm still full of fever from the years I spent in the tropics. Sometimes excitement brings it back."

Morgan said, "I see," and closed the door quietly behind him.

"He's nice," Sherry sobbed. "I—I don't know what we'd have done without him."

"We'd have gotten along," Mercer said. He reached for the phone and dialed his own house number. Magnolia answered. "Get in a cab right away," Mercer told the colored girl, "and come on down to the office building. But don't come upstairs, understand? Wait for me in one of the doorways off the lobby. I'll meet you on the walk a few minutes after midnight. Is that clear?"

She protested, "That clear, Mr. Mercer. But—"

"If you want to see the twins again, do as I say," he said curtly and hung up.

Sherry looked at him strangely.

"No. I'm not crazy," he told her. "I know just what I'm doing."

He made certain that the outer office was empty, then returned to his desk and took a blank scrap of rice paper from his pocket. He had gotten it that afternoon from a Chinese merchant he knew. It was similar in size to the other scraps of paper that Steve had enclosed in his letters. He tore it unevenly on two sides, then laid it on his blotter and took a bottle of ink and a camel's hair brush from his drawer.

Sherry asked, "What are you going to do?"

"Give Nagasaki what he wants," he told her grimly.

Holding the paper in his right hand he took the brush in his left and began. Japanese ideographs began to take form on the scrap of paper as the fingers of his artificial hand worked smoothly, efficiently. "Unfit for combat!" he snorted.

His wife stared at the picture writing, fascinated. When he had finished, she demanded, "What does it say?"

He told her, "Twenty paces toward the old moat, turn toward the sun."

She said, wide-eyed, "You can't get away with it, Matt."

"I think that we can," he said quietly. "And if this doesn't work, I've another joker up my sleeve." He felt the pressure of his guns hard against his chest. "Also two .45s."

He waved the rice paper carefully to dry it and put the brush and ink back in the drawer. "You're going to find this in a seam of Steve's uniform," he told Sherry.

She stared at him a moment, nodded. "Whatever you say, Matt."

Mercer hesitated, said, "We won't even let Morgan in on the fact that I'm trying to pull a whizzer. Let's keep it between the two of us. It'll make the act more authentic."

He folded the paper carefully and handed it to his wife. "The seams of the collar would be a good place to find it," he told her. "I've hidden things there myself."

She crumpled the paper in her palm. Two minutes passed. She began to cry softly again.

Mercer looked at his watch. It was fifteen minutes of twelve. He dialed the hospital to which Irv had been taken and asked to speak to his night nurse. The nurse reported that Irv was conscious and resting nicely. "Tell him it's Matt Mercer calling," Mercer said. "And ask him if Steve said anything in a previous letter about sending the enclosure that Irv found in his letter this morning." The nurse protested disturbing him. "This could be a matter of life or death," Mercer said coldly. "Do as I say and don't argue."

He waited impatiently, listening to the night noises that floated up from the street below and drumming nervously on his desk top with his fingers."

The nurse reported, "He says, no."

Mercer thanked her and hung up.

"I don't understand," Sherry said.

"It took me some time to get it," Mercer admitted dryly. "This deduction business isn't much in my line. But *somebody had to tip off Japanese Intelligence. And I think I know who that someone was. That's why I spent two hours down at the Tribune morgue this afternoon.*"

Morgan returned with the quinine capsule. There were a half dozen in the box. Mercer put one of the gelatinous capsules on his tongue and washed it down with a shot of rye. "Thanks," he told Morgan. "Look. I don't want you to be insulted. *But just what do you really know about Miss Fariday, Ben? I mean, what do you know about her background.*"

"Not much," Morgan admitted. He smiled thinly. "She played the usual stock and vaudeville, I believe. She was a name when she came to me. I don't handle them until they're big enough for me to charge real fees. Why?"

"Someone tipped off Japanese Intelligence," Mercer pointed out. "And that kidnapping of you both this morning could have been a clever stall to divert suspicion from her."

Morgan said, thoughtfully, "I never thought of it that way. But then why did she insist on coming to you with her third of the map."

Mercer drummed his desk top. "Perhaps she hoped I would produce the missing portion of the map."

"I don't believe it," the agent said stoutly. "I think it's more likely that Pulos got drunk and babbled it over some bar."

"Steve drank," Mercer admitted. "But bars are scarce in the Gilbert Islands." He pushed the phone toward Morgan. "Do just one more thing for me. Call Miss Fariday and ask her when she last heard from Steve before she got that delayed letter this morning."

Morgan protested, "But Nagasaki is calling at midnight."

"We still have ten minutes," Mercer told him, looking at his watch.

Morgan made the call, reported, "She said it was the first letter in four months."

Mercer sighed. "That would appear to wash out my theory."

"Unless she is lying," Morgan suggested. He added, quickly, "Not that I think that she is. Bess Fariday means a lot to me."

"You were engaged to her, weren't you," Mercer asked. "I mean, when she left on that U.S.O. tour and came back married to Steve."

"That's right," Morgan nodded glumly. "But why bring that up now?"

"I just thought of it," Mercer said quietly.

Sherry Mercer ripped the last seam on the collar, gasped, "I think I've found it. There's something here in the collar." She opened her palm and exposed the scrap of paper.

Morgan exulted. "It *was* in Steve's personal effects. Don't you see, Matt. Steve didn't mail the third piece of the map after all. He kept it in the collar of his uniform."

Mercer picked the rice paper from Sherry's palm and unfolded it carefully. "I guess this is it all right." He read aloud, "Twenty paces toward the moat, turn toward the sun."

The agent mopped his neck and forehead with his handkerchief. "That's it all right. The plum tree is the starting point. Twenty paces from it—"

The ring of the phone cut him short. Mercer squared his shoulders and answered. It was Inspector Haig.

"Just in case you've changed your mind, Matt," he said grimly.

"No," Mercer said. "I still feel the same as when I talked to you last. Now get off the wire. I'm expecting a contact at midnight."

He hung up and laid his watch on the desk. It was two minutes of twelve. The phone rang again promptly at midnight.

His face an expressionless mask, Mercer said, "Mercer speaking."

The Eurasian's salutation was a question. "You are alone?"

"No," Mercer admitted. "I'm not. Ben Morgan and my wife are here in the office."

"And the police?"

"I just told Haig to get off the line. My boys are all right?"

Nagasaki ignored the question. "You have that which I want?"

"I think so," Mercer answered. "But I asked you a question."

The Eurasian chuckled, "I believe I can reassure you on that point."

A brief pause followed. Then a childish treble quavered, "This ish Matt, Daddy. I don't like it here." The baby voice filled with tears. "When are you coming to take me home?"

His battered face working, Mercer told him, "In just a few minutes, sonny. Stevie is all right?"

"I fine, Daddy," a second treble answered.

Sherry Mercer sat staring at the phone, tears streaming down her face, afraid to trust herself to speak.

"Satisfied?" Nagasaki asked.

"Perfectly," Mercer said. "Where do we make the exchange?"

"We'll come to that in just a moment. Where did you find the third part of the map?"

"In Steve's collar," Mercer lied.

"And you aren't trying to pull a fast one?"

Mercer pointed out, "You have my boys?"

"And the note is genuine?"

Mercer handed the phone to Morgan. "Tell him what you saw."

Morgan said into the phone, "I saw Mrs. Mercer find it in the stand-up collar of Steve Pulos' uniform coat. She ripped the uniform to pieces and that was the last place that she looked."

Mercer took the phone. "Satisfied?"

"I am," Nagasaki admitted. "I knew that it had to be somewhere in the bundle of Pulos' personal effects. But before I give you directions, let me tell you this. If you are attempting to trick me, if you are followed by the police, you know what will happen to your boys."

Mercer said, huskily, "I do."

The Eurasian named a street and a house number on the Northwest side. "Take a Checker Cab," he ordered. "Make certain that you aren't followed. Stop one block from the number. Pay off the driver of this cab. Come the rest of the way on foot. You will be watched from the moment of your arrival. If you have what we want, we'll make the trade. Otherwise—"

He hung up on the implied threat.

Mercer found that his face was dripping sweat. He took another quinine tablet and dropped the box into his pocket.

"I—I can go with you?" Sherry asked.

He kissed her, hard. "No. I have to go alone," he told her. "You and Morgan wait here."

CHAPTER SIX

VOICE FROM A GRAVE

THE QUIET, RATHER SHABBY, RESIDENTIAL STREET lay wrapped in sleep.

The cab stopped under a light. Mercer turned to the colored girl beside him. "You don't have to do this, you know. It will be dangerous. You can go on with the cab if you want to."

She shook her head. "No, sir, Mr. Mercer."

"No what?" the big man demanded.

"I doan' want to go with the cab," she told him. "I want to go with you and get the boys."

He said, "Good girl," and got out of the cab.

The driver asked loudly, "You want me to wait, Mister?"

Mercer told him no, handed him a ten dollar bill. As he waited for his change, he kicked the front tire idly. "You'd better stop at the next filling station and get some air in that," he told the driver. "It looks low to me."

The driver gave him his change and got out to look at the tire. "Low. Hell. It's damn near flat," he cursed. "I'd better change that or I'll be tearing up the casing."

Mercer said, "Good night," and walked on down the street with Magnolia, mentally crossing his fingers.

A faint scuff of feet on the opposite walk warned him that Nagasaki had been telling the truth when he said that he would be watched from the moment of his arrival. He stopped and peered at a house number. It was 3211. He wanted 3231. They walked by several vacant lots. 3231 stood by itself with no house for several blocks on either side. The shades of the house were drawn but light showed in the corners of the windows.

He deliberately paused at the walk leading to the porch, took the box of quinine from his pocket and put a capsule in his mouth.

"Frightened?" he asked Magnolia.

"I is scared to death," she admitted.

A quick step sounded on the street, scuffed across the grass of the parkway and the barrel of a gun pressed hard against Mercer's ribs.

"Nagasaki?" Mercer asked.

"Nagasaki," the Eurasian answered coldly. "You were told to come alone, Mercer."

Mercer answered without turning his head. "Don't be a fool. I don't trust you any more than you trust me. That's why I brought Magnolia. She takes the twins back to Sherry before you get the map."

A moment of silence followed. "I see," Nagasaki said coldly. "Well, we'll discuss that in the house."

The gun in his back, Mercer, Magnolia beside him, walked up the stairs to the porch. The white-haired man he had met in Burke's opened the front door.

"Take his guns, Kane," Nagasaki ordered.

Kane smiled as he slipped Mercer's guns from their holsters and dropped them into his own pockets. "I believe that we've met before, sucker."

Mercer looked over his shoulder at the jaundiced-eyed desk clerk who stood scowling at him from a doorway that apparently led into a kitchen. "Yeah," he answered Kane.

Gray-faced with fear, but determined, Magnolia asked, "Where are my boys? You doan' have no right to worry Miss Sherry so."

"You heard her," Mercer added. He looked around the room. There was nothing unusual about it, no sliding panels or trick walls. It was a typical parlor of a jerry-built bungalow.

The Eurasian laughed. "I really gave you credit for more sense, Mercer. Did you *really* think that I was going to turn your boys over to you and let you walk out of here alive to testify against me in some post-war crime court?"

"I still think so," Mercer said.

Nagasaki raked the sight of his gun across Mercer's injured cheek just hard enough to make it bleed. "So sorry. But you are wrong, Sergeant Mercer. All Americans are too trusting. You are a nation of fools and weaklings."

Mercer reminded him dryly, "From last reports, we're doing pretty well in the South Pacific. That's why you are so damn anxious to get your hands on the loot of Manila. You know you won't be there much longer."

The Eurasian started to strike him again and changed his mind. "All right. Hand over the map."

"First, you hand over my boys," Mercer countered.

There was no mirth in Nagaski's smile. "Very well. If we must take it from you by force, we can."

"I doubt that," Mercer said crisply. He stepped back a step, opened his mouth and held out his tongue. There was a gelatinous capsule on it filled with a white substance. Mercer tucked it back in his cheek, continued. "That's the missing section of your map, Nagasaki. I put the capsule in my mouth when I first stopped out in front of the house. It will take it about five minutes to dissolve. One minute has already passed. I'll swallow it at the first attempt to rush me. You can kill me and cut me open, sure. But by the time you do, my digestive juices will have turned the rice paper to so much pulp."

The Eurasian admitted, grudgingly, "So you aren't such a fool after all."

"You'd better hurry," Mercer reminded him. "Even if I don't have to swallow it, once the capsule has dissolved, my saliva will have the same effect as my digestive juices."

"You win," Nagasaki admitted. He raised his voice and called, "Bring in the boys, Miss Mouton."

The over-stuffed blonde from the Mavis came in from the kitchen holding a squirming twin by each hand. They squealed, "Daddy!" excitedly when they saw Mercer.

"Don't come near Daddy," he told them smiling. "Be good boys and run straight to Magnolia when the lady lets go your hand. Magnolia is going to take you to mother."

The blonde looked at Nagasaki. "Release them," he said sourly. "For the moment, Mercer is holding the whip hand."

The twins ran to the colored girl. She picked up one in each arm. "Now what do I do, Mister Mercer?"

"Go back to the corner," he told her. He paused a moment and listened. There was the faint clang of a tire iron. "The driver of the cab that we came in should be about finished changing tires."

"You planned that," Nagasaki accused.

"You deliberately kicked a valve stem and broke it."

Mercer ignored him. "Take the boys to Mrs. Mercer. She is waiting at my office."

The jaundiced-eyed desk clerk spoke for the first time. "Nix. I don't like this set-up. How do we know the girl won't flag down the first policeman that she sees?"

Nagasaki's eyes were glued on Mercer's mouth. "He has the whip hand," he repeated. "We will have to take that chance." He opened the door for Magnolia.

"Tell the driver of the cab to honk his horn as he passes," Mercer called after her.

Nagasaki slammed and locked the door behind the colored girl. "Now spit out that capsule!"

Mercer shook his head doggedly. "No. Not until I hear that horn." He held the capsule between his teeth so they could see it.

Kane started for him, red-faced with anger. "Damn you, Mercer. You must think that you're dealing with a bunch of punks. I'll—"

"No!" Nagasaki stopped him. "Don't touch him and don't shoot. I know his type well enough to know that he will do just what he says."

They waited in angry silence, their eyes on the dissolving capsule. Then a car motor raced in the night. A moment later it passed the house. A horn tooted and the sound of the cab motor faded quickly into the night.

Mercer spat the soggy capsule on the floor. Nagasaki snatched it up, his eyes glittering with excitement. "You are going to die hard for this, Mercer," he said. "But I expect that you realize that."

He tore the capsule open and unfolded the scrap of rice paper.

"That is it?" the blonde demanded.

"I think so," Nagasaki smiled. He read, " *Twenty paces toward the old moat, turn toward the sun—*' As I recall Manila, that should put it somewhere in the park district, a very likely spot for Osaki to have chosen." He took the other two sections of the map from his wallet and laid the section that Mercer had written between them. The difference was instantly obvious. The ink was a deeper black. The chirography was not the same. The torn edges did not match.

Kane swore, "Tricked by God! Tricked by a flat-footed private shamus."

Nagasaki's lemon tinted face went white. "And I called him a trusting fool." He straightened suddenly and rammed his gun hard into Mercer's stomach. *"You have five seconds to live. Where is the missing portion of the map!"*

Mercer told the truth, "I don't know."

A police siren wailed in the distance. It was joined by a second, then a third.

The man who had posed as a desk clerk swore in German. "Those police cars are coming here?"

Mercer glanced down at the gun in his ribs. "I wouldn't know," he lied.

"He is lying," the blonde screamed shrilly. "Instead of trapping him, we're trapped." She clawed at Nagasaki's face. "We should have known better than to have listened to a dirty Jap even if they are supposed to be our allies!"

The Eurasian pushed her away from him. His eyes had narrowed to slits. Mercer saw his arm muscles contract and flung himself to one side just as the gun exploded in his ribs. The slug burned a furrow across his stomach. Mad with frustrated rage, Nagasaki triggered again. At three feet, he couldn't miss. He didn't. The impact of the second slug slapped Mercer back into the wall as though he had been struck with a sledge hammer. A third, a fourth, and a fifth shot burned through his artificial arm. A sixth and seventh were deflected by his steel elbow and ricocheted angrily around the room.

Still babbling Oriental curse, Nagasaki had to pause to slip a fresh clip into his gun.

The thin-faced German with the jaundiced-eyes had raced to the back door. He returned shouting loudly. "They are already here. The back porch is filled with men. The house must be surrounded!"

Nagasaki turned briefly at the shout. Ignoring his wounded shoulder, Mercer catapulted himself from the wall and attempted to wrest the freshly-loaded gun from his hand. The Jap turned back, screaming, biting, clawing, kicking. He caught a foot behind Mercer's ankle and the men fell heavily to the floor just as a heavy pounding began on the front door.

Nagasaki was fifty pounds lighter but he was fighting with the desperation of fear. He rode Mercer across the floor. Then Mercer rode him back with Kane and the jaundice-eyed German shooting at both men and at the door where the heavy pounding had changed to the thud of axes and the splintering of wood.

Nagasaki tried for Mercer's throat and missed. Then Mercer's fist found his jaw and the man went suddenly limp.

A second slug pounded through Mercer's already wounded shoulder just as his finger closed on the gun. He rolled over on his back in an agony of pain and shot the yellow-eyed man through the throat.

Kane threw up his hands and shouted, "Don't shoot!"

Things were becoming confused in Mercer's mind. He knew that the blonde was still screaming. He knew that he couldn't hold out much longer and the moment that he blacked out, Kane would snatch up his gun and shoot him.

He was suddenly very tired. He wished that Inspector Haig and Colonel Meyers would hurry. He wanted to close his eyes and sleep. His eyelids drooped and Steve's bull bellow burned across his sub-conscious mind, *"Come on. Stay with it, Matt. Don't be a dud!"*

"Dud," Mercer said aloud. "Hell. Of course that's it. I should have known it all along."

Then the crashing of axes ceased. A sudden silence beat against his ears like surf. Haig's lean gray, worried, face swam into his line of vision. The Inspector's voice seemed to come from far away. "We'll take over now, Matt. Are you all right?"

"I'm fine," Mercer answered him. "Fine." He tried to get to his feet—and fainted . . .

When he came to, he was lying on his back with Sherry and Hogan's faces both hovering over him. The police surgeon was packing his wounds with sulfa-sprinkled gauze and assuring Sherry, "Of course he'll be all right, Mrs. Mercer. You can't kill men like Matt by shooting them in the shoulder."

"You can come close to it," Mercer told him. He sat up, supported by Sherry's arm and scowled at the stretcher bearers who were waiting for Hogan to finish. "To hell with that, right now. Let's wrap this up and put it in the files." He asked Inspector Haig, "Nagasaki is still alive?"

He saw the Eurasian then, scowling in one corner of the room, handcuffed to Colonel Meyers. "I've got him on ice, Matt," the man from G-2 assured him. "And Kane is a German agent we've been after for some time."

"Good," Mercer said. He asked Sherry, "I kept my promise? The boys were back by twelve-thirty?"

She kissed him. "They were. But I don't understand, Matt. You told Inspector Haig over the phone—"

Mercer grinned, "That I felt the same as when I had talked to him last. That was about five-thirty, just after I left the Tribune morgue. We planned this whole thing then. Even my cab man was a cop. You see, I knew that I could not trust Nagasaki, but I didn't want to worry you any more than you already were. And I had to figure a way to get the twins out of the joint before the trouble started."

Nagasaki swore at him in Japanese and Lieutenant Carlson cuffed him. "I don't know what you're saying, but keep it up. This is the first chance I've had to slug a monkey."

Mercer looked around the room. "Morgan is here?"

"I'm here," Morgan answered. "But you could have told us, Matt. Sherry and I didn't know what to think when Inspector Haig popped in and bustled us into a squad car not two minutes after you left."

"I'll bet you didn't," Mercer said. He looked at Colonel Meyers. "You know that question you asked me, about who tipped Japanese Intelligence?"

"Yes—?"

"Well, I know who it was," Mercer told him. "I know because I knew Steve so well. The only time that that big skirt-chaser couldn't keep his mouth shut was when he was talking or writing to a woman. God knows how he got it past the censor, but a saw-buck gets you a thousand that he spilled the whole affair in a letter to his wife."

Morgan gasped, "And you mean that your theory was right, that Jennifer Fariday contacted Baron Nagasaki and—"

"No," Mercer cut him short coldly, "you did. She never even saw that letter. You had been engaged to marry her. You were jealous as hell of Steve. And you snaked that letter from her mail as soon as it arrived. Then, being both greedy and a heel, you saw a chance to make a fortune."

The agent smiled weakly. "You're out of your head with pain, Matt."

"Yeah?" Mercer jeered. "Then how did you know that Nagasaki was a Baron? It's the first time that it's been mentioned."

"I—I read it," Morgan explained.

"The hell you did," Mercer told him. "I've been suspicious of you ever since you deliberately threw yourself in my way when I was chasing Nagasaki at the Mavis. You wanted him to get away. That's why I've kept you close to me all day except the few times that I wanted to shake you."

White-faced, Morgan told Inspector Haig, "He's mad. He can't prove a thing." He turned back to find that Mercer had fumbled the Japanese gun that had been in Steve's personal effects from his belt and had leveled it on him. "No. Don't shoot!" he screamed. "Everything that you say is true. I'll talk."

Mercer triggered deliberately. The firing pin clicked metallically on the dud shell.

Haig asked, "What's the big idea?"

Mercer tossed him the gun, "Dig me out that shell, will you, Haig? Hell. Knowing Steve I should have known where he'd stash something really important. But being dumb, he had to comeback and tell me."

Haig pried the shell from the gun with his pen knife, then twisted the lead from the brass and a spill of rice paper fell out. "I'll be damned," he admitted. He picked it up, unfolded it, and handed it to Mercer.

The big man grinned, "I was close." He read, " *'Twenty paces to the morning sun away with the Bishop's palace at one's back,'* that's a famous landmark," he explained to Sherry, " *'even if one walks at snail's pace, one comes at noon—'* " he looked up grinning, "etcetera."

Colonel Meyers took the paper from his hand. "Nice going, Matt. When our boys get back to Manila, all that G-2 has to do is to find this freak plum tree, follow the map and dig. Colonel Osaki looted the town of God knows how many millions. We can use that money in rebuilding Cavite and Corregidor."

"Don't thank me," Mercer said. "Thank Steve."

Baron Nagasaki's black eyes grew resigned. "I have but one request," he told Inspector Haig. "I wonder if I might be allowed to retire into another room and—"

"Commit hari-kari, or whatever you call it?" Haig interrupted him coldly. "Hell, no. The State of Illinois is going to do that for you with a chair and some electricity."

"But I have killed no one," Nagasaki protested.

"Irv died a few minutes before we got here," Haig told him grimly. "It seems that he wasn't resting nicely after all. He was bleeding to death internally from that beating that your boys gave him."

Lieutenant Carlson hustled Nagasaki and Kane from the room. A sergeant followed with the weeping blonde. The stretcher men lifted Mercer.

Colonel Meyers paused beside the stretcher. "Look, Mercer," he said soberly. "I know that you're an ex-Marine. But the Army could use a man like you. I wonder if you'd consider a commission in—"

"In a combat unit?" Mercer broke in eagerly.

Meyers hesitated, "Well, no. Not exactly a combat unit. I was thinking of G-2. After all, you have only one arm and—"

Mercer started to tell him where he could put G-2, where he could put the Army for that matter, remembered his wife was present and said, instead, "No. I don't guess so. But thanks a lot. After all, I am forty-five, a family man with two boys and a wife to support. And, as you say, I only have one arm."

Sherry kissed him full on the lips. "One arm is enough for me," she smiled.

Mercer slipped his good arm around her waist and hugged her as she walked beside the stretcher. After all, there were compensations in being just a civilian.

A MINOR MATTER
OF MURDER

CHAPTER ONE

WAR STORY

IT WAS A NASTY DAY, cold and wet and grey. I had been in Criminal Court all morning and most of the afternoon waiting to testify for the State in an arson case that was tabbed on the court calendar as Illinois vs Monelli.

When I got back to the office there were two lads waiting for me, a husky youngster in his middle twenties and an older man, shabbily dressed, who looked as though he might be a farmer.

Both looked up as I came in but neither spoke.

They both were strangers to me. 1 shook the rain off my hat and walked on into my own private office with Elsie close on my heels.

She told me, "Barney Connell has phoned four times in the last half hour. He phoned, the last time, less than five minutes ago. And he says it is vitally important you call him the moment you come in."

I digested the information as I hung up my dripping top coat. Barney was not a bad lad. But he was a member of the law firm representing Monelli. And my testimony not yet having gone on record I had, or thought I had, a fair idea of what he wanted to talk about.

I said, "The devil with Barney, how about the lads in the outer office?"

She didn't have to look at her notebook. "The young one's name," she said smiling, "is Benny Schermerhorn. He has just been discharged from the Service, he's twenty-four, his home is in Brooklyn, he prefers brunettes to blondes, and he wants to take me to dinner."

I asked, "He didn't by any chance mention why he wanted to see me?"

She said that he had not.

"And the older man?"

She said, "He wouldn't even give me his name. I think it's a shake-down of some kind. I mean I think he wants to sell you some information."

I said it was likely. Most lads with shady information regard private agency men as a sort of verbal pawnshop. Then she wanted to know, it being almost five o'clock, if she could take off a little early as she wanted to change her dress and do a re-paint job before keeping her dinner date.

I said that was all right with me if she would delay her departure long enough to gimmick the board so outside calls would come through. She said she would and would also bend Schermerhorn in.

He came in, grinning, a big lad with the friendly eyes of a cocker pup, just as my phone rang.

I nodded him into a chair and picked up the receiver.

"Tom Doyle speaking."

"This is Barney, Tom," Connell told me. He sounded worried. "Have you anyone in your office?"

I glanced at Schermerhorn. "I have."

"Know him?"

"No."

"Then watch him," Barney warned curtly. "I don't know just what the caper is. But I think I have bumped into something big." His laugh was a trifle forced. "And if we're both alive by morning maybe we can make a deal."

"What the hell are you talking about?" I asked him.

"Murder," he said succinctly. "I—"

His voice trailed off.

I told him to speak up, I couldn't hear him. There was a moment of silence, then a feminine voice broke in. "I am sorry, State 2121 has hung up. Do you wish me to ring them again?"

I thought it over, told her not to bother, and hung up. To hell with Connell and his trades. The more I thought about it the more it sounded like a rib. I was supposed to get all hot and bothered by his pitch—then he'd sell me a bill of goods in an attempt to get me to lay off Monelli. On the other hand—

I looked at young Schermerhorn. His eyes curious but friendly, he was waiting for me to speak. He didn't look hostile to me. I walked by him to the door. Elsie had taken me at my word. But the older lad who looked like a farmer was still holding down a chair.

"It may be some time before I can see you," I told him.

He refused to be discouraged. "That's perfectly all right." The chair was four-legged and solid but he gave the impression of rocking.

I closed the door again and looked over Elsie's date. "Okay. Let's have it, Schermerhorn. How did you hear of me? And what kind of a jam are you in?"

He said Phil Dew at the V.F.W. Hall had recommended me as the private agency man in Chicago most likely to give an ex-Service man a break. "But I'm not exactly in a jam. Look. Let's get this straight, Mr. Doyle. This is the first time I ever hired a private detective. Just how do your charges run?"

I told him, straight-faced, that it all depended on whom he wanted me to kill. If it was State's Attorney Beamer, for example, who was a sad sack to begin with, I would make him a reasonable rate.

He didn't think I was very funny. His name may have been Schermerhorn but there was a kilted McTavish somewhere in his ancestry. "Nix. I ain't kidding," he said. "I want to do what is right on account of I was pals with Jack. But I don't see why it should cost me a lot of money."

I brought us both a drink in lieu of an apology, saying that we could settle the fee once I knew just what he wanted me to do. He told his story slowly, sipping at his rye.

I sat watching the rain scour the accumulated summer dirt off the L girders and the cornices of the building across the way. It was quite a system. Puddles of dirty water would gather on the ledges and the beams, then a gust of cold wind off the Lake would pick it up and spray it on the already sodden pedestrians picking their way through the puddles.

I spotted his yarn as a phoney before he had said ten words. But I couldn't spot the gimmick. Boiled down to its fundamentals, his story was that he and a lad whom he called Jack had enlisted in the Marines at approximately the same time. They had been buddies all through boot camp and later in the Islands.

"Like those two guys Damon and Pythias that I read about in high school," he told me.

He continued. A handy lad with a deck of cards and the 7-11 point system, Jack had built up a bankroll of eight thousand two hundred dollars. But it had been unlucky money. He had been killed during a landing. Before dying, however, he had passed his roll to Schermerhorn making him promise to deliver it to his, Jack's, aged parents in Chicago.

His spaniel eyes slightly misted, Schermerhorn concluded, "So I tried to. I stopped off here on my way to Brooklyn. I went to see his parents this morning. I argued with them for two hours. But they wouldn't take the money."

I played along. "Why not?"

He told me soberly, "They claim that Jack isn't dead. But they know better than that because his father showed me the official notice from the War Department, also a dozen uncashed insurance checks."

I thought I knew most of the dodges and the rackets. But this was a new one to me. I asked, "And just what do you want me to do?"

He unbuttoned his shirt to get at a money belt and laid a thick sheaf of bills on my desk. "I want you to take the money and find some way to make them take it. You can give me a receipt to put me in the clear." He took a slim roll from his pocket and added two ten dollar bills to the money. "It's worth twenty bucks to me to be able to get on to Brooklyn. How about it? It's a deal?"

I fingered through the sheaf. The bills were genuine, mostly fifties and one hundreds. I couldn't spot any obvious markings. I let it lay and walked over to the window. It was a new approach. Connell's phone call was beginning to make sense. It had been a part of the build-up. I took the money, I signed the receipt, and if I persisted in testifying in the Monelli case I kissed away my license. No sane jury of twelve men would believe any such fantastic story.

"It's a deal?" Schermerhorn repeated.

I walked back and slapped him so hard with my open palm that the outline of my fingers showed red against his cheek. "No. It's not a deal," I told him. "I'm not that money hungry. Now pick up the dough and go back to Barney and tell him—"

My back was to the door. It opened suddenly behind me and the husky lad's eyes went wide. But before I could turn, he pushed me backwards, off-balance.

"Down!"

The light went out as he shouted. I lit on my haunches clawing for my gun. Then a gun in the doorway began to bucket. A slug nailed me flat to the carpet. Another one creased my forehead. It had been a long time in coming. But—this is it, I thought.

I had been unconscious perhaps twenty minutes. State's Attorney Beamer and Morgan and Lupe, the aging Mexican fireball, along with a half dozen prowl car cops and the manager of the building had been there when I'd come to. Lieutenant Nobby of Homicide and his squid had arrived less than five minutes later. Schermerhorn, so they told me, was dead. So was the lad in the outer office. And the eight thousand dollars were gone.

Assistant Deputy Coroner Terry was working on my shoulder. No bones, it seemed, were broken. The slug had gone through the muscles and was more painful than serious. It had been the bark on my head that had knocked me out.

Terry wanted to know how I felt.

I told him, "Lousy."

He said that was to be expected, dusted some sulfa in the wound and began to pack it. Nobby came in from the outer office and sat down beside me. "And that's all you can tell us, Tom?"

I said it was. "I was in my own office, minding my own business, when—"

State's Attorney Beamer sniffed, "Ridiculous." A little man with slightly popped eyes, a receding hair line, a blonde eyebrow mustache, and a Little Flower complex slung on a Model T chassis, we the people had picked ourselves a daisy when we had elected him queen of our Mayhem. He high-lighted the story I had told concerning young Schermerhorn and the proposition that he had made me. "And you expect me to believe that?"

I said I didn't give a damn what he believed, that it was bad enough to play clay pigeon without coming to find his ugly face staring down at me. "How do I know? Maybe you shot me," I accused.

He purpled just short of apoplexy.

Cal Morgan chuckled. "No. You have it all wrong, Tom. It wasn't the State's Attorney. I'm the lad who shot you. I did it for the eight grand." He tapped the breast pocket of his coat. "I have it right here now."

Even Nobby smiled at that.

A local paving contractor, and amateur night club entrepreneur, eight grand meant less to Morgan than eighty bucks meant to me.

Looking as expensive as ever, and smelling twice as sweet, Lupe wrinkled her nose at me. "He ees not fonny, no, you theenk?" She patted Morgan's pockets. "Besides he ees not have a machine gun." She imitated one by putting her tongue to the roof of her mouth. "An' thees I am hear weeth my own ears."

It seemed that she and Morgan and Beamer had been on their way to a 1st Ward dinner and rally at the Club Cherie, which Morgan owned, and at which she was the star attraction, when Lupe had remembered that Pete Cooper, whose office was below mine, had promised to have a new orchestration ready. Morgan had come up for the music to find Pete gone for the day. And before he had gotten back to the lobby all hell had burst loose on my floor.

Terry said, "Leave him alone. The guy's been shot."

Nobby shooed them into the outer office and came back mopping lipstick off his under lip. "That dame will kiss anyone," he complained.

I asked if I had to go through a bull session with Beamer. He said I did not, that they had gone on to the rally, and that if there were any points at which we were at variance we could straighten them out at the inquest.

Terry finished with his job and left. I walked out in the outer office and looked at the lad out there. Death hadn't changed him. He still looked like a farmer. I pawed through the stuff Nobby's boys had taken out of his pockets. His name was Fred Able and his draft card was stamped—Local No. 2, Mears County, Cloverdale, Iowa.

Nobby asked if the name meant anything to me. I said it rang a bell, but faintly. To the best of my sober knowledge I had never seen him before.

"And you're not holding out?"

'No. Nothing important," I told him. I wasn't. I didn't *know* that it was important. I merely wanted to talk to Barney before I whacked up his phone call with the law. Someone owed me plenty. I meant to collect.

We walked back in and looked at Schermerhorn. Two wagon men were lifting him into a basket. His face relaxed in death, he looked more like a kid than ever. Benny had fought a man's size war—and come home to this.

Nobby asked, "And that yarn you told us was true? You didn't dream it up to rip the S.A.?"

I lifted my good hand. "So help me. According to Benny he stopped off in Chicago to give the eight thousand bucks to his dead buddy's parents. And they wouldn't tike it, probably because they're trying to kid themselves that maybe their boy will come back."

"But he didn't mention their name?"

I said, "He didn't get that far. I thought he was fronting for Monelli. I thought he was trying to bribe me and I tried to slap him off his feet."

Nobby looked at me over the tip of his cigar. "So—?"

I told him, "So I'm going to get that eight grand back and see that it goes where he wanted it to go. I think I owe Benny that much."

CHAPTER TWO

DEATH WORKS LATE

JIM CURTIS, ONE OF NOBBY'S BOYS, was in the lobby putting the strong arm on Kip the elevator starter. I asked him if he had found out anything.

He said he had not. The lobby had been jammed with home bound office workers. But while everyone had heard the shots no one remembered seeing anyone carrying a golf bag or a violin case that might have contained a machine gun.

Kip wanted to know how my shoulder felt.

I told him, "Lousy," and walked on out to the street. Night hadn't helped the weather. It was raining even harder than it had been. I tried to get a cab, and couldn't. So I walked.

Connell's office was on the fifth floor of 221 N. LaSalle, Adams, Burson, and Connell. The lights were on but the desks were cleared and a scrub woman was emptying ash trays.

She shook her head at me. "Nobody here. All go home five o'clock."

Barney's office was at the far end of a little hall. I could see a light through the glass and I asked her if she had cleaned it yet. She said she had not.

"Then if you don't mind," I told her, "I'll just look in while I'm here. Sometimes Mr. Connell works late."

Her eyes followed me down the hall.

The door was closed but unlocked. I looked in, closed the door, then opened it again. Barney wasn't at his desk. But his briefcase, hat, and coat, were still piled on a chair by the door.

I crossed the office, looked in his private washroom, then went back to the waiting room, plugged in an outside line and called my office. Nobby was still there.

"This is Tom, Nobby," I told him. "I'm over at Adams, Burson, and Connell. I wasn't holding out. I just wanted to check with Barney before I told you. But shortly before Schermerhorn, Able, and I, were shot, Barney gave me a buzz and warned me to keep my eyes open." I gave him the conversation verbatim.

He said it was a fine time to tell him and to put Barney on the wire.

I said, "I can't. He's dead. He's sitting in his washroom with a slug through his left eye."

He was still swearing when I hung up.

The scrub woman stood staring at me pop-eyed, holding an ash tray in one hand and crossing herself with the other.

I debated waiting for Nobby, went down stairs instead, walked through the side door out into the parking lot and cut through the alley to Dearborn. Elsie met most of her dates in the Sherman lobby.

I found her in the arcade standing in front of the flower shop, doing a tap tap on the tile. "That big lug stood me up," she told me. Then she saw the sling under my topcoat and gasped.

I guided her on into the bar and one of the wall tables. "There's been some trouble at the office. But if you faint, I'll fire you." I ordered two double ryes and waited until they were served to tell her that young Schermerhorn was dead.

Her face went white but she didn't cry. It would have been better if she had. I nodded at her drink. She said, "I don't need it. How—why—?"

"That's the eight thousand dollar question," I told her. "Some lad walked in, they say with a tommy-gun, and let all three of us have it. Did Schermerhorn tell you that he was carrying eight thousand dollars in cash?"

She shook her head. "Why should he?"

I said, "It's a temptation to flash a roll."

She caught the possible implication and her eyes went wide. "Oh, Mr. Doyle. You don't think—?"

I patted her hand. "Emphatically not. You going to drink your drink?"

She said she was not. I drank it, then asked her if Schermerhorn had happened to mention where he was staying.

She told me the Devon Arms, a flash joint across the river, and wanted to know what she could do. I asked her to call Sue, tell her I was on a case, and not to expect me until she saw me.

Elsie protested, "But we haven't a client."

"This one is on me," I told her.

I left a bill to cover the check and sweated out a cab under the Sherman marquee. A half dozen police cars, Nobby's car among them, were parked in front of 221 N. LaSalle and the usual crowd had gathered. My driver asked if he should stop and find out what had happened. I told him not to bother.

The desk clerk at the Devon Arms remembered me from a chorus-girl straight man case that I had been called in on some time before. Before I could dig the rain out of my eyes he wanted to know what Schermerhorn had done. I asked how he knew why I was there.

He told me, "Because an H.Q. man just asked for his key and went up to the room." He glanced at his scratch pad. "A Sergeant William Harris."

I thought that over. Bill Harris wasn't from HQ. He worked out of the S.A.'s office.

The clerk added, "He's checked into room 705. But I doubt that you'll find very much. I was on the desk when Mr. Schermerhorn checked in. And all he had in the line of baggage was one of those little canvas overnight bags of the type soldiers and sailors carry."

A goodlooking colored girl ran me up to the seventh floor between dips into a True Love Romance Mag. "Does her husband know that she's seeing this other guy?" I asked her.

"Not yet," she told me soberly. "He—" She gave me a dirty look and banged open the door of the cage. "Seventh floor. Out, please."

Room 705 was one of those rooms they always palm off on the rural trade and lads who aren't apt to be too particular. It was right next to the elevator and its only window opened on an air shaft.

The door was closed and either locked or bolted. I rattled the knob. "Open up, Bill. It's Tom Doyle."

Feet crossed the floor. Someone shot the bolt. I started in, stopped. Whoever the lad in the room was, he wasn't the Bill Harris I knew.

A big man, six feet and better, with black hair and black eyes, he looked like he might be a Greek. He was wearing his hat and top coat but his top coat was unbuttoned and being one of those big bellied lads plenty of white shirt front showed. "I'm afraid you have the advantage," he said. "So your name is Doyle. Am I supposed to know you?"

I said it looked like I'd made a mistake. He wanted to know what room I was looking for. I told him 705.

"Then you banged the wrong door," he said. "705 is next door. This is Room 709."

I turned, instinctively, to look at the plate on the door. It was a mistake. I sensed the blow and turned in time to take the down swing of the sap on my good shoulder instead of on the head.

Breathing hard but saying nothing he lifted the sap again.

I said, "To hell with that heifer dust," and shot him through my pocket twice.

The lead stopped him but not the sap. It slapped into my wounded shoulder and pain turned the whole room green. I leaned against the wall retching, waiting for him to sap me again.

Instead, his face grave, he laced his fingers across his belly, blood welling out between them, and walked soberly from the room. I staggered out in the hall to watch him. He considered the elevator and walked by it to the fire door. Then still holding his belly with one hand he used the other to tug at the steel door. He got it open two inches or so, fell against it heavily and slid down the door to the floor, his hand reluctantly releasing the knob.

A skinny redhead in panties and bra, a hair brush in one hand, had come out into the hall. She pointed the hair brush at me, and screamed, "You've killed him!"

Other doors were opening and faces peering out. I went back into Schermerhorn's room and sorted through the stuff the Greek had dumped on the bed.

There was a shaving kit, a change of underwear, some socks, two campaign ribbons (both with battle stars) a presidential unit citation, a soldier's medal, and the purple heart. There were also a half dozen letters from girls with Brooklyn return addresses, a Japanese imitation of a German Walther P38, a gold handled Kamikaze dagger, and a small bloodstained Japanese flag that looked like it might have been worn as a turban. It made me sick to handle them.

Benny would never tell the boys in Brooklyn how he had done it.

I went through the stuff again. What I was looking for wasn't there. I picked up the phone that had been ringing for some time.

"Yes. There were shots up here," I told the clerk. "But shut up and listen to me. Did Schermerhorn make any calls from this room?"

He said he would check and informed me a moment later that a call to Nagle 4531 was charged against him. By calling the Nagle exchange I learned the phone was listed in the name of Mr. John H. Thompson at 6007 W. Avers Avenue.

The name didn't mean a thing to me. Before I could hang up the clerk broke in again saying he had called the W. Chicago Avenue station and wanting to know if he should call the Bureau. I gave him Adams, Burson, and Connell's number and told him to call there instead. Then I went out to check on the hood.

There were ten or fifteen people in the hall but the big lad by the fire door was gone.

A nervous little man who was polishing his eye-glasses briskly told me, "He wasn't dead. He got up and walked down the stairs."

I asked why he hadn't tried to stop him.

He asked, "Who, me?" He meant it.

I opened the door a crack. The Greek wasn't on the landing. Splotches of blood led down the stairs. I followed them to the basement where a frightened colored fireman was staring out the boiler room door into the rain.

"A man all shot to pieces and bleeding something awful just walked through here," he told me.

I asked him how long ago.

He said, "Not two three minutes ago."

I thumbed the safety off my gun, turned out the boiler room light and stepped into the areaway. It was ankle deep in water. The rain slanting in silver sheets made it impossible to see two feet ahead. I walked slowly up the stone steps to the alley.

The wind on the level was worse. I had to brace myself against it. I doubted the Greek could have gone very far. He hadn't.

I found him twenty feet from the mouth of the alley, face down in a puddle. He was dead. But someone had gotten to him before I had. His pockets were tugged inside out. His sap, his gun, if he had had one, his papers, his wallet, his money, were gone. He was a stranger to me. There was nothing to give me the least inkling of who he was, what he had been doing in Schermerhorn's room, or why he had posed as Bill Harris.

CHAPTER THREE

CALLING ALL CARS

THE BUILDING WAS A TWO STORY yellow brick four-flat in a neighborhood of modest homes. The houses were rather widely spaced. A row of Lombardy poplars that had lost most of their leaves lined the curb. I sat a moment listening to the rain on the steel roof of the cab and looking into one of the lighted windows. The living room I could sec into was comfortably furnished but distinctly working class. I didn't know who the John H. Thompsons were, or thought I didn't at the time, but I did have a fair idea of their connection with Schermerhorn. Their number being the one phone call he had made it seemed logical to assume they were the parents of his dead buddy, Jack.

"You want me to wait?" the driver asked.

I told him I'd get his license if he left me stuck out in the sticks.

"It's a nasty night," he agreed.

Sitting had stiffened my shoulder and the rain hadn't helped it any. It was a job to get out of the cab. As I opened the door a stream of water ran off the roof and down my neck. But it didn't make much difference. I couldn't be any wetter.

The name was hand-printed on a card under one of the bells. I pressed the bell three times and the inner door of the entrance hall clicked as someone in the Thompson apartment pushed a button. I missed the door on the first try and had to go back and ring again. When I did get in a tired-eyed, grizzled, man some years this side of fifty was standing in the open doorway of the left hand first floor apartment. I had evidently called him from his supper as he still held a napkin in one hand.

"Yes—?" he asked me.

His wife, a pleasant-faced woman a few years younger than he was, peered at me over his shoulder.

I knew them as soon as I saw them. It hadn't been the name Fred Able that had rung a faint bell in my mind. It had been his Cloverdale, Iowa address.

"Yes—?" Thompson repeated.

I told him, "You don't know me, Mr. Thompson. But my name is Doyle, Tom Doyle. And I was one of the private agency men called in on the Johnny Doll-Fanchon case."

He said, "Oh, I see. A detective."

He wasn't pleased. I didn't blame him. Both he and Mrs. Thompson had taken quite a pushing around from various sources for merely having the simple courage of their convictions and for refusing to be dissuaded from telling the 'truth, the whole truth, and nothing but the truth'.

My part in the case had been minor. It had broken the year before when, racket rivals for years, Johnny Doll had burned down Frenchy Fanchon in Frenchy's office at the Club Cherie over Lupe's alleged affections.

The shooting had not been entirely unexpected. There had been the usual threats on both sides. But, after the smell of the cordite had burned away, it had been only natural that Johnny Doll had pleaded 'being elsewhere at the time'.

More, his alibi seemed tight. None of Frenchy's employees had seen him at the club that night. The murder gun, left at the scene, could not be traced to him. Johnny maintained that at the time Frenchy had been killed he had been in Cal Morgan's apartment sleeping off a three day drunk. Morgan had sworn on the book this was so.

It had looked like one of those things. Then, several days after the shooting, one of State's Attorney Beamer's bright young boys uncovered the fact that on the night of the shooting a Mr. and Mrs. Thompson had reserved and occupied table No. 26 which, while well back among the potted palms and away from the dance floor, commanded an unobstructed view of the corridor leading to Frenchy's office.

An extensive press and radio campaign had brought them into Beamer's office, timid in unfamiliar surroundings, but willing to tell what they had seen.

A farm couple from Iowa, unable to work their acreage after the induction of their only son into the Armed Forces, they had recently sold their farm and settled in Chicago. Their visit to the Club Cherie had been their first and, they vowed, their last visit to a night club. And while they hadn't seen Johnny shoot Frenchy they had seen him enter the office, they had heard the shots, and they had seen him leave. They picked his picture from the gallery.

They picked him out of a line-up. And he was indicted, convicted, and sentenced to die on their unbiased testimony.

I had come into the case, briefly, when Cal Morgan, admitting to me that he had merely alibied Johnny because they had been boys together and Johnny had sworn on his word of honor that he had not killed Frenchy, had hired me to check the Thompson's background for some possible flaw in their characters at which the defense could pick. But I had been unable to find one. They had lived on the south side then. And while their new neighbors had known very little about them, what they had known was good. A phone call to the sheriff of Mears County had established them, beyond doubt, as a hard-working, religious, prosperous, farm couple whom their former community had been very sorry to lose.

The whole affair had been a headache for Morgan. Due to his political pull he had wriggled out of a perjury rap but it had cost him God knew how much money. His only gain for attempting to give his former boyhood pal a break, had been the dubious privilege of buying the money losing Club Cherie from Frenchy's heirs at about ninety cents on the dollar, and having the fading Lupe choose him as her new 'protector'. He had told me frankly after the trial that if Johnny had been acquitted he believed that he would have shot him for getting him into the mess.

Thompson cleared his throat. "If it's something concerning Mr. Doll, I'm sorry, but—"

I got my foot in the door before he could close it. "I'm not here on Doll's behalf," I told him. "I merely want to know if a young man named Benny Schermerhorn called on you this morning."

Mrs. Thompson spoke for the first time. "He was here right after lunch. I mind I'd just cleared the dishes away." She was indignant about it. "He tried to tell us our Jack was dead. He tried to *pay* us to believe it."

"Wanted to give us eight thousand two hundred dollars," Thompson added.

I said, "But you wouldn't take it because your contention is that your son isn't dead."

"That's right," Thompson nodded. He confided, "You see that telegram from the War Department was a mistake. Oh, there's some reason for us not hearing from Johnny. Might even be that he was took a prisoner." His voice cracked slightly but his chin jutted out to compensate. "But mother and I both know that he is alive and well."

I said I was pleased to hear it. "But about young Schermerhorn. I wonder if I might come in and ask you a few questions concerning his visit here."

He looked dubious. She told me, "Of course you can. Why, you're sopping wet." What with the sapping and the jolting it had taken my shoulder had done some bleeding, enough to soak through the bandage and my shirt. "And you've been hurt. You come right in and dry out and rest yourself a piece."

"Yes'm," I said meekly.

I followed her into the Grand Rapids parlor. Thompson helped me off with my coat. She clucked like a setting hen. "Now you sit here right next to the radiator, Mr.—what did you say your name was?"

I told her, "Doyle."

Thompson brightened a trifle. "We knew a Doyle back home. Fine fellow. And a mighty good farmer, too. Could be that you are related."

I admitted it was possible. "But, now, about young Schermerhorn—"

Thompson sat down on the sofa and leaned over and tapped my knee. "You know what we been thinking?"

I said that I did not.

"We been thinking, he confided, "that money could have been an attempted bribe to get us to change our story about Mr. Doll, now that his end's come so near."

It was an angle I hadn't considered. I didn't think much of it. In that case young Schermerhorn would hardly have come to me. On the other hand, Burson of Adams, Burson, and Connell had been Johnny Doll's lawyer. And the last time we had discussed the case he had admitted the office was still working on several angles in hope of at least a commutation of sentence. I asked if an Attorney Burson had contacted them recently.

Both said that he had not.

I described the Greek I had killed and asked them if they knew him. They said they did not but both brightened perceptibly when I mentioned Fred Abie's name.

"Yes, we know Fred well," Thompson told me. "He farms a hundred and sixty acres just the other side of Cloverdale, up near the county line." He looked at me expectantly. "But what about Fred, Mr. Doyle?"

I told them the story as I knew it, exactly as it had happened. When I finished, her eyes were bright with tears.

"Oh, the poor boy, the poor boy."

Thompson spread his hands in a futile gesture. "It beats me," he admitted. "No one had any call to kill Fred that I know of, or the boy either for that matter." His jaw jutted out again. "But that couldn't have been Jack's money that he tried to give us. 'Cause our boy Jack ain't dead. And the War Department nor anyone else can make me believe it neither."

His wife nodded staunch agreement.

I made no comment.

"Why, say," Thompson continued. "I guess we'd know it if he was." He fished a fat scrap book out from under the table. "And when Jack comes home he's going to get a big kick out of 'em *trying* to worry us so. Here, lemme show you—"

He turned a dozen pages of baby pictures, stock prize ribbons, 4H write-ups, and diplomas, pausing briefly at a page containing a picture of a good looking lad in a Marine uniform.

"That's our boy," Mrs. Thompson said proudly.

I said he was a fine looking boy and glanced at a news clipping on the opposite page.

It was a clipping from the Mears County News regretting the sale of the Thompson farm and the removal of the Thompsons to Chicago.

Thompson continued to turn pages.

"Farm work's awful hard," Mrs. Thompson told me. "That's the main reason we sold. We didn't want Jack to have to feel obligated to work the home place when he comes back from the war."

Thompson found what he was looking for. It was an official telegram from the War Department beginning—

The Secretary Of War regrets to inform you that your son Pfc. John Thompson, Jr.—

Thompson said, "We're saving it to show Jack."

He turned the next twelve pages slowly. Each page contained a monthly government insurance check. "Just like we're saving these." His eyes were wet. "Ought to give him a laugh, eh, Mr. Doyle?"

I didn't say anything. Neither did his wife. He wiped his eyes with the back of his hand and looked down at his shoes. I had it then.

He knew. She knew. They both knew their boy was dead. But miracles did happen. And as long as they refused to admit death openly they had a faint ray of hope to which to cling. The money didn't matter. They had plenty of money. But if they had accepted the money from young Schermerhorn, if they cashed even one of the insurance checks, that last ray of hope was dispelled. Then their boy was dead and paid for and all of their dreams for him were dust. It was easier to pretend.

But I couldn't pretend. Four men were dead. And the Thompsons, pathetic in their grief as they were, were the only common denominator. Young Schermerhorn had been a friend of their dead boy. Fred Able had been a friend of theirs. Burson of Adams, Burson, and Connell, was Doll's lawyer.

I made one last attempt by asking, "When did you last see Fred Able?"

Thompson thought a moment. "It must be over a year. Yes, maybe fourteen, fifteen months. The last time I saw Fred was when we auctioned off our stock. He bought the bay team, and, I think, a couple of Jersey heifers."

"And you know of no reason why he should have come to see me?"

Both said that they did not.

I got up and picked up my coat. "Well, thanks for talking to me."

"Not at all. Glad to help," Thompson said. He helped me on with my coat and both he and Mrs. Thompson walked to the door with me insisting I come again. I said I would, crossing mental fingers.

The rain was still beating at the few leaves on the poplars. The hacker was slumped in his seat listening to police calls.

He straightened, grinning, as I climbed into the cab. "I was beginning to think you'd ditched me. Where now, chum?"

"That's the problem," I told him.

I wanted to check with Nobby on both Barney and the Greek. But I needed a change of clothes. If I went home, once Sue had seen my shoulder, there would be no getting out without a scene. Then I remembered that I had a packed bag at the office and gave him the address.

He switched off the radio and ground the starter. "Some guy named Doyle," he informed me over his shoulder, "is running the cops nuts. There's a Code 32 out on him but they can't find him anywhere."

Unless it had changed in the last few hours Code 32 was murder. I said, "No kidding? Who did Doyle kill?"

The tires made soft sucking sounds on the wet pavement as he swung in a U turn.

"Some guy named Bill Harris," he told me. "A lad out of the S.A.'s office."

CHAPTER FOUR

H.Q. PARLEY

THERE WERE, PERHAPS, a half dozen plainclothes men in the lobby of H.Q. Several looked up as I passed but no one attempted to stop me. I rode as far as Nobby's floor with Simmy Gleason of Morals.

"I hear you killed someone, Tom," he told me pleasantly.

"So I hear," I said. "As a matter of fact. I did. But it didn't happen to be Bill Harris." I gave him the lad's description and asked if it rang any bell. He said not in particular.

There was a cluster of reporters and pic men in the corridor outside of Nobby's door. I told them I had nothing to say at the moment but would male a statement later.

Jim Cooper was on the door. He squeezed my arm as he eased me in. "Give 'em hell, Irish."

I said I intended to.

There was a tight ring of men around Nobby's desk, one of them talking earnestly and banging the wood lightly with his fist to emphasize his points.

I walked up and split the group. "Okay. Here I am," I told Nobby. "What's the idea of putting out a 32 on me? I turned that stiff in the alley in to West Chicago Avenue. And what's more, I told the desk clerk at the Devon Arms to call you at Barney's office."

He pointed the mangled butt of his cigar at Beamer. "It seems to have been his idea."

The sad sack's face turned as white as his shirt. "Now just a minute, Doyle. Let's not be hasty. It just so happened that I got there before Nobby did. And when the desk clerk told me that Sergeant Harris of my office had been killed—"

I said, "You couldn't wait to check. You had to put out a 32 on me. Why I ought to—"

I started to give him the back of my hand across the lips and someone behind me caught my arm.

"Ah ah. Mustn't hit State's Attorneys. Remember you are a papa bird now."

Sue had been crying. I took her in my good arm. "Baby, what are you doing here?"

She said she had been listening to the radio ever since Elsie had called her. "She told me you were wounded."

"When we get home I'll prove it," I promised. "But it just so happens that I stopped in at Doc Fabers for a gauze re-capping job. Also at the office for dry clothes."

The S.A. gave Nobby a dirty look. "I thought you told me you posted Turk Ginnis at his office?"

I said, "He did. But Turk and I were born in the same block back of the Yards. And he was willing to take my word when I said I was on my way here."

Nobby wanted to know how my shoulder felt.

I told him, "Lousy."

Bill Harris had been the lad who had been pounding on Nobby's desk. He insisted on shaking hands. "Kill me again some time, Tom. I'm over in Marty's back room eighty bucks winner playing stud and the cards are just beginning to run against me when the flash comes over the band."

Beamer had recovered his composure. "So I was too hasty in putting out a wanted on you, Doyle," he admitted. "But that doesn't explain away the dead man in the alley. Why did you kill him?"

I said, "Because he tried to kill me. And don't give me that kill-crazy veteran stuff." I told them what had happened, adding nothing, leaving nothing out.

Harris suggested that after the Greek had reached the alley someone had rolled him for a drunk.

I said it sounded more logical to me that someone had been waiting for him and had turned him inside out in an attempt to delay identification.

Nobby agreed, saying that the big Greek's fingerprints weren't in the B. of I.'s files but they were checking with Washington. He wanted to know, "But why should he pick Bill Harris to impersonate?"

Beamer said that seemed immaterial to him.

I said, "Nothing is immaterial in murder. Who knew you were off duty, Bill?"

He shrugged. "Who didn't. I'm working the eight to four. Maybe fifty guys saw me over at Marty's. I think the question is, who knew that the desk clerk at the Devon Arms didn't know me?"

"We could kick that around all night," Nobby told him. He turned back to me. "The squad I sent out to Avers Avenue got there about ten minutes after you'd gone. Are those old folks really that pair of farmers who sat Johnny Doll in the chair?"

I said they were.

He reached for his phone and called the squad room. "In that case I'd better put a stake-out on the building. Although I'll be damned if I can see how anything that has happened tonight could possibly help Johnny."

When he had finished with his arrangements to have the Thompsons guarded, he asked if I thought they were really crazy.

I told him, "Not in the accepted sense of the word. They know their boy is dead, has been dead for twelve months, but—"

"Fourteen months," Nobby corrected. "I checked that angle with the War Department when I checked on young Schermerhorn to make certain his papers were genuine."

I continued, "Their turning down the money that young Schermerhorn tried to give them is merely a defense fixation of some kind. By refusing to believe he's dead they're kidding themselves that—" It dawned on me what he had said. "How long did you say young Thompson had been dead?"

He fished through the papers on his desk.

"Fourteen months. I've got the exact date somewhere. Why?"

I asked Sue if she had a cigarette. She fished a crumpled one from her purse that tasted like perfume.

"Why?" Nobby repeated.

"I just wondered," I lied. Something was screwy somewhere. There had only been twelve insurance checks in the scrap book.

Beamer hooted. "Now don't try to tell me you think the Thompsons killed Barney Connell and the two men in your office."

I said frankly that I knew they had not.

Bill Harris asked, "How about a Monelli angle?"

I asked what he meant by the Monelli angle.

He said, "It's common knowledge that your testimony will send Monelli over the road. But with you out of the way he has a chance of beating the rap."

I said that might explain the attack on me but why kill young Schermerhorn and Fred Able?

He said, "You fry as hard for one as for three. And if Schermerhorn and the farmer saw Monelli burn you down—" He shrugged.

I admitted what he said was possible, but pointed out that after all it was only an arson case. The most Monelli was facing was two to ten and it hardly seemed plausible that he would go out on the big limb for that. Besides, Barney had been his lawyer. At least he'd been one of the firm.

Nobby reached for his phone.

Beamer said, "By all means bring Monelli in for questioning." He looked at me. "But I am beginning to wonder if it is possible that we haven't been able to see the mountain because it is in front of our noses."

I asked what he meant by that crack.

He addressed himself to Nobby. "A young man, a stranger to our city, walked into Doyle's office with eight thousand dollars and a fantastic story. At least, so Doyle says. A few moments later a mysterious killer, whom no one in the building saw, walked in, still according to Doyle, and for no apparent reason shot to death the young man and a client in his outer office, but only mildly injured Doyle. Cal Morgan and the police and I arrived a few minutes later to find him conscious but the eight thousand dollars gone. And not half an hour after Doyle is on his feet again, he *discovers* a third dead man, where again there is no known motive for murder, where again no one saw the killer. Still later a fourth man is killed. And who is on the scene this time? Who indeed but Thomas Doyle."

It was inane. It was stupid. It was Beamer.

My throat tight, I said, "So—?"

He looked at me down his nose. "So I'm beginning to wonder whether I wasn't right in putting out a wanted on you, beginning to wonder whether it might not have been wise to search you when we first entered your office."

I told Sue, "I'm going to do it." She said, "If you don't, I will." Harris caught at my arm. I shook him off and hit Beamer so hard he bounced. He got to his feet with a bloody Chinese mustache screaming for Nobby to arrest me.

Nobby shook his head. "You had that coming. You've no reason to make a crack like that about Tom."

Beamer attempted to dam the claret streaming out of his nose. "He's a kill-crazy vet," he screamed. "He's money mad."

I admitted I liked money. "I like to make it. I like to spend it," I told him. "But I don't see that I'm any different from you. How many of your monthly checks have you turned back to the city?"

He screamed he'd get my license. I said that was possible. "But you make another crack like that and I'll clip you again. I'd clip you if you were the Attorney General of the United States."

Nobby stood up behind his desk. "Cut it out, you two."

Beamer got his nose under control. "You are still suspect in my book," he told me. "And until my office has had a chance to make a thorough investigation, you stay out of this case."

I said, "No dice. That wouldn't be fair to my client."

He screamed, "You have no client."

"Oh, yes, I have," I told him. "Young Schermerhorn paid me twenty bucks to deliver the missing eight grand two hundred to Jack Thompson's parents. And until I do I still have a client and a case."

Beamer said, "You're crazy."

"Indubitably," I agreed.

Sue told him, smiling, "But he is sweet when you get to know him."

He gave her a dirty look, nodded curtly at Harris and stalked stiff-legged out of the office. Harris spread his hands in a futile gesture and followed.

Nobby sat back of his desk again. "You shouldn't have hit him, Tom. After all, he is the State's Attorney."

"It's only a matter of time," I admitted. "If he gets in this coming election I can kiss my license good-bye."

I almost felt sorry for Beamer. He was a living example of the adage, to make a friend let a man do you a favor. To make an enemy do him one. He'd been grand when I'd first gotten out of the Army and opened up on my own after ten years with Inter-Ocean. But he knew, the Force knew, most of the newsmen knew, that the only reason he had gotten a second term was because when I cracked the Hartley and McDonald case I took the cash and I let the credit go—to him. And he'd hated my intestines ever since.

Cole Hooper, Nobby's second in command, cleared his throat softly. "Now—where were we?"

"Right where we started," I told him. "We have four stiffs on our hands. I know why one of them died. I killed him. But I don't know what the Greek wanted in Schermerhorn's room, or what his connection was to Schermerhorn, Able, and Barney."

Nobby bit the end from a cigar. "Just what did Barney tell you over the phone?"

I repeated what I had told him earlier, adding, "I asked him what he was talking about. He said, 'murder'. Then his voice trailed off. I thought at the time it was a rib. But whoever killed him must have walked into his office right then, forced him to hang up and let him have it. No one heard the shot?"

He said they had not. Adams was out of town. Burson had stopped in to say good night a few minutes before five. Barney hadn't been at his desk. But as his coat and hat and briefcase were still on a chair in the office, the presumption was that he was somewhere else in the building and Burson had made no further effort too find him.

"Barney was dead in the washroom then."

"That's what Terry figures."

I said, "Those office walls are practically soundproof. That, and a silencer, could explain why the shot wasn't heard. But how about the receptionist? She must have made a list of his callers."

Nobby said she had. But Barney had no callers after four. However, he pointed out, that meant little as the library door opening into the hall was habitually left open during working hours so the partners could come and go without appearing in the reception room. Anyone knowing that could have come and left unseen by the office force.

"And there is no dissension in the firm?"

"None on the surface." He bit the mangled end off his cigar and chewed it thoughtfully. "Also no fingerprints and no brass. That goes for your office, too. Damnedest case I've ever seen."

I asked if he had checked on Fred Able.

He said Cole had.

Cole told me, "His county sheriff gives him a clean bill of health. The worst thing he could say about him was that he was tight, financially, and drove a pretty shrewd bargain."

"But why should he come to see me?" I thought of what Able had said. "What could he have to sell me?"

Cole shook his head and said he was damned if he knew.

"The Thompsons knew him?" Nobby asked.

I said they did, at least so they had told me. I also said it seemed a trifle odd to me that if Able had known them in Iowa that he hadn't looked them up.

Cole said, "He probably intended to. As far as I could ascertain he only reached town this morning."

Nobby swore under his breath out of respect for Sue. "Which brings us right back to where we were. We have four dead men on our hands and all we really know is that they are dead."

"Well, that's a start," Sue said brightly.

She wanted to know how much longer I'd probably be, as she had called in the girl downstairs to sit with the twins at a dollar an hour. I told her I hadn't the least idea.

"Let's go back to the beginning," I suggested. "You can help us there, Jim. You talked to the starter and all the elevator boys."

Curtis said he had.

"And while no one saw anyone carrying a machine gun, they all heard the shots."

He said that was correct.

"And they are positive it was a machine gun they heard?"

He said they were, that there had been two separate blasts, a burst of three and four the first time. And two and three the second time.

"Then where's the brass?" I asked him

Nobby slid that had been bothering him.

I pointed out, "The average person does not know the difference between the sound of a machine gun, an automatic, a revolver, and a back-fire. Where were Lupe and Beamer and Morgan while all this was going on?"

He consulted his notes, said, "Lupe was in the car. Beamer was in the lobby buying a cigar. And Morgan had walked upstairs to—"

I said, "He walked?"

Curtis looked at his notes again. "That's what I have written here. After all, the cages are pretty busy around five and Cooper's office is only up one floor."

I asked if Morgan had made a statement. He said he had. I asked him to read it to me.

He began, " 'I tried Cooper's door. It was locked. As he had obviously gone for the day I started to return to the car. But on reaching the stairhead I was alarmed to hear a burst of machine-gun fire on the floor above. I debated investigating and decided I had better inform the State's Attorney first. But before I could reach the lobby I heard a second burst of machine-gun fire.' "

I asked how long a time elapsed between bursts.

"Morgan says maybe ten seconds," he told me. "But other folks who heard the shots say longer."

"What the hell?" Nobby asked. "You trying to pin this on Cal?"

"Not particularly," I said. "There's no bad blood between us. But in your opinion, do you think that a former paving contractor would know the difference between machine-gun fire and a rapidly fired revolver?"

He said he doubted it.

"For the record," I told Curtis. "Just where was Morgan when this second burst was fired. How far from the lobby?"

"He was practically in it," Curtis assured me. "Kip, the starter, said he burst out the door almost simultaneously with the second burst of shots, calling that something was wrong on the third floor."

I said, "Then that takes any possible onus off Morgan. Aside from having no motive for being mixed up in this, he couldn't be in two places at the same time. But I still don't understand why there were two spaced bursts of shots."

Cole explained, "That's simple. The killer got you and young Schermerhorn with the first one and Fred Able with the second."

I said, "The hell he did. The first shots that were fired were fired at young Schermerhorn and me. And taking Cal Morgan's estimation of a lapse of ten seconds between bursts, where was Fred Able all that time? Still sitting in a chair in my outer office waiting to be shot?"

Nobby pressed his palms to his forehead and ran them back over his hair. "My old mother, rest her soul, wanted me to be a priest. She—" He broke off to answer his phone, said yes three times, I see twice, and banged the receiver back into its cradle. "That," he told us, "was Washington with the report on the Greek. His name, it would seem, was Bala Gediz, alias Joe Gediz. He wasn't a Greek. He was a Turk. At the time of his arrest he gave his profession as a fry cook. And his only criminal record consists in having been picked up on a Mann Act charge in New Orleans in 1942."

I said, "Well, that clears up everything. When I surprised him in 705, Gediz was undoubtedly looking for Schermerhorn's mother's recipe for wiener schnitzel."

Sue asked Cole, "This goes on for hours."

"And often," he assured her.

I took stock of what we knew. It wasn't much. But it was a start. And the solution of an involved murder case seldom springs phoenix-like from the smoldering ashes. More often than not, you have to sift through ashes and clinkers for days, damn cold ones at that.

"I'm going to call it a night," I told Nobby. "But before I do, there are three things I want to know."

He wanted to know what they were.

I told him, "Why young Thompson's parents have only saved twelve of his fourteen insurance checks. Why the State's Attorney, who was supposed to be at a political rally at the Club Cherie, got the flash on Gediz and arrived at the Devon Arms before you did. Third, and most important, I want to ask Cal Morgan to allow me to check through the social security records of the Club Cherie in an attempt to find out if Frenchy Fanchon ever employed Bala Gediz in the Club kitchen."

Nobby accused, "You've something on your mind."

I admitted I had, but said it was too nebulous to outline. Then I asked Sue if she could eat something.

"At the Club Cherie? Anything," she assured me.

Nobby started to argue with me, changed his mind. "Watch him, Sue," he said. "There's a lot more here than has boiled to the surface so far. In fact, I've a hunch we're handling dynamite."

She brushed my cheek with her lips. "Did you ever try to talk sense to a crazy Irishman?

"I married him because I was tired of being alone nights. I thought we'd sit home and read to each other and talk and listen to the radio like any normal couple. And what did I get out of marriage?" She saw my grin and added, "I'll slap your face if you say 'twins'."

CHAPTER FIVE

COLD ASHES

A THREE-STOREY GRAY STONE FRONT not far from the Drake Hotel, the Club Cherie had begun as a speakeasy under Moran protection sometime during the '20's and had merely continued after repeal, the major changes being in the quality of the whiskey sold and a neon sign instead of a peck-hole.

As the doorman bowed us in, Lupe was singing "Laura." The crow's feet didn't show in the spotlight and she still had all of her curves. She looked like a million dollars in War Bonds. What was more, she could sell a number.

It had been some time since I had given the club a play and the new headwaiter didn't know me. He was *desolado* but if the *señor* had not made a *reservation* he would be *incapaz* to seat us.

Sue wanted to know what he had said.

I said it sounded like "no."

A not too large club catering to the limousine trade, most of the tables were occupied but there were a few bare covers.

She said, "Tell him you know Cal Morgan."

I said he heard that in his sleep and creased a ten dollar bill lengthways. "Stupid of me," I lied. "I remember now. I did make a reservation. The name is Doyle. Remember, I told you over the phone that I didn't care about the location of the table, that in fact I preferred it away from the dance floor."

He palmed the bill and struck his forehead with the back of his hand. *"Si, señor.* I, too, remember now. How *estupido* of me."

I peeled off my topcoat, gave it with my hat to the shapely blonde bandit in the check room and followed him through the potted palms to a table for two with a better view of the corridor and the kitchen than it had of the floor show.

"The steak better be good," Sue muttered. "I thought you said Morgan was losing money."

"His help make more than he does," I told her.

That was factual. He had, considering its seating capacity, paid too much for the club in the first place. The food, the floor show, the service was excellent. But name bands and good floor shows come high. And O.P.A. ceiling prices had cut his net to even less than Frenchy had taken in. And Frenchy hadn't even pretended to make a profit. His specialty had been blackmail. Trying to run the club on the level, Morgan had gone deep in the red.

Eduarado wanted to know if the table was satisfactory. I told him it was fine. It was. It was table No. 26, the one at which the Thompsons had sat on the night that Frenchy had been killed.

As he pulled out a chair I remarked it must be nice for Miss Lupe to have a countryman to talk to.

He told me rather wryly, *"Pardoname, señor.* But the *Señorita Lupe no hablo Espanol."*

When he had gone, Sue asked, "Whose canary did you eat?"

"He just told me the whole thing," I told her. "And is this going to be a blow to Morgan!"

She said, "You mean Lupe is mixed up in this?"

Before I could say yes or no, a waiter put water before us and stood by to take our order. I ordered two steaks medium rare, a bottle of rye and ten shot glasses.

He took it in his stride. "Yes, sir. Very well, sir."

Sue warned me that if I got high she was, steak or no steak, going straight home to the twins. "Besides, you don't dare drink too much. You know what Nobby said."

I told her that I had no intention of pitching one.

She said, "You ordered ten glasses."

"Those are the ten little Indians," I said.

The waiter returned with the bottle and the glasses, put them on the table and started for the kitchen. I called him back, *"Garçon.* Tell Joe to rub my steak lightly with garlic before he puts it on the broiler. He knows just how I like it. Tell him it's for Mr. Doyle."

I could read his mind. He had me tabbed as a tin horn sport showing off before his girl. They get them all the time. They're the same breed of *homo sapiens* as the lads who are willing to pay twice as much for a pair of punched Annie Oakleys as they are for two on the aisle. I could see him debating calling me, then remember that tin horns tip well. "I'll be pleased to tell the cook to rub your steak lightly with garlic, sir. But our present cook's name is Leo, sir. Joe must have cooked here before my time."

Sue said, "I thought you were going to ask Mr. Morgan for permission to look through his social security records."

I said I was taking a short cut and arranged the shot glasses to suit me. A few minutes later Morgan came out of his office, started up toward the front of the place, saw us and came over to the table.

"Why didn't you have someone tell me you were here, Tom?" he complained. "I'd have had them squeeze another table in where you could see the show."

I said our table was fine.

He looked at the shot glasses and grinned. "What's the big idea?"

I said, "I'm detecting. Some lads grow orchids to stimulate their minds. Some take it in the arm. Some even write on dominoes. But I do my best work with glasses."

He told Sue I was a card. Then he wanted to know how I felt. I told him I still felt lousy.

He pulled up a chair and sat down. "With your permission. Anything new on the shooting, Tom?"

I said not on Schermerhorn or Able or Barney and asked him if he had heard of the affair at the Devon Arms.

"Shortly after it broke," he admitted. "In fact I took the phone call for the S.A."

I asked him, "From whom?"

He shook his head. "The lad on the other end didn't say. All I know is that it was a man's voice and he asked me to tell the Slate's Attorney that there had been a shooting at the Devon Arms and he had better get over there as quickly as he could."

I poured whiskey in one of the glasses, telling him, "The dead lad's name was Bala Gediz, alias Joe. And according to the files of the F.B.I, he seems to have been a cook. You wouldn't know, offhand, if he ever worked here at the Club?"

He rolled the name on his tongue. "Bala Gediz. It's not a common name. But I can't say that I recall it. However, he might have worked here while Frenchy was running the Club."

I asked if the name would show on his social security records.

He nodded. "On Frenchy's records, yes. But they are all down in a storeroom in the basement. When I took over, I made a clean sweep. I didn't want anything that even smelled of that blackmailer." He glanced through the potted palms to where Lupe was just finishing her number. "In fact Lupe is the only holdover. It may be she will know if this Gediz ever worked here. We'll ask her."

A waiter brought a check to the table for him to okay. He initialed it without looking at the name or the amount. "It's probably rubber," he told me. "Such a business. I wish I was back paving streets."

I said I had often wondered why he had given it up. He said he had not but that he was making more money renting his heavy road equipment such as bull-dozers and tractors and earth-moving equipment to the government for out of the country jobs than he could make by bidding on local contracts. "They're suckers to pay the rentals, they are," he told me. "But who am I to kick a dollar in the nose?"

Lupe squealed with pleasure when she saw me. "Ees Meester Doyle." She hugged and kissed me soundly, then smiled at Sue. "An' thees ees Mrs. Doyle. I am ver' pleased to know you."

Sue said, "How do you do?"

Lupe wanted to know how I felt.

"He still feels lousy," Sue told her.

Morgan got a chair for Lupe, then nodded at the shot glasses. "Tom is detecting. He says that he does it with glasses."

She nodded brightly. "Eech glass ees stand for a suspect or for a dead man, no?"

I said she was a bright girl and she wanted to know which was which.

I touched a glass standing by itself. "This is Barney Connell," I told her. "These two over here are myself and young Schermerhorn. This is the farmer in my outer office. These two way over here are the Thompsons, the couple who saw Frenchy shot. This lone one is Bala Gediz. And these three in a line are yourself, Cal, and State's Attorney Beamer."

Morgan said testily, "I wasn't aware I was a suspect."

I let him sweat while I sipped at the whiskey in the glass that I had designated as myself. "No, you're in the clear with the department," I told him. "In the first place why should you shoot me, young Schermerhorn, and Able? In the second place, you couldn't very well have been in my office playing trigger man and in the lobby at the same time."

He punched me lightly on the shoulder, grinning. "You son of a gun. You had me going for a minute."

"But tell me this, Cal," I asked him. "Could those shots you heard have been fired from a revolver, possibly two revolvers, rather than from a machine gun?"

Lupe said, "Positeevely not." She imitated a machine gun again. "Thees I am hear weeth my own ears."

Morgan wasn't so certain. All he would commit himself to was that he had heard a lot of shots fired in two separate bursts."

I took his glass from the three in a row and put it to one side. "Okay. We'll pull you out of the picture. Now, Lupe, you tell me this."

She said, "Yes—?" uncertainly.

"You didn't get out of the car until after the shots were fired?"

"I deed not."

I picked her glass from the table. "Which would seem to eliminate you. Now, tell me this." I tapped the glass standing for Beamer. "Where did you and Cal pick up the State's Attorney?"

She wrinkled her forehead in thought. It wrinkled easy. She admitted being thirty but she was closer to forty and despite the fortunes she had spent on them, her face and her curves were beginning to sag. "Eet was not at his office," she admitted. She looked at Morgan.

He sat staring at me intently, trying to read my mind. "Tell Tom the truth," he told her without taking his eyes from my face. "The truth, the whole truth, and nothing but the truth."

She said, "Eet was een front of 221 N. La Salle."

"But the State's Attorney was with you in the car all the time you waited for Cal?" I poised my hand over his glass.

Her eyes widened slightly. "No. He was not. He went eento your office building, he said to buy cigars."

I asked Morgan, "But he was in the lobby when you heard the second burst of shots?"

He was perspiring now, sweat standing out in tiny beads on his forehead. "For God's sake stop beating around the bush, Doyle. What are you driving at?"

I repeated my question.

"I don't recall where Beamer was," he said flatly. "I do remember running out to the car to tell him about the shots and hearing Lupe say that he had gone into the building to buy cigars. Then, I believe, he joined me at the car and we went up to your office together with the building superintendent and a pair of radio car men who happened to be passing by."

I tapped the glass that was Beamer. "Now tell me this, Lupe. Was State's Attorney Beamer here in the club on the night that Frenchy was shot?"

She said she could not remember distinctly but she had a faint impression that he was.

"And what hold did Frenchy have on him?"

Morgan pushed back his chair and got up. "That's enough of that talk, Doyle. The State's Attorney may not be perfect but—"

I pounded, "Think back. Johnny Doll was practically in the clear. He couldn't prove he hadn't shot Frenchy, but the State couldn't prove he had. The case could and undoubtedly would have dragged on for months with a lot of soiled linen being aired. Then, out of nowhere, the couple who sat at this table appeared in Beamer's office and put the finger on Johnny. When he burns next Tuesday night, the case is closed forever. If the real killer confesses Wednesday morning no one would dare to bring him to trial because of the howl that would be raised when the public learned that an innocent man had been executed."

Lupe studied my face thoughtfully.

Morgan poured himself a drink, his hand shaking so badly that he poured most of it on the table. "But I had you check on the Thompsons," he protested. "And they aren't the type who would perjure themselves."

"No. I doubt the Thompsons would perjure themselves," I agreed. "But they naturally were excited at the time and you know as well as I do that no two witnesses to a shooting ever agree on just what happened or what the lad who did the shooting looked like. And suppose they had been shown pictures of Johnny, been allowed to read his record, been told that he was a hoodlum who, having killed before, might even kill again, and that in the opinion of the State's Attorney's office, an office which they respect highly, he was most likely the man whom they had seen."

"I don't know what to say," Morgan admitted. "Johnny still swears he didn't kill Frenchy. And I saw him just the other day after his last appeal had been denied."

Lupe wet her lips with her tongue, then blew up at a wisp of loose hair. "Now I theenk back, ees come to me. Frenchy deed have, how you say, something on Meester Beamer. But what thees ees, I cannot say."

I tapped the glass that stood for Gediz. "How about Bala Gediz? Do you remember him, Lupe? Was he a cook here at the time."

She considered her answer, nodded. "Y-yes. He ees cook here on thee night of thee shooting. But we are call heem Joe. He ees beeg man, seex feet an' dark."

I nodded at the glass in the kitchen door. "And he could have seen everything that the Thompsons saw?"

Morgan said sharply, "Of course he could. My God, how blind we've been. What are you going to do, Doyle? Lay your facts in front of Nobby?"

I scowled at him. "What facts? I haven't any. All I have is a theory. And it takes more than theory to pin a murder on a State's Attorney. Maybe I'm right. Maybe I'm wrong. But before I pull the cork out of the bottle I still have plenty to do."

"Yes—?" Lupe asked.

"One thing that I want to do," I said, "is check on that eight thousand dollars that was taken from my office when Able and Schermerhorn were killed. And if it was Beamer, it shouldn't be too difficult to trace the money to him. He'll be afraid to bank it, so the chances are that he'll stash it in his apartment at least for the time being. All I'll have to do is lure him out of the apartment some way and then go in and pick up the evidence."

Morgan protested, "But assuming it was Beamer who shot Frenchy, supposing he did over-persuade the Thompsons to put the finger on Johnny Doll, why should he have attempted to kill you?"

I pointed out, "Lupe said you picked him up in front of 221. That's Barney's building. Barney was talking to me when he was killed. And it could be that his killer did not know just how much Barney had told me."

The waiter brought in a heavy tray, set it on a service table and looked, hesitant, at the glasses. I told him to take them away.

"You said all you had was a theory," Morgan said. "What would you say would constitute a case against Beamer?"

I said, "Finding the money in his apartment and hearing the Thompsons admit that he had shown them pictures of Johnny before they identified him."

"And your next move is going to be what?"

I said I was going to eat, but that if he wanted to be of help he could send someone to check through Frenchy's records to bear out Dupe's oral assertion that Gediz had worked at the club during the period in question.

"I'll do it myself," he told me.

Lupe stopped to run her fingers through my hair. "You an' your wheeskey glasses. For wan leetle minute you 'ave Lupe worried. I am theenk you theenk I do thees theeng.'"

She followed Morgan down the corridor.

Sue said, "I don't like that woman."

I said there was no law compelling her to like Lupe.

She persisted, "What's more, your theory that Beamer is back of all this doesn't hold water. Granted he is a skunk. Nevertheless—"

"Hush. Eat your red points," I told her.

She poised her knife over her steak. "Besides, when the headwaiter told you that Lupe didn't speak Spanish you grinned like a Cheshire cat and—"

I pointed out, "It cost us ten dollars just to sit down. The steaks and drinks will probably cost fifteen more. Then there's the tip. Now hush and let daddy gormandize in peace or the check comes out of your household allowance."

She gave me a dirty look. "Over my dead and bleeding body."

I glanced over her shoulder down the corridor. Lupe was standing in the doorway of Morgan's office regarding me thoughtfully.

CHAPTER SIX

JOURNEY'S END

DAWN WAS A BLEARY-EYED DISHWATER BLONDE climbing out of the Lake when Curtis and Cooper brought Beamer in. I could hear the little man cursing as soon as they stepped off the elevator.

Morgan cleared his throat nervously.

"I still think you ought to go home," I told Sue.

She pointed out that she had been home for some hours and that before she had returned to Nobby's office she had phoned Elsie to come over and sit with the twins and the dollar-an-hour sitter from downstairs who had been sleeping so soundly that she had been unable to wake her.

Nobby said, "Let her stay." He was nervous. He had a right to be. All I could lose was my license. He had his pension to think of.

Beamer came in handcuffed to Cooper, shaking his free fist at Nobby.

Nobby asked Curtis if they had found the money.

"Yeah," Curtis told him. "We did." He took a sheaf of bills from his pocket and laid it on Nobby's desk. "I make it exactly eight thousand two hundred and twenty dollars. We found it back of the radiator in his bedroom."

Nobby asked me if it was the same money that young Schermerhorn had attempted to give me. I said the amount was correct, but as I didn't have the serial numbers of the bills I couldn't swear it was the same.

"Let's not bother with that right now," I said. "Maybe we do. Maybe we don't. How do you explain the money being found in your apartment?"

"I can't explain it," he admitted. "I never saw it before Cooper fished it out from in back of that radiator."

"You expect us to believe that?"

"It's the truth."

"And I suppose you also deny that you shot Frenchy Fanchon at the Club Cherie some eleven and a half months ago."

His eyes narrowed slightly. "I do."

"And of course it wasn't you who shot Barney Connell, young Schermerhorn, and Fred Able."

The little man stood on his dignity. "Don't be absurd."

"I'll try not to be," I assured him. Cole was standing in the door of the squad room. I asked him for Mr. and Mrs. Thompson.

They came in, eying Beamer warily.

I said, "You, of course, recognize the State's Attorney."

Thompson cleared his throat and said he did.

"And you don't mind repeating in front of State's Attorney Beamer the story that you told Lieutenant Nobby and myself?"

He said he did not. His story was practically verbatim with the supposition that I have outlined to Morgan and Lupe at the Club Cherie. He and Mrs. Thompson had not intended to "come forward," as he phrased it, in the Fanchon-Doll case. But on reading that a city-wide search was being made for them, their sense of duty had won over their dislike of publicity. At their first meeting with the State's Attorney they had told him frankly that their only glimpse of the killer had been a hasty one. But, after he had shown them some dozen pictures of Johnny Doll and had told them of his previous record, they had agreed with the State's Attorney that Johnny Doll, the man already accused of the killing, had been the man whom they had seen.

I said, "And you realize that it was your testimony that convicted Doll and caused him to be sentenced to die?"

Thompson's chin jutted forward. "We do."

"And since then you have had no cause to regret your testimony?"

He started a belligerent denial of regret, changed his mind, and rubbed his chin instead, as Mrs. Thompson whispered something in his ear.

I asked her what she had said.

She hesitated, told me, "Well, it just come to me this minute that the man we identified in court and the State's Attorney are not dissimilar in looks. They are both short, slight-built, light-haired men. And we both remarked to each other the first time we saw him in his office that his face was vaguely familiar."

I expected Beamer to scream that he was being framed. He didn't. His face merely turned a dull brick red as he stared, seemingly puzzled, at Mrs. Thompson.

Morgan got to his feet. "Well, there's your case, Doyle. I'm going to get a little shut-eye."

I told him to stick around while we nailed it down a little tighter. "After all, Johnny Doll was your pal."

He said, "Yes. Of course."

I turned to Lupe. "Now you tell us, Lupe, just where it was that you picked up the State's Attorney this afternoon, rather yesterday afternoon on your way to the rally?"

She looked Beamer in the eyes as she told me. "Eet was een front of 221 North La Salle Street."

"He was just coming out of the building?"

"He was."

"Then the three of you started for the rally at the club. What caused you to turn back?"

"Meester Beamer," she said cruelly. "He said he wanted to buy some cigars." She shrugged. "So, while we were een front of thee building I asked Cal to go up and peek up some orchestrations that Joe Cooper promised to have ready."

"So both Cal and Beamer went into the building. But you remained in the car."

"That ees correct."

"Then how," I asked her, quietly, "did you hear the shots? How did you hear the, you know—" I put my tongue to the roof of my mouth and imitated a machine gun.

"I—" she began, and stopped.

I said, "Hard to explain, isn't it? Especially when we have ascertained by actual test while shots fired in my office can be heard in the lobby, the sound does not carry to the street."

Her palm snaked out and slapped me. "Damn you. Damn you to hell, Doyle. You've been playing cat and mouse with us all the time. You knew when you were at the club. And you'd have made the pinch right then. But you wanted to recover that lousy eight thousand dollars."

I told her, "You're forgetting your accent, Lupe."

She shook her head. "What difference does it make? What—"

I saw the knife in time to slap it from her hand. That finished it as far as she was concerned. She sank down in a chair, buried her face in her hands and sobbed.

Mr. Thompson cleared his throat. "This—er—doesn't seem to concern us. So, if you don't mind—"

I pushed him into a chair so hard that its rungs creaked. It was all I could do to keep from clipping him. "Stick around. So the official telegram was a mistake, eh? So you are saving his insurance checks to give your boy a laugh."

Beamer cleared his throat. "Are you out of your head, Doyle? What's this all about?"

"A minor matter of murder," I told him. "Frenchy Fanchon's to be exact. At least Frenchy's death was the torch that touched off the whole affair."

Beamer protested, "But I didn't kill Frenchy."

I said, "I know you didn't. But you've been as big a sucker as the rest of us. A bigger one in fact. Because you convicted an innocent man on perjured testimony and when this affair breaks in the paper it will probably cost you your re-election."

He stared wide-eyed at the lad I'd pushed into the chair. "Do you mean to tell me that he, that Thompson—"

I said, "I don't know what it is but the chances are that his name isn't Thompson. And if you mean, do I mean that he killed Frenchy, the answer is don't be absurd. Cal Morgan is the lad who killed Frenchy. How about that, Cal?"

He shook his head. "No." It was difficult for him to speak. "No. I didn't kill Frenchy."

I gave him the back of my hand. "The hell you didn't. What's more, it was you who shot young Schermerhorn, Fred Able, and at me. You even had the nerve to confess it because you knew how absurd it sounded. You weren't after the eight thousand dollars. Your hide had begun to smoke and you were trying to turn off the current."

Beamer said, "But he couldn't have shot you. He was in the lobby when the second burst of shots were fired."

I shook my head. "No. He was just the other side of the lobby fire door. And he muffled the shots by shooting into a barrel of sweeping compound." I tossed the six slugs on Nobby's desk. "There's his alibi. Cole and Jim dug them out of the barrel before they went out to pick you up."

Nobby said, "Tell him about Barney."

I said, "It was Lupe who shot Barney. She was as hot as Cal was. So she walked into his office and shot him while she and Cal were supposedly waiting for you. It was Lupe without the phoney accent who told me that State 2121 had hung up and who wanted to know if she should ring them again. When I told her not to bother she recognized my voice and I automatically went on their list, they not having any way of knowing how much Barney had told me. I should have spotted it at the time but I muffed it. *I hadn't called Barney. He had called me. And there was no way on earth that any operator could tell to which number I had been speaking unless she was reading it from Barney's dial!"*

Beamer persisted, "But the machine gun?"

I told him, "There was no machine gun. That was just dust in our eyes. Morgan was carrying two guns, both revolvers that wouldn't eject any brass that might be traced back to him. What's more, he has them on him now."

Morgan got to his feet, both hands plunged deep in his pockets. "That's right. I still have two guns." They said later that he was crazy. I knew it at the time. "And I'll use them if I have to," he warned us. "Lupe warned me at the club that you knew. But you threw me off with your phoney glass act. I thought you really thought it was Beamer."

I said, "So you made arrangements to confirm it, that unfortunately, for you, were observed."

He said bitterly, "More fool I did."

Beamer planted an accusing finger at Lupe. "You planted that money where Cooper found it."

Nobby shook his head in admiration, "Yes, sir. That dame will kiss anyone."

The S.A. admitted, "Okay. So when this breaks in the papers. I'm through. I've been a sucker, But if it was Cal who killed Frenchy why didn't he sit tight? What torched off this whole thing?"

I told him, "Young Schermerhorn and Fred Able." I told the story as I saw it, admitting a lot of it was guessing. "It began at the Club Cherie a year ago. Frenchy was blackmailing Cal. I wouldn't know what about. That is immaterial. What matters is that Cal stood as much as he could and then he shot him. Unfortunately there were witnesses. The Thompsons for two. Bala Gediz the cook and Lupe for two more.

Maybe Cal wanted to give himself up. I wouldn't know. But I do know that Gediz and Lupe wouldn't let him. They had found themselves a gold mine. So Lupe, I imagine, began to arrange things.

"It was easy to pin the shooting on Johnny. They did. But to make it stick they had to get rid of the Thompsons. So they did. And a pair of ringers were brought in. It wasn't difficult. The Thompsons had only been in Chicago a few days."

I stopped talking and there was no sound in the office but Lupe's sobbing.

"Gediz killed them," Morgan said grimly. "And Lupe found this pair of half-witted, small-time tent show actors to replace them."

Thompson showed his first flash of spirit. "We gave a good show. And if that damn farmer and that soldier hadn't shown up—"

Beamer got it and gasped. "But why didn't they just take the eight thousand dollars?"

"For the same reason they didn't cash young Thompson's insurance checks," I told him. "Young Schermerhorn wasn't a fool. He wanted a receipt. And Lupe or Morgan or Gediz had warned them *never to sign anything.* One forged signature could burn them all."

"And Able—?"

"He spotted the Thompsons as phoneys the moment he saw them. But he was looking for a payoff. He tried to get them to pay off with the threat that if they didn't he would go to Johnny Doll's lawyer. He did go to Barney. He told him just enough to intrigue him. He came to me for the same reason. He wanted a three-way payoff. But the alleged Thompsons had called Morgan and he and Lupe and Gediz were caught in the same old trap. They had to kill again to cover the earlier murders.

"They killed Barney. They shot the three of us. They sent Gediz to Schermerhorn's room to make certain that his dead buddy along with the money hadn't given him a picture of his parents. I imagine Morgan saw me go in. He undoubtedly stripped Gediz later to delay identification. And he rushed Beamer to the hotel in the hope he would ball up the issue. They were working against time."

Morgan wasn't a clever killer. His eyes telegraphed his intentions. He said, "Damn you, Doyle!" and shot through his pocket —a fraction of a second too late.

"Justifiable?" I asked Nobby. He nodded.

I jammed my gun back in my pocket. "All right. Let's go home," I told Sue.

She squeezed my arm hard, her eyes bright with tears.

Nobby walked to the door with us. "You look pretty white, Tom. How do you feel?"

I told him I felt fine.

MIGHTY LIKE A ROGUE

CHAPTER ONE

TO THE LAST DITCH

CONNIE LOOKED GOOD TO ME. Six months in the House of Correction hadn't punctured any of her curves. Her tummy was still flat. She still bulged and bobbled intriguingly when glimpsed from the rear of her façade. She still had two nifty pins and the same big blue eyes and baby stare. Her bleached hair had grown out a light brown. I liked it.

When she'd been pinched, she'd been wearing a backless, strapless evening gown torn down to here. When they released her, they gave her a plain cotton dress that made her look almost like the dewy-eyed, simple little country chump she had been when Sir Galahad had ridden into her life in a hot, white convertible. Even without much make-up, what I mean, the kid was really good-looking.

As she walked across the room to where I was feeding some hair to the dog that had bitten me the night before, I couldn't help but think, *"If only she had brains."*

I was glad to see her for two reasons. One, I stood to win over two hundred dollars. Various of the boys had bet me, what with me letting her take the rap on the Schaeffer mugging and not paying much attention to her while she was scrubbing out her time, she wouldn't show back at the apartment. I knew better. I'd picked her out of the hills down in the you-all country.

Down there when a girl promises to love, honor, and obey, until death do us two part, she means it. Once she gets that paper, her man can do no wrong. It's like a religion with the billies.

Then, too, I was tired of Rosita. *Enchiladas* and *tamales* are fine once in a while. But after stuffing on it for two months, a man gets tired of chile powder.

Connie's opening words were typical. "You ran out on me, Willy."

I'd expected a somewhat similar opening gambit, but the words were slightly out of focus. Then I realized why. Six months before she would have said, "You *run* out on me, Willy."

"You've been going to school," I accused.

She bobbed her head. "Four hours every day. I was up to the story about Black Beauty in the fifth reader when my time was up. And I'm going to keep on learning. I like it. And I'm not going to do any bad things any more. Both the matron and Mr. Phillips told me that a girl with my looks and my—" she stumbled over the word—"inherent decency didn't belong in a house of correction and—"

The time to put out a fire is when it starts. I got out of my chair and slapped her, hard. Phillips was the young D.A. who was giving us all a headache. A young punk with a good war record, he'd ridden in on a reform wave. Which was all right with us. You have to expect ups and downs in any business. But the young fool really meant what he'd said. He couldn't be bought.

I slapped her again for good measure. "Don't get too big for your two-way stretch. You're still my dear wife, remember. And you'll take your orders from me."

I thought for a minute she was going to brain me with the lamp she'd picked up. Then a hundred and fifty years of inherited genes came through and pulled for little Willy. Down where she came from, women are used to being pushed around. They like it.

She put the lamp back on the table. "Please, Willy." She sniffed. "Don't hit me." The billy in her came out. "I didn't go for to make you sore. But you did run out on me."

Napoleon was a smart guy. So was Hitler. Up to a point. Both of them went too far. And little Willy learned long ago not to make the same mistake. There are times when women should be clipped—and times when they should be kissed. And as far as Connie was concerned, that was my cue for an osculatory build-up.

I took her in my arms. "I can explain that, honey." I kissed her as hard as I'd slapped her. "And I didn't mean to hit you. But you're so beautiful. And it made me mad to hear you even mention another guy's name."

Connie wasn't entirely convinced. There was still a hurt look in her eyes. "But you did run out on me."

I kissed the hollow in her throat. "For your sake only, honey. You had no record. I have. And if I'd stuck around when the chump blew the whistle—" I shuddered to think of it. "Once the cops had linked me to the deal, you wouldn't have got off with six months. The judge would have thrown the book at you. That's why I ran out on you, honey. Strictly for your sake."

Fluttering the lashes of her big blue eyes, she bought the bill of goods. "I never thought of it that way, Willy. But that's right."

"Sure. Of course it is, honey."

I built her a good stiff drink, but she said if it was all right with me she thought she would just take ginger ale as, while she was in the House of Correction a temperance lady had given a lecture on what alcohol did to the brain, and she didn't want to become stupid.

Coming from her that was a howl, but I added the hair to the pelt I was growing on the dog and let it go at that. There ought, I thought, to be a law. It's positively criminal the things they learn the stupes in jail.

She was glad to be back in the apartment, like any good wife should. She fingered this and looked at that and remembered such and such, as pleased as a kid. She should have been. I'd bought her her first pair of silk stockings.

Down in the hills where she'd come from running water means the nearest branch and the only vitreous china they ever come in contact with is when they handle the souvenir cake plate that great grandfather Zeke stole when Quantrell's guerrillas raided Podunk because Sherman had burned Atlanta.

The next thing she did was take a bath. *"To get the smell off of me."*

I knew just what she meant. I hadn't been kidding about my record. On account of two stupid lawyers and one jury box filled with morons, I'd lost the toss three times. Once more, and they'd etch my number on my hide.

Arturo called while she was in the tub. I told him that Connie was out and home again, he said to bring her over to his place that night to celebrate, and we would combine business with pleasure as he had a little deal he wanted to cut me in on. He also said that an old friend of mine, he wouldn't tell me who, was going to be there. He said I would be pleased to see the guy, however, as we were fellow alumni.

I mixed another drink and told Connie the good news. She was standing in front of the mirror, looking at the expensive lucite brush I'd swiped for her one night.

"The big shot just called," I told her. "Put on something snazzy and we'll drop by there after we eat."

She continued to look at the brush. It made me kinda sore. Any other doll in the city would have been palpitating over the invitation. Arturo wasn't only a big shot. He was the biggest shot since Al Capone lost the fall to Uncle Sam. But Connie had never cottoned to him.

For one thing, he had a habit of liking to wrestle with pretty dolls without stopping to look at the third finger on their left hand. Then, too, she'd gotten plenty sore at him the night he had made all of us but her, laugh by soaking a stray kitten she'd picked up with lighter fluid and then touched off its fur to make a self-propelled cigarette lighter.

I said she didn't seem too pleased, and she turned to face me.

"You don't seem overly pleased to see me, Willy," she countered. Like the dumbest of women will sometimes, she hit the nail on the head. "There hasn't been any other woman while I've been away, has there, Willy?"

I started to say, "Positively not." I laughed. "Why—no," I said finally. "No one I was interested in, if that's what you mean. Why? Why do you ask me, honey?"

I tried to take her in my arms, but she wasn't having any at the moment.

"Skip it," she said. "I just wondered," and walked on into the bedroom.

And that was all right with me. Feeling as I did, I didn't care if I saw any woman, even a little honey like Connie, for a month. I had more important things to think of. I went back into the living room and finished re-pelting the dog.

Things were working out nicely. Arturo was calling me now. That meant I was in. From here on I would move strictly in big time. There would be no more petty capers like the gone-sour badger game.

There would be no more lone-hand filling station and liquor store hold-ups. No more selling hot cars for a fraction of their value because I didn't have an in. I had proven my value to Arturo on the half-dozen little tasks he had entrusted to me. And now I was no longer a wallflower. I was one of the gang. Arturo was calling *me*.

"I have a little deal I want to cut you in on, Willy."

It made me feel like a new man. I bought the new man a drink and sipped it, listening to the radio. With Rosita gone, it was quiet and peaceful in the apartment. There was no more banging of drawers or streams of liquid Spanish curses because Rosita couldn't find something that she wanted among Connie's things. It was just like the old times before Connie had been tagged.

I sat thinking about the three hundred-buck suits I would buy and the block-long convertible I'd drive. I would buy one just like Arturo's. And it would be nice, for a change, to drive a car that every cop in forty-eight states didn't have down on his hot-car pad.

It got so dark I had to switch on the light. The drinks had given me an appetite. I hoisted the six-foot-two of me that had nicknamed me Little Willy to my feet and walked on into the bedroom to see if Connie wasn't about ready to go out and tie on the feed bag.

Dames. Sometimes even a smart guy can't understand them. Here with her time behind her, back home with her loving man, a gold-plated invitation to a penthouse, and the future opening wide for both of us, you'd think she would be jumping with joy. Instead, she was sitting in the dark, on the stool in front of her dressing table, looking out of the window.

I asked her what was the big idea of taking so long, and she told me:

"I've been thinking."

So help me. I damn near burst my sides. Think of it. She'd been *thinking.*

CHAPTER TWO

WILLING LITTLE WILLY

ON THE DRIVE WAS ARTURO'S PENTHOUSE, so high up that on a clear night you could see the lights of Michigan City from the set-back terrace. Believe me. He was one of the boys who had made a chump out of the first panty-waist who cracked that crime didn't pay. It had paid him plenty. He'd made more money out of more rackets than any five big athletes put together. What I mean, he had more pies than he had fingers to put in them.

The doorman fell all over his feet giving us service. I didn't blame him. He knew he was opening doors for quality. It takes a man six feet tall, weighing two hundred pounds or better, to really set off a dinner jacket.

Being fair about it, though, Connie gave us some class, too. The long white organdy evening gown she was wearing was built for curves and shoulders like hers, and her round baby face and straw-colored hair didn't exactly make her look like a hag. But it was her eyes that got men mostly. Most of the time they were just soft and appealing like a kitten's.

But I'll never know how she managed to store up so many watts in nineteen years. When she wanted to turn on the power, she could make an Eskimo melt his igloo just by touching it with his finger. For a dumb little hillbilly kid, she wasn't too bad at all.

Being a big shot as he was, and owning the building besides, Arturo had his own private elevator. Jack Keagle, a punk I'd done time with, was running the cage. He had a grin all over his face.

"Well, it looks like we're moving into the big time, eh, Willy?" he greeted me.

"Yeah. Kinda looks like." I agreed. In the last year, since Phillips had been elected, Arturo had been having a lot of bad luck with his boys. The law had snagged some. Some had gotten cold feet when the new D.A. turned the heat on. Some had opened their mouths too wide. It had been doing a free-lance job on one of them for Arturo that had given me my first in. But Keagle was even newer than I was. He had come into the fold since Connie had been put away.

"Meet the wife," I told him. "Connie, this is Jack. Jade, this is Connie."

Keagle said, "Pleased to meetcha."

"Likewise," Connie said. Then she remembered one of the Emily Posts she'd leaned against in the House of Correction. "I am indeed very pleased to make your acquaintance."

From her, it didn't sound bad.

Arturo's penthouse was really something. The living room was sunken just enough to make it unhandy for a man with one drink too many, and long enough to be a shooting gallery. At the far end of where you came in, French doors led out onto a landscaped set-back, complete with a portable bar and fish pool.

"Now this," I told Connie, "is the kind of a joint that I would like to live in."

I'd expected it to be jumping. It wasn't. Only a half dozen of the boys and their dolls were there. But I was glad I had worn my tux. The boys who were there were creme-de-creme. Gorgo, Chink, Elmo, Farley Gray, Boots Hannon, Tod Wyatt, Petey. I felt even better than before to know Arturo had cut me in on such a gathering.

A butler was passing drinks on a tray, cocktails for the ladies and double-shots for the boys, but I didn't see Arturo. When I asked about him, the butler told me:

"Mr. Arturo is currently speaking on the phone, Mr. Mason. But he requests you and the other gentlemen to join him in the library as soon as he is finished."

I drank a double and took one to hold. Then I saw The Preacher. It was all I could do to keep from giving with a whoop. I hadn't seen the guy in two years, not since we'd knocked over the bank in Mayfield together and had to hole up in the town in which I'd made Connie's acquaintance until the heat had blown off.

The guy was like a brother to me. We'd pushed over our first pushcart together and he'd had the top bunk in Atlanta when we both had been doing two years. Not that rough stuff was much in his line. What he really shone at was con work. He could pose as a doctor, lawyer, preacher, and make the guy he was conning think he was one.

Why, even while we were lying low, I saw him talk a small-town banker into putting up two grand to finance an expedition to Mozambique to dig monobenzyl ether of hydroquinone to sell at one hundred dollars a pint to, as estimated in the 1940 census, eleven million, four hundred and nineteen thousand, one hundred and thirty-eight potential customers.

What I mean, The Preacher was good. But with all of his education and all of the dough he'd grifted, he wasn't above doing a fast favor for a friend. I took a quick look at Connie to see if she recognized him. It could be embarrassing if she did. I couldn't tell, but I doubted if she made him. They'd only met the one time, and then it had been kinda dark in the front room of the farmhouse where he'd been staying.

I patted her and told her to go join the dolls clustered in one corner making snide remarks about each others' dresses. Then I shook hands with The Preacher.

"You old so and so," I told him. "When did you get in town and what are you doing here?"

He was as glad to see me as I was to see him. "I've been in town almost a week," he said. "Arturo flew me in here from the coast as a trouble-shooter. According to what he tells me, this new D.A. has been putting you boys over the hurdle."

I said it was worse than that and started to tell him the whole sad story, but just then the butler opened a big pair of doors and said that Mr. Arturo would now be pleased to see all of the gentlemen in his library.

It looked more like a board of directors' room to me. There was a big polished table in it with chairs along both sides and a bottle of each guy's favorite tipple and a deck of the cigarettes he smoked just to the right of a gold ash tray.

A little rat in his early fifties who looked more like a beat-up second story man than the big shot he was, Arturo was already sitting in a big armchair at the head of the table.

"I guess you boys can find your places," he said, and waved us into our chairs.

I sat between Chink Elmo and Farley Gray, on account of that was where the brand I drank was on the table. Chink asked me if I knew what it was all about. I said I didn't.

Gray poured himself a drink, rinsed it around in his mouth, then, because he was humoring his ulcers, spit it into a gold cuspidor. "Two bits to a dime," he said, "it has something to do with Phillips. We've either got to comb that guy out of our hair or go out of business."

Coming from him, I considered it straight out of the horse's mouth. If anyone knew, he should. He'd been with Arturo for years. I was in the big time and no kidding.

Arturo added another red vein to his nose. Then he told the butler to close the doors, including himself out, and opened the polished table discussion by rapping on it with a gavel just like in a director's meeting in the movies.

"You guys," he began, "are probably wondering why I called you all here tonight. I can tell you in one word—Phillips."

Gray lifted an eyebrow at me as if to say, *"Well, what did I tell you, chum?"*

Arturo continued, "This has been going on now for a year. And it still has three more years to go unless we do something about it. I mean to."

I slapped the table and said, "Here."

Arturo continued, "We've tried to frighten the guy off. We've tried to buy him. We've tried to find out something nasty about him. But he won't be frightened. He won't take dough. And two firms of private detectives have informed me the worst thing he ever did in his life was tip over a cup of coffee at a Methodist church supper. But the fact remains, he *has* to go."

I said, "If I may be so bold as to remark, when I was a kid in school, they taught me the straightest distance between two points is a straight line. How about me shooting the guy?"

"I've thought of that, Willy," Arturo nodded. "And if it does come to that, that will be in your department."

Me, Willy Mason. I was the head of a department. Chink Elmo looked at me with new respect, but The Preacher got to his feet. Pushing the bottle by his place aside, he began to talk.

"Let's hope it doesn't come to that. Not out of any humanitarian precepts on my part. But the murder of a high official, city, county, or state, is always a messy affair. And with the reform party in this town as strong as it is, I am afraid that an outright killing would only add to your troubles."

Gorgo wanted to know who the hell he was.

The Preacher told him. "An expert, punk, on any line of so-called criminal endeavor. And I'm not speaking without official standing. I came here for a fee at Mr. Arturo's request to see if I can't untangle this old man of the sea the voters in the last election have straddled on your necks." He looked at Arturo for confirmation. "Is that correct?"

Arturo said it was. "But one way or another, Phillips has to go. The guy is costing me thousands of dollars every day."

"We'll cure that," The Preacher said. "Now, confirm my own deductions." He looked at Chink. "How old would you say your new district attorney is?"

Chink said, "Twenty-eight, maybe twenty-nine."

"And he's young, husky, human? He likes the girls, would you say?"

Chink colored slightly. "So far as I know. But we ain't never been able to get nothing on the guy. Take it from me, he's cagey."

The Preacher nodded. "In his position, he'd have to be. A reform district attorney, as with Caesar's wife, must be above the suspicion of the vulgate." He lighted one of the strong Turkish cigarettes he smoked.

"But there are means to every end. I've been in town a week looking over the situation, trying to formulate a plan, none too successfully I'll admit." He looked at me, "But when Willy and his little blonde doll walked in tonight, I think, mind you I say I *think*, I caught the glimmering of a solution."

I slipped my rod out of my shoulder holster and laid it on the wood. "You name the time. I'll do the job."

Arturo was impressed. "You're okay, Willy," he told me. "You're okay. I like you fine."

I didn't need a drink I felt that good. From here on it was in the bag. I was already wearing three-hundred-dollar suits and driving the convertible. A nod from a big shot like Arturo is like being knighted by the king and hitting the quiz jackpot all at the same time you are collecting five percent on a new aircraft carrier.

"Laudable willingness, Willy." The Preacher praised me. "But not quite so fast. As I said before, an out-and-out shooting might bring our house of cards and capers tumbling about our heads, and Arturo might find himself in an even worse financial position than he is now."

Arturo patted his forehead with his handkerchief. "Heaven forbid. Put your gun away, Willy. Go on, Preacher."

The Preacher snuffed out his cigarette and looked around the table. " 'Frailty,' " he said, " 'thy name is woman.' Likewise no pair of handcuffs ever forged or no cement kimono was ever half so strong as one fair hair from a woman's head." He added, "Bill Shakespeare didn't say that last, though he might well have."

Chink confided to me, "I used to know Shakespeare well. He was a sergeant at East Chicago. And the precinct station in Logan Square was named after his grandfather."

The Preacher leaned both palms on the table. "Now here is the solution I propose." He looked at Arturo. "But first, let me ask you a hypothetical question. If a young, personable man, currently a district attorney with a bright political future ahead of him, were to fall in love with a little blonde who had done time in the House of Correction, and he had reason to believe she reciprocated his affection, what do you think he would do?"

Arturo thought a moment. "Put on the ball and chains?"

"No, no." The Preacher was patient with him. "He can't afford to marry her. He can't even afford to know the girl. Being a gentleman, he has one of two choices. He can give up the girl. That would be the sensible thing for him to do. Two. He can be a good sport and give you a break by putting a forty-five to his head and blowing out his brains."

Arturo was dubious. "But what if he doesn't want to be a good sport?"

"Right there," The Preacher said softly. "is where willing Little Willy comes in."

CHAPTER THREE

GOLD-PLATED FUTURE

WE WAITED FOR HIM TO EXPLAIN. The Preacher continued: "Let's say some night while he is calling on the doll, perhaps the night he drops in to tell her farewell for ever, Little Willy is waiting in the closet. And if the job is done at close range with the young D.A.'s own gun. and the-girl is brokenhearted all over the place—who is to know that Little Willy and not a tragic love is responsible for the deed? *Especially if the death gun is found in the D.A.'s hand and the doll swears on her love for her dead mother that she saw him clap it to his head and pull the trigger.*"

I got the set-up. It wasn't bad. "Kinda of a high-class badger game, eh, with a homicidal finish?"

He said, "Exactly."

Gray said, "It sounds to me. But what if he doesn't fall in love with the dame?"

The Preacher grinned. "That is the beauty of it. He doesn't have to. All he has to do is be nice to her where people will see it and the public draw its own conclusion."

Chink Elmo echoed Gray. "That sounds to me. But where can we find a doll that we can trust?"

"We can trust Connie," I told him. "And that reminds me, boys. All of you except the boss owe me a little money." They tossed their bets over the table. "She came straight home from the can this afternoon like the little homing pigeon that she is. The kid is nuts about me. What's more, she knows if she doesn't do just what I tell her, I'll slap her black and blue."

Arturo licked his lip. "Heaven knows she is pretty enough. I could go for the doll myself." He looked at The Preacher. "But how are you going to get Connie and the D.A. together?"

"They already been together," I said, "just this afternoon when she came home after doing her time. Connie told me that both the matron and Mr. Phillips had told her that a girl with her looks and inherent decency shouldn't be in a house of correction."

The Preacher dry-washed his hands. "Fine. Fine."

Arturo wasn't so certain. "Okay. So they were together alone, with four hundred girls and thirty matrons. How are you going to get them together now?"

"Why not," The Preacher suggested, "get Connie a job in that restaurant across from the City Hall? Can do?"

"Can do," Arturo said.

"Then there you are. Phillips eats in there every noon. I know. I've spent a week checking his habits. We see that Connie waits on his table. He is surprised to see her. She tells him she is trying to go straight. I'll map out a campaign for her. Maybe she asks his advice about going to night school so she can hold down a better job than hashing. What would you do if you were a young man?" He drew a graphic picture.

"She is standing close to you. She is young and beautiful—and helpless. She's seen the error of her way. She wants to lead a good, clean life. She's standing to close you can smell her perfume. It inflames your senses. So what are you going to do? Are you going to kick the poor kid in the face?"

"Not me," Gorgo said. "Willy is bigger than I am."

The Preacher ignored him. "Of course not. You're going to be noble about it. You're going to give her a helping hand. And maybe get into the habit of dropping up to her room every other night or so—just to see how she is getting along in the secretarial course you suggested.

"The guys in your office, the people on the street, maybe even the kid's landlady, begin to talk. But you are so clean-minded that you don't realize that. Then one night, Willy is there. And when the doll blows the whistle, they find you stiff on the floor with your own gun in your hand and the little blonde doll weeps all over the front pages, *'It just wasn't meant to be.'* "

Concluding, the preacher sat down. "And there you are—rid of Phillips."

All of us slapped the table, saying we would buy it. It was a peach of a scheme, a lulu. The Preacher had come through again. With Connie's looks and the D.A.'s well-known Sir Galahad complex, it couldn't miss. It was a sure-fire pitch.

When we had quieted, Arturo said, "There is just one more thing. Are you *sure* that you can trust her? Can you answer for Connie, Willie?"

I told him, "With my life. Connie is a hill girl from down in the you-all country where women are used to taking orders from their men and a woman's man can do no wrong. It is a religion with them."

"Fine," Arturo said. "Fine. The Preacher can coach Connie later." He got to his feet with dignity. "Well, gentlemen. Shall we join the dames?"

After that, the night got slightly fuzzy. All I remember about it is that we had a barrel of fun. One of the dames got higher than a kite and insisted on doing the routine she used to do on a chorus runway. Another of the dames got a complex she was a gold fish, and we were all of the time having to fish her out of the pool on the terrace, all of us laughing like mad.

Then someone tossed out a pair of dice. After we'd all agreed no passers or miss-outs could be rung in, we rolled them on top of the grand piano with the music rack for a back stop. I built up my roll quite a bit on account of the dice were mine and I had both passers and missouts to match the square dice in my pocket.

We had one hell of a time, and whooped and hollered and wrestled and cut the fool until four o'clock in the morning. That is, all of us but Connie and The Preacher.

They sat most of the night on the sofa while he explained point by point, as to the child she was, just what was expected of her.

Things were pretty hazy along about then, but I remember The Preacher telling me, "She'll do. She'll do, Little Willy. She'll do. If those big blue eyes of hers and that baby stare don't pin a crepe on Phillip's door, I hope I never clip another sucker."

I told him not to be sacrilegious and he added:

"Early tomorrow morning I'm going to get Connie a room in a private house. Something very respectable where the only male caller she could possible have would be a district attorney. So kiss her good-by for a few weeks, Little Willy. We have to play this thing cagey and we don't dare to rush it."

For a moment I was sad, thinking of all an ambitious man has to give up for a career. Then I took another drink and thought, *What the hell? There is always Rosita.*

It was getting light by the time we got back to the apartment. I was so boiled that Connie had to prop up one side and the cab driver another, to get me up the stairs. But I'd never felt better in my life. I wanted to wake up everyone in the building and tell them I was in.

"You're okay, Willy," Arturo had told me. *"You're okay. I like you fine."*

Then the cab driver tried to get tough with me just because I didn't want to pay the fare. I was going to shoot his ears off, but Connie persuaded me to give him a ten of my dice winnings and he slunk off down the stairs.

Even then there were two doors where there should have been one, and I tried to walk through the wrong one the first time and had to clip Connie good because she hadn't steered me right. But she finally got me in.

"Now you get some sleep," she told me.

I said, "To hell with that." I'd never seen her so pretty. I was going to miss her like sin. I grabbed her and pulled her to me. "Did I ever tell you that you were a pretty little doll?"

She nodded like she was frightened of me. "Why, y-yes. You've told me several times, Willy."

"And I'm saying it now," I told her. The frightened look was still in her eyes. "Come on. Tell me, honey. What is eating you now?"

Her eyes filling with tears, she got what was worrying her off her chest. "About, Mr. Phillips. You aren't really going to hurt him, are you, Willy? All you are going to do is hit him, like you hit Mr. Schaeffer."

"Sure. That's all," I lied. "And I don't have to be bad, do I, Willy?"

I kissed her eyes and her lips and her throat. "That's just the point, honey," I told her. "If you were to do anything bad, you would queer the whole deal. Like The Preacher explained, you don't have to do a thing but be good and want to get ahead in the world. You leave everything else to Little Willy. You'll queer the whole pitch if you as much as wink one of those pretty blue eyes at Mr. Phillips."

"I'm glad," she told me. "Because like I told you this afternoon, both the matron and Mr. Phillips told me—"

I'd heard the record before. "Sure. I know," I said. "A girl with your looks and inherent decency doesn't belong in a house of correction. Okay. Now take off my shoes. It's damn near morning." She took off my shoes and untied my tie like a dutiful hill wife should, but she seemed to be having trouble with the zipper of her dress. "You—still awake, Willy?" she asked me. I said I was.

"He—he's nice, in a way," she said. "I mean The Preacher. And even if he is working for Arturo now, he is a real preacher, isn't he, Willy?"

Drunk as I was, I'd never heard anything so funny. I had to hang on to the bed to keep from falling out.

"Hell, no," I told the little stupe. "We just call him that on account of he looks like a Holy Joe. The closest The Preacher ever came to a church was once when he pinched the poor box to buy a quart of rum. He's the cleverest con man in the business."

"Oh," she said. "I see." I tried to kiss her again, but she got up and got the quart I'd left on the dresser. "Let's have a big drink," she suggested. "A great big drink—to celebrate." She handed me the bottle. "Here you take the first drink, Willy."

I was glad to see her in her right mind and forgetting that foolish temperance business about alcohol making you stupid. I tilted the butt of the bottle to the ceiling and let the stuff in it drain down. And it was the one over twenty.

The next thing I knew, it was two o'clock in the afternoon. On Connie's pillow there was pinned a note that read in her misspelled childish scrawl:

> *Mr. Preacher has cum for me to take me to the room he has rented. I start work at the restrant tomorrow morning at ten an work the shift thru until four. Goodbye, Willy.*
>
> *Connie*

I was almost sorry I'd gotten so drunk. Even if she was dumb, Connie was a good kid.

CHAPTER FOUR

FAIR-HAIRED BOY

ONE WEEK, TWO WEEKS, almost three weeks passed. Arturo was biting his nails up to here, but The Preacher told him the same thing he'd told me—we didn't dare to rush the deal. We had to play it cagey.

Meanwhile, the town was going to pot. Cobwebs were forming on the bar stools where the B girls had once made merry chatter to the chumps. Flying squads of picked men from the D.A.'s office knocked over one after another of Arturo's horse-and-poker parlors. Chink Elmo, who handled the hot car-export drop, was tagged by a strong-arm squad and thrown in the clink for three days before Arturo could locate him and get him out on ten-grand bail.

The stick-up boys and muscle men were starving. An Inspector, two captains, a lieutenant, and a short ton of sergeants, were suspended pending charges. It was getting so bad a fellow couldn't even have an over-time parking ticket fixed, let alone square a fast caper.

The first thing I'd done after the party was spend most of my dice game winnings on two three-hundred-dollar suits of clothes. But unless the town opened up pretty soon, I was going to look very silly wearing glad rags like that with holes in both of my shoes.

The only bright spot in the picture was Connie. She'd been a hasher when I met her and a good one. She took to the job in the joint across from the City Hall like benedictine to brandy.

What was more important—from what reports I'd had and what I'd seen with my one eyes, Phillips had fallen for her like a ton of Irish confetti. He used to eat at one, and spend fifteen minutes in the joint. Now he came in for a cup of coffee when Connie came on shift and ate his way through the rest of the day.

What I mean, the guy was on the ropes.

And Connie was playing it smart. From time to time I dropped in for a cup of coffee and a sinker, and saw it with my own eyes. As soon as the chump would walk in the door, she'd flutter those big blue peepers of hers at him like he was the most important thing in her life and she was just as crazy about him, in an innocent way, as he was about her.

Even if he'd just been in five minutes before, she'd say, "Oh, it's you, Mr. Phillips," like her heart was standing still.

And he'd just sit there mooning at her like she was pennies from heaven and keep on ordering coffee and pie for an excuse to look a little longer. Honest. One day I saw the guy eat six bowls of deep dish apple and drink eight cups of coffee.

I didn't blame him for looking. Like the guy said in the book, you never miss the violets until they're gone. And Connie was something to look at in the white nylon uniform. With her straw-colored hair wound in big braids around her head, she reminded a guy of summer and flowers and the sweet smell of hay and the tinkle of a brook and green, living, growing things sprouting up out of rich black earth. The kid only weighed a hundred pounds, but what I mean she was lush.

She was doing good with her homework, too. None of us dared to see her at the restaurant or show at the high-class rooming house where she was living. But like she had arranged with The Preacher, she sent in regular reports. Phillips—she called him Don in her reports—had suggested she take a secretarial course. Even in the short time she had been going to school, it showed in both her spelling and her writing.

He, Don, Connie wrote, said there was no reason in the world why with a little coaching she shouldn't overcome her humble beginning and take her rightful place in society. To that end, he was calling for her almost every night now, escorting her to school, waiting while she learned, then escorting her back to her room and going over her lessons with her.

Even The Preacher was impressed by the way she was following his instructions, and began planning big things for her once Phillips was out of the way.

Then the fly got stuck in the ointment. Arturo, it would seem, just happened to be coming out of a certain office in City Hall, where he had dropped in to try to arrange a fix in the Chink Elmo matter, when he bumped smack into the young D.A.

I wasn't there. All I know is what I read in the papers and what I was told. Maybe Arturo snarled at the kid. I wouldn't know. I don't blame him if he did. But Phillips wasn't having any.

He named Arturo in so many words and told him that now he had him on the run, he was going to run him right back into the hole he'd crawled out of. Then Arturo came back with a couple of hot retorts about Sunday school towns and teaching his grandmother to suck eggs. And the first thing the guys in the hall know, the two are mixing it with their fists.

It takes Gorgo and Farley Gray, an elevator operator, and two Park Board Policemen to pry them apart, before they can make like the gingham dog and the calico cat, while two press photographers who just happened to be passing snapped themselves a twenty-buck raise.

The afternoon papers came out with screamers:

ARTURO AND D.A. BATTLE WITH
FISTS IN CITY HALL CORRIDOR!

CRIME MUST GO, SAYS D.A.
NUTS, SAYS ARTURO!

It was all very sordid and degrading, but I will say for Phillips that he kept his head. He could have jugged Arturo and had him put under a peace bond. But he knew he couldn't keep him in the jug. He also knew all he'd made was talk. He could never get rid of Arturo. Not by any legal means.

Arturo knew where too many lost weekends had been spent. Where too many bodies were fertilizing the daisies. He had too many high officials on his secret pay-roll. Too many aldermen were driving cars and living in houses their smear of the gravy had bought.

So, being a smart lad, Phillips let the affair wind up with a final statement to the press in which he said:

In a younger, more direct, more virile America, what would have been done, what should be done to vermin of Arturo's stripe, is exterminate him. He should be shot down like the mad dog he is.

Arturo blew higher than his penthouse when he read it. "Now the guy is going to shoot me. To hell with this stalling around. Get Phillips out of my hair. Have him rubbed out tonight."

"Okay," The Preacher agreed. "Tonight is as good a night as any. You ready to go to work, Little Willy?"

I told him, "Any time."

He gave me explicit directions in just what part of the house it was and also a key he'd had made for Connie's room and one for the downstairs front door.

"We'll pull it tonight," he said, "when Phillips brings her home from school. You be in Connie's closet and waiting by ten-thirty. When I leave here, I'll stop by the restaurant and tip her off that tonight is the payoff. You remember your instructions?"

I said I did, but The Preacher made me repeat them—how I was to wrap both arms around Phillips and get his gun out of his pocket without marking him in any way that might make the homicide boys suspicious.

"And remember, Phillips is left-handed," he reminded. "Be sure you put the gun in his left hand."

I said I would remember, and he went into more details about how he and two of the other boys would touch off a house a few doors down the block to shill Connie's landlady and her fellow roomers out of the joint, so that no one would see me enter.

Now the pay-off was coming up, Arturo was pleased as a kid. He bought both of us a drink of the good stuff he drank himself, and then slipped me a fifty as an evidence of good faith and affection

"Eat a big steak. Eat two big steaks. Be good and strong, Little Willy," he told me. "And pull that trigger hard."

I promised him I would and rode downstairs. It being then only about two o'clock, and the caper eight and a half hours away. I went back to the apartment to have a few more nips and a nap . . .

It was almost six o'clock when the special-delivery boy banged on the door and poked the letter at me. I tipped him the back of my hand, then ripped open the letter and read it. It was from Connie. On top of her six months training in the House of Correction, three weeks of secretarial school had certainly done wonders for Connie. There wasn't one misspelled word and, instead of a childish scrawl, her writing had character. It could have been written by a governor or even a senator's wife. What I mean, it had class. Some bills fell out in my hand as I opened it. The letter read:

Dear Willy:

Please meet me in Grant Pork by the Buckingham Fountain at exactly seven-thirty tonight. I have something very important to discuss with you. Something vital to both of our futures. If you would like to get rich, if you would like to have as much money as Arturo, don't fail to meet me. And don't tell any one about this. Yours very truly,

Connie

P. S. Am inclosing my two-weeks pay.

It was nice of the kid. It was also an intriguing letter. I couldn't help but wonder what she was on the trail of. Even the dumbest of dames bump into gold mines sometimes, and Connie had had an inside track into the D.A.'s office for three weeks. I burned the letter and put the money in my wallet.

The caper wasn't set for until after she'd come back from school. The Preacher had tipped her by now that tonight was the big night. But I still would have plenty of time to meet her by the fountain and find out what was in her little mind . . .

Since the colored lights hadn't been turned on yet, it was dark in the park by the fountain. But I hit it on the head, and Connie was waiting for me. I took her in my arms and kissed her but something big was eating her and she was too excited to respond.

"Not now, Little Willy," she told me. 'We haven't time." She led the way to a bench and sat down. "Do you remember what you told me that last night, when we went up to Arturo's penthouse?"

I asked her, "What?"

"You said, "This is the kind of a joint I would like to live in."

I was pleased that she remembered. "Yeah. Sure. I did say that."

She took a deep breath. "Well, you can. Listen, Little Willy. I've been thinking."

"No. Not again?" I cracked.

But Connie was in no mood for levity. She had business on her mind. "You've read the afternoon papers?"

"Of course."

"All about where Mr. Phillips said that Arturo should be shot down like a mad dog?"

I laughed. "Sure. And did the little grease-ball hit the ceiling! That's why he said that Phillips had to be—" I remembered her delicate sensibilities just in time—"er—intimidated and disgraced tonight." I wasn't too worried about her reaction *after* the thing was over.

Once I had cut the caper, she would have to string along or find herself tagged as an accessory to murder. And even Connie had brains enough to know what that could mean. "The Preacher contacted you?"

She nodded. "Yes. And that's why I sent you the note." She gave with the brain business again. "And here is what I have been thinking, Little Willy." She patted my sleeve. "You're big and you're strong and you're brave and you're a good shot with a gun."

I was modest. "Oh, I get by. Come to the point, honey."

She said, "I don't like Arturo. And I don't trust him. He burned my kitten. I'd like to see him dead." Then she pulled the snapper and it hit me like a punch in the belly. "So what would happen, Little Willy, if Mr. Phillips tried to keep his threat and he and Arturo did shoot it out—*and both of them were killed?*"

I said, "It would be a mess." Then I saw what she was driving at and the small veins in my temple began to pound. It all just went to show what happened when you bought a pair of shoes for a hill kid and combed the dogwood out of her hair. She got ambitious for her man. I was bigger and tougher than any of the other boys in the mob, The Preacher and Farley Gray included. And with Arturo dead and the snotty young D.A. making the grass greener, there was no reason in the world why I shouldn't take over Arturo's mob and his rackets.

The picture made me nervous, I slapped her. "You've said too much or not enough. Keep talking."

Sniffling a little because I hurt her, Connie explained the plan she'd thought up. It would have to go like clockwork. The Preacher and the rest of the boys would be expecting her to lead young Phillips back to her rooming house for the pay-off and would be busy touching off the house down the block and making certain the road was clear for me to get into her closet. Just on the off-chance that anything should go wrong, Arturo, rat that he was, was certain to be in his own penthouse, perfectly alibied.

Almost breathless now, Connie continued, "So what if exactly at ten-thirty—instead of leading Don back to my rooming house—I suggest he make a personal call on Arturo and have it out with him once and for all? And you are waiting at Arturo's instead of the rooming house? *And when the shooting is over, both of them are dead, the D.A. by Arturo's gun and Arturo dead by his?*"

Once she had made the plunge, Connie was a bloody-minded little wench. It made my skin crawl to hear the calm way she explained it. She concluded:

"Then both of them would be out of your hair, Little Willy. And you could live in Arturo's penthouse and wear three-hundred-dollar suits and drive a big convertible."

It was a pretty picture. "But how do you know you can get the D.A. to go to Arturo's penthouse?"

She made a gesture with her hand "Oh, that. I can wind Don around my little finger. He thinks the sun rises and sets in me and he'll do anything that I ask him."

I thought it over for a few more minutes The more I thought, the better it sounded. Arturo *was* a rat and a cheapskate. What had he given me? A few pats on the back, a few drinks, and fifty dollars.

Connie continued to stroke the sleeve of my coat. "I don't have to tell you. You're smart. But you'll have to time it close. So why don't you get to Arturo's at, say ten twenty-five and, well, get the first part of the business over with. Then when I come in with Mr. Phillips—" She left it there.

"It's a sale," I told her. "I'll buy it." I tried to hug her to me, but she pulled away.

"Please. I'm wearing a brand-new suit and you're getting it all mussed."

The lights in the fountain came on then and I could see her. Feeling as good as I did about what was going to happen and me taking over the whole shebang, I said she looked pretty snazzy. Connie explained it was what they called a going-away suit, whatever that means, and she had bought it with her tips.

"You do like the idea, then?"

There were still a few minor points I would have to work out, like what to do with the butler if he was there, and whether to run the cage myself or trust Jack Keagle. But I'd cut a lot of *ad-lib* capers and I was confident I could bridge any gaps in the mechanics as I came to them.

"Ten-thirty at Arturo's," I sealed it. "And you can quit your job in the morning, Connie. You won't have to hash any more."

"Thank you, Little Willy," she told me.

CHAPTER FIVE

PURE AND SIMPLE

PART OF MY PROBLEM solved itself when I remembered that Thursday was Arturo's butler's night out. After leaving Connie in the park, I took a cab back to the drive and was smoking a butt under the marquee of a joint a few doors up the street, when I saw the butler come out. He was dolled-up to start off on some tom-catting expedition of his own. Working where he did, the guy must have gotten a lot of telephone numbers.

How to get in and out of the joint without being seen was another problem. Then I happened to think that in a swell joint like that they wouldn't bring the garbage down in the front cage. They didn't. Walking around in back of the building I could see a narrow line of lights spotting a freight elevator that ran all the way up to the penthouse.

The entrance, I imagined, was through the boiler room. A quick investigation proved I was right. And Arturo for all his dough was no smarter than the average householder. He had a two hundred dollar a week guard on his front door but he entrusted the back to a two-dollar lock any dime store skeleton key would open.

Satisfied I could get in and out, I walked on down the street and lost myself in a crowded bar for the next two hours. At ten, I called Arturo from a pay station.

"This is you-know-who, boss," I told him. "I'm just calling to have you wish me luck and tell you to be sure to be covered just in case something should go wrong."

It seemed to please him.

"Thanks, I-know-who," he said softly. *"Good* luck." He chortled. "And don't worry about me. I'm sick on the couch with a doctor's prescription. Besides, I've left word for the mayor to call me at exactly ten-thirty, at which time I intend to lodge a protest against keeping in office a certain highly placed official who keeps the low company he does. The nerve of the guy cracking wise like he did about a respectable business man." Then he said, "Thanks for calling again," and hung up.

I smoked a cigarette in the booth. If Arturo was using a sick dodge it was unlikely he had a doll in the penthouse. Besides, once the fat was in the fire, reports from this guy and that would come pouring in over his private unlisted wire and he wouldn't want any doll tuned in.

Some mug opened the door of the booth and wanted to know if I'd rented it for the night.

"If I had time," I told him, "I'd push your teeth down your throat on account of I don't like the tone of that crack. But as it so happens, I'm busy. So, if you will excuse me, chum, I am on my way to earn a million dollars."

He looked after me like I was nuts, as I walked out of the bar. The Indian still having charge of the summer, it was warm. I enjoyed the walk back to the drive. I've thought of it many a time. The thing was a cinch, a pushover. It all just went to show a guy. You went along stealing peanuts for years. Then you picked up a blonde—and whammo, you hit the jackpot.

I walked by in the dark, on the other side of the street, to give it a last quick once-over. Jack Keagle was out on the walk smoking a cigarette with the doorman. When the time for it came, both of them would swear that no one but Connie and District Attorney Don Phillips had asked to be taken up to Arturo's penthouse. I walked on around to the back of the building, in through the open baggage room door, and opened the lock on the freight elevator with my skeleton key.

Closing the door, I pushed the handle forward and started up at exactly the time I should have been sneaking into Connie's rooming house and making like a mouse in her closet.

The cage opened into a service hall with a little better lock on the door leading into the penthouse. I had to use both my pick-lock and my pen knife on it. It must have taken me almost two minutes before I got it open and walked on into the un-lighted kitchen.

I touched the deep freeze as I passed. The thing was big and must have cost two thousand bucks. And it was filled with expensive viands like aged steaks that thick, and quail and frog's legs and quick-frozen pompano. And it all was going to belong to me. All for the price of two slugs. It was the best bargain I'd ever picked up.

Arturo was in the living room, alone. He was propped up on a zebra-striped sofa reading a racing form and nursing a bottle—which must have been the doctor's prescription he'd mentioned.

When he saw me, he squeaked, "Little Willy. What are you doing here?"

I gave him the classic answer like they always do in the films. "Why, me? I'm taking over, chump." I glanced at his wrist watch. It was ten twenty-eight. It was time. "Good-by, Arturo," I told him —and pulled, the trigger of the gun in my hand.

For all of his dough and his rackets, he went out like a switched-off light. I made certain I'd done a good job. Then I lighted a cigarette and sat down to wait for Connie to show up with the D.A.

I'd never known minutes could be so long. It crawled to ten twenty-nine, then dragged on to ten-thirty, and the phone began to ring like mad. That was the mayor. I let it ring. It served him right for a man in his position to stoop to call a rat like Arturo.

From then on time really went slow. It got to be ten thirty-five, and I was beginning to sweat. I could have left any time. The back door was wide open. But I'd only completed half the job. The way it stood now it was murder. Connie *had* to show up with Phillips.

At ten-forty, I unloosened my tie and opened my shirt. I was getting hot—but the stiff was getting colder every minute. If it got much colder even when Connie did show up with Phillips, the boys who make with the thermometers and test tubes were going to be damn suspicious.

My whole body was drenched with sweat. The phone continued to ring on and off. At ten forty-seven I couldn't stand it any longer and picked it up, hoping that it was Connie calling to say they'd been delayed, but she'd be up with the chump in a minute.

It wasn't Connie. It was The Preacher. And he sounded more hysterical than I'd ever heard him before. He thought I was Arturo.

"Both Little Willy and Connie have run out on us," he stormed. "And there's been a tip-off somewhere. Four cops picked me up just as I was about to torch off the house down the block to create a diversion and what I mean—they got me with the goods. But it can't go on the blotter—"

I dropped the phone back in the cradle. To hell with The Preacher. I had troubles of my own. I gave Connie two more minutes, thinking dark thoughts about her, like maybe she'd never meant to show. Then the front door bell pealed. I was never so glad to hear any bell in my life. I'd done the kid an injustice.

Holding the gun in my right hand, I opened the front door. "Come in, Mr. Phillips," I invited. "By all means, come right in."

Captain Miles of the Homicide Squad looked at me like I was nuts. So did the five members of his squad with him.

"Well, Little Willy," Captain Miles greeted me. "Imagine meeting you here. Tell me something, chum. Some dame just called me from Valparaiso. You know, that Indiana marriage mill, just over the state line and down aways. And she told me the screwiest story. She said if we'd chop-chop right over to Arturo's penthouse, we might have the pleasure of making a murder investigation."

That was a long time ago. Nine months to be exact. In the elapsed time, the State has given birth to two murder trials, both of them revolving around me. The first jury was smart. They disagreed. But the second box was filled with morons. They made it 'first degree' with no recommendation for mercy—which means I have to hit the coal chute in a place and at a time as designated by the law. The place is here. The time is two nights from now.

So help me, I didn't have a plea. That guy Phillips is one smart D.A. After him calling Arturo all the things he had, to hear him talk to the jury you would have thought that the little rat was one of the greatest benefactors of mankind. What's more, in both of my trials he got the judge to admit what evidence he wanted on record and to discard all the rest as irrelevant and immaterial and tending to harm and degrade innocent parties involved.

And once he got a look at the pins of the young D.A.'s new wife, even the lawyer appointed by the court to defend me was working for the other side. It was criminal. So help me.

They wouldn't allow him to testify, but they did let me see The Preacher, once. That was just after they'd brought him here to start doing the long haul without any hope of parole. And outside of trying to kick in my teeth, he wasn't too sore about having to take the fall. We both agreed it had been a good idea and I'd only made one mistake.

Those hill kids are funny women. Once they get that paper, they'll stick by their man to the last ditch. They'll work and fight and lie and steal and even kill for him. But they want that paper to be legal. And I'd made a bad mistake by using a phony license I'd just happened to have handy and asking The Preacher to pose as something he wasn't and do something; that he had never been ordained to do.

And that winds it up, I guess. It was murder, pure and simple. Like the guy says in the gag, Connie was pure and I was simple. But I'll see her again. I know. And not too long from now.

The warden doesn't like me either. And he got a big charge out of showing me the invitation to my execution that he sent to Mr. and Mrs. District Attorney Donald Phillips.

RAMBLE HOUSE's

HARRY STEPHEN KEELER WEBWORK MYSTERIES

(RH) indicates the title is available ONLY in the RAMBLE HOUSE edition

The Ace of Spades Murder
The Affair of the Bottled Deuce (RH)
The Amazing Web
The Barking Clock
Behind That Mask
The Book with the Orange Leaves
The Bottle with the Green Wax Seal
The Box from Japan
The Case of the Canny Killer
The Case of the Crazy Corpse (RH)
The Case of the Flying Hands (RH)
The Case of the Ivory Arrow
The Case of the Jeweled Ragpicker
The Case of the Lavender Gripsack
The Case of the Mysterious Moll
The Case of the 16 Beans
The Case of the Transparent Nude (RH)
The Case of the Transposed Legs
The Case of the Two-Headed Idiot (RH)
The Case of the Two Strange Ladies
The Circus Stealers (RH)
Cleopatra's Tears
A Copy of Beowulf (RH)
The Crimson Cube (RH)
The Face of the Man From Saturn
Find the Clock
The Five Silver Buddhas
The 4th King
The Gallows Waits, My Lord! (RH)
The Green Jade Hand
Finger! Finger!
Hangman's Nights (RH)
I, Chameleon (RH)
I Killed Lincoln at 10:13! (RH)
The Iron Ring
The Man Who Changed His Skin (RH)
The Man with the Crimson Box
The Man with the Magic Eardrums
The Man with the Wooden Spectacles
The Marceau Case
The Matilda Hunter Murder
The Monocled Monster

The Murder of London Lew
The Murdered Mathematician
The Mysterious Card (RH)
The Mysterious Ivory Ball of Wong Shing Li (RH)
The Mystery of the Fiddling Cracksman
The Peacock Fan
The Photo of Lady X (RH)
The Portrait of Jirjohn Cobb
Report on Vanessa Hewstone (RH)
Riddle of the Travelling Skull
Riddle of the Wooden Parrakeet (RH)
The Scarlet Mummy (RH)
The Search for X-Y-Z
The Sharkskin Book
Sing Sing Nights
The Six From Nowhere (RH)
The Skull of the Waltzing Clown
The Spectacles of Mr. Cagliostro
Stand By—London Calling!
The Steeltown Strangler
The Stolen Gravestone (RH)
Strange Journey (RH)
The Strange Will
The Straw Hat Murders (RH)
The Street of 1000 Eyes (RH)
Thieves' Nights
Three Novellos (RH)
The Tiger Snake
The Trap (RH)
Vagabond Nights (Defrauded Yeggman)
Vagabond Nights 2 (10 Hours)
The Vanishing Gold Truck
The Voice of the Seven Sparrows
The Washington Square Enigma
When Thief Meets Thief
The White Circle (RH)
The Wonderful Scheme of Mr. Christopher Thorne
X. Jones—of Scotland Yard
Y. Cheung, Business Detective

Keeler Related Works

A To Izzard: A Harry Stephen Keeler Companion by Fender Tucker — Articles and stories about Harry, by Harry, and in his style. Included is a compleat bibliography.

Wild About Harry: Reviews of Keeler Novels — Edited by Richard Polt & Fender Tucker — 22 reviews of works by Harry Stephen Keeler from *Keeler News*. A perfect introduction to the author.

The Keeler Keyhole Collection: Annotated newsletter rants from Harry Stephen Keeler, edited by Francis M. Nevins. Over 400 pages of incredibly personal Keeleriana.

Fakealoo — Pastiches of the style of Harry Stephen Keeler by selected demented members of the HSK Society. Updated every year with the new winner.

Strands of the Web: Short Stories of Harry Stephen Keeler — Edited and Introduced by Fred Cleaver

RAMBLE HOUSE's OTHER LOONS

Alexander Laing Novels — *The Motives of Nicholas Holtz* and *Dr. Scarlett*, stories of medical mayhem and intrigue from the 30s.

Amorous Intrigues & Adventures of Aaron Burr, The — by Anonymous — Hot historical action.

Angel in the Street, An — Modern hardboiled noir by Peter Genovese.

Anthony Boucher Chronicles, The — edited by Francis M. Nevins Book reviews by Anthony Boucher written for the *San Francisco Chronicle*, 1942 – 1947. Essential and fascinating reading.

Automaton — Brilliant treatise on robotics: 1928-style! By H. Stafford Hatfield

Best of 10-Story Book, The — edited by Chris Mikul, over 35 stories from the literary magazine Harry Stephen Keeler edited.

Black Dark Murders, The — Vintage 50s college murder yarn by Milt Ozaki, writing as Robert O. Saber.

Black Hogan Strikes Again — Australia's Peter Renwick pens a tale of the outback.

Black River Falls — Suspense from the master, Ed Gorman

Blood in a Snap — The *Finnegan's Wake* of the 21ˢᵗ century, by Jim Weiler

Blood Moon — The first of the Robert Payne series by Ed Gorman

Case of the Little Green Men, The — Mack Reynolds wrote this love song to sci-fi fans back in 1951 and it's now back in print.

Case of the Withered Hand, The — 1936 potboiler by John G. Brandon

Charlie Chaplin Murder Mystery, The — Movie hijinks by Wes D. Gehring

Chelsea Quinn Yarbro Novels featuring Charlie Moon — *Ogilvie, Tallant and Moon, Music When the Sweet Voice Dies, Poisonous Fruit* and *Dead Mice*

Chinese Jar Mystery, The — Murder in the manor by John Stephen Strange, 1934

Clear Path to Cross, A — Sharon Knowles short mystery stories by Ed Lynskey

Compleat Calhoon, The — All of Fender Tucker's works: Includes *Totah Six-Pack, Weed, Women and Song* and *Tales from the Tower*, plus a CD of all of his songs.

Compleat Ova Hamlet, The — Parodies of SF authors by Richard A. Lupoff – A brand new edition with more stories and more illustrations by Trina Robbins.

Contested Earth and Other SF Stories, The — A never-before published space opera and seven short stories by Jim Harmon.

Cornucopia of Crime, A — Memoirs and Summations of 30 years in the crime fiction game by Francis M. Nevins

Crimson Clown Novels — By Johnston McCulley, author of the Zorro novels, *The Crimson Clown* and *The Crimson Clown Again.*

Crimson Query, The — A supervillain from the 20s by Arlton Eadie.

Dago Red — 22 tales of dark suspense by Bill Pronzini

Dancing Tuatara Press Books — *Beast or Man?* by Sean M'Guire; *The Whistling Ancestors* by Richard E. Goddard; *The Shadow on the House, Sorcerer's Chessmen, The Wizard of Berner's Abbey, The Ghost of Gaston Revere*, and *Master of Souls* by Mark Hansom, *The Trail of the Cloven Hoof* by Arlton Eadie and *The Border Line* by Walter S. Masterman, and *Reunion in Hell* by John H. Knox, and *The Tongueless Horror* by Wyatt Blassingame. With introductions by John Pelan. Many more to come!

David Hume Novels — *Corpses Never Argue, Cemetery First Stop, Make Way for the Mourners, Eternity Here I Come*, and more to come.

Day Keene Short Stories — League of the Grateful Dead, We Are the Dead and *Death March of the Dancing Dolls*. Collections from the pulps by a master writer. Introductions by John Pelan.

Dead Man Talks Too Much — Hollywood boozer by Weed Dickenson

Death Leaves No Card — One of the most unusual murdered-in-the-tub mysteries you'll ever read. By Miles Burton.

Deep Space and other Stories — A collection of SF gems by Richard A. Lupoff

Detective Duff Unravels It — Episodic mysteries by Harvey O'Higgins

Devil Drives, The — A prison and lost treasure novel by Virgil Markham

Devil's Mistress, The — Scottish gothic tale by J. W. Brodie-Innes.

Dime Novels: Ramble House's 10-Cent Books — *Knife in the Dark* by Robert Leslie Bellem, *Hot Lead* and *Song of Death* by Ed Earl Repp, *A Hashish House in New York* by H.H. Kane, and five more.

Don Diablo: Book of a Lost Film — Two-volume treatment of a western by Paul Landres, with diagrams. Intro by Francis M. Nevins.

Dope Tales #1 — Two dope-riddled classics; *Dope Runners* by Gerald Grantham and *Death Takes the Joystick* by Phillip Condé.

Dope Tales #2 — Two more narco-classics; *The Invisible Hand* by Rex Dark and *The Smokers of Hashish* by Norman Berrow.

Dope Tales #3 — Two enchanting novels of opium by the master, Sax Rohmer. *Dope* and *The Yellow Claw.*

Dr. Odin — Douglas Newton's 1933 potboiler comes back to life.

Dumpling, The — Political murder from 1907 by Coulson Kernahan

Edmund Snell Novels — *The Sign of the Scorpion, The White Owl* and *Dope and Swastikas* (*The Dope Dealer* and *The Crimson Swastika*)

End of It All and Other Stories — Ed Gorman's latest short story collection
Evidence in Blue — 1938 mystery by E. Charles Vivian
Fatal Accident — Murder by automobile, a 1936 mystery by Cecil M. Wills
Finger-prints Never Lie — A 1939 classic detective novel by John G. Brandon
Freaks and Fantasies — Eerie tales by Tod Robbins, collaborator of Tod Browning on the film FREAKS.
Gadsby — A lipogram (a novel without the letter E). Ernest Vincent Wright's last work, published in 1939 right before his death.
Gelett Burgess Novels — *The Master of Mysteries, The White Cat, Two O'Clock Courage, Ladies in Boxes, Find the Woman, The Heart Line, The Picaroons* and *Lady Mechante*
Geronimo — S. M. Barrett's 1905 autobiography of a noble American.
Gold Star Line, The — Seaboard adventure from L.T. Reade and Robert Eustace.
Golden Dagger, The — 1951 Scotland Yard yarn by E. R. Punshon
Hake Talbot Novels — *Rim of the Pit, The Hangman's Handyman*. Classic locked room mysteries.
Hell Fire and **Savage Highway** — Two new hard-boiled novels by Jack Moskovitz, who developed his style writing sleaze back in the 70s. No one writes like Jack.
Hollywood Dreams — A novel of the Depression by Richard O'Brien
House of the Vampire, The — 1907 poetic thriller by George S. Viereck.
I Stole $16,000,000 — A true story by cracksman Herbert E. Wilson.
Inclination to Murder — 1966 thriller by New Zealand's Harriet Hunter
Incredible Adventures of Rowland Hern, The — 1928 impossible crimes by Nicholas Olde.
Invaders from the Dark — Classic werewolf tale from Greye La Spina
Jack Mann Novels — Strange murder in the English countryside. *Gees' First Case, Nightmare Farm, Grey Shapes, The Ninth Life, The Glass Too Many.*
Jim Harmon Double Novels — *Vixen Hollow/Celluloid Scandal, The Man Who Made Maniacs/Silent Siren, Ape Rape/Wanton Witch, Sex Burns Like Fire/Twist Session, Sudden Lust/Passion Strip, Sin Unlimited/Harlot Master, Twilight Girls/Sex Institution*. Written in the early 60s.
Joel Townsley Rogers Novels — By the author of *The Red Right Hand: Once In a Red Moon, Lady With the Dice, The Stopped Clock, Never Leave My Bed*
Joel Townsley Rogers Story Collections — *Night of Horror* and *Killing Time*
Joseph Shallit Novels — *The Case of the Billion Dollar Body, Lady Don't Die on My Doorstep, Kiss the Killer, Yell Bloody Murder, Take Your Last Look*. One of America's best 50's authors.
Jvlivs Caesar Mvrder Case, The — A classic 1935 re-telling of the assassination by Wallace Irwin that's much more fun than the Shakespeare version
Keller Memento — 500 pages of short stories by David H. Keller.
Killer's Caress — Cary Moran's 1936 hardboiled thriller
Koky Comics, The — A collection of all of the 1978-1981 Sunday and daily comic strips by Richard O'Brien and Mort Gerberg, in two volumes.
Lady of the Terraces, The — 1925 adventure by E. Charles Vivian.
Lord of Terror, The — 1925 mystery with master-criminal, Fantômas.
Marblehead: A Novel of H.P. Lovecraft — A long-lost masterpiece from Richard A. Lupoff. Published for the first time!
Max Afford Novels — *Owl of Darkness, Death's Mannikins, Blood on His Hands, The Dead Are Blind, The Sheep and the Wolves, Sinners in Paradise* and *Two Locked Room Mysteries and a Ripping Yarn* by one of Australia's finest novelists.
Muddled Mind: Complete Works of Ed Wood, Jr. — David Hayes and Hayden Davis deconstruct the life and works of a mad genius.
Murder in Black and White — 1931 classic tennis whodunit by Evelyn Elder
Murder in Shawnee — Novels of the Alleghenies by John Douglas: *Shawnee Alley Fire* and *Haunts*.
Murder in Silk — A 1937 Yellow Peril novel of the silk trade by Ralph Trevor
My Deadly Angel — 1955 Cold War drama by John Chelton
My First Time: The One Experience You Never Forget — Michael Birchwood — 64 true first-person narratives of how they lost it.
Mysterious Martin, the Master of Murder — Two versions of a strange 1912 novel by Tod Robbins about a man who writes books that can kill.
N. R. De Mexico Novels — Robert Bragg presents *Marijuana Girl, Madman on a Drum, Private Chauffeur* in one volume.
Night Remembers, The — A 1991 Jack Walsh mystery from Ed Gorman
Norman Berrow Novels — *The Bishop's Sword, Ghost House, Don't Go Out After Dark, Claws of the Cougar, The Smokers of Hashish, The Secret Dancer, Don't Jump Mr. Boland!, The Footprints of Satan, Fingers for Ransom, The Three Tiers of Fantasy, The Spaniard's Thumb, The Eleventh Plague, Words Have Wings, One Thrilling Night, The Lady's in Danger, It Howls at Night, The Terror in the Fog, Oil Under the Window, Murder in the Melody, The Singing Room*
Old Times' Sake — Short stories by James Reasoner from Mike Shayne Magazine
One After Snelling, The — Kickass modern noir from Richard O'Brien.
Organ Reader, The — A huge compilation of just about everything published in the 1971-1972 radical bay-area newspaper, *THE ORGAN*.
Poker Club, The — The short story, the novel and the screenplay of the seminal thriller by Ed Gorman
Private Journal & Diary of John H. Surratt, The — The memoirs of the man who conspired to assassinate President Lincoln.

Prose Bowl — Futuristic satire — Bill Pronzini & Barry N. Malzberg .

Red Light — History of legal prostitution in Shreveport Louisiana by Eric Brock. Includes wonderful photos of the houses and the ladies.

Researching American-Made Toy Soldiers — A 276-page collection of a lifetime of articles by toy soldier expert Richard O'Brien

Ripped from the Headlines! — The Jack the Ripper story as told in the newspaper articles in the *New York* and *London Times.*

Robert Randisi Novels — *No Exit to Brooklyn* and *The Dead of Brooklyn*. The first two Nick Delvecchio novels.

Roland Daniel Double: The Signal and The Return of Wu Fang — Classic thrillers from the 30s

Rough Cut & New, Improved Murder — Ed Gorman's first two novels

Ruled By Radio — 1925 futuristic novel by Robert L. Hadfield & Frank E. Farncombe

Rupert Penny Novels — *Policeman's Holiday, Policeman's Evidence, Lucky Policeman, Policeman in Armour, Sealed Room Murder, Sweet Poison, The Talkative Policeman, She had to Have Gas* and *Cut and Run* (by Martin Tanner.) This is the complete Rupert Penny library of novels.

Sam McCain Novels — Ed Gorman's terrific series includes *The Day the Music Died, Wake Up Little Susie*

Sand's Game — A selection of the best of Ennis Willie, including a complete novel.

Satan's Den Exposed — True crime in Truth or Consequences New Mexico — Award-winning journalism by the *Desert Journal.*

Secret Adventures of Sherlock Holmes, The — Three Sherlockian pastiches by the Brooklyn author/publisher, Gary Lovisi.

Sex Slave — Potboiler of lust in the days of Cleopatra — Dion Leclerq.

Shadows' Edge — Two early novels by Wade Wright: *Shadows Don't Bleed* and *The Sharp Edge.*

Shot Rang Out, A — Three decades of reviews from Jon Breen

Sideslip — 1968 SF masterpiece by Ted White and Dave Van Arnam

Singular Problem of the Stygian House-Boat, The — Two classic tales by John Kendrick Bangs about the denizens of Hades.

Slammer Days — Two full-length prison memoirs: *Men into Beasts* (1952) by George Sylvester Viereck and *Home Away From Home* (1962) by Jack Woodford

Smell of Smoke, A — 1951 English countryside thriller by Miles Burton

Snark Selection, A — Lewis Carroll's *The Hunting of the Snark* with two Snarkian chapters by Harry Stephen Keeler — Illustrated by Gavin L. O'Keefe.

Stakeout on Millennium Drive — Award-winning Indianapolis Noir — Ian Woollen.

Suzy — Another collection of comic strips from Richard O'Brien and Bob Vojtko

Tales of the Macabre and Ordinary — Modern twisted horror by Chris Mikul, author of the *Bizarrism* series.

Tenebrae — Ernest G. Henham's 1898 horror tale brought back.

Through the Looking Glass — Lewis Carroll wrote it; Gavin L. O'Keefe illustrated it.

Time Armada, The — Fox B. Holden's 1953 SF gem.

Tiresias — Psychotic modern horror novel by Jonathan M. Sweet.

Totah Six-Pack — Fender Tucker's six tales about Farmington in one sleek volume.

Triune Man, The — Mindscrambling science fiction from Richard A. Lupoff

Ultra-Boiled — 23 gut-wrenching tales by our Man in Brooklyn, Gary Lovisi. Yow!

Universal Holmes, The — Richard A. Lupoff's 2007 collection of five Holmesian pastiches and a recipe for giant rat stew.

Victims & Villains — Intriguing Sherlockiana from Derham Groves

Wade Wright Novels — *Echo of Fear, Death At Nostalgia Street* and *It Leads to Murder*, with more to come!

Walter S. Masterman Mysteries — *The Green Toad, The Flying Beast, The Yellow Mistletoe, The Wrong Verdict* and *The Perjured Alibi, The Border Line, The Curse of Cantire*. Fantastic impossible plots.

Werewolf vs the Vampire Woman, The — Hard to believe ultraviolence by either Arthur M. Scarm or Arthur M. Scram.

West Texas War and Other Western Stories — by Gary Lovisi

Whip Dodge: Manhunter — A modern western from the pen of Wesley Tallant

White Peril in the Far East, The — Sidney Lewis Gulick's 1905 indictment of the West and assurance that Japan would never attack the U.S.

You'll Die Laughing — Bruce Elliott's 1945 novel of murder at a practical joker's English countryside manor.

Young Man's Heart, A — A forgotten early classic by Cornell Woolrich

RAMBLE HOUSE

Fender Tucker, Prop.   Gavin L. O'Keefe, Graphics
www.ramblehouse.com   fender@ramblehouse.com
228-826-1783   10329 Sheephead Drive, Vancleave MS 39565

www.ingramcontent.com/pod-product-compliance
Lightning Source LLC
Chambersburg PA
CBHW030347020726
47493CB00003B/727